Being kissed had made her forget she was a plain woman.

"I want to know why you were in the alley," Worth said.

Caroline groped for a response. "I sensed something wrong. I went to look."

When she lowered her lashes, he lifted her chin so that he could look into her eyes. They glittered with something. Was it, oddly enough, embarrassment? Was she holding something back? It seemed so, but he sensed no direct connection with the murder. "If you think of another reason," he said, releasing her, "be sure and tell me. Meanwhile, we shall take public delight in our new-found love."

Worth bowed and left. Caroline was torn between disbelief and indignation. He had been accusing her of *murder*—or accessory to it. With her passion still roused from the memory of his kiss, indignation took the upper hand. *The nerve of the man!*

Dear Reader,

Our titles for June include *The Lady and the Laird* by Maura Seger, a charming story of mischief and mayhem. Forced to occupy a crumbling Scottish castle for six months or lose her inheritance, Kaitlyn Sinclair is ill prepared for the devilment caused by the castle's former residents—one living and one long dead.

Those of you who have enjoyed Julie Tetel's previous novels will not be disappointed with *Sweet Suspicions,* her first book for Harlequin Historicals, an intriguing romance that pairs a well-connected yet penniless woman with a rich outcast of London society on a hunt to uncover the murderer in their midst.

The Claim is the first of two titles by Lucy Elliot involving the infamous Green Mountain Boys. When frontiersman Zeke Brownwell declares himself the owner of the very same land that citified Sarah Meade believes is hers, the sparks begin to fly.

Captive Kathleen James impetuously marries fellow prisoner John Ashford to save him from certain death in *Pirate Bride* by Elizabeth August. This tale of danger and adventure is the first historical for Harlequin by this popular contemporary author.

Four enticing stories from Harlequin Historicals to catch your fancy. We hope you enjoy them.

Sincerely,

The Editors

Sweet Suspicions

Julie Tetel

Harlequin Books

TORONTO • NEW YORK • LONDON
AMSTERDAM • PARIS • SYDNEY • HAMBURG
STOCKHOLM • ATHENS • TOKYO • MILAN
MADRID • WARSAW • BUDAPEST • AUCKLAND

Harlequin Historicals first edition June 1992

ISBN 0-373-28728-3

SWEET SUSPICIONS

JULIE TETEL

has always loved both history and romance, making it easy for her to love reading and writing historical romances. She is from a suburb of Chicago and currently lives in Durham, North Carolina. She has two sons, two careers, at least two points of view and one husband.

Chapter One

London, 1714

After a pause in the conversation, Richard Worth said, "So, Jonathan. Have I mentioned yet that I've a mind to enter society?"

Seated comfortably in the chair behind his library table, Jonathan Wyndham, Duke of Desford, chuckled. "No, but I suppose that next I'll be hearing that you've been released from the army by favor," he said humorously.

"By purchase, rather," Colonel Worth replied.

"You mean to sell out?" his grace asked, smiling still, pursuing the jest.

"I've already done so."

At the serious note in his friend's voice, the Duke of Desford's handsome face fell. He sat forward. "You've sold out, Richard?" He shook his head. "No. Tell me you are joking."

"I am not joking," Worth said pleasantly. "I have sold out of the army, and I wish to enter society." He paused. "I also wish for your help."

Desford held his friend's steady gaze for several moments before dropping his eyes. He picked up the dagger that lay across one corner of the blotter next to an inkwell. The dagger was long and thin with a carved blade that had no cutting edge. Desford flipped it several times, then looked up. "The army is your career," he said at last. The laugh betrayed his incomprehension. "Good God, it's your entire life! Why, Richard? Why did you sell out?"

Worth was prepared for the question. He was not about to recount how it had been those few months ago, stationed at Antwerp, that he woke up one morning and said, "No more." That was all. No more. No more would the smell of boiled beans and blood and burnt powder fill his nose. No more would the sound of the drum and enemy fire ring in his ears. No more would he awaken to the chill of his spine on hard earth at raw dawn. He wanted no more recruits, no more bounties, no more victories, no more deaths.

Instead, Worth smoothed the fall of lace at his wrist. The harsh angles of his face were softened momentarily by a wry smile. "I was bored," he said. "Yes, bored. Bored with the waiting. The interminable waiting. In the taverns or at camp, it was always the same, with smoke and schnapps and Dutch beer and long, empty stretches of time." He crossed one silk-hosed leg over the other. "Bored, Jonathan."

Desford blinked in some disbelief. "This from the man who often professed his supreme satisfaction to have been born in the age of Marlborough?"

"Those were grand times, you and me and the regiment under Marlborough's command," Worth conceded readily, "and there are no more glorious victories than the ones we savored at Blenheim and Ramillies and Oudenarde. However, if you had not left four years ago when you came into this inheritance—" here Worth let his eyes roam the dustless elegance of the Desford library to illustrate his point "—I wager that you, too, would have tired of army life by now."

Desford leaned back again in his chair. He palmed the dagger and was weighing it. "Perhaps," he said slowly. "Perhaps not."

Worth inclined his head, acknowledging the polite disclaimer. "But now you'll never know, of course, for when you left, you were still having a grand time of it."

"Those were the days," Desford said with a touch of nostalgia, now twirling the dagger idly in his hand. "Blenheim and Ramillies and Oudenarde were behind us. Marlborough was at his most brilliant, and we still had Malplaquet ahead of us. You were being promoted through the ranks at a speed most dazzling and—'' Desford broke off. ''It was during the campaigns of '08, wasn't it, that you caught the eye of that general who was named to our ministry at Hanover?'' His brow furrowed. ''General...General...?''

''Routledge,'' Worth supplied. ''And so?''

Desford nodded. ''That's it. Routledge,'' he repeated. ''Why didn't you go to him, if you were bored with camp life? Wouldn't he have named you to an administrative post of some sort? In one of the German states or the Spanish Netherlands or even here in London.'' Desford shook his head again. ''God's love, Richard, do you realize how drastic is your decision?''

''I haven't cut all my ties to the ministries,'' Worth reassured him. ''I might need something to fill the gap when my commission officially ends in another fortnight, and so I've scheduled several appointments this afternoon at the Secretariat to explore possibilities. But as for Routledge,'' he continued with an ironic twist to his lips, ''he wanted nothing more to do with me after discovering that my character suffered from a fatal flaw.''

''Don't tell me the old scandal followed you all the way—''

''Not at all,'' Worth interrupted evenly. ''Rather, it was Routledge's conviction that all good army men should be married by the age of thirty. I shall spare you the description of his disillusionment the day he learned—two years ago already it was—that I was one-and-thirty and still unmarried.'' Worth shook his head mournfully. ''I sank unredeemably in his estimation, I assure you!''

'''Struth!'' Desford exclaimed.

Worth laughed at his friend's comical dismay. ''Yes, but I wasn't unhappy about it at the time, and I'm not now. I suppose I always had it in mind to sell out and to—'' He stopped abruptly.

''To...?'' Desford prompted.

"To lead a life of leisure," Worth finished smoothly. "In society. After I had made enough money."

"And have you?"

"Enough," Worth confirmed.

Desford ran his eye over Worth's severe but elegant suit of midnight-blue silk. He looked down at the dagger in his hand, regarding it meditatively. Then he pressed the tip of the dagger into the blotter so that it stuck straight up. He placed his palm over the hilt, keeping the dagger poised in its upright position. He looked up and let another moment pass before saying, "It won't be easy."

"I know that."

"What is it you want from me?" Desford inquired. "Shall I sponsor you at the Kit Kat Club? My influence there may just be enough to gain you acceptance."

Worth declined this generous offer and mentioned that he already had membership at the Guard House.

"A tip or two on a house in town, then?"

Worth shook his head. "I am presently negotiating one at St. James's." When Desford looked impressed, Worth commented briefly, "Spoils and victors." He gestured to the uncorked bottle of claret on the desk. "I learned long ago not to throw ill-gotten coin after a flask. No," he said, coming straight to his point, "what I want from you is a wife."

Desford lost his grip on the dagger, and it fell on the blotter with a dull thud. "You have not ceased to astound me these many minutes past!"

"I've left it three years too long already—by Routledge's reckoning," Worth continued, "but I'm ready to get on with it now. Without delay."

Desford was at something of a loss. "I have no sisters," he managed. "Not even a cousin to offer you."

"Which you might not bestow on me even if you did," Worth replied with brutal honesty. "Neither would I blame you. However, I have hardly come to ask for the hand of any of your female relatives. I've come for information. Call it a reconnaissance mission."

To Desford's delicately raised eyebrows, Worth explained, "I've been billeted in town less than a week and do not know the terrain. I want a woman of the highest possible birth and the greatest need to be married. Financial need," he clarified. "Although her case does not have to be desperate, she must be poor enough to have reason to entertain an offer from me." His voice did not falter over the words. "Her social acceptability is my primary concern. Beauty and temperament are of secondary importance. What I want from you is a list of such eligible women, a report on their financial situation and social position, along with knowledge of any other offers they may be entertaining. I require as well a chart of the possible assemblies where I may meet them, preferably within the next few days. I have but one chance, one offer to make if this operation is to succeed, and dare not risk a refusal. I want no mistakes."

To this extraordinary speech, Desford murmured, "One chance, one offer and no mistakes." Then, meditatively, "And it just might work." He regarded his friend with some awe and a little admiration. "You may have sold out, Richard, but you will never leave the army!"

Colonel Worth did not hesitate to say to one of the most exalted peers of the realm, "I did not ask for your opinions. Do you draw me the list willingly, Captain, or must I pull rank?"

Desford expelled his breath on a laugh and leaned back in his chair. After warning his friend that he was hardly the ideal source for information concerning nubile young ladies, he proceeded to brief the colonel on the unmarried portion of his female acquaintance.

Presently, the two men rose. Desford came around the table to escort his old comrade out of the house. Before they had crossed the library, there came a knock at the door. It opened to Desford's answering command, and the duke's steward entered, bearing a silver salver with the morning's mail.

Desford paused to glance idly at the correspondence. "Tedious business," he said with a sigh.

Worth was not deceived. "You seem to have taken remarkably well to the tedium of your responsibilities."

Desford, who had been shuffling through his letters, seemed to check his movements at the last envelope, hesitating over whether to return it to the stack, then deciding that he would not. He looked up, smiling gracefully, regretfully. "Yes, I *have* taken well to my responsibilities—speaking of which, I must take care of this one on the instant," he said, gesturing with the last envelope in his hand. "Along with the most gratifying power and glory, the title comes with an enormous load of duties! But I do not complain and rather fancy that I acquit myself with some merit! Ah, well." He sighed again. "I shall ask Jacobs—" nodding to his steward "—to show you out of the house. Until tonight, Richard."

"Until tonight, Jonathan," Worth replied, "at the London Assembly." He held out his hand.

Desford did not take it but instead clapped his hand to his brow. "But how thoughtless of me!" he said, his mobile face suddenly alive with the smile that was famous for its charm. "I do not know how I came to forget her, but you really must add to your list the name of Caroline Hutton!"

First things first. "Is she well connected?"

The morning mail and the attendant duties were apparently forgotten. "My good man, she is the daughter of a viscount," Desford said happily. "Received everywhere."

Worth attempted to put the name to a face but drew a blank. "Hutton? A viscount? Did I know him?"

"Lord, Richard, *I* don't know! He was reported to have been a high flier in his time, and you certainly cut more of a dash in the old days than I did. But the viscount was twenty-five years your senior if he was a day, so it's possible your paths never crossed."

"Do I gather that the family is suitably poor?"

"Most suitably!" Desford assured him cheerfully. "About three years ago, the old man had to sell off not only his best estates but also his house in town."

"What happened?"

"A spectacular run of bad luck at the tables at the Cocoa Tree together with a packet of investments with the South Sea Company gone sour. He took his daughter and removed to some little place in the country. What's more, I think I heard that he suffered a stroke as a result of his losses." Desford frowned. "Or did he die?" He considered it. "Either way."

"Why did she return to London?"

Desford did not know the answer to that. Nor did he seem to care. "What I can tell you is that she goes about with another woman who is also well connected and not a bad-looking woman, I might add." He frowned again. "Her name escapes me just now." He waved away the memory lapse. "In any case, the little Hutton must be staying with her."

"If she's a gambler like her father, I'll pass on this one."

Desford's brow cleared. "From what I can tell, she's not at all in the old viscount's style!" He laughed. "Let me see." He exhaled gustily. "She's not as young as the others I've mentioned—which might mean, come to think of it," he said, scratching his chin, "that she was already out before she left London, but I don't think I met her then. I'd describe her as a well-mannered little thing. Sensible talk. Nothing to look at, but she's not an antidote or anything of that sort."

"Any musical talents?" Worth asked, seemingly at random.

"The usual, I would suppose," Desford replied without much conviction. "Singing. The harpsichord. But I can't vouch for it personally. Dresses well, though. Good taste."

To this catalog of unremarkable virtues, Worth shrugged. "Entertaining any offers?"

"I never had a head for gossip before coming into the title, and I don't now!" Desford laughed. "But think about it! She's been buried in the country these past three years, so who could have offered for her except some horse-faced farmer's son! And with no dowry that I've heard of, only passable looks and on her second time around, she's hardly a prime target." He smiled and pronounced with satisfaction, "Caroline Hutton. Perfect. I'd make sure you were introduced to her myself, but I've an appointment at the club earlier in the evening. I'll be coming late to the assembly, so you're on your own. Do you remember the conventions?"

Worth assured his friend that he did and thanked him for the new name. He held out his hand and had it taken this time. He then left the room in Jacobs' wake.

"And Richard," Desford called out slyly to his friend's back, "wear your uniform! The ladies are ever dazzled by a redcoat!"

Colonel Worth turned to acknowledge the taunt with an ironic salute. After being led through the echoing halls of Desford House, he collected his things from the footman in the entry, who also opened the front door for him. Cocking his hat, Worth descended the broad stone stairs to the well-swept, well-traveled cobbles of Hanover Square.

On the last step, Worth happened to encounter a distinguished gentleman atop whose bagwig sat an elaborately plumed tricorne. The man was portly for his relative youth, swathed in silks and frothing with lace. A dress sword could be seen peeping through the folds of his coat. He was just then turning to mount the same stairs to Desford House.

The men doffed their hats and bowed to each other. When Worth stood upright, he thought he recognized the man. "Devis?" he queried hesitantly. "Arthur Devis?"

"Worth?" the man answered, equally hesitant, but his hesitation spoke of shock. Arthur Devis had been caught unawares, and his response was unguarded. He took an involuntary step back. "Is it you, Richard? Never thought to see you again! Thought you'd never return! After all these years?"

After all these years. After all these years, Richard Worth had been prepared for such an encounter. Yet, for all his forethought, he had not anticipated how quickly, how completely, the corpse of his past could be revived. It rose whole and skeletal from its very deep grave, all the ghostly horror and spectral shame immediately vivid and haunting. He had not forgotten anything, not how to read the look on a man's face, nor how to interpret the tone in a man's voice. The combination still struck him as physically as a slap. Worth felt the handprint sting red on his cheek. Or was it that, after all these years, the slap had frozen to become indelible on his face, like the spill of an angry birthmark?

Worth's rank and his thirteen years' experience stood him in good stead. His body did not wince, nor did his voice flinch. "Yes, it is I," he replied, replacing his hat on unpowdered hair, "after all these years."

With grim amusement, Worth watched Devis's open scrutiny. "Well, well!" Devis said. "You haven't done badly! Not too badly! Who would have thought... that is to say, looking prosperous. Very prosperous!"

Worth bowed again. "You, too, Arthur."

"Joined the army?" the gentleman inquired, dredging a memory no doubt jogged by the sight of Worth's lean rugged frame, his hard blue eyes and the hair streaked blond by a life lived out-of-doors. "Recall it was the army! Left town. Joined the army. All those years ago!"

"Yes, it was the army," Worth replied evenly, "and it has been very good to me."

"Indeed, indeed!" Devis agreed promptly and then hazarded, "returned for a while? On furlough? Returned on furlough perhaps?"

Worth heard the hope in the question and decided to fire the first offensive volley of his campaign. "Why, no," he answered, smiling, "I've sold out and intend to settle in town."

Arthur Devis cleared his throat. "Settle? In town? Good God! That is—Good! God! Capital!" he spluttered. "Yes, indeed! Settle! In town! Of all places! That is to say, shall look forward to seeing you. Seeing you in town!" Devis uttered a few more extraneous remarks and cleared his throat again. He reiterated his pleasure at the prospect of reacquainting himself with an old friend and bowed several more times. He broke off the encounter awkwardly, pleading a pressing appointment with Des—the duke!

Worth said all that was expected and took his leave of Arthur Devis with Marlborough's first maxim of war ring-ing clearly in his brain: "Pursue one great decisive aim with force and determination." To accomplish that aim he needed the best field position he could command: marriage to a woman of the highest social order and the most desperate need to marry. *No mistakes and no delay!*

Desford had named a dozen women or more who might have answered Worth's specifications. From those names Worth had trimmed an initial tactical shortlist of two women, Julia Stanhope and Angelica Gordon, to which he now added the third name of Caroline Hutton. He passed these names in mental review, wholly satisfied that, though it was mid-November, a full complement of social activities could be counted on to launch the strategic offensive.

He would begin this evening at the London Assembly. He desired to secure for this year, and for all the years to come, warm and comfortable winter quarters. He wanted the kind with thick runners whispering down long hallways, roast beef on the table and music on the air. He wanted a constant fire blazing in the main salon with invitations thrust carelessly in the mirror frame over the mantel. He wanted a personal retreat redolent of leather bindings, beeswax and brass polish.

He attempted to indulge the details of this vision, but they eluded him, as if he had temporarily forgotten a well-known address or misplaced something familiar, like his shaving kit or bootjack. The fraction of an image skittered into his mind's eye. It was the glint of sunlight filtering through a long, high window draped in brocade, the shafts falling to gild a marquetry table. The image did not hold and was blurred by a seeping stain of blood.

The names of Julia Stanhope and Angelica Gordon and Caroline Hutton marched through his mind in much the same fashion as had Blenheim and Oudenarde and Malplaquet on the eves of the sieges of those now-famous towns. After he had studied his position and considered the maneuvers that would win him the most terrain in the least amount of time, he dismissed thoughts of the women and turned his attention to the petition he was about to lay before King George.

Chapter Two

For all the reasons the Duke of Desford had given Colonel Worth and then some, Caroline Hutton had not, in her twenty-three years, received one serious proposal of marriage. The duke was, furthermore, correct in thinking that she might have attracted the attention of a country lad. During the past year, she had caught the fancy of a braw, well-to-do farmer whose interest she had not reciprocated. This was just as well, since he had proved that his intentions were anything but honorable one recent autumn afternoon in the deserted and derelict Hutton Manor stables. Caroline had defended herself efficiently and survived the encounter with her virtue intact. However, the incident had left her shaken, and the rejected lover had subsequently spread a fractured version of the story throughout the Sussex neighborhood.

As for Caroline's father, the duke was correct in thinking that the old man had suffered a stroke three years previously. After hanging on for more than two more years, he had died last March, leaving Hutton Manor in Caroline's capable hands. In the months following, Caroline had discovered that the tangle of the Hutton finances was proving difficult to unravel, given that the family solicitor was in London and not prone to answering her letters. Thus when, a scant month before, she had received an unexpected invitation from her aunt to visit her in town, Caroline had readily accepted.

She had never liked her aunt, nor had she ever thought that her aunt liked her. Nevertheless, she welcomed the invitation and intended to use it to expedite the settlement of what was left of the estate and the payment of the death duties. Although she hardly cared to admit it to herself, she was also happy to visit her aunt while the incident in the stables still tripped off lively country tongues. The village talk had wounded her shy dignity.

However, the duke was wrong in thinking that he had not met Caroline before she left London three years ago. He was also wrong in supposing that Caroline was not currently the object of any eligible gentleman's special interest. She was. And the gentleman was, coincidentally, the duke's own cousin.

It was of this gentleman whom Caroline was thinking on her way to the London Assembly that evening. Her thoughts did not rest on the gentleman, but only considered him as a part of the mass of pleasant experiences she had had in the past days. After having left London under the cloud of the collapse of the Hutton fortune three years before, Caroline had had, naturally, a few qualms about returning, However, she was pleased to discover that her experiences in society were so much more enjoyable now that she expected so little. No longer concerned with finding a marriage partner, she felt no pressure, as she once had, to be sought after. Agreeably enough, this one gentleman, at least, seemed to take delight in her company.

As her aunt's carriage lumbered through the streets, Caroline was musing on how easily she had slipped back into the rhythms of society, how fine it was to renew old friendships, what lovely memories she would soon be taking back with her to Hutton Manor, how perfect this unexpected sojourn in London would have been *if only*—

Next to her, an older woman's voice cut through the mist of her pleasant reflections, dispelling them. "Viscount Weldon will be there tonight, will he not, my dear?"

—*if only she were not staying with her aunt!* Caroline answered, "Yes, Aunt Esther."

"And the Earl of March, one assumes?"

"Oh, yes, Aunt. Surely."

"And the particular young man with whom you danced at the Birminghams' ball last week? Are you expecting him to be there as well?"

Caroline turned to face Lady Esther Besant, her father's half sister, still a handsome woman at forty. It was dark in the carriage. The light of the lanthorns hung out in front of the occasional house they passed intermittently illuminated the interior and highlighted Lady Besant's beautiful, white skin.

"Which particular young man, Aunt Esther?" she inquired.

"I must say that coyness does not become you at your age!" her aunt snipped. "I am referring, of course, to the one who asked you to dance twice, and whom you accepted twice."

"That would be Mr. Kenmure, then," Caroline said. "Yes, Aunt, I expect that he will be attending the assembly tonight as well."

"There, you see! The answer was not so difficult, after all! If such was the style of your conversation before you left London, I am not amazed that you had no offers!" Lady Besant sighed with exaggeration. "When I issued you the invitation, I was expecting that you would be thanking me for giving you a second chance instead of treating me to pert conversation."

Caroline had heard several versions of these words any number of times in the past days. On the previous occasions, she had not felt gratitude, but resentment that she was being made to live down, once again, the failure of her season, which had been sponsored by Lady Besant. She had resented being made to feel, once again, the awkward girl she had been at eighteen, whose plain, young attractions had paled next to the luster of her aunt's mature ebony and ivory beauty.

This time, she still felt the resentment but decided to meet it with resistance; and since she was not going to be a guest in her aunt's home much longer, she felt she could afford to have some fun at Lady Besant's expense. "I do thank you,

Aunt Esther," she said brightly, "for the second chance seems to have been the charm!"

"Whatever do you mean by that, child?"

"Why, if I was being coy with regard to Mr. Kenmure, it is only because I have the notion—and you have guessed it, too—that Mr. Kenmure has conceived a *tendre* for me!"

After a taut little pause, Lady Besant said, "Did I guess that?"

Caroline smiled guilelessly. "Is that not what you meant? After all, you saw the signs at the Birminghams' ball, and you must know that he asked me to dance twice at the City Assembly some weeks ago, and once at Southwark before that," she said, "where we first met."

"And this *tendre*, as you say," Lady Besant asked, frowning slightly, "what do you think will come of it?"

"Why, I think that Mr. Kenmure is going to ask me to marry him," Caroline replied. "Tonight!" From the look on her aunt's face, Caroline decided that this harmless little story was more than worth the telling. Not in her wildest imaginings could she have foreseen the strange consequences that would come from it.

After her aunt had recovered, she asked, "And you, Caroline, my dear. Do you reciprocate his feelings?"

"We share some interests," Caroline said, seemingly serious. "There are the charitable activities that we are both engaged in, for instance, and since he is new to town, I have been able to advise him on projects in some of the more reputable almshouses."

"Yes, he *is* new to town," her aunt agreed, "and my advice is to be on your guard with that one, my dear, for he has recently arrived—poof!—out of nowhere!"

"Not nowhere, Aunt," Caroline replied. "He comes from Leicestershire. Like his cousin. And, by the way, did you not visit Leicestershire just recently, before you invited me?"

"Where did you hear that?" Lady Besant demanded sharply.

"From the upstairs maid," Caroline replied, surprised at her aunt's vehemence.

"Servant's gossip!" she uttered in disgust. She waved it away and continued as if Caroline had not spoken. "Although Mr. Kenmure's birth is good enough—in that he is cousin to the Duke of Desford—his circumstances are hardly better than yours! And there is a shiftiness about Mr. Kenmure's eyes that I cannot like," she continued to Caroline's complete surprise, "and an insinuation in his demeanor that is most suspicious—although I suppose you will tell me that you have seen nothing of the sort! That is because you are no longer used to town ways, my dear, having lived in Sussex these past few years."

"So you advise me to reject him, Aunt?" Caroline asked, amazed and amused by her aunt's strong reaction to Mr. Kenmure.

Lady Besant lifted a thin black eyebrow. "He is an agreeable young man, I will admit, but I wonder, Caroline, if you have not had your head turned by his attentions, for we both know that you have not been accustomed to the little compliments and addresses of gentlemen."

Lady Besant studied her niece's face. She saw brown hair with a light dusting of powder, pretty brows arched over clear hazel eyes, but Caroline's mouth was too wide for beauty, and her nose, though well proportioned when viewed from the front, revealed a distinct bump in profile. Caroline had a nice eye for clothes and knew what coiffures became her, but her coloring was not fashionable.

Lady Besant's words and her critical appraisal would have been frankly insulting, if Caroline had held any illusions about herself. As it was, Caroline submitted to the scrutiny, thinking only that her aunt was overplaying her hand.

"Well, perhaps I am wrong about him, after all," Caroline said with unimpaired good humor. "And if Mr. Kenmure is not truly interested in me and no better prospect turns up tonight, I suppose that I shall simply return to Sussex, once I conclude my business. Ah, well!"

"Your appointment with the estate examiner," Lady Besant said, recalling a detail, "is tomorrow, is it not, my dear?"

"Yes, tomorrow in Birchin Lane with Mr. Gresham at one o'clock," Caroline replied.

"Do you think that you will be able to accomplish all your business with Mr. Gresham in one appointment?"

"I certainly hope so! It was difficult enough to schedule this one meeting with him. The poor, dear man must be horribly overworked. Then, again," Caroline added reasonably, "the difficulties and delays could have arisen from the complications of my particular case. Father left quite a mess."

"Well, my dear," her aunt said in a tone that Caroline guessed was meant to be kindly, "I do hope you do not think to leave immediately, for it is a pleasure for me to have you as my daughter once again. When I invited you, I had hoped you would stay several months—not several weeks. Although we do not always see eye to eye, my dear, I do enjoy your company!"

Caroline had no doubts about why her aunt had invited her, and it was not for the pleasure of her company. Lady Besant was a widow of long standing and a woman who labored under constant financial strain. Caroline guessed that the invitation was issued in the expectation that Caroline would make a gesture of generosity to her aunt when the estate was finally settled. Caroline wanted no more than to conclude her business, sign the papers, pay her taxes, do right by her aunt and return home.

"Why, thank you again, Aunt Esther, and I have appreciated the opportunity—this second chance—to return to town."

Lady Besant relaxed her lips into a smile. "And speaking of better prospects turning up," she said, "I think you might exert yourself to better purpose." To Caroline's look of blank inquiry, her aunt continued, "If I were you, I would cultivate the Duke of Desford, and not his cousin!"

Caroline's response was direct. "If you do not think me capable of captivating Mr. Kenmure, how do you think I could attract the attentions of the Duke of Desford?"

"I rather meant to put you on your guard against Mr. Kenmure's wiles," Lady Besant answered, altering her approach somewhat. "I note that his grace has never failed to speak to you on any occasion in the past weeks. Take the Birminghams' ball, for example! When his grace spoke to you, my dear, I saw from afar that you did not put yourself forward with him. You were almost tongue-tied! Thus you put yourself at a disadvantage and ended by dancing twice with that cousin of his."

Caroline did not immediately respond, for she remembered that occasion well. She mentally winced to avoid the pain of her aunt's shaft, for she had been in love with the handsome duke from the moment she had laid eyes on him four years before.

Few would forget the stunning éclat of the news that the impecunious, though well-liked Jonathan Wyndham, then a captain in Marlborough's army, had inherited the Desford estate through the strange twists of succession; and no woman would forget her first sight of the new Duke of Desford upon his return from the Continent. Jonathan Wyndham had always been a devilishly charming fellow. After his seasoning in the army and his succession to the title, the Duke of Desford was considered positively devastating.

Caroline had hoped to find that three years of sensible country life had cured her of her girlish infatuation with the duke. Although she had grown up in many ways, she had not outgrown her love for the duke. Upon seeing him again, she had discovered that he could still make her weak-kneed. He remained in her young woman's heart no less than her ideal and, with his golden wealth, masculine beauty and silver charm, the embodiment of everything that she lacked.

Although Caroline was at times shy, she was never tongue-tied. If she was relatively quiet in the duke's presence, it was because she considered her love for him a private indulgence, and she did not wish to make herself ridiculous by attempting to attract him with dazzling conversation. On those occasions of late when the duke had chosen to practice his easy charm on her, Caroline understood, as all plain women do who have survived the routine slights and hurts of girlhood, exactly what he must think of her. She wanted to preserve her love for the duke for what it was: a safe harbor for all her girlish fantasies.

She took pains to protect her heart from her aunt's arrows. She was amazed by Lady Besant's uncanny ability to know a person's secrets and weaknesses. She even, reluctantly, admired it. However, she failed to understand why her aunt should fling in her face the Duke of Desford, her pure and hopeless love. She wondered, idly, whether she was being punished for her transparent lie concerning Mr. Kenmure.

"I would think it very much of a disadvantage to put myself forward with the duke," Caroline replied after a moment. "He cannot like such manners."

"Nonsense!" her aunt snapped. "His grace is used to all kinds of manners, he being so handsome and so rich, and so I tell you that the more forward one is, the better! He is sensitive to his duties and must think of setting up his nursery before too much longer. You are, overall, better bred than the silly women he usually makes up to. How do you know he would not choose you?"

"How do I know—" Caroline began, surprised at the extent of what she could only term her aunt's inexplicable maliciousness. "I think you must be joking!"

Lady Besant did not respond to this exclamation. The carriage had come to a halt in front of the London Tavern, ablaze with lights, in whose fine upper rooms was held the assembly, and the door of the carriage had been promptly opened by the driver, who had jumped down from his perch. Following her aunt, Caroline gathered in hand volumes of her cream silk skirts and cloak, and she descended.

Before entering the building, Lady Besant turned to her niece and said in the low voice reserved for threats, "I will expect you to make an effort to come to the duke's attention tonight, my dear. You must make the first move. I have reason to believe that he will not take your advances amiss." Her eyes glittered. "You will see that I am right."

"I shall endeavor to do so," Caroline said slowly, her apparent obedience arising more from puzzlement at this turn in conversation than from true submission to her aunt's wishes.

Lady Besant shot her niece a malevolent glance. "See that you do," she stated flatly. Then she looked furtively about her and clipped with her scissor tongue, "Come, child! Don't stand there! The streets are filled with thieves and cutpurses!"

Caroline was never able afterward to decide whether it was her aunt's strange threat concerning the duke or her reference to the street thieves that caused Caroline's first prick of uneasiness that evening.

The two ladies stepped into a large foyer. To the right was a hallway and to the left was the room where they shed their cloaks. Caroline adjusted the pretty fall of lace at her bosom, and she and her aunt joined in the wake of those ascending the splendid split staircase at a decorous pace eloquent of the height of their wigs and headdresses and the weight of their finery. The upper rooms of the London Tavern were hung in pale green, and lighted with wax whose mellow glow glanced off the branches for the candles, the urns for the tea and coffee and the baskets for the cakes, which were all of silver. For ten nights of dancing, there were two hundred subscribers, so consequently the rooms on any one night were also very crowded.

Caroline and Lady Besant made their way through the throng, greeting their wide and varied acquaintance, heading in the direction of the large recess at the lower end of the main room. There, clustered about the pale green sofas fringed in gold, sat the inner circle of their feminine friends. The newcomers were instantly absorbed into the group and gossip. Caroline fell into conversation, noting within a minute of her arrival that her handsome duke had not yet arrived. She kept half an eye out for Mr. Kenmure, who had been so kind as to distinguish her with two dances the week before.

Mr. Kenmure was not to be the first man Caroline noticed this evening. At one moment, Mrs. Shuttleworth, a rich and very fashionable lady, covered her mouth with the back of her gloved hand and clucked her tongue. "La, a redcoat! There, look! At the door. Is he not handsome?"

All eyes turned discreetly in the direction indicated by Mrs. Shuttleworth's fan. Caroline's gaze was caught first by the magnificent coat smoldering red and gold in the candlelight, then shifted to the man's face, where it lingered. He was looking out over the assembly, his countenance devoid of expression. His face looked, she thought, like the side of a broken cliff, all distant planes and crags. Or perhaps his face had more the roughness of a cast come from the hands of a strong, impatient sculptor and was awaiting the fine chiseling. The face was certainly striking for its irregular features and high cheekbones. Arresting, even, for its look of implacable masculinity. But not handsome. At once attracted and repelled, Caroline looked hastily away.

The words *dashing* and *dangerous* were bandied about, as well as *exotic* and paradoxically, *vaguely familiar.* Lady Besant said, "Military," and almost snorted. Unsuccessful attempts were made to put a name to the man's face. Since the mystery of the newcomer's identity was not immediately resolvable and he had moved away from the door, the talk drifted on to another more tractable topic, namely that of military men in general. It was agreed that the parade of redcoats in town was surely only beginning now since the signing of the Peace of Utrecht. From there it was but a step to venting feelings of outrage concerning the recently crowned German King George, who sat ill on the English throne, and his two ugly mistresses.

However, politics was not a popular subject, and so the topic shifted. Caroline was complimented on her flattering dress of cream and peach, and the talk thereafter drifted to discussion of the toilettes of the less fashionable ladies present, about which there seemed to be a good deal to say. Caroline dismissed speculation about the redcoated man who had stood at the door.

Caroline might have put the man from her mind, but the older half of the assembly did not. Minutes after the man had moved away from the door, the musicians struck up their fiddles, and the polite whispers began, both covered and propelled by the opening airs of the country dance. The name *Worth* was soon rustling about the room like the swirl of silks brushing the parquetry of the tourbillions of autumn leaves in the streets below. Caroline might have heard the name herself had her hand not been claimed for the first set that was beginning to form.

She looked up to see Gilbert Kenmure, young and eager and correct. He was bowing and asking her to dance.

She rose to accept Mr. Kenmure's escort. As they proceeded to the dance floor, she said, looking straight ahead of her as was proper, "Mr. Kenmure, you flatter me. It is a pleasure to dance in the first set."

"It was a boldness, Miss Hutton," Mr. Kenmure said with his smile so endearingly reminiscent of the duke's, "but I could not restrain myself."

Caroline looked up at him quickly through her lashes. "Could not restrain yourself?"

He said low and urgently, "I have discovered something. I must—nay, I am *compelled* to tell you about it, for it has changed my life. It will change yours, too, I hope."

Caroline caught her breath. She could hardly prevent herself from thinking that Mr. Kenmure was hinting at marriage, for nothing else could change her life more. On the heels of that thought came the even more incredible possibility that what he had discovered was his love for her. Had she acquired some magical power, whereby her pronouncement in the carriage, "I think that Mr. Kenmure is going to ask me to marry him," was bound to come true? Or had her frivolous statement merely planted a false seed in her brain?

"You have discovered something remarkable that will change my life?" she repeated, encouraging him to expand, to give her reason to interpret his words otherwise.

"Yes."

Caroline gazed a moment into Mr. Kenmure's eyes. So far from ever having seen the shifty look that her aunt claimed, Caroline had judged him to have very kind, even gentle eyes. This evening, they held unmistakable fire.

Her heart leapt. There was time for no more. The two straight lines of men and women facing each other were forming, and soon the men were bowing to the ladies' curtsies. The figures began with their geometrical designs, and Caroline had to apply herself to minding her steps and executing the arches and the stars and the files and the circles. The figures were manifold, and in their various combinations, the possibilities for the losing and finding of partners were inexhaustible.

Caroline was entirely new to this. These past three years she had been used to the satisfactions of long hours and challenging work, not to the delights of messages whispered on a dance floor. She had long since put thoughts of marriage and children behind her. Now, out of the clear sky, here was a man on the verge of declaring love for her. She did not understand it, but neither did she question it. An unfamiliar sensation percolated inside her. She identified it, tentatively, as happiness.

The next time the figures of the dance brought their hands together, Mr. Kenmure said quietly and quickly, "Downstairs at the end of the hallway off the foyer, there's an alcove. It's next to the side door leading to the alleyway. Do you know it?" When Caroline nodded minimally in answer, he continued, "Can you contrive to meet me there during the second interval in the dancing?"

Good heavens, there was to be romance in his proposal! Intrigue was foreign to Caroline's nature, but she had caught the spirit of the occasion. Her happiness stirred in her stomach, rippled lightly up to her breast, settled back down. An arch had formed so that Caroline was facing the back of the room where her aunt was seated, watching her. She thought it a mean trick of fate that her aunt's speculative gaze should just then prick her happiness, deflating it a little. A second twinge of uneasiness momentarily assailed her.

Caroline collected herself. The arch turned inward. She replied, close to Mr. Kenmure's ear, simply, "Yes."

Their hands parted. At the next formation that brought them moving together, she could not resist asking, "When we are private in the alcove, shall you tell me the remarkable thing you have discovered?''

Before the figure would have Mr. Kenmure fall back, he said, ''I shall *tell* you one thing, Miss Hutton, and *ask* you another.''

She could not possibly misinterpret those words. She was not in love with the man, and had hardly given a thought to whether she would accept him, but her soft, still girlish heart yearned for the gratification of hearing his declaration and receiving his proposal. The dance continued with no further exchanges with Mr. Kenmure, save for the most conventional. When it came to an end fifteen minutes later, Caroline did no more than thank Mr. Kenmure prettily and curtsey. He bowed correctly and led her back to her chair, sparing her only a brief, conspiratorial glance.

After that first significant dance, Caroline was unaccountably popular, more popular than she had been at the Birminghams' ball or the City Assembly or at Southwark; more popular than she had ever been at her most eligible, even before the viscount's financial troubles had surfaced. She thought it a fine, delicious irony that an ordinary young woman with no dowry should never sit out a dance on the very evening after which she might be no longer available.

Caroline discovered this evening the secret that had lain hidden from her ever since her earliest womanhood: that one need only to be desired by one to become desirable to many. She learned that the desperate prayers for a dancing partner she had recited at eighteen had worked to her detriment. Tonight she scorned such worship, and the invitations to dance flowed to her unprayed for. She learned how hungry was her unfed heart. She learned to accept a pretty compliment without a blush. She learned to be cruel. She learned, in short, to enjoy the London Assembly.

One of her partners was a very eligible young suitor to whom she did not throw out even one lure. He was entirely captivated and asked her for a second dance. Another of her partners was the infinitely rich, infinitely silly Arthur Devis. She would have preferred to sit out the dance.

Of the man in the red coat, Caroline saw him in her line of vision on several occasions, for he had entered the dancing, although not as regularly as she. Yet it had not occurred to her to ask any of her partners who the man might be. During the rare occasions she rested, she found herself gossiping and laughing and drinking punch and nibbling macaroons and calmly devising her strategy for being absent from the room during the second interval. She had not given further thought to the mysterious newcomer's identity.

The first interval had come and gone, and the second interval would soon be upon them. She had just been seated by a rather awkward young man who probably meant well but was annoying her, when suddenly there materialized before her one of the patronesses of the Assembly. At her side was a tall, lean man in a red coat.

Experiencing a strange spasm in the region of her heart, Caroline looked up and at the man with the unfinished face, the face as stark as the side of a broken cliff.

Chapter Three

The Marchioness of Margate was performing the introductions. However, Caroline heard only a portion of what that exalted lady said after her initial remark that "The gentleman desires to meet you, Miss Hutton."

Caroline could only hope that she replied just as she ought but a moment later had no recollection of what she had said. Her thoughts were in some confusion. It was one thing for the callow halflings who came in Mr. Kenmure's wake to try their luck with a newly popular lady. It was another thing entirely for a man beyond his first youth who was stamped with style and experience to desire to meet her, and she wondered why. She was not left long in doubt, for he was bowing and saying the most commonplace phrase to be heard at a ball, and yet the most extraordinary. "I beg the favor of a dance, Miss Hutton."

His invitation sounded more like a challenge. A little bemused, thinking, *This must be my night!* Caroline met it with "Yes, sir, with pleasure." She rose from her seat and laid her hand delicately on his proffered wrist.

The marchioness melted away, and Caroline was led to the floor, passing by the group of chairs where sat her aunt. That suddenly poker-backed dame's audible gasp made Caroline alert to the fact that her partner enjoyed a certain notoriety. Crossing to the dance floor, nodding and smiling as they made their way, Caroline observed that her partner acknowledged quite as many names and faces as she did; and although no one cut his acquaintance, he was nevertheless treated with a certain reserve. With a turn of fugitive humor, she could not decide, in having been singled out by him, whether she was being signally honored or slightly tainted. She might easily have fallen prey to the latter interpretation had anyone less than the Marchioness of Margate presented the man to her.

It was necessary to discuss with him where they would take their places, and this topic led them to remark on the loveliness of the present occasion and into further comment on the recent turns in weather. So close to the man now, Caroline realized that he was younger than she had first imagined. She noted with surprise that his eyes were blue, a detail she had not discerned from her brief inspection of him earlier in the evening when he had stood at the door. Neither was his unpowdered hair truly blond, as she had thought at first glance, but only stripped of color in places, presumably by the sun. It was tied back neatly at the nape but still managed to have the same weather-groomed look as his face. She was aware that her heart was racing, but that was surely due only to her imminent meeting in the alcove.

They had joined a set of open couples. The strains of a minuet floated over them, and Caroline cast about for conversation that would suit the stylized refinement of the dance. After she had saluted the spectators with bows and curtsies, Caroline's hand met and joined her partner's. She glanced up at him and found his eyes resting on her. What she perceived in their depths could only be described, once again, as a look of faint challenge. On the instant she discarded the idea of sharing with him her innocuous opinion of the assembly's fine orchestra.

This evening, flushed with her success and bubbling with a tender, still tentative happiness, Caroline had found talk easy enough with the eager young gentlemen who had solicited her hand. She was encouraged to think herself equal to the task of entertaining a military man of some distinction—that is, if the quantity of gold lace on the seams of his coat was any indication of rank.

She admired his gold sash, bold against the scarlet coat. For her opening gambit, she tossed out the question, "Do I suppose, sir, that you have been recently promoted?"

His brief nod seemed to acknowledge her swift change in conversational tactics. "Not recently, ma'am," he replied politely. "I came into my present commission three years ago."

She moved on to flattery. "It must be quite an achievement for one so young to be named to the rank of—" here she floundered, realizing too late that she had grasped but the shreds of their introduction "—of major."

"Perhaps," he replied, adding after the briefest pause, "my rank is that of colonel."

She was immediately vexed with herself and chafed at the figures of the minuet. It was a stately and ceremonial dance, the minuet, but intimate for all of that, with dainty little steps and glides, to the right and to the left, now forward and backward, but never more than an arm's length from one's partner.

She had learned many things this evening, but not how to simper. She smiled up at him apologetically. "I confess that I do not know whether I have just complimented you or insulted you!"

The man looked down at her and said, "You have insulted me, Miss Hutton."

Caroline thought she saw a glimmer of amusement in his otherwise hard blue eyes, and so was not entirely rebuffed. She wondered idly what effect his harsh, rugged features would have when smiling. As his eyes remained on her, she said with aplomb, "I thank you for the lesson. I have now learned that the rank of colonel is superior to that of major." She added reflectively, "So. A colonel, then. An army officer."

"Cavalry," he replied. "First Regiment."

Still regarding him, Caroline felt her smile fade. "Dear me! The cavalry *is* part of the army, isn't it?"

The colonel gripped the tips of Caroline's fingers in one of his hands and guided her in a quarter turn before him. Hand in hand, they approached and retreated, all movements simple and economical, now side by side, now gliding past each other.

When they were facing, he informed her gravely, "Yes, ma'am. The cavalry, which is made up of the Horse and the Dragoons, forms one part of the army. The other parts are the household troops and the infantry."

"Thank heavens!" Caroline said impulsively. "For a moment I had the horrible thought I had made another gaffe. But I suppose," she said reasonably, "that the cavalry would have to be part of the army, wouldn't it, since the only other branch of the armed services I can think of is the navy."

"That is correct. Now, the navy man is generally recognizable for his blue coat," he said instructively. "Shall I outline the various divisions of the navy for you?"

Caroline declined the treat and maintained her composure in the face of what she interpreted as deliberate provocation. First a quarter turn, then a half turn, and she said, "Tell me instead how many witless women have asked you the same idiotic questions this evening."

"You, ma'am, are only the tenth."

She suspected him of horrid exaggeration and answered in kind, with mock-solemn gravity, "How lowering it is to find that one has fallen into vulgar error."

"Would you feel better were I to tell you that you have been the only one?"

Caroline had to laugh at that. Looking him in the eye, she chuckled, "No, indeed not!" The answering gleam in his eyes emboldened her to say, "But if you feel a deep desire to edify me with important information, I wish that you would tell me your name, and then I shall avoid making a further fool of myself! I am afraid that I did not catch it when the marchioness introduced us."

The twinkle Caroline was sure had been lurking in the man's eyes vanished. His blue eyes ran as cool as a mountain stream. "Worth, ma'am. Richard Worth. Your servant," he said after the slightest hesitation. Caroline heard in his deep voice the challenge that she had seen earlier in his eyes and felt in his presence.

But no. There was more in his voice than challenge. There was a defiance, as distinct as the color of his coat and as hard as the planes of his face. She met the defiance directly. "Should I have known your name? I had thought you new to town."

"No, ma'am, not new," was all Worth chose to say.

Caroline did not think it wise to pursue the implication, and she could only wonder what secrets lay behind his air of mystery. "You have been away, then," she said. "On the Continent, I assume?"

"Yes, ma'am. Of late in the Spanish Netherlands, and before that fighting the French at Bouchain."

Now, here was the perfect opportunity to recover from her earlier blunders. She rallied him, "Ah! So *you* are the famous Colonel Worth who rode with Marlborough at Bouchain. It was a marvelous campaign, to be sure, and one in which a certain Colonel Worth was reported to have fought remarkably. I remember it most clearly now!"

Caroline thought she saw his smile edge into existence. His reply, however, was extremely dry. "I doubt you heard anything of the sort."

"In truth, I did," she replied, straight-faced. "How else could I have known that it was a result of that campaign that you were promoted to your present rank?"

"Because you can add. The campaign was in '11, and I have just told you that I was promoted three years ago."

"But that does not explain," she said with a daring that, in a beautiful woman, would have been considered flirtatious, "how I could have heard of your part in the peace negotiations at Utrecht."

Looking down at the woman with the mouth too wide for beauty and a slight smile that was polite and innocent and impudent all at once, Worth thought that Desford might have underestimated Caroline Hutton's possibilities. He had already rated her higher on one score, at least, than the two other beauties he had danced with this evening. He had thoroughly assessed in bluntly masculine, though flattering, terms Caroline's shapely feet, prettily turned ankles, her rounded arms and dimpled elbows and, under the fall of lace at her bodice, the deep shadow between her breasts.

"My last assignment in the Netherlands was at Antwerp," he said truthfully enough, but he suppressed the information that he had been at Utrecht before that. He had come to the London Assembly this evening with a purpose, and it was not to trumpet to the world the achievements of his military career.

Caroline was not abashed. She said with a convincing note of doubt, "Could my memory be so faulty?"

"No, my lady, merely your sources," he replied gallantly.

"My guesses, more like," she admitted with a rueful smile, abandoning the teasing. Then, with sudden insight, "But perhaps I *have* heard of you! You are in the cavalry, First Regiment? Is that not the same in which served the present Duke of Desford?"

"I knew the duke when he was Captain Wyndham," Worth affirmed. He glanced down at his partner and mused, "How selective is the female mind, to remember the number of a regiment, yet be ignorant of military rank."

Caroline immediately regretted the topic. She regretted, again, the intimacy of the dance, first one hand joined, then both hands, searching and evading, one step apart, now one step together. The one step together had brought her a breath away from her partner. In the immediate circle of his compelling presence, she was sure that she was blushing for having betrayed too detailed a knowledge of her heart's secret treasure.

She collected herself with an effort. "Oh," she said offhandedly, "I doubt that I am the only one—man or woman—who remembers the odd detail of the Duke of Desford's regiment. When his grace came into the inheritance, every morsel of his life must have been discussed for days on end—if not months or even years! You know how it is when society seizes hold of a fascinating topic!"

Worth looked down enigmatically at his partner. "Yes, in fact, I do," he stated evenly. "However, do you truly think a topic—even one so fascinating, as you say, as the unexpected good fortune of an army captain—could sustain itself for years?''

"As for years, I wouldn't actually know," she admitted honestly, "since I left London not many months after the duke's succession and have only just returned." Since she wished to distance herself from the subject of her impossible love, she added, conversationally, "For the past three years, I've lived in the country—at quite a remove from the latest London gossip!"

"You are not from London, then?" he asked, as if he did not know.

Caroline answered that, in point of fact, she was. "But I reside permanently now in Sussex, not far from Wych Cross, to be exact. It's lovely country."

Thus far Worth had found nothing in Caroline Hutton's confident directness or shy blushes to have inspired his lover's passion. However, since his presence tonight had so little to do with love or passion—but then again, everything to do with love and passion gone awry—it was enough that the woman he held with the tips of his fingers had given him an opening.

He slipped in. "So your return to London is more in the light of a visit?"

"Yes," Caroline said, politely answering his polite question, "I'm here for a few weeks only, visiting a relative—an aunt—and reacquainting myself with old friends. It's been a wonderful few weeks, but I'll be anxious to get back to Hutton Manor."

"You prefer the country to the city, then?"

"Not exactly. It's rather than in my aunt's house, I have found myself cast in the role of daughter," she said, smiling candidly up at him, "and I have been very much used to being my own mistress for years and years! Why, I suppose that it would not be unlike a demotion for you—say, from colonel to major, perhaps? I think you would find it unpleasant!"

This gentle sally drew from him the hint of a smile that touched his lips and eyes. Caroline was not surprised to see it soften his unfinished features, but she had not expected

the mere hint of his smile to be so compelling, and she nearly
fell under the spell of its promised magic.

"I understand," he said sympathetically, "and I am sure
that I would find it most unpleasant. Do I take it that your
aunt is issuing you orders and behaving in the manner
of—" he sought the appropriate comparison "—an over-
bearing colonel?"

"Not at all!" She chuckled, lying without hesitation.
"My aunt has been very kind and generous, and her invitation has provided me—in addition to these evenings about
town—the opportunity to settle my father's estate. The
matter has been dragging on for months! It's not easy moving the legal wheels forward when one lives buried in Sussex. But I hope to resolve it all tomorrow afternoon during
my appointment with Mr. Gresham, my solicitor, and then
I'll be on my way."

"You are so completely on your own?"

"Yes, legally and financially," she acknowledged. "My
father died last winter, and since I am of age and the last of
my line, I took over. Which explains," she said with a smile,
"why I chafe under my demotion in my aunt's household."

"I see. And yet, having been city-bred, you sound as if
you now prefer the country to the city."

"Perhaps I do," she said, considering the remark, "which
surprises me as much as anyone else. I thought I would
never recover from having to leave London. However,
within a month of arriving in Sussex, I was fully adjusted."

"Could you readjust to city life, if the opportunity
arose?" he asked next, maintaining his show of polite interest.

She could not help it. She blushed. Colonel Worth's
question had reminded her of her meeting with Mr. Kenmure and what he would have to say to her in a very few
minutes, for he had, on more than one occasion, expressed
his preference for city life. In having forgotten the poten-
tially most significant meeting of her life, she could only
suppose that her happiness had bubbled up to her brain and
had addled her wits.

She looked up at Colonel Worth and said, "Yes, I think I could readjust to city life—if the opportunity arose."

The music was coming to an end. The figures required that both hands be joined, and the final pace brought Caroline a heartbeat away from her partner. Still looking up at him, she momentarily lost the ability to breathe normally.

Blue eyes held hazel. "Perhaps that opportunity will arise in the near future," he said.

Caroline had to give herself a mental shake. Her bubbling success of the evening *had* gone to her head, and her effervescence had intoxicated her, for here she was thinking that every man she danced with was falling victim to her charms!

"And perhaps," he continued, releasing her hands and bowing deeply, "I shall have the pleasure of seeing you again, Miss Hutton." He had callously judged his partner "better than expected" and had determined that Caroline Hutton was worth a second assessment, at least.

"Perhaps," she confined herself to saying, now thoroughly bemused at herself and her strange state of mind.

She was required to place her hand again on his wrist as he led her off the floor. She felt his strength, which communicated itself through the tips of her fingers. To distract herself, she looked away, and her eye fell on the dais where sat the musicians. There she saw the fiddlers wiping their instruments with cloths, indicating that they were putting them away for the second interval. When it seemed that her partner was going to restore her to her chair, Caroline said quickly, "Look, there, sir, are some friends of mine not far from the door to the outer room. I have been wishing to speak to one of them the night long. Shall I introduce you?"

Colonel Worth declined the offer and, after escorting her to the group of people by the door, he took his leave of her. Caroline silently congratulated herself in having so well positioned herself to leave the room. After speaking briefly with several people she hardly knew, she was soon enough threading her way through the throngs that were milling about now that the dancing had temporarily ceased. She glanced over her shoulder and scanned the assembly. She was reassured that Lady Besant was nowhere in sight and so could not monitor her movements. Curiously, Colonel Worth's red coat was not visible, either.

Caroline made her passage with difficulty, excited now, exhilarated at what was to come. She was pleased with herself, with her evening, with her success, even with her last dancing partner. She had allowed her happiness to bubble up inside of her and to spill over, so that the tiny pearls of excitement and anticipation and eagerness clung to her, dewlike.

She was almost out of the door and onto the landing that would lead to the stairs when her arm was seized.

When she turned to face her captor, her vague look of irritation transformed itself into pleasure. "Martha! You have caught me!" She laughed, looking into the face of a lovely young widow who had just returned to society after a prolonged period of mourning.

"I have?" Mrs. Sheridan asked, one mobile brow arched. "Where are you going?"

"Nowhere," Caroline lied unconvincingly. She laughed again and glanced down at Mrs. Sheridan's hand on her arm. "Now, let me go, Martha! Do!"

"Not until I congratulate you on your triumph," Mrs. Sheridan said with a sly wink.

"My triumph?" Caroline said quickly. She was amazed that her dear friend, in addition to her aunt, had guessed Mr. Kenmure's interest, when she herself had had no inkling.

"Indeed, yes!" Mrs. Sheridan said. "To have been only one of three ladies asked to dance by the infamous Richard Worth is not merely a triumph, my dear, it is a *coup!*"

Caroline was effectively diverted. "Only one of three?" she echoed, so startled that she did not think to ask about the significance of the adjective *infamous*. "Who were the other two?"

"Angelica Gordon and Julia Stanhope," Martha Sheridan replied impressively. "Accredited beauties, both; and two of the most graceful dancers. You have often spoken of them with just the merest touch of envy. But after tonight, no more! I must tell you that you look a perfect flower, dear Caroline.''

This last comment brought Caroline's feet back on the ground. "What rubbish!" she said frankly. "Next you will be telling me that I am as lovely as a rose, at which point I shall have to discount everything you have said thus far!"

Mrs. Sheridan considered Caroline and the happiness she wore so evidently on her face. "I was thinking more of a modest, late-blooming flower. Would you be better likely to believe me if I compared you to an aster, perhaps, or a chrysanthemum?" she said. "And never mind your protests! Let me tell you about your Richard Worth, of whom I am sure you made a conquest!"

Caroline looked anxiously about her. She saw couples emerging from the assembly rooms and drifting toward the staircase. She did not want to be seen by the entire company sneaking off into the hallway at the bottom of the stairs, and she certainly did not want to keep Mr. Kenmure waiting.

"Better yet," Caroline said, "I'll come to visit you early tomorrow afternoon, and you can tell me all about him then! No, wait! I can't do that! I must go now!" She looked about her anxiously again. "I have . . .''

"An assignation, Caroline?" Mrs. Sheridan had a knowing look in her eye. "But, of course, and why not?"

Caroline blushed and smiled.

"Then, go, my dear!" Mrs. Sheridan waved her on. "Our little talk can wait until later tomorrow, at Lady Purcell's evening musicale. I had anticipated that event being a great bore, but now we can gossip in a corner! Go on!''

Caroline nodded, lifted her skirts and sailed down the stairs. It happened that just as her foot trod the last step, she saw the Duke of Desford enter the front door, cloak and cane in hand. He was just then sweeping his hat off his elegant wig. She had never seen him looking so handsome, or so at ease with himself and the world. She had never felt her love for him more clearly or painfully. Then her happiness fluttered up again and touched her heart when she realized—inadmissible thought!—that, were she to accept Mr.

Kenmure's offer, she would be cousin to the duke for all time.

Desford had paused to exchange a word with the proprietor of the London Tavern, who still stood sentry at the door, waiting to greet the latecomers. Since Caroline hardly wished to be noticed by either of those men, she slipped into the hallway where she would find the alcove. With her first step into the long, darkened hallway, she felt her third prick of uneasiness this evening, and some of the romance drained out of the adventure. It was bad manners to engage in such intrigue. She even felt a spurt of anger toward her swain. Why did he have to choose such a *dark* place to reveal to her the secrets of his heart? Surely he could have declared his love just as well on the morrow, after having made a proper appointment with her!

Still, there was no going back now, and she did not like to think of herself as a scared, kittenish creature. She walked straight into the blackness. The London Tavern was an old rambling building, and she soon discovered a slight corner in the hallway when she stubbed her toe against the protruding wall. She used her hands to feel her way around the corner and then proceeded slowly to the curve that must have been the alcove.

She called softly, "Mr. Kenmure," but there was no response. The alcove felt empty. She waited uncounted seconds, torn between excitement and fear and silliness, until she became chilled by a cold draft of air.

She poked her head out of the alcove. Her eyes had adjusted to the darkness, and she could just discern that at the end of the hallway was a door that most likely gave access to the alleyway that ran down one side of the tavern. The door seemed to be ajar. She sensed something wrong. Still more curious than afraid, Caroline eased down the hall, in the direction of the back door.

She stepped out into the alleyway and registered a series of images, as sharp and clear as the November night: the heaps of ashes piled high at each back door that punctuated the two brick walls lining the alley; the withered apples and shriveled orange peels that mingled with a greasy lump of rags in the gutter; the remnants of a gentleman's wig, which had passed, no doubt, from the original gentleman, to his son, to the coachman, to the gardener, to the secondhand shop, continuing its downward course to the shoeblack's box where it came upon its last usefulness, and from there, it was but the toss of the shoeblack's hand that had landed it in this particular gutter.

These stray images struck her brain and froze as her eye fell on an object about twenty feet away from the door. It was the body of a man, lying broken and pathetic on the cobbles. She could not identify him from that distance, but she felt her prick of uneasiness take definite shape to become a weight of dread that fell from her throat to her stomach. She exhaled, and saw her breath hang for a moment to crystallize on the cold night air. Then her breath vanished, taking with it, she imagined, all her delicate happiness and giddy effervescence. The autumn flower inside her died, and she was filled instead with a cold self-possession. Unable to take her eyes off the body, she stumbled a step back toward the door but fell instead against the wall. The horror of the scene rang down her spine.

One passerby, then two, were drawn to the body in the alley. One shouted for help, the other ran for help, and these actions inevitably brought more people to the scene. Very soon there would be a throng, and the evening would end in shock and scandal.

Richard Worth was the second person from the assembly to find his way to the alley. It was not any one reason that drew him there, but a combination of the muffled shout he heard down in the street mixed with the general smell in the air of danger and death that he had come to know so well over the past thirteen years. After his dance with Miss Hutton, he had withdrawn from the company of the assembly, needing time to be alone, and had descended a back staircase to the foyer. There he encountered Desford, just about to ascend the main stairway to the assembly.

Worth slipped his arm through Desford's, saying by way of greeting, "Come, Jonathan. There's trouble."

Desford was not unnaturally surprised by this and protested that his friend had been away from society and on the battlefield too long. However, he did not resist Worth's insistent tugging, saying that he would do whatever his friend wanted as long as Worth did not ruin the sleeve of his Italian silk coat.

It was with a sigh that Desford followed Worth down the hallway that Caroline had lately traveled. They emerged into the alleyway, heedless of the woman standing rigid against the wall. There in the alley Worth saw what he had feared. A small group of men stood; the curves of their necks and the hushed tones of their voices could only mean that they were looking at a dead body.

Worth pushed forward. Desford followed. They were permitted access into the circle, the men who were already there offering such explanations as "Mohawks!" and "Bloody thieves roam the neighborhood," and "It was a drunken cutpurse that done the deed" and, obscurely, "Wild." Worth stared down at the body of a young man, his blood spilled onto his neckcloth. Not a flicker of an eye betrayed what Worth thought of the gaping slash in the man's neck, the kind he had seen too many thousands of times before on the battlefield. A military cut, he reflected dispassionately, accurate and purposeful. No drunken cutpurse could have been so precise.

"I thought I had escaped this, Jonathan," Worth murmured at last, looking over his shoulder at his friend who stood at his back. "As if we have not seen enough."

The Duke of Desford's handsome countenance was ashen. He said nothing, merely nodded, dazed and dumb.

An off-duty constable had arrived at the scene early on, entirely by chance. He recognized the newcomers as Quality.

"Can either of you fine gentlemen identify the victim?" the lawman asked routinely, in a light Scots burr, his tones of disinterested authority cutting across death and the night air.

The Duke of Desford knelt and touched a disbelieving hand to the victim's neckcloth. He withdrew his hand, and in so doing, his lace cuff came away flecked with red. He glared at the spots in horror. He attempted to say something, had to clear his throat and begin again. In a wavering voice, he said, "The man is my cousin." He stood. He swayed slightly and gripped Worth's arm for support. "His name is Gilbert Kenmure."

Chapter Four

The next afternoon, Caroline had chosen to return on foot from Birchin Lane to her aunt's house in Portugal Row. A few paces behind her trailed one of her aunt's footmen. Although he showed nothing of it on his face, the poor man was vexed that Miss Hutton had unaccountably sent Lady Besant's carriage back to Portugal Row empty. His buckled shoes were pinching his feet.

Caroline had not worn walking shoes either, but she was used to country habits, and being London-bred, she did not need a map to guide her steps. However, it was not for the pleasures of a brisk walk that she was returning on foot. It was rather that she needed the physical outlet, for she was stunned. So stunned she could not feel the ill-laid paving beneath the thin soles of her slippers. So stunned she could not see. She was blind to the colors and the movements of the careless tradesmen—barber, baker, painter, sweep—who plodded their way without caring much whom they jostled; the fights of the carters; the man in the pillory; the chase of the pickpocket; the beau so splendid with his cane, his sword and sash, his mincing gait; the chariot with its painted sides, coats of arms, or nymphs.

She was deaf, as well, to the growl of carriage wheels; the clop of hooves; the hawkers bawling the seasonal plums, pears and walnuts; the newspaper boy running along, shouting the news; the contrasting quiet of the alley; the uneasy creak of the heavy shop signs, swaying over the street.

She was not aware that she was walking on firm ground. She might have been wading through water, swimming even—sinking, more like, her body a deadweight. Then, by turns, she lost all substance and weightlessly bobbled in the air, light-headed and giddy. Word-robbed with shock, she heard baby phrases ring in her brain: *All gone!* and *No more!*

It was not grief at Mr. Kenmure's brutal death that had carved out the hollow place in the pit of her stomach, nor despair that she had suffered a love lost—although it was true that she had not closed her eyes all through the night, mourning the wicked waste of Mr. Kenmure's life. It was rather Mr. Gresham's pronouncements in the dusty front room in Birchin Lane that had so thoroughly undone her. It was shock upon shock. It was death upon death—her father's death, Mr. Kenmure's death—and a loss to her now that seemed so large that it could fill eternity.

All gone! and *No more!*

Caroline dashed her hand in front of her eyes and suddenly recognized by the wooden paling that she was already at Lincoln's Inn Fields. She crossed Holborn Row to a path that cut through the central garden of the square that led straight to Portugal Row, opposite. Just as she arrived at the other end of the garden, which brought her within fifty yards of her destination, she halted.

Amazed and disbelieving, she watched a tall, graceful man descend the steps of her aunt's house. He did not pause at street level, but walked purposefully away, so that his back was to Caroline. A moment later he disappeared down the connecting Pearl Street. If she had been in possession of her normal wits and perceptions, Caroline would have sworn that the man was the Duke of Desford.

She gave herself a mental shake. It could not have been the duke. Lady Besant hardly knew him. Caroline stood at the corner of the garden for another minute or two, until she determined that the news she had received this afternoon, coupled with the shock of the night before, had deranged her senses. She forced her feet forward. On this inhospitable November day, the streets were empty of casual strollers. She encountered no one as she walked up Portugal Row toward the small but fashionable brick house with the black iron railing and green door.

Before she turned to mount the steps, the door opened, and out stepped Lady Besant. Caroline had not seen her aunt since the night before and their stone-silent return through the tomb-streets of the city. Upon rising this morning, Caroline had been told that her aunt was unlikely to leave her rooms before the evening. But here Lady Besant was now, in the act of tying the hood of her purple cloak, as if making a hasty departure.

Upon seeing her niece, Lady Besant's eyes narrowed slightly before she smoothed her features into an agreeable mask. "My dear child," she said, twitching her cloak into place, "I was surprised to receive word that you had gone to meet your appointment. Today of all days. You have uncommon fortitude."

The long walk had exercised the desired effect on Caroline. She felt herself capable of speech again. "I saw no reason to delay it and even thought it beneficial to finish my business with Mr. Gresham. Especially today."

"You were gone far less time than one would expect to finish complicated estate matters."

"It was a short interview and the business brief," Caroline replied.

"When the carriage came back without you, I was worried," Lady Besant said.

"Were you? Surely the coachman informed you that I preferred to walk back. I had no desire to cause you concern."

Lady Besant smiled perfunctorily. "No, indeed. And to relieve all my worries, you must tell me," she said, "how it went with Mr. Gresham."

"Hutton Manor is to be sold to pay off Father's debts. Gambling debts, to be precise." Caroline bit into these cold, brittle words. The unsheltered street struck her as a peculiarly apt setting in which to recount her ruin. "I thought he had quit his disastrous habit after his stroke, but he did not. In paying off the debts, the death duties, the taxes and the lawyer's fees, there is nothing left. Since I am unmarried, Father had legal access to the legacy Mother left me, and he ran through that as well. All of it. It is gone. There is no more.''

Caroline stopped short of saying that it was, finally, this plunder of her legacy that was so deeply galling. She had expected to come out of the financial tangle with Hutton Manor and a small, but respectable, competence. She had even contemplated an act of largess toward her aunt, as a conciliatory gesture. Now, irony of ironies, she was at her aunt's mercy.

"He ran through the *whole* fortune, my dear?" Lady Besant said on a note of amused disgust. "How like him!"

Caroline could hardly believe her ears, for her aunt sounded almost nonchalant. Again, Caroline thought her senses must be deranged. She said nothing, for there was nothing more to say. She braced herself for the inevitable *What will you do now, my dear? For you cannot expect me to support you!*

Instead, her aunt surprised her with the comment, "Well, that is too bad, but perhaps something else will come up."

"Too bad?" Caroline echoed, amazed. "Come up—?"

Lady Besant shrugged. "I do not mean to sound callous, my dear, but I must admit I am not entirely surprised that James was incapable of containing his folly! Oh, I agree that it is *indecent* that he ran through such a *large* fortune, but there it is! And perhaps I am taking your news...somewhat less seriously than I might have under other circumstances—" here Lady Besant had the grace to look truly stricken "—given the tragedy of last evening. Speaking of which," she said, her eyes darting speculatively away and then back to Caroline, "you might wish to speak to the Duke of Desford about your plight."

Caroline could only ask, stupidly, "Why should I wish to tell the Duke of Desford about my plight?"

Lady Besant's hard beauty was well framed by the purple hood. "You recall our little talk on the way to the London Assembly last night, my dear? It was most informative! I was quite persuaded, during the course of the evening, by what you had to say earlier in the carriage. I am sure that many others at the assembly perceived it too! The point is, my dear, that you have suffered a . . . disappointment with Mr. Kenmure's quite horrible death, and I think it only right that the Duke of Desford should know about it."

Caroline blinked. "So I *did* see him leave the house just now!"

The tiniest pause seemed to indicate that Lady Besant had to revise what she was going to say next. Perhaps she had not been going to divulge that the duke had come to Portugal Row. She arranged a complacent smile on her face. "Yes, of course, you must have seen him, for he just left," she said easily.

Caroline was acutely conscious now of her surroundings and the chill that had invaded her bones. Her voice was little more than a glacial whisper. "Do not tell me that *you* told his grace what I said about . . . about Mr. Kenmure wanting to marry me!"

"Calm yourself, Caroline. Of course I did not!"

"Then why did his grace come to see you?" she demanded.

"He did not come to see me," Lady Besant returned. "He came to see you."

"But—but *why?*"

"It seems his grace feels it necessary to visit everyone who had close contact with Gilbert before his death," Lady Besant explained, "to make sure that they are not suffering unduly. He was desolated to find that you had gone out, and he told me that he intends to return. Perhaps not today, however, given the many demands on his time these days. His grace is so sensible of his duties! And, given that, it occurs to me, my dear, that you may wish to tell him, when next he comes to visit you, of your expectations with Mr. Kenmure." She smiled. "You never know how his grace might respond."

A bitter anger momentarily surged through Caroline's ice-cold veins. She imagined that her teeth had just sunk, hard, into the sourest of lemons. "I have no wish to profit," she said with acrid distaste, "from Mr. Kenmure's death."

"Of course you do not, my dear," her aunt said. "However, you are hardly now in a position to ignore any possible sources of help. Neither am I—as you well know—in a position to encourage you to ignore them."

Never had Caroline felt a more rigid dislike of her aunt. She thought it just as well that her face was already pinched from the cold and her loss, for she made no attempt to conceal what she was feeling. "I am not completely helpless," she said flatly. "After all, I am used to these circumstances."

"Are you, indeed?"

"I have faced financial adversity before," Caroline reminded her aunt.

"But you have never had such a severe case of it."

To this Caroline remarked dispassionately, "I have a disease. A poverty disease."

Lady Besant was hardly amused. "We have all suffered from the untoward events of the last evening," she said repressively. "You, my dear, have suffered a double shock, so I will not reproach you." She looked about her, as if recalling the fact that they were standing in the street. "This is hardly the moment to discuss such delicate business. I must be off now. Please be ready at five o'clock so that we may be prompt at Marylebone."

"We attend Lady Purcell's musicale today?" Caroline asked with real surprise.

"There will be no music, to be sure," Lady Besant said.

"Then what is the point? No one will come."

"I predict that Lucy's house will be full to overflowing," Lady Besant said. "Everyone will come. To commiserate."

"And the duke?" Caroline wanted to know.

"The only person not likely to attend will be his grace, who is in mourning." Lady Besant smiled a rather tight little smile. "Now, run along inside, my dear, and consider in better circumstances what you will say to his grace when he comes to visit you." With that, she strode off in the direction the duke had taken minutes before.

Caroline stood in the street a few moments longer, prey to a paralyzing series of emotions. On top of her disbelief and grief, anger at her aunt's suggestion warred with a horrible suspicion that Lady Besant was not telling her the whole truth about the duke's visit, until her disbelief, grief, anger and suspicion were washed away in a wave of pure weakness.

Financial disaster, like an illness, had struck her three years before, and it had recurred unexpectedly this morning. She remembered the symptoms. They were stronger now, more debilitating. A well-bred woman, alone in the world, could die from such a disease. She wanted nothing more than to take to her bed for the rest of the day and night in the hopes of awakening from this bad dream. However, she had had enough experience with the poverty disease to know that inaction would, indeed, be fatal. Only one vague course of action occurred to her: to go to Lady Purcell's and to speak with Martha Sheridan.

Later that afternoon, at the appointed time, dressed and coiffed, Caroline and her aunt were once again in the Besant carriage, following the progress of bricks and mortar west to the agricultural estates which a handful of aristocrat landowners had opened up for housing. The strange conversation she had had with her aunt earlier in the day was not mentioned. Lady Besant was quiet, with a slight air of preoccupation. Caroline gazed sullenly upon the passing gridiron of streets that was imposing its pattern on the emerging map of London, imagining that the urban evil of the kind that had visited Mr. Kenmure was dogging their trail, nipping at the back wheels of the carriage, urging them forward.

The geometric scheme of this westward march of streets was marred only by the occasional irregularity, such as the meandering course of Marylebone Lane. Taking that ancient thoroughfare, the Besant carriage arrived in the vicinity of Purcell House. Caroline saw the drive, as well as the entire street leading up to it, clotted with carriages, bearing out her aunt's prediction that Lady Purcell's gathering would be the most well-attended event of the London elite that day.

As the carriage drew up to the entrance, Lady Besant turned to Caroline and said, "Would you mind it if we do not mention the duke's visit today? Then you will have nothing to explain."

"Good heavens, no!" Caroline replied promptly. "I should not mind it in the least! Do not mention it to anyone!"

"Then I will not, my dear," her aunt said, smiling sweetly.

They descended. In the shadow of the chaste Palladian facade of Purcell House, they hugged and embraced others who had come to offer sympathy and find it themselves. Inside, a subdued atmosphere reigned, the tone set by the black crape that hung on the cherubs adorning the pedimented doorcases. To any other signs of mourning the hostess was not entitled. Lady Purcell was there, at the foot of the lavish staircase, greeting her guests and directing them to the drawing room.

Upstairs, in the restrained grandeur of Lady Purcell's home, Caroline felt curiously soothed. Her losses of the morning were not less real, and she still felt physically weak. Yet she found comfort in sharing expressions of horror at the brutal murder. She felt her newly diagnosed poverty disease go into slight remission.

As Caroline moved slowly through the noble apartment, greeting, nodding, embracing, her calm increased when no one treated her as having any special claim to mourning. It was noted, of course, that she had danced with poor Mr. Kenmure the evening before, but then again, so had several other ladies present. She had been among the first at the scene of the crime, but no one was commenting on the order in which the crowd had gathered. Caroline was heartily relieved that there was no public acknowledgment of her relationship with Mr. Kenmure. Thus, no one—besides her aunt—was likely to mention such a relationship to the Duke of Desford.

The only one who might have guessed would have been Martha Sheridan. It took only the opening exchange between them for Caroline to realize, with further relief, that

Martha's thoughts were entirely preoccupied with the horrors of Mr. Kenmure's murder and not with Caroline's assignation the night before. Upon encountering each other in the drawing room, the two friends had fallen into each other's arms. When they drew apart, they were still clutching hands.

"And to think that the last time we saw each other, we did not have a care in the world!" Mrs. Sheridan said with a sad, entrancing smile and sad, beautiful eyes.

"So horrible," Caroline agreed.

"It could have been any of us," Mrs. Sheridan continued, drawing Caroline over to a sofa next to a harpsichord whose graceful wing was closed for the evening. "Any one of us could have been victim to the assault." She waved a hand, gesturing randomly at the crowd of people in the room.

"Which is why, in part, we are all here," Caroline replied. "Safety in numbers. I felt it, too, on my way through town, the sense of insecurity, the tingling down my spine."

"It affects me particularly since I have just come back to society after Humphrey's death—which was not at all the same thing, I know! His was grave illness—nothing to be done!—and not the act of savage criminals who I hope will be brought to justice! But the feeling is curiously the same, and the result in both cases so harsh and final and so...so..."

"It's a blow to us all," Caroline agreed, patting Martha's hand.

Martha looked at Caroline and smiled a less troubled smile. "I *knew* I would feel better once I had seen you!" she said. "Just hearing your voice is so very soothing, my dear!"

"I'm glad then," Caroline confined herself to saying as she continued to pat Martha's hand. It had been her intention to unburden herself to Martha, but she saw now that Martha's need for comfort was the more immediate. Caroline was disappointed, but she understood that this latest death had brought back the sadness of Sheridan's death.

"Mr. Kenmure reminded me of my gentle Humphrey, of whom I was so very fond," the widow said with a catch in her voice. "You see, I rather liked Mr. Kenmure."

Caroline released her friend's hand. "You did?" she said in a strange voice.

"Not in the way that you think!" Martha laughed shakily at Caroline's expression. "I do not suppose that I knew Mr. Kenmure better than anyone else, but he was such a nice man and... and as of yesterday, so *alive!*" Martha put a hand to her forehead. "I have not slept a wink since last night. I could not even close my eyes for a rest earlier today! Nor have I eaten! It was all I could do to allow myself to be dressed to come here. To think that it could have been anyone! But it was not anyone. It was Mr. Kenmure. I thought perhaps it was because he was so new to town and not wary enough in the streets, but no—" She stopped, then smiled a wavering smile. "Forgive me. I ramble."

Caroline had the fleeting thought that if the beautiful and wealthy Martha Sheridan had shown the least interest in Mr. Kenmure, Caroline must have seriously misinterpreted Mr. Kenmure's reasons for the assignation in the alcove. She shook her head, in part to rid it of her own improbable fancies, in part to reassure her friend.

"I haven't slept either," Caroline replied, "and in addition to that, I had particularly bad news earlier today—well, never mind that just now," she added, fully aware of her friend's distress. "I'll tell you later! But just look around you. Everyone is overset and living on nerves. I doubt that anyone present has a word to speak beyond the tragedy!"

Martha's sad smile steadied. "That is true, of course. I have no right to take so much on myself—to take it so personally!" She exhaled and sank back into the sofa. "I haven't drunk anything, either, all day." She clutched a hand to her throat. "I'm parched!"

At that moment, the bulk of Arthur Devis came into view on the immediate horizon. He bowed as deeply as his girth would allow and, after the briefest of greetings, offered to fetch the ladies a drink. "Need another one myself. Been drinking since last night. Began after the ruckus. Can't seem to stop. What's more, don't want to. Awful." He held up his empty glass. "Not the stuff they're serving here. Why, Leland has one of the best cellars in town. No. What happened at the assembly. Awful." He nodded his head decisively. "Need another drink, myself. Can I fetch something for you, ladies?"

Martha stretched out her hand to touch his sleeve. "Make it tea, Arthur dear. I need something soothing. Anything stronger will undo me!" She turned to Caroline. "And for you?"

Caroline agreed that the only drink she could swallow was tea, and Mr. Devis took himself off to procure the necessary. He returned with a full glass of sherry for himself and a footman bearing a tea tray in tow. He pulled up a chair, and when the ladies had full cups and saucers in hand, he said, "To think that I just missed seeing the poor blighter yesterday afternoon!"

"Who?" Martha asked, puzzled.

Mr. Devis looked surprised by the question. "Kenmure, of course, rest the poor blighter's soul. Awful!"

"Do you mean that you went by Mr. Kenmure's rooms?" Caroline asked, when Martha did not pick up the topic of discussion.

"By Cavendish Square," he said, nodding. "Not far from here, don't you know! Sold him a horse. A week or two ago. Went by his rooms to have him pay me."

"Mr. Kenmure left debts?" Caroline asked.

Devis waved this away. "Nothing to signify. Sold him a horse, that's all, and he hadn't paid me yet. Wouldn't call it a debt. Nothing of that sort. Still, went by his rooms yesterday. Midafternoon, it was. Told he wasn't at home."

"I am sure that the duke will make good on all his cousin's encumbrances," Caroline said, thinking inevitably of her own unenviable place on the duke's list of duties.

Devis fortified himself with a deep drink. "Don't need the money," he said, hardly slurring his words. "But went by his rooms and asked to see him. Told he was out." He winked suggestively. "Wasn't out, though. Saw someone at the upper window. Not Kenmure. Someone else." He nodded. "Entertaining. Didn't want to be disturbed."

Caroline misliked the implication. "I am sure that he planned to pay you," she said, to defend Mr. Kenmure's honor.

"Sure of it," Devis agreed. "What I mean was, entertaining a woman. Saw her at the window."

Caroline's brows snapped together. She felt distinctly uneasy at this news, but hardly had a moment to consider it, for Martha had given a little squeak.

"Oh, look, Caroline!" the widow exclaimed, clucking her tongue in disgust, "I've spilt my tea upon my skirts." She set down her cup on a low side table and began brushing the spot on the silk ineffectually with a lace napkin. Caroline lent her napkin to the task, as well.

Devis was nodding continuously. "Meant to pay me. A good man, don't you know. Not one to run out owing a man money. Didn't deserve the stab in the back he got last night. Awful."

Still ministering to Martha's skirts, Caroline looked up at Devis and felt her throat tighten. She was incapable of response.

Martha had mopped what she could of her stain. She had taken up her cup again, and as she was leaning back once more into the sofa, her eye drifted across the room. "Well," she said, her voice steadier, "there is Richard Worth, speaking with Angelica Gordon. In the press of events, Caroline, I completely forgot to tell you about him." With a kind of relief, she asked, "Should you like to hear about him now?"

Caroline turned to glance hastily in the direction Mrs. Sheridan had indicated. She, too, had completely forgotten about the mystery of the "infamous Richard Worth." She, too, desired a change in subject. "Oh, yes, tell me, Martha!" she encouraged.

Devis tossed off the rest of the sherry in one gulp. "Worth. Been away a long time. Back for good. In town. Means to settle down." He glared into his empty glass. "Awful."

Chapter Five

Moments after stepping into Lady Purcell's crowded drawing room, Worth had gauged the temper of the occasion. He knew from long experience how to assess the mood in camp on "the day after." These troops, though decorous and dressed in silk, were nervous. A strain of fear ran deep, but they had closed their well-knit ranks and were ready to defend themselves from further attack.

Within a minute of his arrival, Worth had circulated enough to perceive that the reserve with which he had been treated the night before had vanished, or was held in abeyance. All expressions of horror and scandal on this occasion were saved for the fellow who had met his end the night before in the alley that ran alongside the London Tavern. By the time he had worked his way past the first few clusters of people in the room, Worth had come to the unexpected, satisfying realization that the shock gripping the assembled company was serving to smooth his return to society. Being completely unacquainted with the victim, Worth thought of the murder in practical terms as a great piece of perfectly timed luck. The benefits to his own plans were apparent, and he did not intend to squander his advantage.

He glanced around the room and was satisfied by what he saw. Angelica Gordon and Julia Stanhope were present. So was Caroline Hutton, seated on a sofa with the woman he had once known as the incomparable Martha Stowell. Next to them, nodding fatuously, was Arthur Devis. Beyond them stood a harpsichord of walnut that Worth guessed at a glance to be of English origin, possibly from the craft shop of Plenius.

Worth strolled the room. He bowed to any number of people, who offered the distant, though conventional "Didn't have a chance to speak to you last night. A pleasure to see you again." There were those who greeted him with the distracted bluntness of "Gad, Worth, I suppose you've heard the news?" However, no one unbent far enough to offer any greeting so friendly as, "I heard you rode with Marlborough. Lucky chap!"

Worth was passing by one group when he overheard a man say, "Strangled," to which a second rejoined, "And with his own neckcloth, too!"

Worth stopped to listen, his curiosity piqued. He recognized the first man, an older, very correct gentleman. He searched his memory and found the name of the peer Bromley. He mentally winced at the memory of their previous encounter, thirteen years before.

"It's a scandal!" Lord Bromley was expounding. His voice rumbled with barely suppressed outrage. "Violence and plunder are no longer confined to the highways! The field of action is removed, and the streets of the City are the places of danger! Our wives, our daughters, why, our *selves* live in constant threat of violence, perpetrated by the thieves and cutthroats who run the City! Something must be done!"

"The police are afraid," a second man complained.

"The police are *collaborators!*" a third responded.

Talk flashed. Corruption in Bow Street was discussed with animation until the solemnity of the occasion was recalled. A sudden, somber silence fell. Bromley broke it with the pronouncement, "It was Wild's doing, or one of his men."

Worth had heard the word *wild* the night before, as he had entered the circle of men surrounding the dead body. However, he had not recognized it as a name. Since this scandal-preoccupied occasion had afforded him an excellent field position, he decided to skirmish on the border of his social acceptability. "You mention a man named Wild, Bromley?" he ventured.

"Mr. Jonathan Wild, if you please," the older man explained, turning to his questioner, "the most notorious thief in all of London!" Facing Worth now, Bromley paused, the surprise of recognition flickering across his face. Worth had no difficulty interpreting the consternation that swiftly followed. After the merest hesitation, Bromley chose to continue his answer. "Wild and his men have terrorized the streets of London for the past several years." As judge, he passed sentence. "He belongs in Newgate."

"Or hanging from the branch at Tyburn tree," the second man opined, taking up the role of executioner.

"At the end of Kenmure's neckcloth!" was the third's idea of just punishment.

It was testimony to the extreme feelings of the occasion that no one rose to protest the ghoulish lack of taste of the last suggestion. The subject of Jonathan Wild began to be elaborated with zest. Having won a valuable scrap of social territory, Worth bowed himself away from the group and furthered his acquaintance with Angelica Gordon. At one moment, he glanced beyond Miss Gordon's shoulder to verify that Miss Hutton was still seated on the sofa. He saw that she seemed to be engaged in inspecting something on the incomparable Martha's skirts. She was brushing at it, as if something had spilled. He concluded his conversation with Miss Gordon and moved in the direction of the sofa next to the harpsichord. As he approached, he noted that the two women looked up and broke off their low conversation. Their expressions were carefully composed.

Worth bowed correctly to Miss Hutton, whose pale face showed none of the pastel gaiety he had seen the night before. She raised her eyes to his and greeted him by name. He acknowledged Arthur Devis, whose drowning wits surfaced enough for him to offer a sodden, automatic "Servant" in return. Then Worth turned to the incomparable Martha and said, "The last time we saw each other, I knew you as Miss Stowell." His smile was one of regret. "I am afraid that I know no more."

Martha held out her hand to him. He took it. "You knew me as Martha," she corrected, returning the pressure of his fingers, "and since we last saw each other, I have been married to Humphrey Sheridan," she said, "and widowed."

Worth released her hand. He took the news with no outward display of emotion, but Humphrey Sheridan had been a good friend who had stood by him longer than most. After a brief "May I?" he drew up a neighboring chair and sat down. "When I returned last week," he said, "I had not expected that all the news I would catch up on would be good. Still, Sheridan—" He exhaled slowly. "Not recently widowed, I assume?"

Martha gestured minimally to her dress, which was not even the mauve of half mourning. "A year ago this month," she said. "High fever and wrenching chest pains. We suspected that it was his heart. His father died of the same thing." She shrugged. "At the same age." She bridged the respectful pause that followed with a short laugh. "I have only just returned to society—not unlike yourself, Richard."

"The cases are hardly parallel," Worth said without expression.

Her smile was kind and including. "You've been gone and now you're back," she said, with no hint of slyness or insinuation, "and seeing you again reminds me of the old days, when we were happy! So long ago it seems, and yet a happy time is no farther away than yesterday! However, today it is difficult to believe that we were ever so carefree as we were fifteen years ago, so innocent or so—" Her voice crumbled.

When Martha was unable to continue, Caroline came to her friend's aid. She took one of Martha's cold hands in her warm one. She looked at Colonel Worth and said a little ruefully, "Before you came up, we were discussing—what else?—last night's tragedy." This was the perfect truth, for in recounting Worth's scandalous past, Martha had got no farther than the tantalizing opener: "Many people said he was guilty, you know, but *I* never thought so." Caroline continued. "Mr. Kenmure's death has affected all of us deeply, and all of us differently. For Martha, it has had the unfortunate effect of refreshing a bereavement that is not so very distant.''

"I understand," Worth said, turning from Mrs. Sheridan's face, whose delicate loveliness was enhanced by her trembling, vulnerable grief. "And for you, Miss Hutton?''

Caroline found it disconcerting that Colonel Worth should focus on her. Martha Sheridan's beautiful distress should have drawn him far more than her own uninteresting sadness, but his eyes did not waver from her face. The intensity of his blue gaze and the severity of his body clothed in a suit of deeper blue struck her with a curious, physical effect that she could not quite define. Caroline answered, "It is the horrible waste of Mr. Kenmure's life that overwhelms me.''

Slouching slightly in his chair, Devis roused himself enough to insert, "Good man, Kenmure. Didn't deserve the stab in the back he got last night. Awful!''

Caroline was glad that Worth's attention swerved to Devis. "Stabbed in the back?" Worth queried. "How do you know?''

"Common knowledge." Devis nodded wisely. "Got there myself before the body was carted away." Devis blinked heavily and sat up with deliberation. "Beg your pardon, ladies," he enunciated. "Not polite conversation, but it's the topic of the evening, don't you know." Caroline murmured something to the effect that it would be unnatural to avoid it, and Martha waved away with a limp gesture any objections she might be thought to have. "Saw him lying there," Devis continued. "Covered with a sheet by that time.''

Worth pressed. "So you did not actually see the wound?''

"Didn't have to," Devis informed him. "When they took the body away, saw the blood on the cobbles. Awful! Stabbed in the back. Everyone said so. Must have been robbed. Poor old blighter." He raised his glass to his lips and frowned at it, astonished that it was empty. He lowered the glass. "Now, me. Tell you what I'd do. In a street, or in an alley, I'd give the thief my valuables. 'Have the watch!' I'd say. 'Have the notecase, too.' Damn, I'd give him the jeweled pin in my cravat, see if I wouldn't!" Pot-valiant, he added, "My ring, too! No sense dying for a few trinkets. Got more of 'em!"

"Entirely senseless!" Martha agreed, weakly.

Worth said, "So Mr. Kenmure was robbed, in your opinion."

Devis nodded with drunken emphasis. "Not just my opinion. Everyone's opinion. Jumped on from behind, unawares. Stabbed in the back. Robbed. Poor old blighter. Awful!" Devis's weaving attention was caught by a passing footman to whom he gestured with his empty glass. Before the footman could pour, Devis wrapped his hand around the bottle and took it off the tray. The footman bowed and withdrew. Devis splashed some sherry into his glass, not spilling more than a drop or two on his breeches. However, when the bottle ran out before his glass was even half-full, he spluttered, "How's a man to get a decent drink? Bad service, I call it." He struggled to his feet and had to grasp an arm of the chair to stand steady. "Must be a loose board here," he commented, peering owlishly down at the floor.

The next moment he swayed, and Martha had to hold out her hands to prevent his falling on her. With a meaningful glance at Caroline and Worth, Martha rose and grasped Devis's arms. "Come along, Arthur," she said, "I'll find you what you need."

"A full bottle, by God," was Devis's response. With a painfully precise bow to Caroline and Worth, he excused himself and took his leave on the words, "Fellow needs a drink at a time like this. Bad service, I call it."

Martha turned back and said over her shoulder to Worth, "Come visit me soon, Richard." To Caroline, she said, "I'll speak to you later tonight, my dear. Or tomorrow."

"Wobbly floorboards here," Devis said, leaning heavily on Mrs. Sheridan as they moved away. "Have to speak to Leland to get them fixed. Did I tell you Kenmure owed me money? Not that it signifies. The man's dead. Gone. Don't need the money. That's that."

Caroline was about to excuse herself as well, when Worth asked, "Do you agree, Miss Hutton, with the theory that

Jonathan Wild, or one of his men, is responsible for the murder?"

Caroline checked her movement to rise. She made it look as if she were resetting her skirts. "Oh, is that what's being said?" she replied, looking up. It surprised and even calmed her to think of the murder in terms of a murderer. Until now, she had conceived of Mr. Kenmure's death only as a manifestation of a nameless, faceless, urban evil, all the more fearsome for its lack of human agency.

"Such is Bromley's opinion," Worth said.

Caroline raised her brows. "And yours, as well?"

"I have no opinion," he returned. "I only heard of this fellow Wild a few minutes ago. I understand he's a notorious robber."

"That's right," she replied, "Mr. Wild is at the head of the most infamous gang of robbers ever to plague London. He must have begun his career some five years ago already—before I left for the country. But, no," she said, considering, "I do not think that Mr. Wild could be responsible."

"Why not?"

He wishes to converse with me, Caroline realized with some astonishment. In her weakened condition, the topic of Mr. Wild spanned safely before her like a bridge over the frozen stream of her emotions. Standing on her mental bridge and alone with Worth now, Caroline found the words to describe the effect of his presence. Colonel Worth, she decided, was like an unwise sip of champagne in an already hung-over state, for he had stirred in her blood the bubbling memory of her giddy happiness of the evening before.

Caroline smiled. "Mr. Wild is certainly a rascal," she answered easily, her tongue loosened by nothing stronger than a cup of tea and the stark, challenging presence of the man seated across from her, "and will come to no good end, but never before has one of his victims been murdered."

"There is always a first time."

She shook her head. "No," she said quite definitely. "That would be bad for business." From her years of charitable work at the St. Mary's almshouse at Cripplegate, she was familiar enough with Mr. Wild's methods. She explained, "Mr. Wild profits only from theft, not from murder. You see, the man has become so famous that whenever a person has been robbed, he knows to go to Mr. Wild's office. Yes, his office!" She chuckled at Worth's expression. "He has established it in a fine house in Cock Alley, by Cripplegate. So, the victim goes to Mr. Wild's office, and for the fee of a crown he is allowed to enter and to describe the items stolen. Mr. Wild says that he will investigate the matter. Do you see the trend?"

Worth was not slow. "Wild investigates and usually recovers the stolen items."

"Not usually," she said, "invariably! And never before two or three inquiries, after which, he explains to the victim that a friend of his, an honest broker to be sure, has stopped a parcel of goods upon suspicion. Mr. Wild discovers that these goods match precisely the description of the items stolen. Mr. Wild asks the victim only that some coin be paid the broker in consideration of his care, out of which Mr. Wild no doubt takes some profit. In addition, he pockets all the entry fees."

"And from this, Wild has a business?" Worth asked, a little doubtfully.

"A flourishing business," Caroline assured him. "Once the victim has thoroughly described what he has had stolen, the thieves seldom dare to conceal anything from Mr. Wild, and if they do, it is at their peril. So everyone wins. The victims recover their goods with as little trouble and expense possible, the 'honest broker' is paid, as well as the thieves who surely take a portion of the broker's fee. As for Mr. Wild, why, he reaps pure profit at no risk to himself."

"Ingenious," Worth commented.

"Very," Caroline concurred, "and so far from dirtying his hands with the stealing and being thereby unprosecutable, he is seen more in the light of a friend to the victim."

After a moment, Worth said, "I see your point that murdering the victim defeats the purpose."

"Yes, and it must be that Lord Bromley is unfamiliar with Mr. Wild's methods," Caroline suggested, "to have identified him as the murderer. Lord Bromley thought of him only because Mr. Wild is the most prominent of the practitioners of vice in the City."

"And how comes it that you, Miss Hutton, are so well acquainted with Mr. Wild's methods?" Worth wanted to know.

"Oh, it is because I was brought up in London," she said, offhand, hardly wishing to expose her association with the neighborhood of Cripplegate and her butter-soft heart, "and know the City and its ways well."

"No wonder, then, that you conceived a preference for the country, being so well acquainted with the varieties of vice in the City," he observed.

She felt two spots of color stain her cheeks. Although she was flattered that he had remembered their conversation from the night before, surely she was not such a goose as to blush at a modestly engaging, personal comment from a man. Perhaps it was merely a relapse of the fever weakness of her poverty disease. Weak or not, she was never diffident and met Worth's eye. He was, indeed, regarding her with interest, but what she read in the lines of his lean, irregular features and in the depths of his blue eyes was not flattery. He was assessing her, and his assessment puzzled her.

"Do you suggest," she asked directly, "that I have grown unaccustomed to the ways of the City in my years away?"

He smiled slightly. "I do not presume to know," he said. "However, it is possible that in the intervening years Mr. Wild's methods have grown less genteel."

"It is possible," she agreed, acknowledging the truth of this. She looked away. Her eye fell on Lady Besant who was regarding their tête-à-tête with palpable disapproval. "My Aunt Esther," she said, unable to keep the sour note out of her voice, "certainly thinks I have become countrified and am no longer used to town ways." Her eyes shifted back to Worth. "She said as much to me on the way to the assembly last night."

"Your Aunt Esther?" he queried, quick to pursue.

"Yes, Lady Esther Besant."

He stated, more than asked, "Lady Besant is a relative of yours, then."

"Yes, she is my father's half sister," Caroline informed him, "and I have been her guest in London these past few weeks. She thinks me little more than a bumpkin now."

Caroline Hutton might not have lit in Richard Worth the fires of passion, but with these simple statements, she awoke all his husbandly desires. He had wanted a good field position, but he had not expected anything this good. Marriage to Caroline Hutton would put him squarely behind enemy lines.

Caroline was unaware of the arrested look in Worth's hard eyes, for she had glanced back at Lady Besant. She acknowledged her aunt's basilisk stare with a nod and a placid smile. When she returned her attention to Worth and their conversation, Worth's expression was bland.

"So it is perhaps as you have said," she continued. "Mr. Wild's ways may have grown more dangerous in the past three years. It is possible that one of Mr. Wild's men—a novice—might have been frightened and bungled the robbery."

"Kenmure might have put up a fight," Worth suggested, seconding her idea.

"Not if," she said, puzzling the matter out, "he was jumped on unawares and stabbed in the back." The thought confused her. Some aspect of Mr. Kenmure's murder suddenly did not add up, but she could not think it through. Agitation overtook her, and she rose from the sofa.

Worth misinterpreted her reaction. "Forgive me, Miss Hutton," he replied, rising with her. "I did not mean to cause you pain. My interest in the affair must seem callous to you. It is only because I am unacquainted with the victim."

"Yes, of course," Caroline replied. She looked up at him, still puzzled. "Yet, given that lack of acquaintance, you seem to have more than a passing interest."

He smiled the smile that held all the elusive charm Caroline had seen the night before. She was partially reassured.

"I thought I had left the dangers behind on the battlefield. It comes as something of an unpleasant reminder that death awaits the unsuspecting in the City streets," he explained, reasonably enough. "I shall have a care to avoid the winding ways and dark alleys."

As he took her hand in parting, pieces of a thought strained to come together in Caroline's mind: *And why was Mr. Kenmure in the dark alley instead of the alcove?* Before settling into a whole, the pieces scattered like heaps of alley ashes in a light wind, for the moment after she had risen with Worth, a friend of hers chanced by and stopped to chat. Caroline was instantly occupied in presenting Colonel Worth to that lively, curious lady. Only after the introduction was made did Worth release Caroline's hand, and he did not think the significance of that gesture would be lost on anyone in retrospect.

Caroline might have excused herself from his presence. However, it happened that her popularity of the evening before had carried over into this occasion. After the first introduction, a great number of Caroline's many—equally curious and lively—friends came up to her, one by one. Out of the corner of her eye, Caroline perceived Lady Besant's spine-stiff posture, watching the proceedings. Caroline took a defiant pleasure in very graciously introducing her many friends—or reacquainting them, as the case might have been—to "Colonel Worth, of the First Regiment" or "Colonel Worth, who rode at Bouchain" or "Colonel Worth, of late under Marlborough's command." It was a puny defiance, but it felt good, even healthy.

When the little, spontaneous procession had ended, Worth turned to Caroline and made his first move. "I wish to call on you tomorrow morning at your home, Miss Hutton. Will that be possible?"

Caroline could not have been more surprised. In her distraction, she repeated a point of information. "Yes, of course. Have I mentioned that I am staying with my aunt—"

"Esther Besant," he said. "You have mentioned it."

"Shall I give you her address?"

"Portugal Row," he said, surprising her yet again, and even stated the correct number. "Until tomorrow morning."

"Until tomorrow," she repeated.

He bowed and left her. It had been his plan to speak next with Julia Stanhope, but that intention was now abandoned.

Caroline watched him as he was absorbed in a new group. Then a cutting voice at her side said, "You have become quite the popular young lady!"

Caroline turned to see her Aunt Esther measuring her. "I have many friends, yes," she answered flatly.

"I am referring to your apparently continuous conquests! That man you were speaking with just now...I have never before seen you so chatty, or that man so interested!" Lady Besant lapsed into abstracted reminiscence. "He was quite sought after once. Years ago already it was. Women seem to have found him attractive. *I* never thought so, myself, but there is no accounting for taste. Some might still find him attractive—perhaps even more so." Lady Besant recalled herself and smiled. "Did you have an interesting conversation with him, my dear?"

"Most interesting," Caroline replied, fighting down the flush she felt creeping over her cheeks, "under the circumstances."

"Under the circumstances," Lady Besant repeated. Then, shrewdly, "And the circumstances are so very much to his advantage. The present scandal of your Mr. Kenmure's death has overshadowed that man's return." She flicked a glance across the room at Worth. "It should not have been so easy for him. Perhaps it will not be, once the immediate furor dies down, and his greater crime is remembered."

"A greater crime than senseless murder?" Caroline scoffed.

"How have you remained so innocent," her aunt mused, mocking in turn, "after all your hours of good works at the almshouses?" Lady Besant did not lower her voice and recounted the old scandal with a casual disregard for who might overhear it. "You were too young at the time to remember that your latest gallant's father was a marquess." She smiled at Caroline's sudden change of expression. "Yes, a marquess. That man's mother died when he was young, and his father was unwise enough to remarry a beautiful young woman when that man was no more than twenty. It was not long before that man began to desire his new mother in a most inappropriate way and eventually satisfied his desires with brutal thoroughness."

"You can't know that for a fact," Caroline denied, but her throat was constricted, reducing her voice to a whisper.

Lady Besant's response was trenchant. "But I do, you see. The second marchioness was my best friend. And when the marquess discovered what his son had been doing, he killed his beautiful young wife, then turned the pistol on himself."

Chapter Six

Caroline's interview with Worth the next morning might have been less of a disaster if he had not arrived in Portugal Row so soon after Lady Besant's stunning announcement at the breakfast table.

Caroline had spent a fitful night, haunted by dreams of disease and death and blood and pistols. She arose late and heavy-eyed. She dressed and descended to find her aunt already in the breakfast saloon, seemingly recovered from her brittle temper of the day before. When Caroline entered the room, Lady Besant put down the letter she had been reading and favored her niece with an extremely bright smile. Lady Besant was looking particularly hard and glossy and satisfied this morning. She was elegant in a gown of patterned puce silk.

Caroline took her place at the table. She made a show of interest in food, although she had little appetite for ham and eggs.

"Well, my dear," her aunt opened, "I trust you slept well."

"Tolerably," Caroline said, shaking out her napkin and placing it on her lap.

"I am glad to hear it," her aunt replied. "I, myself, slept like a baby. Heaven knows we needed a peaceful night after all the wretchedness. My, but I feel better today! Even all the usual bills that are such a struggle to pay," Lady Besant continued, sweeping her hand across the litter of her morn-

ing's correspondence, "cannot spoil my mood. How a good
rest makes all the difference in one's outlook!"

When Caroline did not respond to these chipper remarks, Lady Besant's sharp black eyes surveyed her niece
critically a moment. "Your dress is charming, my dear. You
have an eye for what becomes you, I grant you that."

Caroline's ensemble was, in truth, rather fetching, being
a simple pearl-green linen dress with a square bodice lined
with white and faced with pink silk. Over this, for warmth,
she had added a hip-length damask jacket of darker green,
of a close-fitting waistcoat cut with a flare at the hips. The
neck was round, the cuffs deep and turned back, and the
whole was lined in leaf-green moiré. The jacket lent at once
an old-fashioned air and an unusually new look to the out-
fit, for Caroline had replaced the buttons and ribbons with
accessories of Oriental inspiration. The entire effect became her.

After another moment, Lady Besant added, "Yes, it will
do for today."

"It will have to do for today," Caroline said. In the long,
restless watches of the night, she had imagined her dreary
return to Hutton Manor to salvage those few personal pos-
sessions of no particular value, before the rest was sold.
Beyond that activity, however, she had not the faintest idea
where, or how, she was to live. "I must return to Hutton
Manor—for the last time. Today is as good a day as any
other to get started."

"That will not be necessary, my dear!" her aunt objected cheerfully. "I must tell you that the duke intends to
make up for your loss in an extremely handsome manner—"

"I told you yesterday," Caroline interrupted, "that I have
no intention of profiting from Mr. Kenmure's death."

Lady Besant's smile was truly ingratiating. She held up
the letter that she had been reading upon Caroline's entrance. "I told *you* yesterday that his grace wished to speak
with you. The letter I have just received from him expresses
his intention to visit you today."

"Must I repeat that I have no intention of telling his grace my plight, as you put it yesterday, or of suggesting that I was expecting a proposal of marriage from Mr. Kenmure?"

"You do not need to do tell his grace anything," Lady Besant assured her.

Caroline swallowed a bite of egg. "I am glad that you have realized it."

"You do not need to tell his grace," Lady Besant said, "because Mr. Kenmure had apparently already done so. And since you have suffered incalculable loss at Mr. Kenmure's death, the duke writes that he is coming to rectify matters." She paused dramatically. "I believe he intends to offer you marriage himself."

"Good God!"

"And is it not the perfect solution?" Lady Besant continued, ignoring her niece's strong, negative reaction. "Having lost all, you stand now to gain exceptionally."

Caroline had choked. "No," she gasped, with horror. She coughed once and managed, "I want to gain nothing from Mr. Kenmure's death. How could you even think of it?" she accused.

"I did not," Lady Besant replied. "It was the duke's suggestion that he himself be the agent by which to restore what a murderous street thief stole from you."

"I do not believe it."

Lady Besant handed the letter across the table to Caroline, who accepted it with nerveless fingers. "Read for yourself, my dear."

Caroline attempted to decipher the missive, but the letters of the spidery scrawl danced before her eyes, and she could make no sense of it. She was too astonished to consider the oddity that his grace had written to Lady Besant and not to her. She put the letter down and looked at her aunt levelly. "This is preposterous."

"Not at all. It is perfectly logical. The duke is such a good, honorable man. His grace had expected that he would soon have cause to welcome you into the family as a cousin. Now it will be as his wife." When Caroline did not respond, Lady Besant continued in silky tones, "I thought you would be pleased by this news, my dear."

Caroline's heart had split into two and was thumping madly at her temples, making it difficult to think. "It is not right," was all she could think of to say. "It is wrong. The duke is grief-stricken. He is overreacting. Yes, I see that he wants to do right by the memory of his cousin, but—"

"But you will not refuse him, when he comes to offer for you," Lady Besant finished.

When he comes to offer for me! "And when did you say that was to be?"

"Sometime today," her aunt repeated.

"Sometime today," Caroline replied mechanically.

"Which makes it unnecessary," her aunt said smoothly, "for you to consider undertaking a return to Hutton Manor today—or any other time soon."

Caroline attempted to concentrate, but her brain was spinning out of control. She willed herself to behave normally until her wits could function properly. Though her temples throbbed and her throat ached, she picked up her fork and struggled with another bite of egg.

"And, in fact," her aunt pressed, "it is quite unnecessary for you to make any other plans for today, either. You would not wish to risk being out when the duke calls."

Caroline's impulse was to flee the house, or to take to her bed with grave illness. That was it: she felt ill. She did not immediately understand it, but the incredible possibility of becoming the Duchess of Desford seemed only to make her feel physically unwell. Yet she knew she could not refuse to see his grace without handing him undeserved insult.

"Certainly, I shall remain at home today," Caroline said, struggling for calm, "in order to receive the duke whenever he calls."

Lady Besant paused, then said with a slight air of caution, "I cannot help but wonder, my dear, whether you might not, after all, have conceived an attachment to your Mr. Kenmure—an attachment that makes you reluctant to accept the duke's offer?" When Caroline found herself incapable of responding, Lady Besant favored her niece with a long, penetrating regard. "Yes. Well. I would have thought, on several occasions, that you held his grace... in special affection."

Caroline had regained a measure of self-control. "That is because his grace is such a good, honorable man, as you say," she said evenly. Not for the world would she expose the wound to her weak spot that her aunt had unerringly touched.

Lady Besant left it at that. "Very well, then," she said, rising from her chair and walking toward the door. "I have several matters to attend to just now that will take me out of the house for most of the day. When I return... later, you may tell me the pleasant details of his grace's visit."

When her aunt had left, Caroline abandoned all pretense of eating. With great precision, she laid her fork across one corner of her plate and stared at it in abstraction. Then her gaze fell on the duke's letter. She picked it up and attempted to master its contents. Phrases swam before her eyes: *...deep concern for Miss Hutton's well-being... exceptionally fine woman... greatly admired by my deceased cousin... Gilbert's last visit to me on the afternoon of the London Assembly... will come today in Gilbert's stead... continue what he was unable to complete...*

She put the letter down. She recognized the duke's elegant scrawl, but she could not quite rid herself of the notion that her aunt had guided his grace's hand. But it made no sense. Esther Besant hardly knew the Duke of Desford. Caroline's eerie impression that her aunt was behind this wild scheme was surely a product of her own disordered senses. No one could command a duke to do what he did not want to do—but why should the duke want to offer her marriage? The answer came to her: shock and grief and a strong sense of duty. The duke wanted to do something right in a world that had gone very wrong. He wanted to honor his cousin's intentions. But what would happen when the duke recovered from his shock and grief and found himself dutifully and honorably and lovelessly married to *her?*

The turmoil in Caroline's breast began to swirl at the idea of entering into a one-sided marriage with the man of her dreams. She could imagine no humiliation more exquisite, no pain more vivid, no hunger more constant than to live with the man she loved, knowing that he did not love her in return. One clear thought stabbed through her brain and down through her heart: it would mean death to be married to him, a slow and painful death, an emotional and spiritual death, the dying coming a little more every day, his careless and easy indifference for a wife of no wit and less beauty eating away at her heart and soul. Already weakened from her poverty disease, Caroline felt now positively debilitated.

Would she be strong enough to refuse him?

Caroline lost track of time. She remained at the table, staring into space. Suddenly she was roused by the ancient butler, Marston, who entered to announce that she had a caller.

"A caller?" she said quickly, her heart beginning to thump unpleasantly again.

"A gentleman to see you, miss."

So soon? She had not expected it. However, the meeting could be neither avoided nor deferred. "Show him to the anteroom, if you please," she said tonelessly. With an afterthought, "Is the fire laid?"

"Yes, miss."

She nodded and smiled distractedly, and said she would receive the gentleman presently. She folded her hands on the table and considered her intertwined fingers at length. Then she drew a deep breath and rose. She left the room to greet the Duke of Desford.

Upon stepping into the adjoining anteroom, Caroline saw a man gazing into the leaping flames on the hearth. She halted abruptly on the threshold, registering first the scarlet coat so vivid against the walls stylishly hung in moss-green silk. When the man turned, Caroline was gazing into dark blue eyes and an unfinished face. "Oh! You!" she said involuntarily, and instantly wished she could retract this utterly tactless greeting.

"Miss Hutton, good morning," Worth said, maintaining the proprieties in the face of the painfully obvious. Although he had not flattered himself that she would be waiting breathlessly for his arrival, he had not expected that she would have completely forgotten his request to call.

Caroline shut the door behind her and forced herself to advance into the room. "Yes, of course, that is to say, Colonel . . . Colonel—" she began, swallowed hard and cleared her throat. "Colonel Worth. Good morning."

Better and better! Worth thought with irony as he moved from the fireplace to meet her. He bowed correctly over the hand she extended him and returned the conventional greeting. He knew by the way she had choked over his name that she had been told the old scandal, no doubt by the Besant. By the time he had released her hand and straightened, he had already determined grimly, *And it's just as well she's heard the worst!*

Caroline rose from her curtsy, her color heightened. "Pray excuse my distraction," she said, attempting to recover from this opening disaster. "I fear that no end of untoward events have pressed upon me in the past forty-eight hours." She added, for the sake of form, "Your kind visit provides me now with pleasant respite from this morning's new worries." All the while, she was devising ways to rid herself of him in order to prepare for her interview with the duke.

An experienced strategist, Worth had already altered his plan of attack. He was quick to assess the strength of her defenses. He was quicker still to take the offensive. "Do I gather that your new worries concern, perhaps, the difficulties arising from your presence in your aunt's household?"

Caroline's brows rose. She said rather coolly, "Why should you imagine that I might experience difficulties in the home of my relative?"

Worth bowed. "Because you told me at the assembly that your aunt behaved in the manner of an overbearing colonel, and because, when you entered the room just now, you had the look of an underofficer contemplating desertion."

Caroline smiled a little ruefully. "Are you always so acute?"

"A matter of professional survival, on the battlefield and off."

Caroline's smile was replaced by a little frown between her brows. Something in his tone and stance suggested that he had come for a determined purpose and was not going to leave before he made it known. Caroline gestured for him to be seated as she disposed herself in the opposing wing chair. Arranging her skirts, she said, "In fairness toward my aunt, I must insist that her welcome to me in her household remains warm."

Worth accepted this disclaimer without demur. "Then your new worries must stem from your meeting with the family solicitor."

Caroline was again unable to hide her surprise. "How could you have known?"

"About your appointment?" he returned. "You also told me at the assembly that you had come to London to meet with your solicitor."

"Did I?"

"Your appointment was yesterday. In the afternoon, if I recall correctly."

"Yes, but I fail to see how—"

"With a Mr. Gresham."

"Yes, but—"

"In Birchin Lane."

Further protest died on her lips. The interview was taking a decidedly strange turn. "That is the one. But still, sir, what makes you think that my worries this morning stem from my visit with the solicitor?"

He watched her closely as he answered the question behind her question. "I have heard nothing in the general way of gossip, if that is what you are asking." He did not, of course, add that he had visited Birchin Lane this morning before arriving in Portugal Row and had paid Mr. Gresham handsomely for some highly satisfying information. "I only inferred from your statement of new worries that they have come in addition to the emotional distractions of the recent murder." His approach was bold. "Perhaps your difficulties are financial."

Caroline was amazed by his directness, but not disconcerted. She held his eyes steady with hers. His manner did not suggest sympathy, and she was at a loss to understand it. "I hardly know how to respond," she said at last.

"You need not respond at all," he replied. "You need merely hear me out."

A long regard arched between them, inquiring on his part, wary on hers. In his presence, she felt again that sensation of having stepped out onto a mental bridge, of being suspended above the tumult of her emotions. It was a strange calm, as if his intuition of her difficulties had relieved her, temporarily, of the need to be preoccupied by them. And yet, so removed from her feelings, she felt distinctly uncomfortable.

She nodded for him to proceed.

"You wondered," he said, "at our first meeting whether I was new to town. Perhaps you know now that I am not."

The terms of the interview thus far hardly required polite dissimulation. She said, simply, "That is correct."

He continued, "I have not come today to discuss my past and to justify myself. Nor even to exculpate myself. I will allow whatever account you have heard of my past to stand."

Chilled by his tone and thereby emboldened, she matched him for directness. "Then why have you come?"

He rose and stood before her, "To extend to you an offer of marriage."

Caroline was looking up at him, her eyes resting on the hard planes of his face, the high cheekbones, moving upward to his blue eyes, then down to his uniform, so smart and official, masculine and threatening. She was confused. It had been a trying morning. Her thoughts, evidently jumping ahead to the duke's impending visit, had taken a strange, romantic flight. "In my distraction," she answered slowly, "I am afraid that I have not heard you aright."

His perfunctory bow bordered on the uncivil. "An offer, Miss Hutton. I have come with an offer of marriage."

His manner was so blunt that Caroline persisted in doubting her ears. She gave her head a little shake. "Forgive me," she said and explained, "but I thought I heard you say 'an offer of marriage.'"

Worth was far from pleased. "I have come," he repeated, "with an offer of marriage. From me. To you." Again, curtly, "Marriage, Miss Hutton." Of all the reactions he might have imagined, he had not anticipated blank incomprehension. He continued brutally, "Perhaps you are unused to such occasions and are unaware that the customary response to such a proposal is either 'yes' or 'no.'"

Worth immediately regretted the insult. Yet, so far from seeming to take offense, Miss Hutton laughed. He could not have guessed, of course, that her amusement arose from the opposite circumstance: that here could be the third man in as many days to wish to marry her—that is, if she counted Mr. Kenmure's near proposal and the duke's impending one.

"But—but, why?" she managed, not bothering to suppress her amused disbelief.

The words broke from his mouth like chips of ice. "Because I am a rich man and can offer you a home on St. James's Square and a generous allowance."

Again, Caroline laughed. Not immediately realizing that he would think his suit required justification, she clarified, "No, I mean, why would *you* wish to marry *me*? As long as we are speaking frankly and since you have very nearly guessed it anyway, I may as well as confess that I am destitute."

Worth looked down into Caroline's face and made a tactical error. At the moment when it would have served him to have maintained the usual sweet illusions of a marriage proposal, he was cold and soldierlike, regarding Caroline as a town to storm and conquer, and a relatively insignificant, poorly defended one at that. Perhaps because he found her pale face unappealing; perhaps because he wanted to punish her a little for having forgotten his visit; perhaps because he was embarrassed at having betrayed himself with the bald statement of his wealth; perhaps because she was so evidently amused, he said, "Because the scandal caused by the murder of that fellow at the assembly has provided the perfect opportunity to reestablish myself in London. I want to settle down, and settling comfortably involves a wife." Fortunately, he had lost enough patience to stop short of admitting that her poverty was her most attractive attribute. He demanded, "And now for your answer."

Her amusement vanished. Thoroughly offended, Caroline nevertheless knew what her answer must be. It was a matter of her life. Survival. Feeling precariously suspended on her mental bridge, she uttered a bald, unromantic, "Yes."

Her hands were taken in a light grip, and she was pulled to her feet. She was so close to him she could see the tiny design in the brass buttons at his collar and the stitches in the gold braid. The pulse in his sun-darkened throat was strong and steady. He smelled of shaving soap, clean wool and white linen. Reliving her first impression of him, she was at once attracted and repelled by the power balanced in his body.

He released her hands, moved away and bowed again. He expressed his entirely conventional happiness and moved on to practical matters. "We must choose a date, then, and I am not inclined to wait to proclaim the banns. I should like it done as soon as possible. Do I understand that there is no one else I should apply to for your hand?"

"No, no one. Yes, as soon as possible," Caroline murmured, answering at random, frankly distracted by this extraordinary turn of fate and by his touch. "As soon as possible." She needed to stall and found the tactic. "Of course, we cannot choose a date before we consult the almanac."

"Very true, although my guess is that it will have to be within the next two weeks," Worth replied, conversant with the prohibitions on the choice of days for weddings. "In any case, we can announce the engagement before setting the date. Would you object to a notice appearing in the *Morning Herald* and the *Times*—say, as early as tomorrow?"

Events seemed to have taken on a momentum of their own. Having agreed to marry him, she could hardly balk at the placing of an announcement in the newspaper. It was the very speed of the entire affair that prompted her to ask, "If we are to announce our engagement and to marry so quickly, what are we to say to the world about our reasons for haste?"

Worth had the proper answer to that, though it came too late in the proposal to have the desired effect on Caroline. "Miss Hutton," he said, bowing formally, "you do not flatter yourself."

Caroline looked into his gem-hard blue eyes and felt once again more amused than offended. "How could I," she wondered sweetly, "have overlooked the obvious? I shall be sure and explain to my aunt that we have conceived a violent attachment to each other."

Unmoved by her irony, he continued smoothly, "Speaking of whom, is Lady Besant at home?"

"No, she is out."

"And when does she return?"

"She will likely be out for most of the day."

"So." He paused to review his plans for the day. "Well, then. I should like to go now to the newspapers, while you, no doubt," he said, punctuating this statement with a bow, "shall wish to consult the almanac. Would it meet with your approval if I were to return this evening, to settle the date and to discuss the particulars of our wedding plans? I should like, as well, to provide you with a ring. It will also give me an opportunity to pay Lady Besant my respects," he said, smiling with undisguised relish, "and to give her an opportunity to wish us happy."

Caroline could only agree to this. A few extraneous remarks were made and parting civilities were exchanged. Caroline escorted Worth to the door of the sitting room.

"I shall send you round a note this afternoon telling you when I shall come," he said. He stretched out his hand.

She surrendered hers. "Very well," she replied.

"Until tonight," he said, bending and kissing her hand.

"Until tonight," she repeated, snatching it back, a little too quickly.

Plain, disagreeable woman, he thought as he bowed himself out of the room, *but she serves my purposes!*

Rude, disagreeable man, she thought as he left her, *but one who has just rescued me!*

After she had closed the door behind Worth, still dazed and disbelieving, Caroline crossed the room to stand before the fire. She was attempting to grasp the wholly incredible thought that her poverty disease had been miraculously cured. She was no longer homeless and penniless. Neither was she at her aunt's mercy. Nor was she in the ignominious position of having to accept an offer from the duke. In waves of relief, she felt her strength return. She was not going to die, physically, financially or emotionally. *I've been rescued,* she thought again. *And all because Mr. Kenmure was murdered and Colonel Worth wishes to reestablish himself!*

With that, Caroline's fragile mental bridge collapsed. For the first time in two days, she was free from the burden of worry for her immediate future. As she recalled Mr. Kenmure's murder, the images of the alley that had been frozen since two nights before suddenly broke up, slowly, like ice in spring. In her mind's eye, Caroline saw Colonel Worth emerge into the alley, brush past her and press his way into the crowd of men surrounding Mr. Kenmure's body. She remembered that Colonel Worth had been one of the first at the assembly to arrive at the scene of the crime.

She recalled as well Worth's conversation at Lady Purcell's. He had quickly questioned Arthur Devis's assertion that Mr. Kenmure had been jumped on from behind and stabbed in the back. Now, if Worth had seen Mr. Kenmure's body before it was covered, then he would also have seen how Mr. Kenmure had been murdered. It suddenly occurred to Caroline that something in Devis's story must not ring true. Although her mind winced from the memory of Mr. Kenmure lying on the cobbles, she forced herself to consider it, for she, too, had seen his body uncovered. The

image came to her vividly and unmistakably: Mr. Kenmure
had been lying faceup.

Her thoughts moved more swiftly now, tumbling, confused, and in the tumult the vexing question resurfaced:
*What had Mr. Kenmure been doing in the alley when he
should have been meeting me?* Hard on the heels of that
came: *And if he was not jumped on from behind and
robbed, how and why was he murdered?*

She struggled with these questions until she remembered
that, when Colonel Worth had pressed his way in to see Mr.
Kenmure's body, he had had the Duke of Desford in tow.
Here Caroline's thoughts took a sharp turn away from considerations of murder, motive and method and veered toward musings on her heart's desire. She could not help but
compare Colonel Worth to the Duke of Desford and find
Worth wanting.

Where the duke was easy to smile, quick to laugh and as
charming as mercury, Worth was as hard and cold and blunt
as iron. Caroline was glad to be spared the pain of the duke's
offer, but a tiny corner of her young woman's heart cried
out: *Oh, to be loved by a man like Desford!* To which her
plain, practical head replied: *But far, far better to be the
wife of a scandal-tainted outcast than the object of scorn
and pity as your precious duke's unloved wife!*

With her most immediate worries behind her, Caroline
banished her plain practicality and gave her heart its day.
She beguiled herself in pleasant reverie, weaving a highly
satisfying, highly improbable scene with the duke. She
would tell him of her engagement to Richard Worth. He
would protest vehemently, sweep her into his arms and
whisper cherished words into her ear. Because it was her
daydream, after all, to do with as she pleased, she made sure
that her nose was perfectly straight and a quarter-inch
shorter, her mouth a cupid's bow, her hair a rich chestnut
and her fortune intact.

These pleasant thoughts might have continued indéfi-
nitely had they not been interrupted by the announcement
of her second masculine caller of the day.

Chapter Seven

As he left Lady Besant's house, Worth felt pleased. His pleasure was purely professional, similar to the kind he had taken on campaigns, when he knew his troops to be on high ground and well covered. This was security—or the nearest thing to it one could experience on the battlefield.

Since he had chosen the role of infantryman for the day, he was pursuing his battle plan on foot. By the time he had descended the few steps of Lady Besant's house to the street, he had already decided to head first in the direction of Fleet Street and the offices of the *Morning Herald* and the *Times*. From there he would go to the Guard House and spend a few hours socializing with his cronies, circulating his news.

Hardly had he turned the corner to Pearl Street before he crossed paths with a military man, to judge by his uniform. Worth vaguely recognized the man but could not place him. Worth hesitated, then stopped. The recognition was apparently mutual, for the other man stopped as well. They approached each other, measuringly, before the man in the uniform ventured, "Colonel Worth?"

Worth affirmed the guess and gave himself another moment to further assess the man. He was perhaps ten years Worth's senior, if the graying at the temples was any indication. Otherwise his body was as hard and fit as that of a twenty-year-old. His heavy features were softened by a pair of beautifully formed lips and highlighted by a pair of keen gray eyes above which hovered thick chevrons for eyebrows. The coat that brushed the tops of his boots was neat and in good repair, but its army red was long since drained from the fabric, making it a pale salmon in contrast to Worth's lobster.

Worth, the ideal officer who knew all his men by name, drew a blank. "Army man?" he queried.

"Formerly. The Twenty-first."

Worth was impressed. "The Royal Scots Fusiliers. You marched with Marlborough, then." He flicked his glance over the man's coat, which had plainly seen better days, and added with a touch of sympathy and irony, "The Peace of Utrecht has put a number of us out of business."

The man gestured to his thigh. "I took a bullet at Bouchain and so beat the peacetime rush to find a new employ."

Worth found the warm burr in the man's voice strangely immediate. He had heard it far more recently than Bouchain, which was three years before. "Fair enough," he said. "Should I know you?"

The man shook his head. "It wouldn't be from the Continent, if that's what you're wondering—although I knew of you, sir, by reputation! No. Two nights ago it was we met, standing in the cold over the body of the cousin of your friend." The man saluted. "Chief Constable John Locke, at your service."

Worth returned the salute. "Ah, so that's it," Worth said, matching the voice to the face in daylight. He recalled a detail. "You were off-duty then." With an afterthought, "And not wearing your uniform."

"Observant," the chief constable said. His smile was pleasant. "Aye, it's a poor, underpaid profession, the keeping of the king's peace—as you've suggested, there's more profit in war!—and so it's a saving that makes one uniform serve the needs of another. Then, too," he said with a wink, "it commands a certain respect."

"Let us hope," Worth agreed pleasantly but noncommittally. He would have brought the encounter to its natural conclusion, but then Constable Locke said, almost casually, "A troublesome case, this one."

Worth's ears pricked up. "You speak of the London Assembly murder, I presume. Has any progress been made?" he asked, affecting only mild interest.

"Great progress," Locke replied and pulled at his ear. "I've been assigned to the case."

Worth smiled obligingly. "You told me at the time that the vicinity of the London Tavern was out of your jurisdiction."

"Most observant, as I've said," the chief constable remarked, nodding appreciatively. "The locale is out of my jurisdiction, but the case interests me." He did not elaborate on how he had come to be assigned to the case. Instead, he asked casually, "And what brings you to this neighborhood?"

Worth thought the opportunity well favored to try out his news. He informed the chief constable that he had just extended a proposal of marriage and had had it accepted. He was on his way now, he explained, to the newspapers to insert notices of his forthcoming marriage in several of the daily papers.

"Congratulations are in order," Locke replied with a mobile smile that produced deep creases in his jaw. "Who is the lucky lass, then?"

"Miss Caroline Hutton has done me the honor of accepting to be my affianced wife."

The chief constable's smile froze an instant before he said, "Then I shall be able to wish her happy myself, since I am on my way to pay her a visit. Miss Caroline Hutton," he said, withdrawing a notepad from his coat and consulting it. "Yes. Resides at the home of Esther Besant. Portugal Row." He recited the number.

"You are paying Miss Hutton a visit?" Worth asked, justifiably curious.

"Nothing significant," the chief constable said affably, keeping a professional eye on Worth. "All in the line of duty, mind you. Since she was identified by one of my sources as the first person in the alleyway the night of Gilbert Kenmure's murder, it is necessary for me to interview her before anyone else."

Ambush! Worth felt as if he were suddenly surrounded by danger. An experienced cavalryman, he wisely did not jump for cover. Instead, he maintained position. "Yes, of course," he said calmly. "I see, then. That would naturally cause you to wish to interview her."

"And to wish her happy, as I've said."

"And to wish her happy."

As the two former military men regarded each other, the moment lengthened. Worth's thoughts churned rapidly. He recalled himself and said, bowing, "Let us imagine, then, that we shall be seeing each other again, Chief Constable Locke."

"I am quite sure of it, Colonel Worth," Locke returned, sketching a salute in parting that Worth returned. "It's a certainty we will be seeing each other again soon."

With that the men parted, each to his own errand.

During the short passage to Fleet Street, Worth had reason to look grim. His first thought was not to announce his engagement to the newspapers, to withdraw his offer from Miss Hutton. She—*his affianced wife*—had been the first in the alleyway? With a sixth sense that was never dormant, he hastily recreated the scene of the crime. He had a vague recollection of having brushed past the shadow of a woman slumped against the outside wall of the tavern. Miss Hutton? Worth thought farther back. Minutes before, Miss Hutton had been dancing with *him*.

What had she been doing in the alley? And what the *devil* was her association with Kenmure?

Of all the potential disasters he had foreseen for his return to England, Worth had not anticipated being yet again stained, if only by association, with murder. This time, of course, the victim was a man he neither knew nor cared about, a fact that nevertheless filled him with a frustrated rage he remembered well. This time, however, he was no longer a raw, passionate young man with a wound bleeding of pain and defiance and humiliation. This time, he was angry.

His anger shot out in different directions and flew briefly in Jonathan Wyndham's direction: Jonathan, the Duke of

Desford, his only friend in town; Jonathan, whose blasted cousin had been murdered; Jonathan, who had recommended Miss Hutton. The anger did not quite reach that mark, however, for it had honed in on its real target.

No mistakes and no delay! Worth had vowed to himself. To be sure, he had acted without delay. However, he had made a grievous mistake. He had ignored one of Marlborough's most important defensive tactics: that of holding troops in reserve to stand directly behind the front. From that position, they could attack the flank of the enemy columns seeking to envelop. Worth had left himself exposed and had just been jumped on from behind, unawares, victim of a surprise attack.

He had, in short, drastically underestimated Miss Hutton. If he had dismissed his bride-to-be as an uninteresting woman only minutes ago, he now had cause to assess her afresh. He would have done well, he realized, to have retained the image of Miss Hutton at the assembly, a poised and popular young lady, whom he had rated "better than expected." However, he had too easily accepted Desford's characterization of her as negligible. Even the subdued, yet composed, woman he had encountered at Lady Purcell's should have indicated to him that Miss Hutton might be involved in intrigues of her own. Instead, without making one inquiry into her life beyond her finances, he had offered marriage to the creature. She had laughed in his face and then accepted him!

He had arrived in Fleet Street. For several long moments, he stood in the street, motionless, expressionless, jostled by the occasional passerby, rapidly reviewing his options. He could withdraw his proposal on the possibility that Miss Hutton was, somehow, connected to Kenmure's murder. More to the point, he could withdraw it on the possibility that Chief Constable Locke suspected her of some involvement, either with Kenmure or the murderer. And where did he, Worth, now fit into Locke's thinking? In light of the fact that Worth had just announced his engagement to the chief investigator of the murder, any retraction might incriminate himself in a way that was, as yet, unknown to him. And assuming Miss Hutton had nothing to do with the murder, if Worth withdrew his offer now, she could ruin him socially in the space of an afternoon. Less.

He had had one chance, one offer. He had made it, and it was a disaster.

But he was not without experience. He was not without resources. In time of war, Worth had always tried to have the probability of victory on his side. But that was not always possible. Often he had had to act against that probability, when there was *nothing better to do*. Were he to have despaired then, he would have abandoned the use of reason just when it had become most necessary, just when everything seemed to be conspiring against him. Worth had not been one of Marlborough's most brilliant field officers for nothing, for he knew precisely how, when the undertaking was at its most impossible, to make the best use of the few means at his disposal.

The murder of Gilbert Kenmure had piqued Worth's interest from the beginning. Now he would have to investigate it himself. Worth remembered with cold detachment the slash in Kenmure's neck. Was Miss Hutton capable of such an act? He did not think so, but he was long past the point where he could be surprised by what a man, or a woman, might do. Was she accessory to it? Or had her presence in the alleyway been inadvertent? Had she, like him, sensed something wrong and gone to investigate?

He reviewed all that he knew of Miss Hutton in the past few days and recalled, in particular, the interesting conversation he had had with her at Lady Purcell's. Suddenly, he knew what plan of action to take. He headed decisively for the *Morning Herald* and the *Times* where he paid handsomely for several large and elaborate engagement announcements, then set out purposefully for Cock Alley by Cripplegate, near St. Mary's.

Later, Worth presented himself at the door of an obviously well-to-do establishment in Cock Alley. He trod the well-swept step and plied the shiny brass knocker. The door was opened to him by a respectable-looking matron in a crisp linen smock and neat mobcap.

Worth requested an interview with Mr. Jonathan Wild. The housekeeper nodded, cast an admiring glance over his uniform and asked for his name. He obliged her. The housekeeper bobbed once and withdrew. She returned almost at once and invited him into the house, informing him that he was in luck. "Mr. Wild is in, sir. Follow me, Colonel Worth, sir, and I will show you to my master's office."

When she stretched out her palm, Worth knew enough to cross it with a crown. She thanked him prettily. With the first trace of amusement he had felt since his encounter with Locke, Worth reflected that this courtesy befitted the most respectable businessman in town and not the "Thief-Taker General" of all of London.

When Worth was ushered through the foyer to the adjoining room, he found the well-appointed office entirely that of a prosperous, respectable businessman. The room was bright and sunny, with a bow window giving onto the street. The walls were lined with bookshelves crammed with leather-bound volumes, and in the center stood a desk appropriately littered with important-looking documents. From behind that desk came an extremely dapper man, short and a little thick but not quite to the point of squat, with a light tread, a lively eye and an enormous wig, overcurled.

This was Jonathan Wild. "How may I help you, sir?" he asked, holding out his hand to pump Worth's vigorously. "Or should I say Colonel? Now, it's always a pleasure for me," he continued elaborately, "to enter into a piece of business with a military man! So efficient! So aware of the best, most direct methods! An officer, in fact! Yes! As I was saying, how may I help you? Have you lost something of value?"

Before Worth could reply, Wild thrust out his chest, which was crossed with a profusion of gold chains. "I flatter myself that I have something of a reputation for helping gentlemen to recover stolen property—but, of course, you know that! Else you would not be here! I am proud to offer something in the way of a community service, especially in these difficult, rather lawless times—if I may say so." Then, mellifluously, "Perhaps you would care to describe the items that have been stolen from you, Colonel?"

Worth said that he had not come because he had been the victim of any robbery. "It is rather that I have some questions to ask you."

Wild did not miss a beat. "Then you have come for advice," he rejoined affably. "I am known for dispensing advice as well! You must have heard of my reputation—sound advice for difficult times such as these! Lawless, even! So then, sir, how may I advise you? Perhaps you are married?"

Worth answered that, in point of fact, he was not married. "I am, however, engaged, and you will read of it tomorrow in the papers."

Wild nodded his bewigged head sapiently. "Then my advice in that case is to avoid a Fleet wedding. Oh, my, your fee of a crown will have been well spent here if you follow this piece of advice, Colonel! No Fleet wedding!"

"I had not planned on it."

Wild nodded judiciously. "Very wise. I must ask, as well, whether your bride-to-be is in debt."

"Not in debt, no," Worth answered.

"That, too, is a good sign. Many a woman desires to marry in order to shift her debts to the shoulders of her husband. Of course, there's many a foolish man ready to marry and to take over any amount for the pleasures of the marriage bed! I must say, however, upon making your acquaintance, you do not strike me as a fool. And in your case, sir, being a soldier—and an officer!—you cannot be arrested for debt. Oh, I warn you! There is no end of trickery that women will employ!" Hardly pausing, he asked, "Perhaps you've heard of the case of Deborah Nolan?"

Worth understood that he must play along. He stated that he had not heard of Miss Nolan.

Mr. Wild assumed a serious mien. "Well! Miss Nolan desired to rid herself of her debts by marriage yet shrank from putting herself in the power of some low ruffian. So her bridegroom was a woman dressed as a man, who called herself John Ferren, Gentleman. Need I mention that so irregular a marriage could only have been a Fleet marriage? Of course Miss Nolan's creditors might look for John Ferren, Gentleman, as long as they pleased.''

"I fail to see how this pertains to my case."

"Eh? What's that? Well! No, indeed not, sir! It's a cautionary tale I tell, that! It bears repeating."

From the tone of Mr. Wild's voice, Worth imagined that the man's desire to tell the tale stemmed wholly from his admiration of Miss Nolan's resourcefulness.

"It's a scandal, and so I've always said," Wild continued. "The Fleet wedding is for those who wish to marry secretly and irregularly. So, you have relieved my mind that you plan no Fleet wedding, sir!"

"I'm posting banns, procuring a license and, as I've said, putting notices in the newspapers."

"Nothing cheap about it, then," Wild said, apparently pleased. "Not rushed, I hope! A hasty marriage is almost as bad as a Fleet marriage! I don't advise it! How long have you been engaged?"

"Since this morning," Worth answered.

"And you plan to be married soon?"

"Within the fortnight, I hope."

" 'Happy is the wooing that is not long a-doing,' " Wild quoted, heedless of the glaring contradiction of his stricture against hasty marriages, uttered the few seconds before.

Worth did not mistake Wild's erratic discourse for that of an idiot. Wild was as shrewd as they came. However diverting Worth found this interlude, he had other business to accomplish. "I've not come for your advice," Worth reminded him, "but to ask you some questions."

"Eh?" Mr. Wild frowned. "Although I hesitate to pronounce it, the word *interrogation* comes to mind."

"Perhaps you might read it like that."

"This is most unusual."

"Is it?"

"Ah, I see what it is! You are unacquainted with my methods! *I* ask the questions, sir," Mr. Wild said, all amiability, "and *you* describe to me the objects that have been stolen from you."

"I have had nothing stolen," Worth repeated and came to his point. "I am interested, rather, in the murder of a man named Gilbert Kenmure. Two nights ago, at the London Tavern. Have you heard of it?"

Mr. Wild's affability was replaced on the instant by a blustering dignity. He stiffened dramatically. "Of course I have heard of it. Why should I have not?"

"I should think you would have," Worth answered, "which is why I came to discover whether you knew anything more about it. That is all."

When the occasion warranted, Wild could come to the point. However, he rarely abandoned his histrionics. With grand indignation, he sputtered, "Have you come, sir, on the wholly inexplicable errand to accuse me of this—I do not shrink from the vile word—murder?"

"Indeed not," Worth answered calmly. "You have identified these times as lawless and yourself as a man who helps to recover stolen property. I would be interested to know whether you have heard tell of any items belonging to the murdered gentleman that might have been stolen from him. I am rather more interested in the motive for his murder. Perhaps he was robbed."

Wild changed tactics. He began twirling one of the curls of his wig, thoughtfully. He asked, with interest, "Was the gentleman carrying his notecase on his person? Did he have in his possession, perhaps, an exchequer bill? Was he known to wear jewels?"

Worth did not know the answer to these questions.

Wild frowned. "Then, I must ask *you*, sir—since it is customary, as I have said, that *I* am the one to ask the questions!—what your interest in the murder could possibly be? Did the poor victim—the streets have become increasingly dangerous in London, we have agreed, have we not?—owe you money? Or was he carrying something of yours that night that you have not recovered? In brief, sir, what is *your* interest?"

"Kenmure was a great friend of mine," Worth lied smoothly, "from the army. Upon my recent return from the Continent, I intended to reestablish our friendship. His death has shocked me."

"A military man shocked at death?" Wild asked succinctly.

"On the battlefield death is not called murder."

Wild took a step back at the note in Worth's voice. "You think me acquainted with the murderer?" he pressed.

"As one acquainted with the lawlessness that reigns nowadays," Worth said, "I thought you capable of providing me with clues to the murderer."

Wild resumed his grandiloquent indignation. "I am known far and wide for my genius for recovering stolen goods and not for the sordid details of murder, sir!" Wild had plainly had enough of Worth, for he went to his desk, took a pamphlet off the top of a stack and returned to Worth, taking him by the arm and leading him to the door. "You may read about my views in this pamphlet, sir," he said, handing Worth the object in question. "It is my testament, which I have published—at great expense to myself, I do not mind telling you—under the title *The Regulator: or a Discovery of Thieves and Thief-Takers*. In it, I describe the method of one Charles Hitchin, who was a city marshal, suspended for malpractice, and who now carries on a lucrative profession of—yes, I say the word—*thieving!* It is he to whom you should next address yourself if you are looking for a criminal behind your friend's death!"

Worth accepted the pamphlet, and at the door to Wild's office, took his leave of the dapper little man with a bow.

"Once you have visited Mr. Hitchin," Wild said to his client "do not hesitate to return to me. I shall make inquiries for you. Oh, yes! Inquiries! Who knows, but in a day or two, that I might not have more information for you."

"Who knows?" Worth repeated. It was difficult to determine, given the little man's bombast, but Worth would have said Wild's sudden interest in items possibly stolen from Kenmure was genuine. It fitted his profile as a thief, not a murderer, and seemed to suggest that Wild was not directly involved in Kenmure's death. If the deed had been done by a common cutthroat, it was possible that Wild might learn his name and be willing to divulge it for a price. "And if I return, will it cost me another crown?"

Wild smiled rather apologetically. "For my trouble, you understand! An honest businessman must pay his bills, after all!" To Worth's brief bow, Wild made a flourishing leg. "Return in a day or two, Colonel! I shall not disappoint you a second time. Your humble servant!"

Worth left Wild's establishment, tapping the pamphlet meditatively in an open palm. He seriously doubted that Charles Hitchin, whose methods were exposed in Wild's pamphlet, would know any more than Wild, for Worth had an excellent idea that Hitchin was nothing more than Wild's greatest rival in the thieving business. Hardly had the door closed behind him and he had stepped out into the street, than he came face-to-face with the very man he had predicted he would see again.

"Chief Constable Locke," Worth said.

"Colonel Worth," the chief constable replied. "It's a step ahead of me you are today, I perceive."

Chapter Eight

Altering his plan to go to the Guard House, Worth went instead to High Holborn and the premises of Roger Plenius, Harpsichord Maker. Indulging in an unnecessary transaction, he sought solace amidst the rhythms of craftsmen at work, the sweet smell of resins and the cushion of wood shavings underfoot. Worth took great interest in Plenius's excited description of an Italian pianoforte that had been recently introduced in London and that contained the secrets of enabling the harpsichord to produce gradations of tone.

While Worth was listening to the new musical mechanics that substituted for the crude harpsichord jack, the intricacies of springs, guide wires, dampers and wooden hammers fitted with pads of leather, Caroline was in her aunt's anteroom, speaking to her third visitor of the day.

"Don't go, Martha," Caroline was protesting. "Not yet. You have just come!"

Mrs. Sheridan laughed lightheartedly. "You've outlined the essentials," she replied, rising from her chair.

Caroline rose with her friend, shaking her head. "You've hardly been here five minutes—ten, at most! You can't have come all the way across town for a five-minute visit!"

"Ah, but now I have such delicious news to spread!"

"No, really, Martha, stay. I feel so much better with you here."

"You don't need me to hold your hand," Martha replied airily, "for you seem quite capable of managing your affairs on your own." She crossed to the anteroom door. "Most speedily, in fact!"

Caroline followed. "Too speedily, perhaps?" she asked.

Martha considered this. "Oh, I was surprised when I first got your note, but then I thought, 'Why not?' I've never believed in love at first sight or mad flights of passion, but what do I know, after all?" Martha winked conspiratorially. "The London Assembly is a lovely place to fall in love and by what better means than an assignation? It's a time-honored custom!"

"I never said I was going to meet him," Caroline faltered.

Martha gave Caroline's shoulders a playful shake. "And neither did you have to, my dear! Richard danced with you, found you to his liking, kissed you a few times in a dark corner and came this morning to ask you to marry him. The most natural thing in the world!"

"Is that how you see it, Martha?"

Martha hugged Caroline affectionately. "I see it as a most welcome respite from talking about—" she paused "—death." She drew away from her friend. "Unfortunately, however, I fear your good news will be overlooked in the continuing gloom of Mr. Kenmure's murder! For the next few weeks, at least, all social engagements will be little more than mourning parties. Ah, no, the only negative aspect to your engagement is its timing."

Caroline's smile went slightly awry. Remembering that the timing of Mr. Kenmure's murder had provided Colonel Worth with the reason for his offer, Caroline ventured, "Might not another negative aspect be...the scandal?"

Martha waved this away. "Ancient history!" She linked arms with Caroline, and they proceeded through the door and began to stroll down the vestibule. "Only the harpies will remember it."

"It cannot be as simple as that."

"Well, no," Martha conceded, "for it was an extraordinary scandal. However, in my opinion, Richard has already paid long and dearly, and you, my dear," she continued, with a playful tap on Caroline's wrist, "are well connected and well liked. I cannot predict, of course, who will and who will not cut his acquaintance, but at least you will know who your friends are.''

"Aunt Esther will not like it," Caroline said.

Martha said, surprised, "No? What is her interest in Richard Worth? But let me see, now, I *do* seem to remember that she— Oh, never mind all of that now!" Martha did not appear to want to give the troublesome matter of Richard Worth's social acceptance or his history with Esther Besant any more thought. She changed the subject. "Now, the best part of your news is that you will not be leaving London to bury yourself at Hutton Manor. Only last week you declared this to be your firm intention—I might say what I liked!—and now here comes a man in two days to persuade you otherwise! So much for friendship!"

To these teasing words Caroline had no response. She was exceedingly grateful just now to her friend, for her loving support, for her acceptance of this strange, sudden engagement, for her genuine sympathy for Worth. When Martha had first arrived, Caroline had had the impulse to tell her all. Now, however, Caroline saw no reason to burden her friend with her emotional alarums, the sale of Hutton Manor or the real reasons Worth had proposed and she had accepted. Martha's presence had been calming and beneficial enough.

Caroline said simply, "Thank you for coming, Martha."

Martha laughed. "After receiving your note, I could not do otherwise! 'Dearest Martha,'" she quoted, "'I have just received, and accepted, an offer of marriage from Colonel Worth. I would desire to speak about it some time with you, however, I dare not leave the house this day, given the many things I must do.'" Martha gestured to herself. "How else could I have responded?"

"I certainly did not expect you to respond in person."

"I wanted to be the first, in person, to wish you happy."

"But you weren't," Caroline said suddenly, without thinking. "Chief Constable Locke was. He had the news from Colonel Worth, who had just left the house, not more than an hour ago."

Martha slanted Caroline a glance. "A chief constable?" Then, quickly, "Mr. Kenmure?"

"Yes, it was about Mr. Kenmure's murder." It dawned on Caroline that she could not give a completely accurate account to Martha of her movements the night of the London Assembly without having to explain the real story behind her engagement to Richard Worth. "Chief Constable Locke is interviewing all those people who were at the scene of the crime...early on."

"You were there early on?"

Fortunately, Martha's earlier mistaken impression gave Caroline a ready explanation. "Colonel Worth was there as well, you see, and I, we..."

"Ah!" Martha broke into this. "The London Tavern is known for its secluded alcoves in the hallway by the alley! You need say no more! But why were you being interviewed—or any one of us who attended the assembly? Was not Mr. Kenmure's death the work of a ruthless cutpurse?"

"So it seems," Caroline answered. "Chief Constable Locke was, in his own words, following routine. He wanted any information I could give him. Anything to help him bring the guilty party to justice. I only wish that I *had* seen or heard something to tell him," she continued, quite honestly now, "but I did not." Caroline shuddered. "It was so *strange* to be interviewed about a murder—although the chief constable's manner was most proper—and he's rather attractive, really, in his own particular way!"

Mrs. Sheridan showed no interest in a man of justice, attractive or otherwise. She was nodding, with a sad, wry smile. "There, you see, Caroline, it's as I've said. Mr. Kenmure's murder will overshadow your wonderful, happy news." Running an assessing eye over Caroline's neat dress, she said on a lighter note, "The jacket becomes you, my dear. I've been admiring your buttons—or whatever you call those fastenings."

"I call them 'frogs,'" Caroline replied. She explained how she had replaced the old cloth buttons with the kinds of closures she had seen on representations of Chinese jackets. She had interpreted these fastenings in looped knots of silver silk.

"I see. Very innovative," Martha commented admiringly. "Where *do* you get your ideas?"

"From pictures mostly, I suppose," Caroline answered. "I think I got this idea from a tapestry I saw some months ago."

"Well, it's a very stylish effect," Martha stated. "I shall most likely be imitating you!"

Mrs. Sheridan departed soon thereafter, leaving Caroline prey to contradictory emotions. She was partially relieved to have had the news of her engagement so joyfully received. She was partially unnerved by the half-truths she had been forced to tell concerning Richard Worth, Gilbert Kenmure and herself, both to Martha Sheridan and to Chief Constable Locke.

She had hardly been in a position to tell Chief Constable Locke the *truth* about why she had left the assembly rooms that night. Since the constable had greeted her by wishing her happy on her engagement to Colonel Worth, Caroline was not about to divulge that she had been expecting to meet Mr. Kenmure for amorous adventure and a possible marriage proposal. However, she had not precisely lied to the chief constable, either, for she had not seen anything or anyone possibly connected to the crime. She had only seen a body, lying there in the alley, one that she would have been unable to identify as Mr. Kenmure's.

And how was it that Miss Hutton was the very first to have arrived at the scene of the crime?

She explained that she had left the ballroom and gone below stairs for a breath of air, slipping into the hallway at the foot of the stairs. The constable did not appear to think that behavior so very odd. Neither did he find remarkable her true statement to the effect that, upon feeling the draft from the open door at the end of the hallway and sensing something wrong, she had gone outside to see for herself. It was shocking, she recounted, to see a body lying there, alone, not another person in sight. She was able to discern, from the man's dress, that he was a gentleman, of course, and she naturally assumed it was someone who was attending the assembly. However, she did not approach the body and did not know who it was.

Was Miss Hutton acquainted with the deceased?

Caroline affirmed that she was and volunteered the information that she had been the first one to dance with Mr. Kenmure that evening.

Chief Constable Locke wrote it all down, thanked her for her time and entered into her regret that she had had nothing particular to tell him. He left her with the impression that he would not have to importune her again.

So, where was the harm in what she had said? Nowhere, as far as she could tell, and now that she was alone, Caroline turned her attention to the dozens of things she had to do. However, the unsettling effects of the chief constable's visit along with the last, brief passage with Martha stayed with her, niggling at the back of her mind.

On the whole, however, Martha's breezy visit had cheered her. In the subsequent peace and quiet, she wrote some business letters concerning the estate and the dreary business of selling Hutton Manor. She wrote some personal letters concerning her engagement. She consulted the almanac. The duke did not come. Neither did her aunt return. She ate lunch. She went through her belongings and arranged her clothing. She received a note from Worth, informing her of the time of his visit this evening, but there was still no word from the duke.

It was not until very early evening that his grace, the Duke of Desford, was announced. Tall, graceful and sober in his mourning, he was ushered into the anteroom. The wall sconces there had been lit, as well as two candelabra on the deep mantelshelf. The fire was ablaze. Caroline was still in her pearl-green dress, but she had shed the damask day jacket for a beautiful shawl of eggshell silk, embroidered *à la chinoise* and with a heavy silk fringe.

She rose from the elegant little japanned bureau cabinet where she had been leafing through an illustrated auctioneer's pamphlet on ceramics. She closed it and crossed the room to greet her visitor, dropping into a deep curtsy. Desford's greeting was equally formal. She allowed him to lead her to the wing chair by the fire where she had, earlier in the day, received Worth's proposal. Had it not been for that proposal, Caroline would have been a mass of nerves. As it was, she settled her skirts calmly and folded her hands in her lap.

When he had seated himself opposite her, Caroline said without evasion, "You must forgive me, your grace, for addressing first the topic of your recent bereavement."

His handsome face was drawn. "I have been grieved."

Caroline nodded. "Upon my father's death," she said, "I noticed that expressions of sympathy, instead of increasing my pain, actually helped to alleviate it! I cannot explain why that is so. Nevertheless, I hope that when I express to you my deepest sympathy at the tragic loss of your cousin, my words will have a beneficial effect on you."

"Why, thank you, Miss Hutton, and very prettily said," Desford replied. "It is indeed inexplicable the way fellow feelings in time of need provide comfort, but so it is."

He smiled at her, sadly. His expression was heavy. Caroline thought the new and solemn dimension of mourning ennobled his easy charm. "I am glad, then," she said.

He drew a long breath. "I am in a state beyond grief, rather approaching disbelief—call it shock, if you will." He was regarding his hands meditatively. "Gilbert's death seems unreal. A fiction." He shrugged. "A tale told."

She felt his grief. She wanted to release him from its weight, so that he might once again smile his mobile smile. She said with all gentle sympathy, "I understand. The reality of it is not increased for having been witness to your cousin's horrible fate only moments after it occurred."

Desford looked up sharply.

Caroline felt a stab of pain at her blunder. "I have been morbid and must beg your pardon!" she said immediately. "If I have spoken amiss, it is because the incident has been on my mind the entire day. Earlier this morning, I received a visit from a Chief Constable Locke, concerning your cousin's murder." To the duke's strange expression, she continued, "But I do not think to excuse myself, your grace!"

Desford drew a ragged breath and stood up. "No offense is taken, Miss Hutton," he said quite gently. He walked to the fireplace, then turned to face her, hands clasped behind his back. The fire and the candles flickered behind him. Caroline could not quite see his expression, for his face was shadowed. Still, she had never seen him so handsome as he was in his black silks, white lace and curled wig. "A chief constable—a Chief Constable Locke, you say?—has come to you concerning Gilbert's death?" he asked gravely. "Why, pray?"

Caroline was more than happy to give his grace an account of the interview she had had with the chief constable. She explained how it was that she had come to be in the alleyway, mentioning how she had seen his grace there, in company of Colonel Worth. She omitted again the part about her plans to meet Mr. Kenmure in the alcove. However this time, her reason arose from the fact that to have mentioned it to the duke would have been indelicate, and indeed, now, irrelevant.

"I see. Very interesting," he said when she was done, "and thank you. It does bring some comfort," he said, "to think that officers of the law are treating Gilbert's death— no, then—his *murder* seriously." He held up his hand. "Not that I am expecting any miracles of justice in this case."

"Chief Constable Locke did think it would be difficult to bring the criminal to justice," Caroline offered, "especially if he belongs to a band of common street thieves. I mention this not to cause you further pain, your grace, but only so that you will not build false hopes."

"I shall try not to," he said. Then he straightened and took several steps toward her, so that he was standing directly in front of her. He bowed formally. His expression was intent, even resolved. He began, "Perhaps, Miss Hutton, you have guessed why I have come to you this evening."

Caroline was prepared for this. Her heart was pounding wildly, but her voice remained calm when she forestalled

m by saying, "Allow me first to tell you my news, your
ace, which you might not have heard, it being so recent
d you, of course, being bereaved." She had mentally re-
arsed it a hundred times. "I am engaged, as of this
orning, to Colonel Worth." It came out smoothly, and she
as pleased.

Caroline saw surprise flicker in the depths of Desford's
es. She had expected it. However, she had not expected his
sponse to be, "Ah, so! But, of course!" Nor had she ex-
cted his look to change, instantly, to one of assessment.
e felt that he was truly seeing her for the first time. As a
oman. Caroline felt a deep blush begin at her throat and
awl up her cheeks. As if aware of her embarrassment,
esford dropped his eyes and took several steps back.

The strange moment passed, and Desford's following
eech was smooth and conventional. It pleased her, of
urse, to hear his grace acknowledge a friendship with
chard Worth, one that had grown in the army despite—as
esford charmingly pointed out—Worth's superior rank.
e stated that Colonel Worth was ever a man of decisive
tion. With a devastating smile that made Caroline's heart
rn over, he added that Worth had now proved himself to
a discerning man as well.

Caroline did not hear this cheering, charming tribute with
l the usual pleasures of a newly engaged young woman.
he very impossible possibility of becoming the Duchess of
esford had teased and tantalized her throughout the day.
'ith Desford's ready acceptance of her engagement to an-
ther, her brief, beautiful dream had died.

Nevertheless, Caroline had not truly cherished false hopes
out herself or the duke or their future together. It was easy
ough to mask her pain, and her reply was polite. "I am
eased to accept your good wishes, your grace." She added,
ut of concern, "although I am sorry to have to think that
y news has made your visit a useless one."

"Not at all! The news of your engagement has made my
sit, on the contrary, a most pleasant one!" Desford said
romptly. "It is always a blessing to receive happy news in
e midst of mourning."

Caroline agreed with that and responded appropriately. She began to rise, assuming the interview would now be over. She was happy—though the happiness was bitter-sweet—that it had passed with so little awkwardness; and she loved the duke all the more for concealing what must be his profound relief to be honorably released from what he perceived as his duty toward her.

However, the duke chose that moment to reseat himself. "And now, Miss Hutton, for the purpose of my visit."

Caroline sat back down. "Your grace?"

"I am visiting everyone who had close contact with Gilbert before his death—to make sure that they are not suffering unduly. It is the least I can do. Needless to say, I am reassured that you, Miss Hutton, are in state for which I can wish you joy."

"Yes, indeed. Very kind," she murmured, torn between admiration at his fine sense of duty and sudden puzzlement over the purpose of his visit.

Desford's earlier gravity was gone, and his easy manner restored. His smile was charming. "As I wrote to your aunt this morning—she is an estimable woman, by the way, and I am so delighted to be getting to know her! Yes. Well. As I wrote her, I am come on what is a rather special errand."

Caroline did not understand the drift of this remark. "I am afraid that I . . . that is, I had thought—about Mr. Kenmure—"

To the duke's look of polite inquiry, Caroline shook her head and declined further speech. She gestured for him to explain himself.

"Yes," he said, "I am come to ask for your help—your help in fulfilling Gilbert's wishes. You see, Gilbert came to me on that last day. It was such a delight to see him. He was so animated!" Here Desford stopped. He put his thumb and forefinger to the bridge of his nose to relieve the painful pressure of the memory. The gravity returned momentarily. "Yes, so animated! But I had many visitors that day. Why, Arthur Devis came to see me and so did—"

Again Desford broke off, but Caroline did not think that this time it was from pain. He smiled slightly, shook his head and continued, "A lapse, Miss Hutton. Pardon me. As I was saying, Gilbert came to see me. He was brimming with importance! However, I did not allow him to speak his mind because we were interrupted by one of my bailiffs. I sent Gilbert away. I now regret it deeply! The business ended by being a trivial matter. Far better would it have been to have heard Gilbert out!"

Caroline was slowly absorbing the import of this speech. "And, what, in your opinion, your grace, does this have to do with me?" she asked quite deliberately.

"Why, Miss Hutton, I was hoping that you would tell me," Desford returned. "I had gathered that Gilbert wanted to tell me something concerning you. Perhaps he was going to enlist your aid in some charitable project of his. Ever since his arrival in London, he had been interested in undertaking charitable projects. He was not a rich man— which makes his generosity all the more to his credit. Perhaps you knew of this?"

Caroline did. However, since she had imagined a different purpose for Desford's visit—an extraordinary purpose, a wholly unthinkable purpose—she was incapable of speech. She nodded.

"In honor of his memory, then," Desford continued, "I wished to complete whatever project it was he had in mind, and I have come in his stead to discover what it might be. I had understood that you, Miss Hutton, were a friend of the poor. Or do I refine too much on your good offices?"

This time she managed a wobbly "No. That is, yes, I have been engaged in charitable projects." All the while she was recalling the phrases from the duke's letter this morning: *will come today in Gilbert's stead . . . continue what he was unable to complete.* It fitted together now, with horrible, humbling, hilarious good sense.

"Then perhaps you can tell me what was on Gilbert's mind, Miss Hutton? I believe you danced with him at the assembly. I had hoped he had mentioned something to you!" He peered at her. "I say, Miss Hutton, is there something that amuses you?"

Caroline schooled her features and marshaled all of her calm, good sense. She now had cause to reinterpret Mr. Kenmure's words, spoken to her during their dance at the London Assembly: 'I shall *tell* you one thing, Miss Hutton, and *ask* you another.' He was evidently going to tell her about his latest project and ask her to join him in it. She might feel the fool, but at least she did not have to act the fool.

She met Desford's eyes directly. Both her gaze and her voice were level. "I am sorry to disappoint you, your grace, but Mr. Kenmure and I had no private conversation that night." She smiled and entered once again into the duke's feelings of bereavement. "I do sympathize with you and deplore his death most sincerely! As you say, it is a pain and a grief to think of that happy, animated spirit now gone forever, and his last wishes—whatever they may have been— left unfulfilled."

Desford looked distressed. However, after Caroline's quick apology, he assured her that she should not imagine for a moment that she was at fault for not being able to help him complete what he had sensed were his dead cousin's intentions.

There was little more to be said after that. The usual civilities were exchanged, the funeral plans briefly touched upon. Caroline rose, and Desford with her. He kissed her hand and departed.

Desford made his way down the vestibule to the front door. He received his topcoat, hat and cane from the footman and was on the point of leaving when Lady Besant returned. Upon seeing this distinguished peer of the realm, she paused on the threshold, before entering her own house.

"Desford," she said bluntly, "you have come only now?"

"I have many duties these days," he replied.

"And your duty here?" she inquired.

Desford regarded Esther Besant speculatively. "I wonder, Esther," he said low, "if I misunderstood your intentions."

"I do not think so."

Desford's brows rose slightly. The easy charm for which he was known was absent. A hard look had set his handsome features. "I did not think I had, my dear, after our most...informative conversation yesterday. You are a well-informed woman. So well-informed! I have always admired that in you."

Lady Besant smiled. She held up her hands in a gesture of mock helplessness. "What's a poor woman to do? When she has no money, she must be resourceful, and information can prove so valuable."

"Indeed. But could it be that you missed a very valuable piece of information—right under your very nose?" To Esther Besant's look of inquiry, Desford said, "Your niece is engaged to be married, as of this morning, I believe." Her look changed, and Desford remarked, "Ah, so you did *not* know it!"

"What are you talking about, Desford?" Lady Besant hissed.

"I shall let Miss Hutton inform you," Desford replied. "How I look forward to our next conversation. It will, no doubt, be *most* informative." With a last provocative regard, he was gone.

In the anteroom, Caroline was rooted to the spot where the Duke of Desford had left her, her hand tingling with the sensation of his lips upon it, her spine tingling with the knowledge that she had just avoided true disaster. Her crazed sense of the humorous in the situation had vanished, and she was left with a sense of humiliation. With sickening clarity, she imagined how she might have acted if Colonel Worth had not offered for her. What if she had determined to accept the offer the duke would not have been making? What if, to Desford's statement "Perhaps, Miss Hutton, you have guessed why I have come?" Caroline had replied "Yes, and I am pleased to become your wife?"

Pathetic woman!

Gusts of emotion blew inside her, gathered and began to whirl, funnellike. Lying untouched in the eye of the storm was her love for the duke, her secret love, a calm lagoon. However, she wanted no safe harbor from the anger she had turned in on herself. She wanted to feel the pain and rage; and then the door to the anteroom was thrown open.

Lady Besant swept into the room. To Caroline, she appeared as if she had sprung, full-blown, like a fury out of the floorboards, a beautiful witch from the underworld.

"*What* is this extraordinary news I hear about your engagement?" Lady Besant demanded at her most brittle.

Caroline did not flinch from the shards of the splintered tone. She did not assume her mask of genteel compliance. She did not deign to answer the question. Her inner storm surfaced in full force. "Well, it is not to the duke! Why did you lead me to expect that he would...would offer me *marriage?*" she demanded in turn, her voice rich with emotion. "Did you wish for me to appear truly idiotic? I suppose the only thing more extraordinary than your interpretation of Desford's letter is the fact that I believed you!"

"Desford had every intention of offering for you!"

"He had every intention of completing what Mr. Kenmure was unable to complete!"

"Which was to offer you marriage," her aunt shot back.

"However, he died before he could do so," Caroline retaliated hotly, "which makes my claim on him negligible, and all but nonexistent in the case of the duke!"

Lady Besant's eyes had narrowed to black slits. She asked quietly and icily, "Who is it you are to marry?"

At that moment, Richard Worth entered the room, unannounced. He felt the tension, immediately sized up the situation and took action. As if in answer to Esther Besant's question, he crossed to his bride-to-be and took her purposefully in his arms, thereby deploying the strongest weapon of offensive warfare.

Wholly surprised, caught off guard, Caroline had no defenses and so submitted, unresisting, to this possessive and passionate embrace.

Speaking against her lips, so softly that only Caroline could hear, he commanded, "Return my kiss."

Chapter Nine

"Yes," Worth murmured quiet encouragement, "that's right. Now, place your hands on my shoulders. There. Good. Very nice. Yes." Then he abandoned speech and devoted himself to the kiss.

Worth was as surprised as Caroline, for, in seizing this moment, he had unexpectedly seized her storm, and the success of his maneuver exceeded his expectations. Her mouth, which was too wide for beauty, was sweet and quivering and responsive. A honeyed mouth. A generous mouth. A kissable mouth.

Having so easily won that strategic territory, he struck out for further gains, to trace his lips down the column of her throat, so slim and white and vulnerable, then back up to reclaim her lips. And her body. It was full and soft and round. Her breasts were pressed to him, her waist and hips curved to his hands. His. His field. A lily field. White flowers. To pluck. White-hot kisses to pluck. But he knew nothing of the lily field. He knew only the battlefield. The battlefield, where hearts raced and blood beat. A new battlefield, this kiss. A glorious battlefield where pain and hatred were slain, where murdered souls came to life.

He did not know what had produced the storm he had caught and captured on her lips. Nor did he care. It was enough that in this brief moment he had tasted the honey on her mouth, caught the scent of her desire and held her storm in his arms. Yet, having experienced the promise of her fullness and passion, having found in her kisses the para-

doxical satisfaction of wanting more, he was not thereby
pleased.

Neither was Caroline. Her emotions were truly storm-
tossed now. In the past five minutes, she had been flung on
many rocky shores. She had borne the ache of love's possibility truly lost. She had experienced humor and suffered
humiliation upon hearing the duke explain the purpose of
his visit. She had surged with hot, righteous anger at her
aunt. She had been incredulous at her own credulity. Now,
she was surprised into the first passionate response of her
life, fired by the kiss of Richard Worth.

She could not deny her response to his lips and hands
upon her. Yet she resented him, for her passion and her fire
were not for him, but for her impossible love, the Duke of
Desford. She was outraged at the audacity of Richard
Worth to march in and capture what was not his.

The hard, brass buttons on his soldier's coat were bruising her breasts. She recovered from her surprise and submission and struggled against him.

At the first sign of her resistance, he broke the kiss and
looked down at her face and into her hazel eyes, glittering a
tempestuously. "Miss Hutton," he said, still holding her
against him. "Good eventide."

She did not return the greeting. Instead she whispered
angrily, "How dare you?"

His answer was for her ears only. "We are supposed to be
in love, remember?"

She responded by flashing him a fiery look, which he
alone could intercept, since he stood between Caroline and
her aunt. He did not respond to her mute reproach, but
rather continued, now in audible tones, "We are being rude,
my dear, and must defer our eagerness until we are private." Then he turned, with an arm around Caroline's
shoulder, to face the woman across the room.

There she stood before him. At last. The secretive, se-
ductive woman who had kissed him, caressed him and condemned him. The beautiful woman with the onyx eyes who
had whispered accusations behind his back, but never to his

face. The lacquer-hard woman who had brought him to ruin.

Esther Besant had not moved a muscle. She stood as if turned to stone.

"Allowances must be made for the newly engaged," he commented, by way of explaining his behavior. His tone was that of the satisfied suitor, but his words were a slap in her face. "I have come this evening to discuss the particulars. Do you care to join us, ma'am?"

Esther Besant's worst fears were confirmed. She was not about to respond to his invitation to join them, much less accept it. She flicked a regard over Caroline. At Worth's handling, several tendrils had escaped Caroline's coiffure and were curling behind her ears. Her shawl had slipped from her shoulders and was draped from her elbows so that the fringe touched the floor. The whole effect was one of charming dishevelment. For such a plain, unpromising woman, her niece was looking fresh and flushed and well kissed. And very much in love.

Esther Besant's lip curled. Caroline and Worth in love. Love at first sight. She almost believed the evidence before her eyes. Almost, but not quite. She knew too much of Worth's past and guessed too well his motives. He was paying her back, settling the score, and she knew it. She was almost flattered. Almost, but not quite. She had teased him. He had teased in turn. She had almost had him, all those years ago. Almost, but not quite. It was an unimaginably ill wind that had blown Worth into London this week of all weeks. But here he was in her anteroom, against all her expectations, almost the same man she remembered so well. Almost, but not quite.

He had the same unfinished face and moved with the same raw passion, but he was older now, and so was she. She would not panic. "My niece—" she began. She loathed the role of guardian but would play it. "My niece, I am concerned for her. What do you have to offer her?"

"My devotion," Worth answered promptly and bent to place his lips on a warm, fragrant spot on Caroline's neck.

"What, no title to offer her? You are titled, are you not?" She smiled. "And land? Do you not have land?"

"Surely you recall that I renounced my title and estates before I left England," he replied without a trace of emotion and without mention that he had applied to have his title restored.

"I am afraid that I did not attend the details of your departure." She appraised Worth's jacket. "I recall now that there was talk you had joined the military."

Worth did not mistake Esther Besant's opinion of his profession. He was determined to enjoy this encounter and knew just how he would take his extremely belated satisfaction. "I did," he replied, "as you can see. However, I have recently sold out. My commission ends within the fortnight, in celebration of—" he shifted a loving gaze to Caroline "—my marriage."

The curl to Esther Besant's lip was pronounced. "Before taking that rash step, did you, in the heat of your...love, consider the state of my niece's finances?" She paused. "I ask out of concern, mind you, since eager young couples are often blind to the practical considerations in life."

"In deep appreciation of your concern," Worth said with a half bow, "you shall be the first visitor at our home at St. James's Square."

"St. James's Square?" Lady Besant repeated in complete surprise. "That is not possible, unless you bought—"

It was Worth's turn to smile. "Yes, I bought Montague House, which just came up for sale."

Lady Besant's tongue was working faster than her brain. "But that must have cost a—" she began before she realized that she had no desire to complete the thought.

"A fortune," Worth completed smoothly. "Yes, and although my birth and breeding taught against discussion of finances, I am aware that in the present circumstances, some mention must be made." He would turn all her insults to good account. "I did well in the military. Very well. This afternoon, I opened up an account at the Bank of England for my wife-to-be. Shall I tell you the amount of the allowance that will be transferred to her account there every quarter?''

Esther Besant was stunned. After a frozen moment, she collected herself. "That will not be necessary," she said. Then, to Caroline, "Love *and* wealth. You have done well for yourself.''

Caroline confined herself to a simple "Yes.''

"We shall talk about this in the morning," Lady Besant said. She did not trust herself to speak further to Worth. Without another word, she left the room as abruptly as she had entered it.

Caroline was stunned herself. She had paid little heed to the actual words spoken between her aunt and Worth. Instead, she had listened as if she were holding two halves of a broken plate. But when she put the two halves together, the pattern still did not match, for too many chips were missing. To gather her thoughts, she needed to distance herself from Worth, his touch, their pretense. Before she could move out of the protective circle of his arm, she found herself turned to face him.

"Now, Miss Hutton, we have much to discuss," he said. His one arm remained on her shoulder. The other hand he placed at her waist. He wanted to be touching her so that he could sense her most minimal reaction to what he had to ask her. He looked down at the woman he had lately kissed, whose pale skin was glowing in the flickering light of the fire, whose hair was falling in pretty disarray, whose breath was coming rapidly, to judge by the intermittent, feather-touch of her breast against his. His feelings for her were far, *far* different than when he had left her this morning, and not all of them were unpleasant.

"We do," she agreed, struggling a little to be free of him, but with no success. She thought a repellent question might obtain her release. "To begin with, you may tell *me* the amount of the allowance to be deposited every quarter in my bank account.''

He did not release her. "I had every intention of informing you of your new financial status in the, ah, accepted manner. I've already instructed my man of business to come

round to you on the morrow to discuss your account." His
hold was gentle, but firm. His smile was cynical when he
said, "Were you being deliberately vulgar to ask, Miss
Hutton?"

"Oh, not *deliberately*," she retorted. "Why should you
think so?"

"Because you had ample opportunity to inquire into your
new financial state this morning, if you were so interested."

"But I wasn't then," she said, still squirming.

"And you are now?" he queried. Without further ado, he
named the figure. "Five hundred pounds."

"A *year?*" she gasped, awed by the amount of what she
knew was pin money, not a household budget.

"No, every quarter."

She ceased to struggle against him. She suddenly realized
how little she knew about her husband-to-be, his former life,
his former friends, the fortunes of his military career. Very
slowly, she said, "That is a considerable sum, especially
when I bring nothing to the marriage."

"No dowry," he agreed, "but no debts either. And you
have other assets."

She considered this. "Two thousand pounds a year for a
wife's allowance and a home in St. James's Square," she
stated. Then, directly and with genuine curiosity, "How did
you acquire so much, after having lost all?"

He dropped his arms and took a step back. "Perhaps it
is as well you know now that I am a merchant, of sorts." He
waited for some sign of distaste from this daughter of a viscount. When none came, he continued, "While on the
Continent, I discovered that I had a head for business, and
I allied it to my taste for music. I began to trade in harpsichords."

"Harpsichords?" Caroline echoed, surprised by this odd
turn.

"Yes, and more recently the pianoforte."

All she could think of to say was, "I am not familiar with
it."

"The pianoforte is a new instrument. I believe it will catch on in England," he said. "I did well with it on the Continent."

"How extraordinary!"

"Not at all," he replied. "The instrument has a very attractive sound, and much music is already being composed for it."

Caroline laughed. "I meant rather that it seems an extraordinary occupation for a soldier," she said. "Musical instruments are not usually found on the battlefield!"

"As an officer, I had entrée to the courts and the salons at my various posts where the latest music was to be heard."

"Yes, but nevertheless, I imagine that you had to start somewhere," she pressed, "and you did not enter the army as a colonel. You began with nothing."

Although this was apparently his night for disclosures, he would not detail the less than admirable customs practiced by a victorious army over a losing countryside. He explained briefly, "In the immediate past, when I was not on the battlefield, I spent my time in the craft shops. I was in the Low Countries," he reminded her, "and the Dutch are among the premier instrument makers. However," he said, turning the topic, for he wanted to blot from his mind further thoughts of the brutality that had brought him wealth, "I have returned this evening to discuss the more pressing matter of the date of our union. Did you consult the almanac?"

The fragile calm that had carried Caroline through most of this remarkable day threatened to desert her now. "As to that," she said, hedging, "we should not choose an unlucky day."

"Certainly not."

"Advent and, of course, Christmas fast approach," she observed, "which makes the coming season ineligible."

"Wholly ineligible."

"And we cannot proclaim banns in one quarter of the year and be married in the next quarter."

"Indeed, that is illegal."

Caroline drew a breath. "Since December and January are out, it seems that we must be married before Advent Sunday."

Unlike Caroline, Worth was pleased. "I suggest no further delay, then," he said, bowing. He withdrew a small ring box from his coat and opened it. He reached for her left hand. "May I recommend Sunday next?"

"Sunday next," she repeated apprehensively, as a cold band was slipped onto her third finger. She looked down and saw a ring of threefold gold fashioned into a lover's knot, the symbol of constancy and of willing bonds.

Not letting go of her hand, he took another step toward her. She took a step back. He shook his head and said, "This is no minuet, and you have yet to bestow my ring on me." He gestured with the box in his other hand. "There is a second ring there."

When Caroline had slipped the ring onto his finger and he had pocketed the box, he took her hand. Now both of her hands rested in his. His look was intent. He bent his head toward her slightly. Thinking he was going to kiss her again, she turned her head away. Although that had not been his intention, he asked, "You object to a kiss, Miss Hutton?"

"It is not right."

"We were agreed that love was to provide the explanation for our hasty marriage."

"That was *your* idea," she pointed out.

"Which you put to immediate use," he returned.

Puzzled, she looked up at him.

"Martha Sheridan," he explained succinctly.

"Ah," Caroline said, holding his eyes, coloring a little.

"Yes," he said, "I paid her a visit this afternoon and heard a most interesting story. A charming story, really."

Caroline felt a wash of color seep up her neck and over her cheeks. She was aware that something had changed between them. She could see it in his face. She could feel it in his nearness. She could no longer look Worth directly in the eye. She dropped her gaze to his blaze-red coat. The color was a shock, an offense. It offered too violent a contrast to the sober black that Desford had worn so nobly and whose sober nobility had deepened the ache in her heart.

"I do not reproach you, Miss Hutton," Worth said. "In fact, I am pleased that Mrs. Sheridan should think that we are in love. Before returning to London, I had remembered only how much society honors wealth. I had forgotten how much the world loves a lover. As your aunt aptly observed, love and wealth—it is a powerful combination. I wish to maintain our sweet illusion."

"But only in public, I would imagine, sir. Your earlier attentions to me," she said, looking up at him through lowered lashes, her color still high, "were for my aunt's benefit, I must suppose."

He was suddenly curious to discover whether a second kiss would have the same effect on him as the first. Looking down at her, he focused on her mouth, her generous mouth. "Then we'll call in a footman or two to make it legitimate," he said. He drew her to him and pressed his lips to hers.

He sought and found her storm. He was enjoying this kiss, the feel of her body, her scent, her response. He was surprised at how much he was enjoying her, and his surprise, in turn, increased his enjoyment. He was fired most immediately by Caroline Hutton, the woman in his arms. His flame was fanned, more subtly, by the encounter with Esther Besant and the belated satisfaction she had provided him. And with the satisfaction surfaced ancient memories. Ancient memories that he had learned to keep at bay by losing himself in battle and ambition.

As he held Caroline and kissed her very kissable mouth, the memories danced on the edges of his consciousness, memories of the last blood-red day of his youth. He had spent it toying with Esther Besant. It had not been a serious dalliance. Not on his part. She had been a beautiful woman who had married unwisely. A beautiful woman who was condemned to travel on the fringes of society. A beautiful woman who was hard, even then, in a magnetic kind of way. A married woman with an appetite. A hungry woman and expensive. And he had been rich, but the young man he had been did not foresee how much she was to cost him.

Murder. Suicide. Whispers. His name bathed in blood. Blood. Everywhere. Whispers. Everywhere. Death. Everywhere. Gaping flesh. Warm flesh. Sweet lips. This kiss. His thoughts meandered back to his purpose. He moved his lips across her cheek to her ear.

"I wished to sample, in earnest, what had reportedly been mine. In private. During our assignation. At the London Assembly." With that, he moved his hands boldly from her back around to her waist, then up to her rib cage to stop just below her breasts.

Caroline's heart had begun to thud at his rough touch, and she was dissolving against him. He had tantalized her with his hands and the promise of his touch. He had tantalized her with his lips and the promise of his tongue. She had never been kissed at all, and it seemed she did not need experience to know how to respond.

On the surface, her response was spurred by the blaze-red of his coat, the warmth of his lips and his taste, the working of his shoulder muscles under her fingertips, the feel of his palms nearly cupping her breasts. Deep inside, she felt herself responding to the recent memory of noble, sober black and the Duke of Desford's handsome gravity. Deep inside, she felt the storm of her emotions swirling furiously around that untouched eye, her secret love.

"And speaking of the assignation we never had," Worth continued lazily, moving his lips to rest lightly against her neck, "how was it that you were the first person to appear in the alleyway on the night of Gilbert Kenmure's murder?"

Her storm wobbled akilter, blown off course by the events of the day and of the past minutes, thrown awry by the man she had touched with her lips and hands, near whose heart her own was pounding. At the question, she momentarily lost the ability to breathe normally and to speak.

He felt her change. He was regarding her intently. "You told Martha Sheridan that we had had an assignation, but that is not, I think, what you told Chief Constable Locke."

"I did not *tell* Martha that I had gone to meet you," Caroline replied quickly. "She inferred it. And you cannot be unhappy about it, for it preserves the...sweet illusion of our marriage, I think you said."

"True," Worth agreed, "I am not unhappy about it." He repeated, "Why were you the first in the alleyway?"

"Why do you ask?" she countered.

"Because announcements of our marriage are to appear in tomorrow's newspapers," he said, "and because I want no breath of scandal to taint my name."

"Do you think I had another assignation?"

"No."

Of course he would not. Being kissed the way she had been kissed had made her forget that she was a plain, undesirable woman. She *had* had another assignation that evening, but its probable purpose and her wild flight of fancy about it humiliated her. She flushed.

"But I want to know why you were there," he said.

She groped for a reasonable response. "I was below stairs, taking the air," she told him as she had told Chief Constable Locke. "I sensed something wrong. I went to look. That is all."

Worth regarded her a moment longer. When she lowered her lashes, he lifted her chin so that he could look into her eyes. They glittered with something. Was it, oddly enough, embarrassment? Was she holding something back from him? It seemed so, but he sensed it had nothing directly to do with the murder. "If you think of another reason," he said slowly, releasing her, "be sure and tell me. In the meantime, we shall take public delight in our newfound love."

Worth bowed over her hand. When he had left, Caroline was torn between disbelief and indignation that he had not been accusing her of an assignation, he had been accusing her of *murder*—or of being accessory to it. With her passion still roused from the memory of his kiss, indignation initially took the upper hand. *The nerve of the man!*

Yet he was the only person in the world who knew for sure that she had not had an assignation with him. The fact remained that she had been the first in the alleyway, and he knew it. She had lied to Martha Sheridan, and he knew that, too. If he was suspicious of her, at least he had good reason.

He was bound to her, a woman he did not love and one he did not trust. And she was bound to him, a rough, passionate man, whose kisses touched a storm that was not for him. Earlier in the day, Caroline had wondered what the harm would be in the half-truths she had told Chief Constable Locke and Martha Sheridan. Now she knew.

Chapter Ten

The next day when Caroline awoke, she lay in bed far longer than usual, savoring the wholly incredible fact that her fortunes had changed, quite literally, overnight.

She rose only after the upstairs maid had delivered the message that Worth's solicitor would arrive within the hour to review the accounts, as Worth had promised the evening before. She spent a good two hours with Mr. Thornton, during which she demonstrated her hard head for household finances and made clear her desire to hire the housekeeper herself and several upstairs maids; she devised a financial plan to save Hutton Manor; she made provisions for a handsome cash settlement to her aunt.

By the time the interview drew to an end, Mr. Thornton had decided that the young marquess—or Colonel Worth, as his client must now be called!—had shown excellent judgment in his choice of bride. The solicitor had been less than optimistic the week before, when the marquess had returned, stating his desire to enter society. Mr. Thornton had been impressed with the size of the marquess's bank balance, but he remembered all too well the kind of woman who used to hover around the marquess in his younger days. He recalled, with a deep shudder, the former marquess's second wife.

Lady Besant had arranged her morning's affairs so that she would be on hand when Caroline's interview ended. Like Caroline, she had had the night to ponder the startling effects of blind fortune. Unlike Caroline, she was deeply displeased, for she saw blind fortune operating to ruin her most carefully laid plans. When she considered the full implications of those ruined plans, her displeasure turned to an apprehension that contained the first tricklings of fear. Twin dangers were apparent to her, but the devil of it was, she did not know which man presented the greater danger. To judge from the look on Richard Worth's face the night before, she had reason not to underestimate him.

"Well, my dear," she said after Mr. Thornton had departed, "how did your interview go? No unpleasant surprises?"

"If there are to be any unpleasant surprises, they are not financial," Caroline said evenly.

"That is reassuring," Lady Besant said. "So. All the surprises are on my side."

"Not unpleasant ones, I hope."

Lady Besant smiled tightly. "I make no secret that I was not transported with delight to discover that you had allied yourself to Richard Worth, my dear."

"I am aware of your prejudice against him," returned her niece. "In spite of that, he rather swept me off my feet. It was fortunate that he returned my feelings."

Lady Besant was certainly not going to argue the question of the betrothed couple's feelings for each other. "Pray forgive me, my dear, if I spoke too frankly yesterday evening! However, I do not regret it, and I shall continue my frank approach—for your sake, my dear! In all good conscience, I must ask you if you are quite sure you wish to ally yourself to a man whose past is scarred by murderous scandal."

"However scandalous his past, it remains a fact that Colonel Worth was not the murderer," Caroline said loyally.

The beginning of a plan momentarily dazzled Esther Besant. "No, he was not," she replied slowly. Then, more briskly, "But let us turn our thoughts to more pleasant subjects. Have you set a date for the wedding?"

When Caroline told her, she looked at her niece anew. "Sunday, is it?" Lady Besant said, agreeably enough.

Could Worth, indeed, be the eager bridegroom? Smiling sweetly, she unconsciously echoed Martha Sheridan's prediction, but with less genuine dismay. "The one regret, of course, is that your wedding will be entirely overshadowed by Mr. Kenmure's funeral, which is scheduled for the day before."

Lady Besant had the right of it. Mr. Kenmure's funeral was to overshadow any other event in all of London that week, even the king's dinner with the City at the Guildhall on Lord Mayor's Day. The probable cause of Mr. Kenmure's death had created sensation enough, added to which, no Londoner of any consideration, especially cousin to a duke, could be buried until he had had a lying-in-state. This period traditionally began on the third day after death and continued for two full days after that, to culminate in the ceremony at the parish church cemetery.

Because Mr. Kenmure had only recently come to London from Leicestershire and because Desford was the head of what had become a very small family, the lying-in-state had taken place at Desford House. Thus it was that an enormous number of mourners had come to Desford House, whose largest and most elegant drawing room had been the setting for a hemorrhage of fear and indignation for the past several days.

By Saturday afternoon, Hanover Square was thronged with carriages filled with mourners, come for the procession from the house to the cemetery. By Saturday afternoon, as well, the murder had become so celebrated in town that a full complement of the London middle class and a strong representation of riffraff had come to line the sidewalks for a glimpse of the proceedings.

The gawkers were not to be disappointed. Desford House, solemn and majestic, was draped in black. On each step of the stairs to the front door stood a footman bearing a black pole ornamented with three black plumes. All afternoon long, elegant mourners with black scarves descended from carriages adorned with black streamers and disappeared into the house.

Inside, the mourners put aside for the day their fear and indignation, out of respect for the dead. They offered condolence to the duke, who stood at the threshold of the room that held the coffin. Beneath the black bunting and in the light of black wax candles, they murmured and milled in small groups, clusters of no more than three or four, centered around the coffin, whose lid had been closed that morning. Although the atmosphere was hushed, a certain restlessness reigned. The mourners moved sedately, yet constantly, in and out of the room. Desford House, large and accommodating, was full.

Lady Besant had come early and alone, and she had greeted the Duke of Desford with the reserve one would expect of distant acquaintances. Arthur Devis had come early as well, apparently intending to drown his deep sorrows at the death of Mr. Kenmure in Desford's excellent drink. Worth wished to make his presence felt, and he had arranged to escort his bride-to-be, as was proper for a public occasion so close to their nuptials. Caroline had steeled herself for this next meeting with the duke after his private visit to her earlier in the week. However, instead of feeling a renewed sense of humiliation at her pathetic love, she was rather taken aback by the warm look Desford bent on her when she curtsied to him. Martha Sheridan arrived late, looking heartbreakingly beautiful in her grief. The black pomp and circumstance of the occasion had brought back sharp memories of her husband's funeral.

In short, everyone was there. Everyone including Chief Constable John Locke.

As it happened, Worth had encountered Chief Constable Locke that very morning in the same neighborhood where he had last seen him. Worth had made a point of returning to the office of Mr. Jonathan Wild and, for no particular reason, he had chosen the morning of the funeral. He imagined that enough days had elapsed since his previous visit to Mr. Wild for that efficient businessman to have made the requisite inquiries into possible clues concerning the identity of the murderer. Worth was anxious to discover whether Mr. Wild had recovered any items that had perhaps been stolen from Mr. Kenmure at the time of his death.

However, Worth had arrived at Mr. Wild's office in Cock Alley a few minutes too late. At the moment that he stepped up to the spruce establishment and was about to ply the shiny brass knocker, out walked Chief Constable Locke.

Worth gave him a greeting and said, "So our positions today are reversed. The last time we were here, I was leaving just as you were entering."

Locke acknowledged the remark with a salute and returned the greeting. Then, "Have you lost something, Colonel Worth?"

Worth shook his head. "Just interested in the case. That is all."

"The case?"

Worth was unable to read Locke's face. He saw no reason to deny the obvious. "I'm interested in the London Assembly murder. I heard Wild's name mentioned in connection with it," he explained, "and came to pursue my own little investigation."

"Oh, aye, you're interested, then," Locke concurred easily. With more the inflection of a leading question than a statement, he continued, "But, sure now, your interest arises from your friendship in the army with the victim."

Worth was about to disclaim any acquaintanceship with Kenmure and any knowledge that Kenmure had been in the army, then remembered having spoken of such an army friendship to Mr. Wild the few days before. Worth had already determined that Locke had been put on the case for a reason, and it was not because he was incompetent. He guessed that his lie about his relationship to Kenmure was transparent and, possibly, incriminating. He felt himself on low, indefensible ground and reckoned that further dissembling would possibly create unnecessary suspicion. A bold move was called for.

"I did not know Kenmure from the army," Worth admitted, "and doubt he ever served. I'm guessing that you know it, too."

Locke smiled in approval. "That I do." Then, with a meaningful look directly into Worth's eyes, he said, "Do not let your interest carry you too far. You might not like what you find. Good day to you, sir, and give my greetings to Miss Hutton."

With another salute, Locke was gone, leaving Worth to wonder whether the chief constable was friend or foe.

Since that question could not be immediately resolved, Worth turned his attention to a second one: should he enrich Wild by a crown to discover what Locke had already discovered? Feeling that little would be lost either way, he spent the crown to learn from Wild that no progress had been made on the identity of the murderer. It cost Worth a further crown to learn that Wild had discovered an interesting item, possibly stolen from the victim. It was a kind of knife, as Wild described it, rather more of a dagger, and not of English origin. It cost Worth a third crown to learn that Wild had relinquished the knife in question—most reluctantly and with no profit, Worth supposed from Wild's aggrieved tones—to Chief Constable Locke's official keeping.

Worth dismissed the incident, for he had more immediate legal matters to accomplish concerning his marriage the next day. When he saw Chief Constable Locke later that afternoon at Desford House, he did little more than bow to him. Worth briefly watched the chief constable's progress through the fashionable throng. With his unpowdered hair, his powerful build and the suit he wore with more comfort than elegance, the police officer certainly stood out in the crowd. However, if Locke was uncomfortable traveling on the crisp of the upper crust, he did not show it. All in all, Worth thought, Locke was cool and canny. Worth turned his attention to Miss Hutton and the quiet conversation she was pursuing in their small group.

In truth, Locke was not in the least uncomfortable rubbing shoulders with the ton. He was investigating a murder, pure and simple, and he had come prepared. Two days before, he had obtained the Duke of Desford's written permission to attend the funeral. The duke's response had suggested that he welcomed Locke's presence. The day before

Locke had investigated Mr. Kenmure's movements on the days preceding his murder. Locke had gone to Cavendish Square and interviewed the housekeeper where Mr. Kenmure had rented his rooms. He had caught a whiff of Kenmure's amorous adventures. He had studied the names and family histories of those people most likely to be connected with Gilbert Kenmure, and he had learned quite a bit about a class of people with whom he did not normally associate. That morning he had retrieved an interesting item from Jonathan Wild. In final preparation, he had donned his fawn-colored, full-skirted suit and laced waistcoat, which, though far from new, would make him less conspicuous than his army coat.

Locke ran a professional eye over the fashionable assembly and spotted first Arthur Devis. Since Mr. Devis had already been imbibing for at least the hour past, Locke had no difficulty learning that Kenmure had owed Devis money. Devis also confirmed that Kenmure had been entertaining a woman on the day of his death. When Devis's conversation—if such a rambling mixture of disjointed sentences could be called a conversation—dissolved into maudlin childhood recollections, Locke sought out the Duke of Desford who, upon receiving the last of his guests, had moved from the threshold into the drawing room.

It was easy enough for Locke to establish with the Duke of Desford the common ground of the army. Desford accepted the point of contact by reminiscing briefly on his captaincy in the First Regiment.

Locke knew his business and came straight to it. Except for the fact that he had had to shrug into his gray suit, the occasion was little more than routine for him, a day's work. He withdrew his notepad from his coat and held a strange graphite rod in his hand. Although the rod was as thick as a woman's forefinger, in Locke's large fist it was dwarfed to little more than a twig. Locke handled it with practiced ease.

"I'm needing to know, your grace," he began, with the rod poised over the paper, ready to write, "the exact family connection between yourself and the deceased."

Desford nodded his understanding of what the chief constable in the murder investigation needed to do. He answered willingly, "We are cousins through our grandfathers."

"Brothers, your grace?"

"Yes," Desford said. "Gilbert's grandfather and my grandfather were brothers. Gilbert's had no sons and one daughter. She married a Kenmure."

"Did you come into the title directly, your grace?"

Desford smiled. "No, the title and estates had passed directly through the Wyndhams of Yorkshire. Gilbert and I grew up in Leicestershire. My great-grandfather Wyndham must have been a long-headed man, for he made out his strict settlement to the rather distant cousins. The long and short of it is that my grandfather was the second son of the original line, and Gilbert's grandfather was the third."

Chief Constable Locke was neither insinuating nor accusatory. "What happened to the male heirs in the direct line of third generation, your grace?"

"There was only one male heir in the third generation. My grandfather's elder brother had one son who had a son. The grandson, then, married a woman who was, to say the least, fertile, for she had given birth to three daughters in the first three years of their marriage and was expecting a fourth child at the time of her husband's death."

"Which was four years ago, when you inherited, your grace?"

"Yes. The direct heir died in a riding accident, and his wife gave birth soon thereafter to a fourth daughter. I was in the army—in Flanders, as you know—and was not aware of the succession proceedings. I was not even aware of the strict settlement provisions made by my grandfather, which prevented common law rules of inheritance to prevail when the line unexpectedly died out. In any case, in default of direct male issue, the settlement turned back two generations and made its way to me. I was called home."

"You were not aware of the provisions, your grace?"

Desford shook his head. "Neither me, nor anyone else, it seemed, besides the lawyers," he explained cooperatively, taking no offense at the possible reason why Chief Constable Locke might have to ask such questions. "The Wyndhams, represented by Drummond, were, needless to say, surprised to find the entire inheritance slip away from the branch of the family the widow married into, but financial arrangements were certainly made on her behalf and that of her daughters. More to the point, however, was that I had never given a thought to the possibility that I might succeed."

Locke listened to this recital with great interest. He cleared his throat, but his eyes never left the duke's face. "And who is next in line, your grace?"

A truly charming smile lit Desford's handsome countenance. "You don't like asking such questions, do you, Chief Constable Locke? It's a damnable business you're in, but I'm glad you're in it! I have a younger brother, Robert, who has three sons, so the current succession is not in doubt, whether I marry tomorrow or not! A rather quiet man is Robert. He did, however, come from Leicestershire for Gilbert's funeral." Desford smiled kindly. "Shall I introduce you?"

Locke was an old hand and a difficult man to disconcert. "You were wrong that I minded asking the questions, your grace," he said, his heavy eyebrows lightening, "but you were right that your few answers gave me ones to many questions more. And, aye, I'd like very much to meet your brother, your grace."

Locke was led to the rather taciturn Robert Wyndham and got little out him beyond the fact that the direct heir to one of England's greatest fortunes was more interested in farming than power and glory. The undemanding conversation gave Locke time to digest the fluent information the duke had given him. That information was subject to verification, of course, and Locke would verify it come Monday, but he doubted he would learn from the lawyers anything other than what the duke had told him. As for immediate confirmation, he had only to cross the room and ask the widow of the direct heir how widely known were the details of the great-grandfather's settlement.

His preliminary conclusion was that no angle on the matter of succession would easily figure into Gilbert Kenmure's murder. His efforts this afternoon had definitely not yielded what he had expected. He scribbled a few more notes and replaced pad and crayon in his coat. He was beginning to think, against his first instincts, that the murder of Gilbert Kenmure fell into the pattern of dozens of other such crimes: a petty murder, with petty motives, by a petty criminal. It was a routine lacking in surprises.

Then he crossed paths with a beautiful woman, a fair and fragile woman, with eyes the misty blue of the Isle of Skye and lips that promised heather honey. He presented himself to her—as the job demanded, of course—and when she treated him with suspicious reserve, he felt the routine investigation develop an interesting new dimension.

"Was your husband acquainted with Mr. Kenmure, ma'am?" Locke inquired, permitting himself the license of the question.

Martha Sheridan's reply was cool. "My husband died last winter."

A widow, then. The investigation had taken on a *very* interesting new dimension. "I see," Locke replied, "well before Mr. Kenmure's arrival in town—" he withdrew his notepad and consulted a page "—last month."

"Well before," Martha concurred.

"And you, Mrs. Sheridan? Were you acquainted with the victim?"

"I knew him the way the others did. No more, no less," Martha was careful to say.

"And your opinion of the man, Mrs. Sheridan?"

Martha slanted a glance at the rough-cut, unfashionable man with the powerful build and the beautiful lips. The inflection in his voice, with its light burr, was subtle. But her reaction to him was not. It was strong and immediate and complex. How much did the chief constable know? How much did he guess? His eyes were far too keen.

She said, "Mr. Kenmure was a charming man, with a kind and gentle nature. Not a likely target for a murder." Under the scrutiny of his gray eyes under the heavy eyebrows, she felt strange: halfway between awakened and violated. Because she was reacting so strongly and so incomprehensibly to the man, she wanted to put him in his place. She continued, "Kind and gentle, as I've said—" here she ran a slightly disdainful eye over the chief constable's unfashionable habit "—with a kind and gentle sophistication."

"Sophistication, Mrs. Sheridan," he replied, his Scots burr pronounced, "is a skin that covers many blemishes."

Martha felt as if she had just been slapped, lightly, across a cheek. Or was it that she had been spanked? The thought of Locke's hand on her rump was perversely stimulating, and again she felt torn between attraction and dislike of Chief Constable Locke. She was torn, too, between excitement and shame that she should feel such feelings in the midst of a funeral—a funeral for a kind and gentle man who reminded her so much of her kind and gentle Humphrey. Dislike and shame took the upper hand.

"Indeed, sir?" she said with a nice blend of disbelief and superciliousness. "Sophistication for Mr. Kenmure was not a veneer, as I think you are suggesting, but something rather deeper."

If Locke was to have found himself at a loss in this crowd, it would have occurred far sooner than this conversation. "But then, ma'am, how could you tell?" he replied. "Unless you knew him better than most."

The man is a barbarian! Martha thought. "One can determine quite a lot about a person after just one conversation, Chief Constable," she retorted tartly. "Good evening."

"Good evening, Mrs. Sheridan," he replied, with a half bow, thinking that it was not heather honey on her lips but, possibly, something less sweet, far more delectable.

Martha moved away too hastily to have perceived the satisfied look on Chief Constable Locke's face, and sought out Caroline, who was speaking in a group that included Worth. Martha greeted them perfunctorily and drew Caroline aside.

"Could it be, Caroline," Martha said, her blue eyes far from misty and rather gem-hard sparkling, "that this Chief

Constable Locke is the same one who visited you the other day? The one whose manner you said is so proper? The one, you said, who is attractive in his own particular way?''

"Why, yes, I saw him here a while ago," Caroline said, looking around. "He is still here, is he not, investigating the case?"

"He is still here," Martha rapped out quietly.

At her friend's tone, Caroline peered closely into her face and asked, "But what is it, Martha? You are red as a beet!"

Martha fought down her uncharacteristically fierce blush. She composed her voice. "I do believe that your Chief Constable Locke has just insulted me." She did not really care to expose herself further, even to Caroline. Enunciating each word with deliberation, she added, "I think that I shall procure myself a cup of tea. A very bracing cup of tea. Excuse me, my dear."

Caroline returned to her circle. Worth bent to her ear attentively and asked, "A problem?"

Caroline shook her head. "Pique, nothing more, as far as I can tell." She smiled up at him tentatively.

He responded with a nod and a smile, less tentative, far warmer.

The thundercloud that had hovered between them on the evening of their engagement had changed character. This afternoon a cloud still hung between them, but it was less stormy, more billowy, rather difficult to define. This subtle change was due in part to the fact that, in observing Chief Constable Locke's behavior at the gathering, Worth sensed that Locke was pursuing a line of investigation into Kenmure's murder that did not include Caroline Hutton. (Worth had also had several days to think through the real unlikelihood of her involvement.) Then, too, maintaining their "sweet illusion" required loving glances and light touches, and these inevitably inspired in Worth thoughts that centered more immediately on his wedding night than on lining up suspects in a murder.

For her part, Caroline found it impossible not to respond positively to a man who was treating her so well. She was able to carry out her part of the illusion, although it was not easy under the circumstances: the context of Mr. Kenmure's death; the strange attentions from the duke, which wrung her heart; the hostility that simmered against Richard Worth from some of the men; the curiosity that buzzed in every word spoken to her by some of the women; the humming consciousness that she was to be married on the morrow. As the afternoon wore on, she was beginning to feel the strain. Thus, she was not unhappy when evening had overtaken afternoon, the black wax candles had burned low into their sockets, and it was time to leave for the church.

Outside, the cold gray of the day had turned to a colder, grayer drizzle. Even so, the gawkers on Hanover Square had remained for more glimpses of the aristocratic mourners. Again, they were not to be disappointed, for this funeral procession was to be all that was expected of a cousin to the Duke of Desford. The gawkers were to follow the procession around the corner and down the street to the low stone wall encircling the parish church of St. Michael.

Preparations to leave Desford House were made. As the mourners filed out the front door, they were presented with black scarves and weepers, black cloaks, black gloves and rings. Everybody carried a sprig of rosemary. Because the funeral was conducted at night, the mourners carried torches. The procession, in its short, wet walk to St. Michael's, was headed by several beadles. Twelve men came next displaying the heavy cloth pall, which was adorned by the Desford coat of arms. After them and before the hearse were the footmen carrying the black poles ornamented with the black plumes. The hearse that bore the coffin was painted black. The driver was dressed in black. The horses pulling the hearse were black. The black plumes attached to their harnesses nodded limply in the rain. The mourners followed two by two.

In the church, the mourners' torches smoked. The atmosphere was dank. The service within was elaborate. The graveside ceremonies were mercifully short, but not lacking in respect. Before the coffin was lowered into the ground, the embroidered pall was thrown over it. After the coffin was settled, everyone tossed in the sprigs of rosemary. The mourners turned away, putting out their torches by knocking them on the ground, and left the last sad acts to the spades of the sextons.

It was at that moment, in the cold, black drizzle, that the hostility simmering against Worth the evening long flared out momentarily. As he was turning to leave the graveside, his right arm linked to Caroline's left, he was jostled by a man. He ignored it the first time. The second time he could not. Nor could he ignore the vile epithet spoken low as the man passed by.

Chapter Eleven

It was strange, Worth thought dispassionately. The last time he was accused of this unnatural relationship with his stepmother he had been brought to the peak of blind rage. This time the ugly word had little effect. Nevertheless, when he heard the curse, Worth released his hold on Caroline, whirled and caught the arm of the man who had spoken.

Worth was surprised at the man's identity, but only mildly, for no one of his former acquaintances had been eager this week past to come forward as his friend. He knew that emotions had been running high since Kenmure's murder and that the anger had been deliberately suppressed for the day. Thus, aware that he was but an easy target for the release of some of those emotions now, he might have dismissed the man's comment. However, he never missed an opportunity to disarm the enemy when he met it.

"You mistake the matter, William Langley," Worth said instantly and with complete sangfroid, still gripping the man's arm, "if you think I will not challenge that statement."

"You are quick to take offense, sir," Langley said, attempting to shake his arm free of Worth's murderous grasp.

"And you are very slow to cast down the gauntlet, my boy. It has taken you thirteen years, to be precise. Do you care to repeat, very slowly and for all to hear, what you just said to me?"

William Langley was looking as if he now thought the better of his rash words. Perhaps he remembered Colonel

Worth as a hotheaded young man. Perhaps he had heard that Worth had faced legions of enemy troops and never lost a battle. Perhaps he realized he could not repeat his exact words in public. Whatever the reason, Langley declined to repeat his statement, but not without a further attempt to insult Worth. "I don't think the occasion right for me to stoop to satisfying your desire to defend your honor."

Worth turned the intended insult to good account and managed a further threat. "Your observance of the proprieties, though belated, is most wise." Only then did he release the man's arm, and Langley had to shake it to restore the flow of blood.

With all the manner of a ranking officer who had just reprimanded a soldier for insubordination, Worth looked calmly about the small group that had gathered, then nodded once, as if dismissing his ranks. It worked. The crowd dispersed. Langley's departure from the graveside was singularly abashed.

Worth knew the three main objects of warfare: to conquer and destroy the armed power of the enemy, to take possession of all his sources of strength and to gain public opinion. In warfare, Marlborough had proved that public opinion was won through great victories and the occupation of the enemy's capital. In Worth's case and for his campaign, he did not think to gain public opinion by winning great social victories with his personal charm of manner. It would be won by securing respect through defeating every challenge to his name and his past. He imagined those challenges had begun, tonight, here in the cemetery, just seconds after Kenmure had been interred, the moment when proper, mournful behavior no longer held in check the hostility against him.

Yes, the most difficult, and ultimate, goal of warfare was to gain public opinion. Worth was ready to meet all challengers. But what of private opinion? He turned to Miss Hutton, still at his side. While the last of the onlookers drifted away, Worth and Caroline exchanged a long, wordless regard. He could not quite read her expression in the pitch and with the hood of her cloak cast over her head. In any case, it was cold and drizzling and time to leave the graveside. He offered his arm. She accepted it, and they made their way down the short path toward the church, slowing their steps to allow distance between themselves and the others.

"Did you hear what Langley said?" Worth asked at last, looking straight ahead, not a note of emotion in his voice.

"Yes," Caroline admitted, glancing up at him.

"It can only have shocked you."

It *had* shocked her. "But not in the way that you think," she said. "I was not shocked by the reference to you, only by the fact that someone would say such a thing out loud."

"Would it shock you further to know that I have heard it said out loud more than once and in reference to myself?" he said in the same expressionless voice. Then, with regret, "I am sorry for it. For you, Miss Hutton."

"It wasn't your fault, sir," Caroline said.

He laughed softly. "That, Miss Hutton, is the point of contention."

They had come to the end of the path. The door of the iron grille gate had clanked shut at the passage of the couple ahead of them. They were the last ones on the path, and they stopped before the closed gate.

"That was not what I meant," she said, looking up at him. "But you know that." Her face caught the rain. "You handled Mr. Langley very well, by the way."

"Thank you."

"In something of the style of an overbearing colonel, I think."

"My specialty."

At this nearly lighthearted turn, she opened her mouth to speak again, but closed it. She had been about to ask him, directly, whether the story about his illicit liaison with his stepmother was true. She decided against doing so on the wholly arbitrary grounds that a woman could not ask her husband-to-be such a question with drops of water running off her nose.

He did not volunteer the information, either. Instead he said gravely, "You see what awaits you as my wife. I am afraid that I cannot assure you that this will be an isolated instance.''

''I doubt Mr. Langley's comment was intended for my ears,'' she said. ''It may not be an isolated incident in your experience—and for that I am sorry!—but as for me, well, I cannot imagine being similarly insulted a second time.''

''Not in so many words, perhaps, Miss Hutton,'' he replied, looking down at her intently. ''Think carefully about it now, however, while you still have time to cry off. You may not wish to sink so low.''

Caroline knew she must look a fright. Her curls were wet and plastered to her forehead. Her nose felt red, and her skin was not the kind to take on an interesting pallor in the cold. She knew her face must be unattractively blotchy, even in the wan light emanating weakly from the church portico. Under other circumstances, she would have felt acutely uncomfortable to be seen at such a disadvantage. Under other circumstances, she would have been sure the gentleman wished for her to cry off so *he* could be free. Under these circumstances, however, she was not worrying about how she looked. She was responding only to what she heard between his words.

She said the first thing that came to mind. ''I was facing financial ruin, Colonel Worth. Without a farthing to my name, I would not have merited even Mr. Langley's scorn, so far beneath his notice would I have been.''

Worth almost smiled at that, but then his expression changed to one of steely self-possession. ''Do you understand,'' he began, ''do you fully understand, Miss Hutton, that my father killed my stepmother, then committed suicide?''

Here, in the cold and rain, at the edge of the cemetery, was a question Caroline could comfortably confront. ''Do you feel similar murderous impulses, Colonel Worth?''

''I worked them all off on the battlefield, over a period of thirteen years,'' was his immediate reply. His next remark came more slowly. ''Consider, please, Miss Hutton, the step you are to take tomorrow. Now is the time to change your mind, if you will. Now, and no other. Consider it well.''

Caroline did so. Financial rescue was, of course, only half the reason she had accepted Worth's offer. The other half was to save her from the temptation of accepting an offer from the duke. Would she have accepted Worth, if she had known the duke had had no intention of offering for her? That was a difficult point to decide.

Now that she was given an opportunity to cry off, Caroline did not know why she did not want to. It occurred to her that there might be something about Colonel Worth that she actually liked, and at that point her thoughts fell into confusion. Cutting through the confusion, she asked herself the most basic question: should she believe that Worth harbored no murderous impulses similar to his father's?

She said directly, ''If you had no murderous impulses before your father's actions, I can certainly understand that you might have had some afterward. Needless to say, I am glad to hear that you have worked them all off. It seems, then, on a number of scores, that the army served you well.'' She drew a breath and answered Worth's question. ''We shall have to muddle through this together, I suppose.''

Worth opened the gate and ushered her before him, then passed through himself. ''You are honest, in all events.''

''Yes, I am,'' she agreed forthrightly, ''and while we are listing my qualities, I might mention as well that I also have a good sense of social limits. I think we have reached ours tonight. We did well enough a while ago at Desford House. However, I recommend that we do not attend the late supper that is soon to begin there.''

They were heading down the now-deserted street back toward Hanover Square. Her suggestion found favor with Worth, and he nodded agreement. He said that he would have his carriage brought around upon their return to the duke's, and he offered to escort Caroline directly to Portugal Row.

They walked on a few more paces and turned the corner before Worth said, ''A good sense of social limits, you say, Miss Hutton? Then, tell me your assessment of the terrain we shall encounter in the weeks ahead.'' He slanted her a glance. "I ask, you understand, in the spirit of an over-bearing colonel."

They were nearing Hanover Square. In the light of Desford House, now magnificently illuminated, she looked up at him and caught the gleam in his eye and a glimpse of the broken architecture of his cheek and forehead against the surrounding night sky. She smiled slightly and looked quickly down again. He was joking, but only halfway. Some part of him thought of their marriage on the order of a military expedition.

"Before I answer you, Colonel," she said, "I need to establish my rank."

"Your rank—?" he began.

"Yes, rank," she said, "so that my assessment is cast in the appropriate terms. The word *general* has a nice ring, I think, although—as you know—I do not have a head for the fine points of military hierarchy!" Then, assuming a serious mien and a deeper voice, she continued authoritatively, "The terrain will be rough. However, our field position on St. James's Square is good. We have some friendly troops behind us, and Martha Sheridan can be counted on to smooth the rougher passages. In terms of heavy artillery, we have the Duke of Desford on our side. Our marriage tomorrow might have been an occasion vulnerable to gossiping attack, but with his grace's offer to serve as a witness, we will be unusually well defended." She paused. "That's my report, sir."

"Most accurate. I thank you," Worth replied pleasantly, looking down at her. "However, generals do not ordinarily report to colonels, since generals have the higher rank." He added provocatively, "in case you did not know."

She met his look directly. "Oh, really?" she said and smiled what he had come to know as her impudent smile. He had an impulse to kiss her but did not give in to it. They had reached the front steps of Desford House. He told her to wait for him in the foyer while he went round to the stables and got the carriage himself. Caroline's smile lingered as she followed him with her eyes until he was swallowed by the black mists.

* * *

The unsavory incident in the cemetery with Mr. Langley had had the unexpectedly happy result of providing the occasion for this frank conversation, which, in turn, had produced an easy, almost friendly aspect of their relationship. Unfortunately, that easy friendliness did not survive their wedding day. The rupture between them was not caused by the weather, or the fact that their wedding conformed so little to custom, but by a discussion that Caroline overheard between Worth and Desford after the ceremony had taken place.

The weather on their wedding day was, in truth, depressing. The morning dawned dark and damp and dreary, with the cold gray mist drooping on the chimney pots of London. The drizzle had thinned to a spit. Caroline refused to take the weather as an omen.

Caroline also refused to allow herself to be cast down by the hastiness and paltriness of her wedding. No gay group of bridesmaids would come this morning to deck and dress her bridal bed. They would not adorn it with ribbons of blue and green. They would not tie sprigs of herbs dipped in scented water to the posts. They would prepare no wedding favors. There would be no streamers of blue and green ribbons for the girls, no topknots or cockades in the same colors for the young men's hats. The ladies would not solemnly inspect her trousseau, which did not exist. She would be given no teacups, no silver spoons.

These omissions did not truly bother her, and the event began well enough. Worth presented himself promptly at ten o'clock in the entry hall of Portugal Row to escort her to the church in the parish of St. James. In his suit of midnight-blue silk, his hat and his dress sword, he was extremely handsome, in his own particular way.

"Miss Hutton," he said, bowing over her hand, "you are looking most lovely. Most lovely, indeed."

Caroline was naturally pleased and thanked him accordingly. However, since Lady Besant was also ready and on hand to hear it, she imagined that the pretty compliment was as much to maintain their "sweet illusion" as to continue their friendliness of the evening before.

Worth's admiring scrutiny was acute. "And is that not the dress you were wearing," he continued, "the evening I met you at the London Assembly?"

For her wedding, Caroline had chosen her peach and cream ensemble, cut low at the breasts with a fall of lace. "Yes," she said, "and now that you mention it, I recall having worn the gloves that match. Excuse me while I go to fetch them."

When Caroline left and Lady Besant found herself alone with Worth, she was suddenly wary.

"I would hope, Esther," he said smoothly and with a bow, "that you could wish me happy on my wedding day."

She realized that nothing was to be gained by being unpleasant. "But, of course, Richard, I wish you happy."

"And now that we are family," he continued, "I expect that we shall be seeing quite a bit of each other."

She slanted him a glance and liked what she saw in the hard, blue gaze he had focused on her. She knew what admiration looked like in a man's eyes. "Perhaps."

"Surely, Esther, you have not become so diffident, since last we were together?"

She was wary, but also, despite herself, curious. Was there a hidden twist in his game? She quirked an exquisite black eyebrow—the only sign of interest she would betray—and said, "You may call on me anytime. As family."

Worth merely nodded to that, for Caroline was coming down the hallway, and he went forward to meet her and to help her on with her cloak. There was little more to do than to depart in Worth's carriage, which was adorned with the traditional white plumes. Lady Besant took her own carriage to the parish church.

Martha Sheridan was already at the church when Caroline and Worth arrived. She had arranged for the escort of Arthur Devis, who was not at first eager to oblige. (Upon being issued Martha's invitation, his exact words were: "Awful! Miss Hutton deserves better!" but then he must have remembered that Worth's father, the old marquess, had kept an exceptional cellar and that he could count on something half-decent afterward at Worth's home on St. James's Square.) Martha greeted the bride and groom with hugs and kisses and extravagant compliments on Caroline's loveliness, on Worth's handsomeness. Lady Besant arrived shortly thereafter with Mrs. Shuttleworth, who had engineered an invitation from Caroline. Caroline had not objected, for Mrs. Shuttleworth, though a curious old tabby, was rich and fashionable, and her presence could not hurt.

The duke arrived betimes, still dressed in mourning. He graciously thanked Caroline for having kept the wedding party to an absolute minimum. Had she planned a large wedding, he said, he would not have been able to attend, for such an occasion would have counted as "going out in the society" and, thus, would have been an inappropriate activity for him so soon after Mr. Kenmure's death. In this perfectly charming way, the duke made it seem as if the wedding party had been kept small on his account and not because of haste or because of the scandalous past of the groom. His grace complimented Caroline, kissed her hand, smiled warmly into her eyes and congratulated Worth on his great good luck.

Caroline was too preoccupied to do more than thank the duke rather absently for his kind words. The flutter in her breast at his presence was minimal. She was also too preoccupied to notice that, once, when the duke and her aunt were in a private conversation, they were speaking in a way to suggest that they were more than distant acquaintances.

"And what of your pretty plans now, my dear?" Desford said to Lady Besant in passing. It was a taunt.

Lady Besant took this without a blink. "Don't try me too hard, Desford. Do you forget how well informed I am?"

"You will not let me forget it, my dear," he returned. "Going to Leicestershire for your information was a brilliant stroke. I wish now that I had thought of it myself!"

It was Lady Besant's turn to taunt. "You are short on thoughts, as recent events indicate. My latest plan is a very pretty one. If you are interested, call on me tomorrow morning."

Desford was interested enough to agree to that, and they turned away from each other to be absorbed in the wedding party.

Caroline and Worth exchanged their vows in the presence of five witnesses, a priest and two altar boys, and were pronounced husband and wife. Worth kissed his bride, and when his kiss lasted longer than the usual peck, Desford began the typical wedding party ribaldry with the comment, "You shall have to wait until you are private, Richard, to complete *that* kiss!" Devis was moved to second it with a "Hear, hear!" Then, in an audible aside to Martha, he nodded his head in Caroline's direction and said, "A taking little thing! Hadn't noticed it before last week. Nice-looking female. Good figure, too!"

Caroline glanced up at Worth and blushed. Worth returned her look with exactly the kind a groom would give his bride upon sealing their vows with a kiss. Her blush deepened.

Caroline signed her new name in the parish registry, along with Worth, and all seemed to be going well. In the carriage adorned with the white plumes, Worth escorted Caroline to Montague House. They were followed by three other carriages bearing the witnesses, who had been invited to St. James's Square for a meal. Caroline had never been inside Montague House, but she knew it from the exterior, and it was similar to the house she had grown up in. Because of her foreshortened engagement and the events of the week—mostly notably, the funeral the day before—Caroline had not previously visited her new home. She entered Montague House for the first time as its mistress.

Worth escorted her over the threshold, and Caroline saw that her new home was indeed very similar to the former Hutton House, except for the fact that it was virtually bare of furniture. It was a lovely structure, however, with handsome floors and ceilings, built in the middle of the previous century and freely inspired by the old classical patterns of symmetry and balance. In the entry hall several retainers were waiting to greet the new Mrs. Worth. The other guests arrived soon thereafter, and Worth led them into the dining room, which was the only room that was furnished.

The meal was a success. The talk ran merrily and in a light vein. Lady Besant's behavior was exemplary and subdued, and so did not set Caroline's teeth on edge. It had been agreed beforehand that the occasion would be an abbreviated one, because of the atmosphere of mourning that still reigned. The guests left several hours later, all thanking Caroline and Worth for having provided an oasis of happiness in an otherwise very dark week. No direct mention of Mr. Kenmure or the funeral was made.

The rest of the afternoon was easily and companionably occupied with a complete inspection of the house. The ground floor was grand and had great possibilities. Caroline noted with some relief that both the master's and the mistress's chambers on the first floor had beds. The second floor, for servants, badly needed a thorough cleaning. Together, Caroline and Worth inspected a dozen rooms and poked their heads into as many cupboards.

Such domestic activities were not a bit tiring to Caroline, although they did help her raise an appetite. Worth had ordered a light supper for two in the dining room, complete with champagne. Seated at the table, Caroline realized that the "sweet illusion" they maintained in public for the day had carried over into their private dealings. Worth was nothing less than the attentive bridegroom.

The bubble of the sweet illusion went to Caroline's head. She felt effervescent, and it was a feeling she was beginning to associate with Worth's presence. It had little to do with the champagne they were drinking and much to do with the way he was looking at her. She felt desirable. She felt her deep-down singing self come alive. When the talk turned to music in general and Italian opera in particular—about which Worth was extremely knowledgeable—she decided to share with him a pet theory of hers. Just when she was ready to expound her theory, and just when their friendliness seemed to become something warmer, there came the clang of the front door bell.

Worth frowned. Because the household was not yet running smoothly, he decided to answer the door himself. Rising, he bade Caroline remain seated so that she might enjoy the rest of her cake undisturbed, saying he would return to her immediately. He left the room.

Several moments later, Caroline overheard two friendly masculine voices, one Worth's, fade down the vestibule in the opposite direction from the dining room. After a minute or two, Caroline decided that she could greet the caller herself. In the spirit of a happy bride and housewife, she went down the vestibule, crossed the entry hall and stopped at the door to the parlor, where she heard the men talking low. Her heart leapt to perceive the second voice to be that of the Duke of Desford.

She took a moment to smooth down her skirts before entering the room. She had a greeting fluent on her lips and had made a movement forward when the significance of the phrase she overheard registered in her brain with a shock. In that second, the words died in her throat and her step froze. Instead of entering the room, she flattened herself against the outside wall to listen, with a sinking heart, to the conversation within.

Chapter Twelve

At the clang of the front doorbell, Worth's first thought was that someone of Langley's stripe had come to call him out on his own terrain. He did not want one of his retainers to handle the caller, nor did he wish Caroline to have to face a second such incident.

He excused himself and told her not to trouble herself with getting up. Upon leaving the room, he took a lit taper from the branch of candles on the sideboard. Cupping his hand over the flame as he walked down the vestibule to the entry hall, his thoughts were grim. Upon his opening the door, however, his face was transformed into a smile.

"Jonathan!" he said. "What brings you to the neighborhood? Didn't have enough of witnessing my married bliss earlier?"

"Is that sacred state so blissful?" Desford replied, stepping through the door that Worth had opened wide for him.

"I would not yet know," Worth said, closing the door behind his friend.

Desford smiled at that. "Ah. Do I intrude?"

Worth was, in truth, annoyed to have been interrupted at just that promising point in the conversation with his bride. It was months since he had been with a woman—not since the last, horrifying encounter with his Flemish mistress. That had been a truly gruesome episode, and Worth remembered it now, fleetingly. However, he was good at suppressing unpleasant thoughts, and he pinched this one before it could flower.

"Not quite," he replied, "but almost. Do you join us for cake?"

Desford shook his head and said he had come for his cane, which he had left, he believed, in the parlor. Crossing the hall, Worth led his guest down the vestibule to the parlor. Sure enough, when Worth lit a wall sconce, they saw Desford's cane lying across the closed wing of a magnificent rosewood harpsichord of Dutch craftsmanship, which was the only piece of furniture in the room. Desford picked up the cane but displayed no inclination to depart.

The two friends commented on Worth's fine new house, the wedding, their respective plans for the coming week. Finally, Worth said, "I wish to thank you, Jonathan, for volunteering to be a witness at the wedding today."

"It was nothing," Desford disclaimed gently.

"No. It was kind and very brave," Worth said. "I would not have asked you, you know."

"I know. The damnable business with the funeral prevented you from asking any favors of me, which was why I volunteered. It is hardly a kindness to do what one wishes, and as for bravery—why, you may acquit me of that, dear boy!"

To this disclaimer Worth said, "I assume, then, that in attending my wedding today, you have remained ignorant of the depth of feeling that is still harbored against me. You also did not hear, at your cousin's funeral, Langley's opinion of my morals."

Desford had a knowing look. "Shall I guess what he said?"

"You hardly need to guess."

Desford looked sympathetic. "I told you it would not be easy."

"Which is why I must thank you for having supported me so publicly," Worth replied.

Desford smiled a sad-hearted smile. "Although my rank comes with a heavy load of burdens—this week has been the most onerous of my past four years—it does put me above considering what Langley might think." He tapped the handle of his cane against his palm. "It was the least I could do, to attend your wedding. After all, it was I who recommended Miss Hutton to you as a woman who met all of your specifications."

Worth thought he heard the rustle of skirts at the door, but when no one entered, he decided he must have been mistaken. "Yes, you did, and I thank you for the recommendation."

"Do you?" Desford pressed the tip of the cane into the floorboard, spread his palm over the handle and leaned into the cane. "How was it that you chose her, by the way, over Julia Stanhope and Angelica Gordon?"

"You fault me for my taste?" Worth felt vaguely insulted by the question. "You mean that the other two are accredited beauties."

"I mean no such thing! I ask out of curiosity. Merely."

Worth was conscious of a desire to return to Caroline and their discussion. To bring the present conversation to a rapid conclusion, he answered hastily, "Would it satisfy you to know that the principal reason involved the old scandal?"

"Interesting," Desford commented. "Do you care to elaborate?"

"Not at the moment," Worth said flatly. Then, hearing his own rudeness, he laughed apologetically, "Pray excuse me, Jonathan. In response to your kindness and, yes, your recommendation of Miss Hutton, perhaps I *do* owe you an explanation. However, not," he repeated, "at the moment."

Desford did not press the point. Nor did he take the hint that their interview was at an end. Instead, he eased away from the cane and leaned now against the harpsichord, seeming inclined to linger. "Tell me, Richard," he said. "How was it that Miss Hutton came to be the first from the assembly to arrive at the scene of Gilbert's murder?"

Worth had the sudden, uneasy sense that Desford had left his cane on purpose and that he had returned to fetch it in order to ask this very question. Worth did not feel ambushed now, the way he had when Chief Constable Locke had first disclosed this fact to him. Still, he paused a long moment before he replied, "It would be ungentlemanly of me, Jonathan, to answer that question."

Desford laughed softly. "Such a man of decision!" he admired. "And such a fast worker! You met Miss Hutton and immediately persuaded her to join you in—what is the quaint phrase?—amorous congress in the infamous London Tavern hallways?"

Worth kept his countenance admirably bland, and Desford rolled an amused eye. Then he looked back at Worth and cocked his head. "But, wait. I recall that you accosted me that evening just when I was going up the stairs. I believe you came toward me from the cloakroom, at the left of the foyer."

Too late Worth perceived his error, and he did not like to be forced into a lie. "No, I came from the long hallway to the right," he stated, "the one that gives onto the alleyway."

"Did you?" Desford queried. "Yes, that is the one famed for its alcoves. But it makes no mind where you came from or where you chose to pursue your lovemaking." He straightened now, as if finally ready to leave, and tucked the cane through his arm. "I am only sorry that Miss Hutton was so unfortunate to be the first at the scene. It cannot have been pleasant for her."

"Indeed not."

As the two men walked toward the door, Desford said easily, "Yes, I must guess that she has discussed so extraordinary a circumstance with you."

They turned into the vestibule, which was empty. Worth lied, just as easily, "A little, but not at length. There's been no time, you see, and it is, as you say, most unpleasant. Should you care to ask her about it yourself?" Worth offered, nodding ahead, toward the dining room.

Desford declined politely, saying that he had troubled Worth quite enough this evening, and the two men made their way through the entry hall. At the front door, Desford turned. His expression was unreadable, but his voice held a sincere note of regret. "But it is such a curious affair, Gilbert's murder. I am sorry that Miss Hutton—that is, Mrs. Worth—should have had to be there, so early on.''

Worth had had a few moments to think through the implications of his story and was glad of the opportunity to plug the holes in his account. ''Yes. I hold myself partly to blame. We were in the hallway, you see, when we heard the shouts from the alley.'' Worth opened the door to let Desford out. ''Although we both sensed something was wrong, our thoughts were elsewhere and, well, I made the decision to go into the tavern to find help before going out in the alley, never dreaming that Miss Hutton—Caroline—would take it upon herself to go outside before me.''

''Oh, yes. I quite see how it must have been,'' Desford said. ''Do not blame yourself, old boy. With your wife-to-be in your arms, I am sure that your thoughts, as you said, were most certainly elsewhere. And on that note,'' Desford said in a teasing voice, ''I shall leave.'' As he descended the steps, he expressed, in blunt, though not quite vulgar terms, the hope that Worth would enjoy his wedding night.

Since Worth planned to do exactly that, he wasted no time returning to the dining room. There he saw Caroline, seated at her place, just as he had left her.

However, Caroline was not at all the same woman she had been before the interruption. Outside the door to the parlor, she had overheard how it was that she had been brought to Worth's notice, and she had stayed at the door, immobile, until Worth had explained her presence in the alleyway to Desford, using the same excuse that she herself had given to Martha Sheridan. She dared listen no longer and so crept back down the vestibule to the dining room.

Reseated at the table, her heart pounding irregularly, her stomach feeling sick, she needed to pull herself together before Worth returned. She tried to convince herself that she should feel good that her husband had defended her against any suggestion of being involved with Gilbert Kenmure's murder, but she failed. She tried to convince herself that she had known all along that her husband had had a motive in having offered marriage to her that had nothing to do with her particular attractions. Again, she failed. She remembered the night of the London Assembly and recalled that Martha Sheridan had mentioned that Worth had singled her out, along with the very poor and very beautiful Angelica Gordon and Julia Stanhope. Two days later, Worth had come to her to propose marriage. That evening they had set the date. And that kiss!

Caroline looked over at the fire on the hearth. Before the interruption it had been bright and dancing. Now it hissed at her. Before the interruption, she had felt bubbly. Now she felt flat. Before the interruption, she had thought that Worth had been looking at her as if, in a moment, he would rise from his chair, lift her into his arms. Then the doorbell had clanged.

She looked down at her intertwined fingers. Facing the truth directly, she identified the source of the sick feeling in her stomach. Yes, she admitted to herself, somewhere deep inside, she imagined that Worth had offered for her because he fancied her. She was shamed by her vanity.

Of course, the most painful revelation had been that the Duke of Desford had suggested her to Worth as conforming to his unspecified "specifications." (If she had needed further proof—which she did not—that the duke did not think that Gilbert Kenmure intended to offer for her, it was surely the fact that the duke had callously recommended her to another man as an available *partie*.) She could imagine the conversation that Worth and the duke must have had about her. She burned with humiliation. But the worst of it was that she felt unattractive. Downright *ugly*. She had never felt so ugly—not as the disappointed debutante unable to attract a dancing partner, not as the ruined heiress who had no hope of contracting an alliance. It was such an old, *familiar* feeling, this one of ugliness. Only it was stronger, as if a little fox had been living dormant in her stomach all these years and had suddenly awoken this evening. It gnawed at her now with its sharp teeth and claws. She hated it. She hated herself.

When she heard Worth's footfall in the vestibule outside the dining room door, the little fox bit more deeply. Worth entered the room and took his place at the head of the table with her on his right. She glanced up at him briefly, attempting a smile, then back down to her plate of uneaten cake, saying nothing.

After a moment, Worth said, "That was Desford."

Ugly and stupid, she apostrophized herself. Any normal person would have asked who had come calling at such an hour. "Oh?" She sounded dull, to her own ears. "What did he want?"

"His cane."

"Did he leave it?"

"Yes, in the parlor."

"Oh."

A small space of silence. Then Worth put his elbows on the table and leaned toward her. He said pleasantly, "Yes, he left it on the harpischord. Which reminds me of music and the point you were making when we were interrupted. Now," he continued provocatively, "where were we?"

"I do not know what you mean." Caroline peeked up at her husband again briefly.

Worth smiled, and Caroline blushed. "You had just advanced an interesting theory, a pet theory of yours."

Caroline looked away. She could say that she did not remember. However, since less than ten minutes had elapsed since they were interrupted, she could hardly make such a statement without appearing unutterably idiotic or even churlish. Whyever it was that Worth had offered for her, he did not deserve either an idiotic or a churlish dinner companion.

Although the bubble of their sweet illusion had burst, she saw no reason to evade the issue. She cast him a fleeting glance. "Oh, yes, of course. Harpsichords and music. That is the connection. I had advanced the idea that singing was an extension of speaking, another form of expression." She picked up her glass but put it back down before taking a sip. She was too sober now for champagne. "Or, perhaps, it is more accurate to say it the other way around—speaking is an extension of singing." She paused and glanced at him again. His expression was interested, his gaze intense. She summoned her courage to continue. "I was saying that every woman has a vocal range and a register. Every woman has a singing self." She drew a breath. "That's my theory."

Worth was content to play along. "I take it that the woman's singing self does not refer to musical talent as such."

"That's right," she answered. "Martha Sheridan, for instance, has a very musical voice and a well-developed singing self, I would say, although she does not care to actually sing." Caroline was aware of the pretentious absurdity of the topic but would pursue it until she could think of another. "It could be that all men have a singing self as well, but I have not noticed it so much. Perhaps I suffer from being a selective listener or am simply more naturally attuned to the voice of another of my sex."

Worth considered the point. He thought, inevitably, of the many sounds of men he had heard on the battlefield. It was not the fierce calls of "Charge!" or the battle cries that he heard in his inner ear, but the thin thread of a sound, the faint, chilling rattle that rose from the throat of a dying soldier as he breathed his last.

"And your singing self, ma'am?" he asked. "To what degree is it developed?"

She dared another glance at him. He was smiling and looking at her, she thought, in just the way he had before the interruption. However, by now, she had pulled herself together and had mastered the effect that her intoxicating husband had on her. She answered him forthrightly. "Well developed and allied to a natural ability. In fact, I pride myself on my singing voice. Though not strong, it is pure and, I have been told, sweet."

He was charmed by her forthrightness and by other of her assets: her skin in the candlelight, the shadow beneath the fall of lace at her breasts and her generous, kissable mouth. "And do you play the harpsichord as well as you sing?"

She shook her head. "Only indifferently."

His eye fell on her neck. He remembered the fragrant spot there that his lips had touched. He was acutely aware of the fact that he had not kissed her since the night of their engagement. "You are honest," he remarked.

"Along with my ability to sing, honesty is another of my qualities," she replied, having found again her rhythm in the conversation, "as we agreed last evening."

"Along with your fine sense of social limits," he added promptly. "Highly desirable qualities. In a wife." He pushed back his chair and rose, extending a hand to her. "Will you sing for me now? I have already lit the candles in the parlor. I can easily fetch a chair to listen to you play the harpsichord indifferently and sing purely and sweetly."

She laid her hand in his, and he helped her to her feet. She shook her head again. "Not tonight, sir, if you please. You would be heartily disappointed." He did not immediately release her hand. She felt his strength and intuited his desire for her. She did not understand it and drew away slightly. He let her hand drop. "But we can go to the parlor, and I shall describe to you the plan I have for it."

"The plan?"

She laughed a little at his surprise. "You may have noticed that it has no furniture."

Worth took the nearest branch of candles from the table, and they proceeded toward the door. "You saw it only once and very briefly this afternoon," he said, "and you already have a plan for it?"

"Oh, easily," she said. "I mentally decorated it at least three different ways and have chosen one."

In the vestibule, he took her arm and placed it on the wrist of his hand that held the branch of candles. With the other hand he shielded, more or less, the half dozen flames from the drafts. Their pace was leisurely to accommodate the flickering candles. Worth was enjoying her nearness and her scent.

"Three different ways?" he echoed on a note of admiration. "You did this in your head? I do not see how that is possible."

"I am in the habit of it. Sometimes when I lie abed in the mornings or even before falling asleep at night," she said, "I imagine rooms and decorate them. A variety of ways with different furniture. The exercise amuses me."

He looked down at her. "Does it?" he replied.

Something in his voice signaled to her that she had made an extremely suggestive remark. It had been quite innocent, this reference to her bedtime fantasies. She looked up at him and realized, not for the first time, how attractive her husband was. With the branch of candles held out before them, his cheekbones were thrown into high relief, accentuating the unchiseled quality of his features, giving him that rough, unfinished look that was more appealing in a man than beauty. His dark unpowdered hair was bound at the neck and blended into the surrounding darkness, a negative halo.

She was not going to be undone by him. "It does amuse me," she insisted, meeting his eye, "and in addition to having decorated the parlor, I have peopled it. We must entertain. To begin with, we might hold a small, intimate musical evening. At the end of next week would be good, I think." Although her voice was decisive, her eyes unconsciously pleaded the message: *I may not be as beautiful as Angelica Gordon or Julia Stanhope, but I can decorate a room to perfection and entertain admirably.*

He intercepted her look but interpreted it wrongly. He had noticed the change that had come over her since Desford's visit. *Nerves,* he thought, naturally enough. *The virgin bride.* He had no doubt of his ability to gentle her into acceptance of him and to find the passion she had given him a few days before in her kiss. The look he returned said as much. It also said he was eager for what lay ahead, but not impatient.

Caroline glanced away, confused.

"You already imagine entertaining?" he said.

"As soon as possible."

"Is that a good idea?" he persisted.

She overcame her confusion. "An excellent idea," she said confidently. "I have already discussed it with Martha, and she agrees with me. Music, some cards, a small group. Subdued entertainment. I plan to send out the invitations tomorrow."

"But is it wise?" he protested again.

They had arrived at the door to the parlor. She paused on the threshold. "Do you doubt me?" she queried. "I am the one with the fine sense of the social limits, remember."

"The key word being *limits*."

"And they need to be pushed, in our case," she replied immediately, "without delay." Before she could put a guard on her tongue, she said, "You, sir, are a colonel in the army and should know about the advantage of speed upon the battlefield. Or was it your tendency to hesitate that prevented you from being promoted to the rank of general?"

Worth, who was not known for a tendency to hesitate, laughed at that. "I bow to the superior rank and withdraw my objections to the commanding officer's excellent plan."

"Very well. Now listen to my decorating idea," she began.

They were interrupted just then by the footman who had served them at dinner and who was currently doubling as the butler. He had come in search of his master and mistress to complete their wishes for the evening.

Worth handed the retainer the branch of candles and bade him light the candles in the bedchambers. He dismissed him with an absent smile and nod and turned his attention back to Caroline. The light from the sconce in the parlor spilled across the threshold where they still stood, illuminating their profiles as they faced each other. The moment was charged.

Worth's expression was inviting. "Tired?"

Caroline shook her head and covered the moment in talk. "Now for my plan, sir," she said, "I have in mind an Oriental motif. Do you have any objections to chinoiserie?"

"I don't think so," Worth answered her lazily, somewhat at random, "and even if I did, you would override them. I shall leave the decorating of the chamber in your capable hands." At that, he picked up one of her hands and brought it to his lips.

She continued quickly, "I envision a lacquer cabinet in that corner there and several Chinese chairs and an Anatolian carpet. A settee for three, I think, should go under the window. The centerpiece of the room, of course, will be the harpsichord, but I shall balance it with a ceramics cabinet.''

He kissed her hand. "A worthy plan. I approve," he murmured against her knuckles.

"I am particularly fond of Kakiemon jars—you know, the Hampton Court vase—and the blue and white Chinese designs in plates and bowls. I do not think such a display will detract from the harpsichord, since it is so very fine—do you?"

He kissed the back of her wrist. "Yes. Er—no." He looked up at her, teasing, tantalizing. "What was the question?"

The strain of the past minutes had taken their toll. Her temples were throbbing. "You aren't paying attention."

"No, I am not."

She drew away her hand before he could kiss it again. She was feeling very tired and very hurt and wanted nothing more than to take to her bed, alone.

She must have looked how she felt, for Worth said with some concern, "You are tired. It is time to retire." With a smile in his voice, he said, "I cannot say that I am sorry about it. I shall accompany you upstairs."

Chapter Thirteen

"That won't be necessary," she said.

"Not a necessity. A courtesy, merely," he agreed softly. "Come. You have no woman, as of yet. I shall help you."

She did not move away from the door. "I am used to managing alone. Pray, do not trouble yourself."

"It is no trouble. A pleasure, rather." He pulled her by the elbows away from the doorframe.

She was standing so that her forehead nearly touched his nose. She felt his lips near her temple. It began to throb harder. She did not move. Her eyes were fixed on the pulse in his throat. The wide set of his shoulders blocked out the rest of the world. In a wooden voice, she repeated, "I am used to managing alone. I prefer it."

Nerves, he thought again. He was willing to make allowances. He stepped away from her to grab a single candle from the sconce, and snuffed the others before leaving the room. Caroline quickly moved out into the vestibule. "Very well," he said, following her, "I will give you time alone. But then I shall come in to bid you good-night."

Caroline stayed a pace ahead of him, finding the blackness less fearsome than his touch. "That will not be necessary, sir," she managed.

This was taking skittishness to the extreme. He took command of the territory. "It is most necessary, ma'am," he said pleasantly, even politely, but in a tone that left no room for argument.

They exchanged no further words on that subject and confined themselves to the usual things two people walking through a darkened house would say to each other regarding the negotiation of the hallways and staircase.

At the door to her bedchamber, he asked, "Will a quarter hour suffice before I come to you?"

"Oh, but I don't think—" she began.

"I can easily make it ten minutes," he said. "Or even five."

"Fifteen, yes. Fifteen," she managed.

He left her with a correct bow and the promise to see her presently.

"Dear me," she breathed, entering her bedchamber. She closed the door and sank against it, closing her eyes. Lively ponies galloped away in her temples. The little fox gnawed at her stomach. She opened her eyes and stared a moment at her bed, a large, delicately wrought mahogany piece, with yellow silk curtains. A branch of candles glowed with a mellow light on the bedstead table. An inviting fire mulled on the hearth.

She closed her eyes again and, with an effort, tamed the wild animals roaming through her body. Contradictory images warred in her brain: the memory of Worth's kiss and their unexpected passion; the thought of the terms in which the duke and Worth must have discussed her as a possible marriage prospect; the pleasant, provocative intimacy of the wedding meal before they were interrupted; the excruciating hours she had spent at balls as a young woman waiting for a gentleman to ask her to dance; the sharp pain she had felt upon hearing the duke's words: "After all, it was I who recommended Miss Hutton to you as a woman who met all of your specifications."

The wild beasts strained at their leashes.

She pushed herself away from the door. Her hands shook as she unpinned her coiffure and unlaced the back of her dress. Her favorite peach and cream creation fell to the floor, and she was so distracted that she left it in little more than a silk heap where she had stepped out of it. Her clothing had been packed the day before and brought to St.

James's Square. The trunks had been shoved in a corner of her bedchamber, and she went to them now, opening the one where she had put her nightclothes.

She knew that she did not have much time to compose herself. She attempted to reassure herself that she could put her husband off. She was unattractive. Ugly. But as she tied the ribbon of her nightdress at her breasts and smoothed the mauve satin over her hips, she did not think that the bump in her nose, her too-wide mouth or her unfashionable coloring would stop him. She knew what men saw in her. She knew what he wanted. It had happened to her before. The ponies pawed their hooves. The little fox bared his teeth.

She had had several days to contemplate her wedding night. She knew what was expected of her, and she had had no fears about meeting those expectations. No qualms. Not even any twinges of apprehension. Why, she might have almost been eager—

No. Not *eager.* Calm, maybe. Confident, rather. Confident that she would be well treated.

That confidence had come to her the evening before, after the strange passage in the cemetery with William Langley. In that conversation, she and Worth had come to some kind of understanding, she would have said. It was as if they had converted their initial wariness into a respectful friendliness, without having spelled it out in so many words.

When he had subsequently helped her down from the carriage at Portugal Row, where she was to spend her last night as Miss Hutton, he had taken her hands in a warm, reassuring way. He had asked, "Do you have a woman friend whom you can talk to about tomorrow?"

She had smiled up at him, grateful for the delicacy of his consideration. She nodded. "I do, but I don't think any little talk will be necessary."

"It's just that sometimes," he explained himself, "on a woman's wedding night—"

"I'm not eighteen," she reminded him, "and . . . and I'm not uninformed."

"Not worried either?"

She shook her head. "Not worried."

"I'm glad."

He pressed her hands with his fingers. He bent and brushed her hand with his lips. Once she was safe inside, he had climbed back in the carriage.

Perhaps she *had* been a little eager.

Now everything was different. The circumstances were different. *He* was different. She *knew*. She knew now what she had not known yesterday. He did not truly want her. He was going through the motions. She was ugly, and she had put him off. He did not want to come to her anyway. He would not bother her.

Worth tapped once at the communicating door between their chambers and entered. Caroline had not quite shrugged into the light violet dressing gown that covered the mauve sheath beneath. Her nightdress was pretty but practical and not that of a temptress. Yet with the gown falling about her white shoulders, she had the look of a ripe, half-peeled plum or an exotic flower aching to be plucked.

Worth responded to the sight. Seeing the blaze in his eye, she moved into the center of the room, a strategic defensive gesture, so that she would not be caught in the corner.

Worth advanced. He had undressed. He was wearing a dark blue silk dressing gown with robin's-egg-blue revers. His hair was unbound but still brushed back behind his ears. He was holding out a hand toward her. He was smiling. He said something to her. She did not register it. He came within a step of her.

She stepped back immediately. She saw a little frown come between his eyes, eyes as dark blue as his gown, eyes kind and concerned. He said something. It might have been: "Don't be afraid. I won't hurt you." She was not sure.

Without putting his hands on her, he bent and kissed her. It was a lovely kiss, soft, tentative, preliminary, promising. She wanted more. No. She wanted no more. She wanted to escape.

He lifted his head, withdrawing so that he might see her better. His expression was intent, determined, desirous. When he stretched out his left hand, reaching to cup her neck at the place it curved into her shoulder, her senses began to swim. She felt faint. She was not quite sure whether she was in her bedchamber on St. James's Square or in the stables of Hutton Manor. She was not quite sure whether the man before her was her husband or the braw, well-to-do Sussex farmer who had courted her over the course of the past year.

The farmer had been handsome enough, she had thought, and he had liked her well enough. She had permitted him to kiss her, though not in the way Worth had kissed her, for she was curious, too. They had kissed more than once, and that had been a mistake. He became bolder and had tried to touch her breast. He wanted her. He wanted her enough to marry her. When she refused, he came one afternoon to take what he wanted. In the deserted Hutton Manor stables, he had ripped her bodice and lifted her skirts. He had called her a comely wench. A real beauty. Beautiful body. Beautiful breasts. Beautiful thighs. He had invited her to open her basket and share a meal for two in the hay.

Only a farmer would want such an ugly wife. He had not even respected her. It had been lust, just lust.

"Caroline, my dear," Worth said the next second, placing his hand at the very spot he wanted. He bent to kiss her there, a fragrant spot. "Such a lovely neck."

She closed her eyes before he touched her and caught a glimpse of the gold glint of the wedding band on his finger. She was not lovely. The circumstances were humiliating. She opened her eyes to see his head bent to her neck. Who was this man? Wedding band. Husband. She felt the warm pressure of his lips at her throat. It was a pleasurable, tingling. Dark hair, sun-streaked. A man who lived outdoors. The kiss was insistent. She knew what he wanted. It had happened to her before.

The contradictory images fused in her brain and the feelings became increasingly dissonant. It was the farmer who had come to rape her. No. It was a man who had brutally forced himself on his stepmother. A different man, but still a rapist. She was in her bedroom. She stumbled back a pace, knocked against the footstool at the edge of her bed. No. She was in the stables. She had nearly tripped over the milking stool as the farmer had ripped her bodice and lifted her skirts.

Worth was a little drunk on her scent. Just before taking her fully in his arms in order to blend his lips with hers, he said, "You are very beautiful, Caroline."

That was it. At those words, the wild animals broke their leashes and had their way. She was ugly. Undesirable. But not defenseless. And not without her dignity. In a flash, she bent to grasp the footstool. In the stables, she had cracked the farmer smartly across his head with the milking stool, sending him flying backward to land in the slops.

However, the man kissing her now was no cloddish farmer. He was a battle-trained officer who could defend himself against any assault, even one that came with no warning and no seeming cause. Hardly had Caroline lifted the stool, than Worth guessed her intention to use it against him. Caroline was quick, but Worth was quicker still. Before she had raised the stool above her head, he had knocked it out of her hand, grasped both her wrists and sent her sprawling backward across the bed, with him stretched out on top of her. The moment they landed, he pinned her between his knees. It had been ridiculously easy for him, and it was over in the space of a heartbeat.

Swift effort and surprise quickened their breath. Caroline was lying beneath him, breathing hard, her hands held back against the bed above her head, her eyes wide. Worth was above her, looking down into those wide hazel eyes, struggling to understand what was going on. *No gentle seduction, this night!* he thought, with labored breath.

The evening long, he had enjoyed the soft, slow flames of good food, champagne, flirtatious conversation, a blushing bride, knowledge of pleasure to come. This hand-to-hand combat had fanned those flames and aroused his quick desire. His blood was racing with anticipation. He could enjoy it this way, too. Rough and ragged. He could shift his body and have what he wanted. In a second. Then he could have it later, too, in a smoother, silkier manner, more befitting a wedding night. He had been without for a long time. He would take it whatever way he could get it.

But he did not understand the assault. Nor did he understand the look in her eye. It was certainly not passion or desire that he saw there. Neither was it fear. He knew what fear looked like in a man's eyes. It was mostly dull and blunt, only glazed with excitement. The look in Caroline's eyes was sharp. It stabbed. It looked less like fear and more like pain. He was puzzled.

Caroline had had the wind knocked out of her, but her senses had returned. She spoke first, but did not attempt to explain her extraordinary actions. She said the first thing that came into her mind. "I—didn't kill—Gilbert Kenmure."

Worth's puzzlement was not lessened by this admission. Nevertheless, he replied simply, "I know you did not."

"How can you—be sure?" she said. She fought for breath. "I was not with you—in the alcove—of the London Tavern—as we are both—claiming."

Worth gulped and caught his breath. "If I had had any lingering doubts, they were dispelled by the dress you wore today."

"My dress?" she managed.

With Caroline stretched out beneath him, he had to struggle to restrain himself. He knew something of his own strength and relaxed his hold on her wrists, but did not release her. Otherwise, he did not move. He took another deep breath. "Is it not the one you wore at the assembly?"

She nodded, dumbfounded.

"There's no blood on it," he explained. "I had ample opportunity to inspect it throughout the day. There is no blood on it. Nor are there any marks to suggest that any stains have been cleaned."

Her wits were still moving slowly. "I don't understand."

"The slash in the neck that killed Kenmure could not have failed to spurt blood on whoever held the knife."

"Are you so sure?"

He knew precisely how the blood left a man's throat after it was slashed. He nodded. Experimentally, he released her wrists. He directed at her a look of inquiry. When she did not lunge at him, he placed his hands on either side of her. In another moment, he would lower himself and try for a more loverlike embrace. It was not a bad position to be in, and it had certainly aroused him.

His breathing had steadied from the momentary struggle. "In any case, I did not think you capable of such a gash."

"I did not see—who did it, either. I truly know—nothing," she said. She struggled to regain normal breathing, but her whirling emotions prevented it. They whipped her, like a flag in a windstorm, between fresh pain and embarrassed surprise and old hurt and continuing humiliation and unacknowledged desire for the man who held her.

Worth was having trouble, too. The topic of murder was not the usual bedtime talk—not in his experience, anyway. It had its stimulating effect: this confession, the talk of blood and gaping flesh. Yet he knew himself to be thinking with the wrong part of his body, and before he lost control completely, he wanted to turn the talk to bring less pain and more pleasure into her eyes.

"But, my dear—Caroline. Good God! Why do you bring this up?" he asked at last, thoroughly baffled.

He saw the pain in her eyes become pronounced. "The other day," she said, suddenly fighting back tears, "you wanted to know why I was the first one in the alleyway. You said you wanted no more scandal attached to your name. I understand your concern—your suspicion! You said that if I should ever think of another reason why I was there, I was to tell you. I merely sensed something was wrong. I went outside. I saw the body lying there. That's the truth."

Worth believed her, but he hardly needed this confession to know that she was telling the truth. After the surge of emotion they had both just experienced, he realized that the confession must have been important to her, that it weighed heavily on her. Although why it should be so important *now*—

The answer came to him. He remembered the rustle of skirts outside the door of the parlor when Desford had come for his cane. She had overheard their conversation, at least the part when Desford had asked about Caroline's presence in the alleyway. Worth did not immediately remember the specifics of what else they had said, but the general outline came to him as an explanation for all Caroline's actions since Desford's visit.

He exhaled, extended his arms so that his body was not touching hers, bowed his head and looked away. He looked back at her, and what he read in her face confirmed his suspicions. He eased himself up from his advantageous position.

Could one make love to a woman who felt she had just been profoundly insulted? One part of his body responded: Of course! His head warned him sanctimoniously: win the battle but lose the war! He could have her now, but at what cost? Caroline was his wife. He had no experience with wives. Nevertheless, it was his wedding night, and he knew what was due him. He looked back into Caroline's eyes, deep, wide, hurt pools of hazel. She had choked back her tears. She was not going to cry. A brave soldier.

He could woo her with sweet words. That sometimes worked. "Caroline, my dear," he said. He bent his lips again to her neck. "This is hardly the moment to explain. But I think I can. Nor is it the moment to assure me of your innocence. You have drugged me, you see, with your beau—"

Caroline turned her head sharply away. Her mouth was muffled in the counterpane. Her words came indistinctly, but her meaning was clear enough. "When you proposed to me," she said, "you said that the scandal of Mr. Kenmure's murder had provided you an opportunity to reestablish yourself in London."

"Did I?" His miscalculation shocked him.

"You did. And to reestablish yourself, you needed a wife—a woman of little wealth and few attractions." He was about to protest that description when she added, "You had your choice of Julia Stanhope and Angelica Gordon, and you chose me."

Worth was at an impasse. If she could not tell by the state of his body how much he wished to touch and taste her passion, he did not see how words and explanations would serve him. He looked away again and cursed. It was a mild invec tive, considering. After a severe struggle with himself an with utmost reluctance, he stood and secured the tie of hi dressing gown. He thrust a hand through his unruly hair. H saw, with great clarity and equally great disappointment how the rest of the night would unfold.

Caroline propped herself on her elbows. She was stunned but aware the storm had passed. She opened her mouth t apologize, but closed it again, deciding defiantly that sh had nothing to apologize for. Instead, she said, "Do yo understand?"

He glanced at her, a curious, attractive mixture of emo tions chasing across his face. Understanding was there. Rue too, as well as a certain kind of battle-hardened calculatio of how best to retreat in the face of defeat. A glint of desir remained in his eyes when he cast them over her, saying "Yes."

She struggled to rise. Her hair was gloriously tangled. He nightdress was invitingly askew. He did not help her up "Well, then," she said. Deep chagrin over this episod would settle in her much later during the sleepless watche of the night. At the moment, she was in control of herself She managed to say precisely the right thing. "You came t wish me good-night, I think, sir.'

Many, many things occurred to Worth to say. He con fined himself to "That is correct, ma'am. I wish you good night." And he withdrew from his wife's chamber, closin the communicating door with a soft click behind him.

Chapter Fourteen

Worth's night was as sleepless as Caroline's. However, he
spent no time, as did Caroline, writhing in a vise of chagrin. He was surely sorry that she had overheard the conversation between himself and Desford, but he did not
agonize over it. To his way of thinking, what was said was
said, and could not be unsaid. He never wasted time in idle
speculation on "if onlys." He was angry, too, but not at
himself. For the second time in recent days, Desford served
as his convenient target. Worth was sympathetic to the distress that Desford must be feeling, but to have interrupted
him on his wedding night and to have bothered him with
pointless questions was an action unworthy of even the
rawest recruit. On his wedding night! Now here, Worth's
thoughts took a sharp turn, and—although not given to
pointless musings on "if onlys"—he wasted a deal of time
dwelling on his frustrated desires.

When he could tear his mind away from Caroline, her bed
and the feelings inside him when she was stretched out beneath him, vulnerable, hurt and very desirable, he attempted to concentrate on strategy. Yes, strategy. A strategic
campaign, that was what he needed. Strategy was chosen
according to the goal. The better defined the goal, the better the chances of victory. He had the goal of this particular campaign in sharp focus. It lay just beyond the
communicating door.

He still needed a strategy, a strategy that acknowledged
the facts that his wife had heard the conversation between

himself and Desford and that it had not been flattering to her.

Marlborough's first aim of war floated through his mind: *Pursue one great decisive aim with force and determination.* He had already formulated such a decisive aim: to reinstate himself in society. His marriage was to have gained him ground, like the capture of the next most important city that lay just outside the capital, defending it. Caroline Hutton. Caroline Worth. A city to storm and conquer. Perhaps it would help him to refigure her in his mind, not as the *next* most important city, but as the capital itself. The seat of power. The citadel. The inner city. The inner sanctum. To which he wanted access.

The image seemed all too appropriate. He began to sweat lightly.

He tossed restlessly in his bed and cast his mind back to strategy. It was definitely an offensive he needed to devise. Offensive. He grunted. No doubt to Caroline. All right, then. Offensive. *The strategic offensive pursues the aim of war directly,* Marlborough had taught him, *aiming straight at the destruction of the enemy's forces.* Enemy? To describe his wife, the term should surely be "partner," no? He weighed the two words, enemy and partner, and chose "enemy." It operated as a better stimulant to his thinking. Enemy, then.

Two principles, and two principles only, were needed for offensive warfare: *The first is constant replacement of troops and arms.* He had troops and arms in abundance for this campaign. And two: *Even under the most favorable circumstances and with greatest moral and physical superiority the aggressor should foresee a possibility of great disaster.*

Worth reassured himself that any future disaster could be no greater than this evening's. He considered this. No, in fact, this evening's could have been *far* worse. He pillowed his head in his hands. A good sign.

Maybe.

Back to strategy. Heading: Principles Governing the Use of Troops. *Cavalry must not be used before the enemy has suffered considerably from our infantry and artillery.* From this it follows: *We must place the cavalry behind the infantry.* Place the cavalry behind the infantry? Not a useful thought. Scratch cavalry. Move to artillery. *Artillery fire is much more effective than that of infantry.* Artillery. Artillery fire. Yes. Good analogy. *We should begin combat with the larger part of our artillery.*

Worth had to pause in his musing. He groaned. Then his body shook with silent, unamused laughter. His big cannon had not been fired off, and he was feeling a good deal of physical discomfort because of it. He paused an extra moment—thinking about his thinking about strategy while lying in bed—and hoped that Caroline was not lying in her bed, awake, and mentally *decorating rooms,* of all things, for God's sake! (This fleeting thought seemed to indicate that he had not lost his sense of humor, completely.)

And so it went, on into the night. Once he got past the grossest, most obvious aspects of his offensive strategy, he began to refine more subtly on his amorous campaign and on the citadel in question who was Caroline Worth. Just before gray dawn came to pearl the mists that smothered the London sky, he came up with a plan—an extremely simple plan, the second oldest in the book—and fell asleep.

It must be said that neither Worth nor Caroline was in a good mood later that morning, but for different reasons. Worth was grumpy, but watchful and ready to implement his plan. Caroline was acutely embarrassed.

She rose well before Worth. She breakfasted early and alone, then prowled the house, hoping to work off some of her embarrassment, dreadfully avoiding her next encounter with her husband. Finally, she could avoid it no longer. She knew what she had to do this day and that was compose the guest list and write out the invitations for the musical evening she had planned for the next week.

Since there was currently only one table in the house and that was the dining table, Caroline was compelled to go to the dining room with pen and inkwell, paper, sand and blotter. The room was still empty, but she did not think it would remain so for long. She sat down at the foot of the table where she had eaten this morning, not to the right of the head of the table where she had sat last night. She began to write.

Not much later Worth arrived. She looked up from her work and murmured a greeting. He did not return it. Her heart quailed. Although his clothes were neat, he looked like the devil. Nevertheless, he bowed, and then even smiled at her. He took his place, rang the silver bell, growled for some coffee and was quickly gratified.

Caroline continued writing in silence. By the time Worth had finished his ham and eggs, she had finished her work. He had pushed back his chair, was folding the *Morning Herald* this way and that, and was sipping coffee in a rather leisurely fashion. Caroline gathered her courage and rose from her chair.

She cleared her throat. "Pardon my intrusion, sir," she said clearly, bringing Worth's head up and his gaze on her, "but I wish to consult you about several matters." She began to walk the length of the table toward him. No few feet of space had ever seemed so long.

Worth kept his eye on her the whole time. For all his aura of early-morning, ill-rested grogginess, his regard was uncomfortably perceptive. Under the heading: Know the Strengths and Weaknesses of the Enemy, Worth had spent part of the night cataloging his wife's qualities. (Spiritual qualities, that was, for he already knew her physical attributes.) He had composed a preliminary list: a good ear, good taste, honesty and a sense of the social limits. He had noted other characteristics: both shy and forthright, seems to be wounded easily. However, he was not sure whether these last characteristics were qualities or faults, and he was a long way from understanding the entire episode in her bedchamber and the source of her strength.

Now, he was extremely interested by the fact that she had taken the initiative this morning, and he was admiring her composure. As she walked toward him, he lengthened his list to include courage and dignity.

With a half smile playing about his lips, he said, politely enough, "Yes, my dear. How may I help you?"

Caroline's step did not falter, and she was glad. She stood before him and handed a short list of names to him. "I wish for your approval of the guest list for the musical evening I spoke to you about," she said. "Last evening. You remember. You did not think it was such a good idea. But I persuaded you otherwise. And then—" she broke off.

He had settled comfortably in his chair and was smiling up at her blandly. He said with a remarkable matter-of-factness, "And then you attempted to crack me over the head with a stool." He took the paper from her nerveless fingers and perused the list of ten names. "If you had hit your mark, I might well have forgotten all that came before, but, fortunately, I still have all my wits." He glanced up at her and saw her struggle with her composure.

All heart, he thought, *and no wisdom.* She was entirely too courageous for her own good, and he reckoned that the effort to maintain her dignity was costing her more than the encounter was worth. If she had been a soldier under his command, he would have schooled her in discretion. He would have told her that she should have saved her forces, that the first move should have been his.

After all, he wanted her far more than she, evidently, wanted him, and she could have easily repulsed any friendly advance from him. However, she was not under his command, she had not saved her forces, and she had met him head-on. He found her courage and her lack of wisdom endearing. He was less pleased by her dignity—though admiring it—for he thought it might prove a formidable defense against him.

She accepted the paper from him. "Yes. Well," she said, a little nervously, then with more conviction, "it *is* fortunate that your wits have been preserved, for you can advise me on the propriety of inviting the FitzHughs." She pointed to the fifth name on the list. "I am not sure they will accept."

"Then do not invite them," Worth suggested helpfully.

The corners of Caroline's mouth turned down. "Oh, but I think they will be *curious,* you know, and possibly even offended if I do not invite them."

"Then by all means, invite them," Worth said agreeably.

Caroline paused, then slipped the list into the pocket of her day dress. "You're no help at all," she said. "I shall make the decision on my own."

Worth was surprised. He made a mental note that his strategy might need adjustment. It was his general plan to make himself altogether agreeable to Caroline and win access to her chambers not through force, but through seduction. He thought he had been being agreeably helpful just now, but apparently all women did not find agreeableness, well, *agreeable*.

"But I do need your approval of my decorating plans for the parlor," she continued.

"Ah, yes. You have chosen the Oriental motif, I believe."

"Yes, that is the one I have settled on."

To her tone of faint surprise, he looked up at her again and saw her color with pleasure. *That* was more like it! With a wicked look in his eye, he said, "And you thought I wasn't paying attention to you last night."

"I did not say that exactly," she protested.

"You said that exactly," he countered. "You see, I was rather more interested in kissing your hand just then, but I *was* listening."

Caroline saw that he was trying, very deliberately, to disconcert her. He was good at it. She clung to her dignity. "I plan to start contacting furniture makers immediately. Do I have your permission to send round some notes to tradesmen so that I may consult them here?"

Worth graciously granted her permission and said he would take care of sending the notes by linkboy.

Caroline steeled herself to continue. "And for the better part of the day," she said, "I shall be interviewing servants. I set up the appointments last week. The first applicants are due to arrive any minute, and I believe I shall need the dining room, since that is the only room with chairs. However, since you have descended late, I do not mean to disturb you and can easily have several chairs placed in the parlor."

Worth pretended to consider this. "I had imagined that you would sing for me this morning," he said with charming disappointment. "However, I suppose you have your work to do. And so do I. Yes," he said, rising, "I am finished and see no need for you to use the parlor."

"Thank you," Caroline said, a little surprised to find her wishes so easily granted and the interview so cordial.

"You are most welcome," he replied, taking her hand and bowing over it but not touching it with his lips. "Do not hesitate to call me if you need me to do anything else for you today." He crossed the room to leave it. At the door he turned and said, "Perhaps you will sing for me this evening."

Caroline was feeling somewhat dazed. "This evening? I don't think so. That is, we are engaged to go out. Did I not tell you? At Mr. Kenmure's lying-in-state, Mrs. Shuttleworth told Lady Purcell of our wedding plans, and it seems that Lady Purcell was sorry not to have been invited. So at Desford House she invited us to her home for this evening. Of course, it was her musicale the other day that was spoiled by Mr. Kenmure's murder. Oh, that's right! You were there, so you know!" Caroline stopped. "Was Lady Purcell a particular friend of yours... in the old days?"

Worth shook his head. "Not in my set, but she was polite enough to me the other evening at her home." He smiled. "Interesting invitation. No doubt due to the fact that Desford witnessed our wedding. I'm glad to think his influence is already having a beneficial effect."

Caroline was glad of the length of room between them, and she attempted to hide her wince at mention of the duke.

Worth realized his mistake and smoothly recovered. With another bow, he said, "You see how helpful the duke has been to us. To me." Before she could respond to that, he asked, "At what time are we to be there?"

"About five o'clock."

"Then let us leave at four-thirty, say."

"Four-thirty," she agreed.

"Until then, my dear," Worth said, bowing a third time.

For the rest of the day, throughout the long, often tedious, but productive interviews, Caroline felt light-headed, mostly with relief. Her husband had chosen to treat the miserable scene in her bedchamber lightheartedly. (He could have forced her, too, the night before. He had had every right. The thought embarrassed Caroline and made her realize, in retrospect, how little her husband had in common with the Sussex farmer.) The little fox in her stomach was lulled and went back to sleep. At four-thirty, she had changed and was looking forward to the evening's entertainment.

Worth had brought around his open perch carriage for two. The sky was still overcast, but it was not raining, and he wanted the pleasure of driving them through London alone. Caroline donned bonnet and gloves and a heavy cloak, and Worth had provided a rug for their legs.

They set off, with Worth announcing that he knew a shortcut from St. James's Square to Marylebone that would avoid the clot of traffic on Oxford Street.

They started off at a spanking pace, and the chill fanning their cheeks felt initially good. They conversed on desultory topics for quite a while. The short November day had darkened, and soon it became apparent that they had spent more than the usual half hour to get to where they wanted to go. When they had passed one row of houses twice, Caroline turned to Worth and stated the obvious. "We are lost, you know."

"No, we are not."

"Yes, we are. We've passed this row of houses twice now, and—wait! Don't turn here! We have already been down this street, as well. Ten minutes ago already, but we were traveling the other way. Don't you recognize it?"

Worth shook his head. "Not at all. This is an entirely new street."

"But I remember that red door. There. Yes, and there was a green one next to it. We have been on this street before, I tell you! We are traveling in circles."

"We are not. I was born and bred in London, do not forget."

"So was I," Caroline replied, "and it is precisely my very good sense of London streets that tells me that we are lost!"

Worth favored her with a rather superior look. "You have been gone these past three years and have forgotten."

"*You* have been gone these past thirteen!"

"Ah, but I was older than you when I left."

"You were not."

"How old are you, ma'am?" he asked with a satisfied smile.

"I am three-and-twenty, sir. How old are you?"

"Three-and-thirty," he said, his smile fading.

Caroline bit her lip and sternly resisted temptation. "I *won't* say it!" she managed with great restraint.

Worth was losing this one. "We might have been the same ages when we left," he said, "but I got around much more before I left than you did."

"This is an absurd conversation, sir! We are completely turned around now! No, don't go here! This is a dead end. I am sure of it! Where are we? Brekeley Street and Portman Square? The coordinates are certainly north and west, but how to get back to Marylebone Lane, I do not know!" Caroline was exasperated, and the chill on her cheeks was slowly seeping into her bones. "We are lost, and we should ask directions."

"We do not need to ask directions," Worth snapped back. "I know my way perfectly."

"Oh, yes! The shortcut!" she retorted, her voice heavy with sarcasm. "Now, stop, do! Look! There is a man of whom we can ask directions."

Worth was rapidly abandoning his strategy of being always agreeable to his wife. "It is pointless to stop and ask a complete stranger," he retorted testily. "How do you know he knows the neighborhood? Why, he might not be from London at all. He might not even be English!"

"I have no idea as to his nationality. Nor do I care," Caroline said, becoming rather testy herself, "but from the fact that he has just taken a key out of his pocket and is inserting it into the lock of that door, I would say that he is most certainly from the neighborhood and can at least direct us out of it!''

When Worth drove right by the man at a rather rapid clip, Caroline huffed and was about to deliver herself of her most immediate feelings when she broke into laughter.

"And what, may I ask, amuses you, ma'am?" Worth demanded.

"You are just like my father!"

"I fail to see how... *traveling* through London can be compared to the habit of gambling!"

"Oh, not gambling," she said dismissively, still chuckling, "but *he* wouldn't stop and ask directions either, if his life depended upon it!"

"And I suppose that you, ma'am, ask directions the first moment you think yourself lost?" he demanded.

"Not the first moment, perhaps, but often the second, and certainly the third. And sometimes I ask directions *before* I get lost!" she said cheerfully. "Now, my father—! Well, we were sometimes—not often, mind you—hopelessly lost, and the last thing he would do was to stop and ask directions." She shook her head, still amused. "Why not the *last* thing at all, for he wouldn't do it, not even last! We would wander until we found our way!" She looked at Worth. "It is the most curious coincidence!"

"I fail to see the connection. We are *not* lost, and—"

Caroline paid him no heed. She mused, "Is it just you and my father, I wonder? Or all men?" She looked at him with polite interest. "Can you enlighten me, sir?"

Under the heading of Know the Strengths and Weaknesses of the Enemy, the list of Caroline's faults was growing longer in Worth's mind. He added three new ones: typical female wrongheadedness, self-righteousness, inelegant sense of humor.

She chirped on. "And it seems that this inability to ask directions is allied to the male aversion to discovering a tradesman's hours before setting off for the shop. It is always five o'clock when a gentleman desires something most desperately and sets off, not knowing whether the tradesman in question closes at five or five-thirty or six!"

Worth ticked off number four: an unbecoming tendency to rub things in. He fumed silently.

"I think it is a male trait," she pronounced. She nodded her head once, decisively. "Definitely a male trait. I am quite sure of it."

Worth made a stab at defending the Men of the World. "And you know of no woman who ever sets off at the end of the day without knowing whether the shop she is headed for is open or closed?"

"In my case, sir," she said, smiling at him, "I keep a list of the shop times of all the tradesmen I frequent."

Number five: overly organized. "What an excellent idea, ma'am," he said, with no hint that he thought it so.

"It works well for me," she informed him with unimpaired affability. "And look, we have hit upon Marylebone Lane, quite by accident. Now, if you are careful to turn *left* here, sir—to head north, you know—"

"I *know* to turn north here, ma'am!" Worth said through clenched teeth.

Not too many minutes later, they were coming to a halt at the Palladian facade of Purcell House. Worth jumped down and came round the carriage to help Caroline down from the perch.

"Well, we made it," she said pleasantly. "The shortcut did not increase our time above forty-five minutes, I would say!" She accepted his hand and hopped down.

Worth had regained his temper. In a voice that nicely blended silk and steel, he said, "So far today, my dear wife, I have treated you with a geniality that you do not exactly deserve, considering the outcome of our wedding night. If you continue in this most...provocative manner, I cannot be held accountable for my actions later on tonight."

Not daring to push her luck further, Caroline hurried on up the steps to the front door, giving him a nice view of an angry swish of her hips.

He followed Caroline, considering her backside with much appreciation. He bethought himself of an attribute of hers to count in her favor.

No, that one already *was* on his list.

So, put it on twice.

Worth's thoughts were given an entirely new direction when the front door was opened, giving him a view of the entry hall. There at the foot of the grand staircase, he saw Lady Purcell in conversation with Chief Constable Locke.

Chapter Fifteen

Worth and Caroline shed their cloaks, relinquished them to the waiting footman and greeted Lady Purcell. She expressed her heartfelt congratulations on their marriage and thanked them for coming to her house for the evening's entertainment.

"Entirely modest entertainment, of course," Lady Purcell warned them, "as it must be, but so much more *pleasant* than the reception—I hesitate to call it a true mourning party—we held last week! How delighted his lordship and I are to be celebrating a happy occasion tonight. What an inspired idea it was of yours, Colonel Worth—for I understand it was your impatience, no?—to think of getting married at such an otherwise unseasonable time!"

That was as much acceptance as Worth could have expected or even desired at this early date, and he thanked Lady Purcell accordingly for her sentiment. She then brought Chief Constable Locke to their notice. The chief constable greeted Caroline now as Mrs. Worth and saluted his former army superior.

"You have come to join us this evening?" Worth asked.

Locke shook his head. "I'm on the point of departure," he replied. "It's a useless errand I've come on, it seems, and I am sorry to have troubled you, Lady Purcell."

Lady Purcell insisted that she was always willing to be of help, especially when it came to apprehending the criminals who were overtaking the City. After saying goodbye to the officer of the law, she drew Caroline's arm through hers, and the two women began to ascend the staircase.

Just as Locke was turning to go, Worth said, "A development in the case, then?"

Locke paused and turned back toward Worth. "Oh, no, nothing so fine as a development," he answered. "I've come in search of his grace. Have you perhaps seen him today, Colonel?"

Worth said that he had not seen Desford since the night before.

"I was told at Desford House that he was either at his club or here," Locke said, "but I have been unable to locate him. Lady Purcell told me that her guests have been here this past half hour at least, except for the duke and you and Mrs. Worth, which made me think," he continued in the casual manner that was so effective at retrieving information, "that perhaps the three of you were together."

"The lateness in our case," Worth said with a glance up the circular staircase at Caroline, who was just disappearing through a door, "was due to what my wife would describe as 'being lost.'"

Locke's eyes twinkled responsively. "Which you were not."

"Assuredly not, but it does not do to contradict a wife so early in a marriage."

Locke laughed. "Most unstrategic," he murmured.

"My thoughts exactly," Worth concurred. "Married?"

"No, sir."

"Wise man."

"So I've been told." Locke had had a moment to think through the possibilities that this encounter presented. They were alone in the entry hall, save for the shadow of a footman hovering disinterestedly by the front door. Locke came to a swift, risky decision. He said, still with that effective, casual tone, "But it's well met we are this evening, and seeing you now might save me some steps on the morrow." He withdrew a cloth from his inside coat pocket and unfolded it to expose a glint of steel. "Have you ever seen this, by chance?"

Worth looked at the object in question and with a leap of intuition said, "You retrieved that the other day from Jonathan Wild, did you not?"

Locke hesitated before he smiled and said, "Yes, I did."

"Wild said that he had come across a knife, possibly belonging to Kenmure or his murderer. But that's no knife, it's a dagger," Worth said, "and as for having seen it before, why, I must have seen hundreds just like it. It's common enough."

"Not in England," the chief constable pointed out.

"No, but on the Continent. I hardly have to tell you that," Worth said easily. The dagger was long and thin with a carved blade that had no cutting edge. "From the ornamentation I would say it's Italian. A stiletto. Every other soldier and his brother had ones similar." Worth peered at it. "Perhaps not as finely carved, though." He looked up at Locke with an ironic eye. "And you say there are no developments?"

"Who's to say if this dagger had anything to do with the murder? I have only Mr. Wild's supposition."

"True enough," Worth agreed.

"And I am not entirely sure whether this dagger could have produced the slash in Kenmure's neck. What's your professional opinion, Colonel Worth?"

Worth evoked the sight of Kenmure's wound and dispassionately considered it. He glanced down at the dagger, then back at Locke. "It could have, yes. In the hands of someone with experience. When it came into your possession, was there any blood on it?"

"No," Locke answered, "but there was ample occasion for it to have been washed before I—or even Wild—ever got hold of it." He asked again, "So you've never seen this one, then, in England?"

Worth shook his head. "It's a stabbing weapon, and we've many an English-made dagger for that. This one has more the look of a novelty item—bought in a curiosity shop to be used for slitting envelopes."

At the moment he said the words, the image sprang into his mind. Or perhaps it was that latent image—in the Duke

of Desford's library—that caused Worth to think of the
stiletto as an item on a gentleman's library table. Worth had
seen that very dagger—he was nearly sure of it. Seated at his
table, Desford had been toying with it, palming it and
twirling it, when Worth had come to him and asked him for
a list of names of marriageable young women.

"Yes, Colonel?" Locke prompted, seeing the flash of
recognition on Worth's face.

Worth lifted his eyes and looked straight into Locke's.
There was no point dissimulating. Indeed, Worth had no
cause to say anything other than, "I have seen one like it."

"Where?"

"In the Duke of Desford's library. On his table."

"How recently was that, Colonel?"

"On the morning of Kenmure's murder."

Locke folded the cloth over the stiletto and slipped it back
into his coat pocket. "I was wanting to track his grace down,
you see, to ask him whether the item might have belonged
to his cousin. I thought it a long shot—since Mr. Kenmure
would hardly have been likely to carry such a thing on his
person." Locke smiled enigmatically. "Now I can ask his
grace whether his own stiletto is missing."

Worth nodded. "Desford's might still be in his library,
and as you say, Kenmure would not have been carrying such
an item on his person. Since the Peace of Utrecht, regi-
ments of soldiers have been returning from the Continent,
and dozens of similar daggers might be circulating
throughout the City. It is far more likely that this one belongs to a nameless soldier—quite unconnected to the murder."

"Far more likely," Locke agreed affably. "I am sure the
matter will be instantly cleared up once I meet with his
grace. I must thank you for your help."

"You are very welcome," Worth replied, then recalling a
detail, "but since you came across this item Saturday
morning, just before Kenmure's funeral, could you not have
cleared it up that afternoon with Desford? Or was it your
delicacy of manner, given the situation, that stopped you?"

"Delicacy of manner?" Locke echoed, seeming amused. "Caution, rather. It's a cautious man I am, Colonel Worth. And neither of us knows yet where the dangers lie in this case. I thank you again for your help."

Worth replied just as he ought, and the two men parted, both with brains seething with conjecture. Worth turned to climb the stairs and was crossed by Martha Sheridan, who was floating down those same stairs.

Just as Locke was turning to go a second time, he caught a glimpse of the woman coming down the stairs. He retraced his steps and stopped at the foot of the staircase. He placed his hand on the knob of the carved newel post, his eyes lingering on her form as she descended. The soft dazzle of her golden beauty tempted him. His eyes touched her heather honey mouth, a burnished curl at her ear, the curve of her breast. With the pieces of his case falling into an intriguing pattern, Locke felt indulgent, with the world, with himself. He indulged himself by mentally undressing the woman approaching him. Her gown permitted it, invited it. He improved his fantasy: he imagined her undressing herself for him. He imagined what must follow.

He stood watching her descend, imagining her nakedness and her responsiveness. He had smelled the strong scent of a good lead in his conversation with Colonel Worth. That was heady enough, but he reckoned that the encounter with Mrs. Sheridan promised to be even more interesting—for different reasons.

She arrived at the last step and paused. She was suddenly hesitant, instantly attracted, instantly on her guard. They exchanged a wordless regard. Martha was shocked by her reaction to him, which was as strong and contradictory as it had been two days before, when she had first met him at Desford House. Shocked though she was, she would have been vastly disappointed had she had a lesser reaction to him now.

She had an impulse to wrap her shawl around her shoulders to cover her décolletage. She resisted it. *Let him look!* she thought. She wanted to tease him. He had gotten the better of her in their last encounter, and she wanted the satisfaction of putting him in his place—even if it meant coming after him to do it.

"Chief Constable Locke," she said. "You wished to see me?"

He shook his head slowly. "I did not ask for you to come down."

Martha was certainly the equal of handling this rebuff. She looked up at him boldly. She was excited by this meeting and by her feelings. The little devil that had been nipping at her so relentlessly of late urged her on. "You asked Lady Purcell whether I was here, did you not?"

"I did."

He met her boldness with boldness. His eyes raked her skin, her curves. She tingled and almost lost her nerve. She had to take the last step down so that she could dangle herself right under his nose. She wanted to draw him near, then push him away. She wanted him to suffer. She took the step.

He was not a tall man, and her eyes wee at the level of his beautifully molded lips. She lifted her eyes to meet keen gray ones. "And you told Lady Purcell that you would not trouble me now, but would have to consult me at another time, did you not?"

"I did."

"Why is not now as good a time as any, Chief Constable Locke?"

"Because, Mrs. Sheridan, I did not wish to trouble you before I had a chance to make other inquiries," he said. This was true enough, but what he had just learned from Colonel Worth at once simplified and complicated his dealings with the beautiful widow.

Martha continued to look into his eyes. She cast her line and attempted to reel him in. He did not take the bait. She felt desperate to keep the conversation going. "Trouble, Chief Constable Locke? Why all this talk of trouble?"

Her eyes were the depth and color of a Scottish loch on the fairest summer's day. A man could get lost in them. He must remember that. "Because a man has been murdered."

"Yes, but what does that have to do with consulting me at another time? Or consulting me at all? I have nothing to hide, Chief Constable Locke."

He had no difficulty understanding her. She was not hiding anything. Not from him. He had never met a woman so available to him. "If I am to consult you," he said, "it must be at another time. When we are private."

Her smile was condescending. Her voice was condescending. "Private," she repeated. She ran her eye over his suit. "I may not wish for a private consultation...later. So. What is to prevent you from consulting me now?"

Locke leaned into the newel post slightly. It was as close as he dared come to her, which was close enough to feel her heat and her desire. The combination of her nearness and his fantasies of her nakedness had formed a potent aphrodisiac that swirled through his senses. The drug nudged him into unwisdom. The caution that he claimed for himself dissolved in her presence. The stiletto in his jacket was forgotten. He said low into her ear, "Merely a desire to avoid interrogating you in this public setting, Mrs. Sheridan—"

"Is not the word 'consult,' Chief Constable Locke?"

"About your presence in Mr. Gilbert Kenmure's rooms on the afternoon of his murder."

She felt naked, covered only by his Scots burr, which was warm and woolly. She felt many things, except surprised. She would have been disappointed had he not by now discovered that she had been in Gilbert's rooms on the day of his death. Kind, gentle Gilbert, who reminded her so much of her dead husband. Kind, gentle, malleable Gilbert, who reminded her nothing of the man standing before her.

It was more from coyness than from a wish to hide the nakedness of his assertion that she veiled herself in a laugh and the words "What a charming fairy story, Chief Constable Locke. Do you expect me to confirm it?"

"I expect you to tell your motives for being there," he replied.

"My motives? They are none of your business."

"I have made them my business." He had already thrown caution to the wind. For piquancy, he added, "A very serious case of murder has been committed, and I am the chief investigator. All in all, it will go better for you if we defer this discussion until later. When we are private."

She was breathing quickly now, her color heightened. "But there is nothing to discuss."

"I shall call on you later," he repeated, "at your home."

"I shall not let you in."

"It will go much better for you," he repeated, stepping away from her now and bowing ironically, "if you let me in willingly, and with a smile."

The men she wanted had always melted in her presence, and she could bend them as she pleased. The man before her was already molten. He had stood in her fire and was unchanged. He excited her in a way she had never been excited. She taunted, "Do you think me capable of murder, Chief Constable Locke?"

"Aye, Mrs. Sheridan, that I do."

She nearly gasped. Her condescension was pronounced. "I do not need to let you into my house for any reason, Chief Constable Locke."

"And then you will tell me quite specifically," he continued, as if she had not spoken, "why you were in Gilbert Kenmure's rooms—"

"My house shall not be violated, by the chief investigator of a murder or anyone else! You have no legal right!"

"On the afternoon—"

"I do not have to endure this!"

"Of his murder. I shall listen with rapt attention to your account. You will begin with your motives. I am sure they will interest me."

He turned on his heel and left her. She could hardly wait for him to come. She hoped, crudely, that it would be tonight.

Locke strode across the entry hall, collected his coat from the footman, whose face betrayed nothing of his lively interest in that tête-à-tête, and walked out into the street. After the heat, the shock of the cold blasted through him. He felt like a rod of red-hot iron dipped in the tempering bath. He sizzled, and as the steam escaped him, his senses returned, but only in part. He had acted from impulse, not caution, but he did not regret it. He did not think he was wrong about her and yet . . . and yet . . . what if he were? He imagined that his curiosity, if nothing else, would be satisfied. Would his curiosity, like the cat's, prove fatal?

Martha ascended the curving stairs to the drawing room abovestairs, feeling breathless and frustrated and alive. Hardly five minutes before, she had descended those stairs, spurred by her strange, unmediated attraction to Chief Constable Locke, by her sense of superiority and by her desire to even the score. He had stripped her of everything but her attraction to him, and he had added a new dimension of fear. Did he truly think her capable of murder? Or had he said that to tease her flames, to thrust a poker in her fire? Did he expect to come and seduce her into a confession? What then?

Fortunately, both her exit from and her return to the drawing room went unremarked by Lady Purcell's guests. When she sat back down on the sofa next to Caroline, she discovered that the center of attention of a dozen pairs of eyes was, not surprisingly, Richard Worth.

Worth's entrance to the drawing room had been delayed because of his conversation with Chief Constable Locke. When he entered a few minutes after Caroline, who had already been duly congratulated on her nuptials, Lady Purcell had asked him, naturally enough, "Tell us, sir. Were you discussing Mr. Kenmure's most horrible murder with the chief constable? Is there any further news?"

Worth lied without hesitation. "The chief constable and I were discussing old times in the army. We were on the Continent together."

The topic was easily turned, for now that Kenmure was buried, Worth's return and his sudden marriage could occupy center stage. One of the gentlemen, the very correct Lord Bromley, whom Worth had spoken with last week in this very drawing room, ventured, "I heard from Desford that you, sir, were in the cavalry, First Regiment."

Although Bromley's voice was cool, Worth heard an overture of friendliness in the comment. "That's right," he affirmed.

"The King's Regiment of Dragoon Guards," Bromley continued, displaying a tidbit of knowledge, "with the blue facings on your uniforms. Desford was excessively proud of those facings!"

Lord Purcell, who was refilling everyone's glass, chimed in amiably, "We thought we'd never hear the end of it, when Des returned from the Continent. A captain he had become, so he was happy to tell everyone he encountered! Said he wouldn't have left his commission for anything less than the title!"

A volley of supporting comments followed. "Such a surprise it was to all of us when he inherited."

"Surprised him, too, more than anyone!"

"Never thought Des would take to the position so well."

"No, indeed. No one did! Especially not Des himself!"

"Unusual—a strict settlement through the grandfathers!"

"Very unusual, but scrupulously legal!"

Then the mournful comment, "A pity about his cousin."

"It's been hard on Des."

"Hard on everyone."

"He was supposed to be here this evening, was he not?"

This last query was directed at Lady Purcell. "Yes, and that is why the chief constable came, to see whether his grace had yet arrived," she answered. She glanced at Worth. "Isn't that right, sir? Did I not hear him ask you the same thing?"

"Yes, he asked me if I had seen Desford today," Worth replied. "However, when I had not, we fell to reminiscing."

"The chief constable was in the army, you say? What unit?"

"Infantry," Worth replied. "The Twenty-first."

"Royal Scots, of course," said one. "To hear the man talk!"

"The Twenty-first marched with the First, then?" asked another. "Is that how you knew this fellow Locke?"

Worth nodded and stretched the truth, to draw the conversation away from Kenmure's murder. "We knew each other from the campaign of '11. We were in Flanders together."

Caroline's ear had been carefully attuned to the dynamics of the evening. She had noted the subdued interest the group had taken in Worth's return and the tentative attempts to learn what he had been doing for the past thirteen years. She had heard, too, the distance in Lord Bromley's voice. Furthermore, she did not believe that Worth and the chief constable had been in amiable discussion of shared army experiences past.

Caroline chose to enter the conversation. "My husband rode at Bouchain," she offered, glancing around the group calmly. "I am sure we all remember the English victory in Flanders."

Noises of admiration and appreciation were made. This new subject generated animated talk. Worth looked across the room at his wife and nodded to her. She smiled back at him. His gaze lingered. The vision of her warped and blurred, as if he had drops of water in his eyes. He blinked, and when she came again into clear focus, she looked very different to him.

Worth began to appreciate his wife's methods. Without seeming to conduct the conversation, Caroline kept the focus of discussion on the military, weaving a deft course between general comments on English victories and specific aspects of her husband's personal accomplishments. Worth replied in a straightforward manner to all the queries and questions that came his way. He discussed the heat of action without glorifying himself. He discussed the aftermath of battle without a sense of the maudlin or the grotesque, but with compassion and regret for the tragic necessity of war. He discussed the intricacies of the Flemish campaign without bogging down in boring detail.

"The French were rightly flummoxed, then, you say, Worth—they with the superior forces and so close to home?'' one gentleman asked with obvious relish, wanting to hear more.

Worth nodded and deftly recounted Marlborough's strategic brilliance, to the obvious delight of his listeners.

"And how long did this campaign take?" another inquired.

Worth's gaze had once again fallen on his wife. Seeing her with new eyes, in this setting, as they were, among friends, he felt his heartbeat and breathing affected. After his entirely boorish manner of proposing to her, after all the insults she rightly inferred from his proposal, here she was actually helping him to reestablish himself. She was putting him in a good light. She was helping to rub off his tarnish. She was making him shine. He was filled with a new and unidentifiable longing, which merged with his immediate physical need to win access to her bed. He suddenly realized that he had forgotten an essential aspect of planning his strategy: he had devised no timetable.

"And how long did this campaign take?" the man inquired again, after a moment of silence.

Worth roused himself and transferred his gaze to his questioner. With lingering abstraction, he said, "Five months." He looked back to Caroline and calculated rapidly: *Five months for my present campaign? Impossible! Five weeks? No. Five days? Better. Five hours. Aha!*

Caroline was blushing rosily, for Worth's gaze was transparent. Little more than this brief passage was needed to convince the very perceptive audience that, as far as the newlyweds were concerned, she was in love, and he was besotted.

Thereafter, the initial constraint caused by Worth's presence eased somewhat, and the evening unfolded pleasantly. It also passed quickly and with no sign of the duke. Soon enough, it seemed, it was time to go.

In the entry hall, the guests were muffling themselves in their cloaks and scarves and bonnets and gloves. Worth had drawn Caroline aside, into a shadowy recess provided by the curve of the staircase, and was helping her with her cloak. As he enfolded her in its warmth, he took the opportunity to take her into his arms. He had been aching all evening to kiss her. She was more than ready to accept that kiss and raised her face willingly. Their lips met, and the first strong breeze, signaling the storm to come, rose between them.

Just then, Lord Bromley walked by and saw their embrace. He had warmed up to Worth during the evening and said affectionately, "Good God, Richard! Always after a pretty woman in a corner! As lusty as ever—and as bad as your father!"

It had been meant as a joke.

It had been exactly the wrong thing to say.

Bromley realized it. He froze, aghast.

Caroline realized it. She felt Worth's reaction like an electrical shock.

Worth drew his head away from Caroline. He turned slowly. Every nerve ending bristled with the point of a little knife. Thousands of knife points pricked at his skin from the inside. He looked at the older man levelly. His voice held neither malice nor apology, nor any other emotion, and that very lack gave it a frightening quality. "Except that, in my father's case, he rarely married the women he kissed and rarely kissed the women he married."

Chapter Sixteen

Worth's pleasure in the evening was slain. He managed to take his leave of Lord and Lady Purcell civilly enough. He was only vaguely aware that Caroline carried them through their goodbyes, just as she had managed—as far as was possible—to smooth over the hideous moment with Lord Bromley.

Their return in the open carriage passed in a numbing silence. Caroline felt helpless. By the time they arrived at St. James's Square, she was outwardly frozen and inwardly chilled by the knowledge that she had no way of reaching her husband through what she guessed was his haze of pain. She regretted, not for the first time this day, that she had rejected his advances on their wedding night.

She was not a dewy-eyed demoiselle ignorant of the ways of the world. So what if she was plain? So what if her secret heart held the vision of another man? So what if Worth had not married her for love? He had saved her from financial ruin. He had treated her with respect. The least she could do was to help him when he needed it. However, she did not know the words to say that would not salt his deep wound, and she had cut off the possibility of offering him physical comfort.

Worth would not have accepted her comfort, in any form. He did not accompany her upstairs. He dismissed the retainer who had awaited their return with a branch of candles, and bade Caroline a remote good-night in the entry hall. She did not ask what he intended doing, but it was clear that he was not headed for his bedroom. She feared for the possibilities of how he might spend the rest of the night.

Worth's actions would not have caused Caroline concern. He took the branch of candles and repaired to the parlor. He set the candles on the rosewood harpsichord and walked to one of the long uncurtained windows that gave onto the square. He clasped his hands behind his back and stood straight, witnessing, with no apparent interest, the moon stealing through the gauze of clouds in the vast wastes of the night sky.

He had been about to kiss Caroline when he had heard the words: *Always after a pretty woman in a corner! As lusty as ever—and as bad as your father!* They had slipped past the lines of his defenses and struck him in the heart of his camp.

He remembered the hard-drinking, hot-blooded, spend-thrift, arrogant young man he had been. He could drink all night and still drink more. He could bed six different beauties on six successive nights and still pant after a seventh. He could throw his quarter's allowance away on horses and women, and still spend more. There had always been more: more drink, more women, more money. It had seemed inexhaustible. Until the afternoon he had entered the drawing room and had seen the results of his father's last mad act of passionate excess.

He might have told Bromley that he had become a sober man—an unusual breed in this age of hard drinking. He might have told Bromley that he had become a chaste man— a rarity in this age of libertinism. He might have told Bromley that he craved the solidity of *things*—an odd quirk in this age of wild speculation in the South Sea Company. He might have told Bromley all of this, and it would have been the truth—yet not the whole truth. His old passions and appetites had not died. But never again would he be their slave. Never again would he be their victim.

Victim. His father's victim.

His father. Unbidden, there arose a vision of a man astride a heavy black charger. He was handsome. He was in the prime of life. He was a commander of men. He wore large-topped boots and a full-bottomed wig and a scarlet coat, laced with gold. He held a bayonet high above his head. He sounded an order and was instantly obeyed. The vision filled with the smoke and roar of cannon fire and the charge of battle cries. Worth shook his head. His vision was of Marlborough. It was the trick of the victim's mind: to confuse the agent of terror with the savior.

A second vision came of a man astride a black stallion. He was big, very big, or so he seemed to a little boy. He was handsome. He was in the prime of life. He wore riding boots and a beautifully curled wig and gray silks with white lace. He held a whip high above his head and was beating a snarling stable dog. The man was going to kill it. The man was laughing. It was Worth's earliest memory of his father.

Various memories jostled one another. The death of the stable dog skidded into the death of his mother. His father had killed her, too. His adult mind knew that she had died in a riding accident, but the child that dwelt deep in his breast carried the knowledge that his father had killed her: with his excess of women and wine; with his ungoverned passion for fast living and fast horses; with his unharnessed desire to eat the most, drink the most, rut the most. Memories of a hundred women, his father's women, collided into an imperfect composite of one woman: glimpses from his early boyhood supplied her with white dimpled arms, bared white breasts and full red lips that parted to emit sounds of giggling satisfaction.

Other sounds, less distinct, darker and heavier, were supplied by memories from his later boyhood, along with her avid black eyes, sinuous movements, the musky sticky-sweet scent of desire, a tuft of hair not otherwise visible, the back of a knee, a strange, impossible fascinating position. The incoherent composite fused into an individual woman: his first, a castoff from his father, thrown to him as one would throw a still-meaty bone to a hungry dog. To reverse the image: was he the meaty bone thrown to the hungry woman?

Then—his young manhood and a sea of beautiful feminine flesh. He swam in it. He drowned in it, happily so. He had his father's appetite. He had his father's skill. He began to have his father's women, not his castoffs. He rivaled. He surpassed. He was guilty of every sexual excess, save the one for which he had been condemned. Not that he had not thought about his stepmother as a possible conquest. Not that he had not known that his father had married her in order to taunt him. Not that she had not seen in the son more of what had attracted her to the father.

But he had not hated his father enough to have acted on his illicit thought or to have reacted to his father's taunt or to have responded to his stepmother's advances.

No, that deep hatred had come only after the scene of unspeakable horror in his father's drawing room. The hatred was no longer a driving presence in his body, but it was easily revived, like a sleeping snake; and it had been stirred to venomous life this evening with Bromley's ill-considered comment. It had stung him in a way that Langley's charge of "mother fucker" had not.

He had been warned that his return to society would not be easy. Before lapsing into cold, black, wordless despair, he entertained the flickering hope that this night would be the worst he would have to endure.

He was wrong.

The next morning, Caroline awoke with a start. A fearsome feeling spread through her limbs that Worth had spent the night in a drunken stupor or some other form of debauchery. Thus, she was a little amazed and a little relieved when she descended to the dining room to see her husband seated there, calmly working on some papers. The remains of his breakfast were at his side, suggesting that he had been up for quite some time. At her entrance, he looked up, smiled at her politely, half rose from his chair and bowed to her. His clothing was fresh, his hair was neatly tied, he was well shaved, and his eyes were clear, though somewhat shadowed. This was not a man who had indulged in wild excess the night before.

If anything, he was too much in control, Caroline thought, as they exchanged intermittent remarks at the table. With no trace of emotion, he explained that he had business to attend to this morning and that he would return in the early afternoon, in order to be on hand when the first furnishings for his library were delivered. He asked after Caroline's plans for the day and accepted, again without emotion, her information that she would be occupied in the parlor for most of the day. In rising from his chair to leave, he asked about their plans for the evening.

"We are engaged to go out again," she said, looking up at him. She saw, at last, a trace of emotion cross his features.

"And the nature of the engagement?" he inquired.

"A card party, at Mrs. Shuttleworth's. A larger party than last evening." She tried to sound casual. "Which is all to the good, for I believe there will be more people that you and I know better, perhaps, than there were last evening."

He hesitated.

She put out her hand and laid it on his forearm. She looked up at him earnestly. "I think we should go."

He looked down at her, his expression unreadable. "Do you?"

"Yes," she said quickly. Then, with more confidence, she repeated, "Yes. I think we should. It is important."

"Very well."

She removed her hand from his arm. He bowed and left the room. Not much later, she had donned a pinafore and was busily at work in the parlor with one of the maids she had engaged the day before. From there she would organize the rest of the house, and the parlor had been piled with pillows and cushions destined for other rooms, and box upon box upon box. As she inspected the ceramics she had had sent from Hutton Manor, she reflected that money was an extraordinary commodity, operating with a magical quality to make objects appear from thin air. The beautiful carpet had appeared this morning, for instance, as well as the china cabinet.

She unpacked the porcelains lovingly. Her best piece was a blue and white Kakiemon jar, which she placed on the mantelshelf, below which a comfortable fire burned. As she dusted her other pieces and put them on display in the lacquered cabinet, she pondered the problem of her husband's past and their present together. He had been plainly more shaken by Bromley's unintentional insult than by Langley's deliberate curse. That much she knew.

She picked up her plates and began to wipe them. Tigers and herons and peacocks passed through her hands, a brilliant, enameled, exotic bestiary. She paused to peer into one dish that pictured the serpentine Chinese dragon, which, she had read, in the Mandarin language was called Lung. It had five claws and was the symbol of imperial authority. So different from its European counterpart, the Chinese dragon was a creature not of fire but of water. She thought of Worth. A dragon, and yet not? A man out of his element? A man as fierce as the mythic animal and as fragile as the porcelain? The comparisons did not seem wholly apt. She put the plate away.

She worked through lunch. In the middle of the afternoon, she heard the sounds of her husband's return. After a few minutes, when he did not come to seek her out, she went in search of him. She went into the vestibule, still wearing her pinafore, her hair bundled in a scarf. She heard another man's voice in the entry hall, speaking low. Desford again? Her heart sank.

When she turned into the entry hall, she saw it was not his grace but Chief Constable Locke. One look at her husband's face told her that something was amiss.

"Chief Constable Locke," she said and was greeted in return. She turned to her husband, drawing the scarf from her hair, which tumbled to her shoulders, several curls escaping their pins. "Richard," she said. She stood on tiptoe to kiss him on the lips, making a show of a united front.

He grasped her shoulders and drew her to him. "Caroline," he replied, kissing her. It was almost with regret. He put her away from him and said, looking away from her, "Do not trouble yourself, my dear. The chief constable has come to talk to me."

"That's right, ma'am—" Locke began but was cut off.

"To *us*, you mean, surely, my dear?" she said to her husband and turned back to the chief constable. "Let us not stand about in the drafty entry hall. Will you come into the parlor, so that we may speak at our leisure? I have a feeling that we shall be seeing much of you in the next few days." Before the constable had a chance to demur, she linked her arm in his, firmly taking control of the situation. Worth had no choice but to follow them. "Pray, excuse my housewifery," she continued, gesturing to her pinafore, "but I am in the midst of establishing my rooms."

Chief Constable Locke privately thought that he had never seen Mrs. Worth look so attractive as she did in her pinafore, with her hair awry, her cheeks flushed from housework. She looked serene. She looked dependable.

On the way down the vestibule, she gave orders to the footman to fetch some chairs. She handed her head scarf to the maid in the parlor, who was dismissed. She and the chief constable settled themselves in the makeshift seating arrangement that the footman had quickly set up. Worth took a standing position at the harpsichord, facing them.

She placed her hands in her lap and came straight to the point. "I imagine that you have come with regard to Mr. Kenmure's murder."

"That's right, ma'am," Locke began again but was cut off a second time.

"Locke has recovered the possible murder weapon," Worth said to his wife. "It is a dagger. An Italian stiletto. I told him last night that I had seen a similar one in Desford's library last week, on the morning of the day of Kenmure's murder. The chief constable checked into the matter this morning, and it seems, in fact, that Desford's stiletto is missing. Desford is naturally distressed by the loss, which he had not noticed."

"Naturally," Caroline said, placidly. She sent her husband a loving smile and said, "And what does that have to do with you, my dear?"

"Unfortunately, I was the last one to have seen it," Worth replied.

"Unfortunately?" Caroline questioned.

"I believe that I am under suspicion of murder, my love," Worth said bluntly.

Caroline looked quickly at the chief constable. "I'm just doing my duty, Mrs. Worth," he said stolidly.

"Good heavens!" she exclaimed. A cold dread gripped her stomach, but her wits did not abandon her. She noticed that a curious glance—not quite hostile, yet not quite conspiratorial, but somewhere between the two contradictory poles—passed between the chief constable and her husband. She picked her words with care. "If my husband was the last one to have seen the dagger, is he not more accurately under suspicion of *theft?*"

Locke met Caroline's eye levelly, without flinching. "That might be a more accurate way of putting it, yes, ma'am," was his reply.

Something struck Caroline as very odd in this encounter. Was her husband being accused, or was he not? She continued, "It is a rather large step, is it not, from my husband having been in the presence of the possible murder weapon to his act of actually killing a man?"

"A very large step," the chief constable concurred.

"And is there some reason why my husband should fall under suspicion of a theft that is possibly connected to a murder?"

Worth chose to answer that question. "It is my violent past, I believe, that lends support to such a theory."

Caroline looked at her husband, and the question came involuntarily to mind: *What if he is Mr. Kenmure's murderer?* Aloud, she said to him, "But you did not even know Mr. Kenmure, as I am sure you have told the good chief constable! And in addition to lacking a motive," she continued swiftly, "you also lacked opportunity." She turned back to the law officer. "I think you recall, Chief Constable Locke, that I was the first person from the assembly in the alleyway. When you questioned me the other day about my presence, I said that I had gone downstairs from the ballroom to catch a breath of air. Need I mention now that I was not alone?" Her explanation was ready-made, for not only had she given it to Martha Sheridan, she also knew that Worth had given it to Desford. "My husband was with me at the moment Kenmure must have been murdered. Any number of people can confirm it.''

She wondered whether Locke knew the story for a lie, but she could not tell. He seemed satisfied by it and said, ''I am happy to have heard the account from you, ma'am. It does make Colonel Worth's part in the deed—'' here he glanced at Worth ''—most unlikely.''

''Most!'' she agreed. ''Surely you have other, more likely suspects to investigate.''

''Surely,'' was Locke's reply.

''But I am somewhat at a loss! Does someone—did his grace *accuse* my husband of, first, the theft of his dagger and, then, the murder of his cousin?''

''No, ma'am, his grace did not exactly accuse Colonel Worth,'' Locke said. ''He merely confirmed that his dagger was missing after I told him this morning that the colonel had identified it as being similar to one he had seen in his grace's library on the morning of the murder. His grace was distressed, as I've said, that the object was gone. He could not account for its disappearance—and he could not recall having seen it after Colonel Worth's visit.''

''This is quite nonsensical, Chief Constable Locke,'' Caroline said roundly. ''In addition to having no motive and no opportunity, my husband would not have the least reason to *acknowledge* having seen a thing he stole and then killed someone with. Why, *anyone* might have taken the dagger from Desford House! A servant! Another visitor! There must have been other visitors to Desford House that day besides my husband.''

Worth's memory was jogged. ''I met Arthur Devis,'' he said, ''coming to Desford House just as I was leaving that morning.''

Locke repeated with interest, ''Mr. Devis? And about what time would that have been, Colonel Worth?''

''Let me see,'' Worth began. ''I was not there above an hour, and I must have come at, say, ten o'clock. I remember now that, just as I was leaving, the morning mail arrived. Then came Devis a minute or two later.''

"Anything of importance in the mail?" Locke wanted to know.

Thinking it through, Worth said, "Perhaps one letter at the bottom of the stack." He shrugged. "Estate business, no doubt."

"No doubt," Locke echoed.

Caroline waved away the business with the mail. "Although it is extremely distasteful to start casting aspersions willy-nilly, one might suspect *Arthur Devis* of having stolen the dagger and of having killed Mr. Kenmure. He, at least, had a motive! Mr. Kenmure owed him a bit of money."

"Yes, I knew about the deal over a horse," Locke said. "But I did not know that Mr. Devis had been to Desford House."

"Is it important?" Caroline asked.

"Possibly," Locke said. "Now that we know the murder weapon comes from his grace's library, I am interested in all of the visitors to Desford House that day."

Caroline's heart leapt to her throat. "Mr. Kenmure visited Desford House, as well, on the afternoon of his murder."

After a moment of utter silence, the chief constable asked, "Mr. Kenmure told you that, Mrs. Worth?"

"No, his grace told me." She explained how it was that the duke had come to Portugal Row for an interview with Caroline, to discover whether Mr. Kenmure had told her anything about his latest charitable plans during their last dance at the London Assembly. To the chief constable's quick question, Caroline answered that Mr. Kenmure was indeed involved in charitable projects. More quick questions followed. Caroline answered them all to the extent her knowledge permitted, and then asked a question of her own, "But did not his grace mention Mr. Kenmure's visit?"

"No, he did not, Mrs. Worth," Locke answered, glancing briefly at Worth, "but then again, his grace was mightily upset by the loss of his dagger—and the possible implications of it having been used against his cousin—and Colonel Worth's association with it."

"I see, then," Caroline said. "Yes, his grace has been much grieved this week. I am sure we can all understand his . . . his distraction."

It was better to say less just then, than more. Locke departed soon thereafter. When the chief constable had gone, Worth said, "I must thank you, ma'am, for having protected me."

"I defended you to the chief constable, as you defended me to Desford," she said. At mention of the conversation she had overheard between her husband and the duke, she flushed, but she did not lower her lashes. She added belatedly, "We're married now."

It was a charged moment. Her gaze roamed his face, the high cheekbones, the blue light of his eyes, which returned her gaze steadily. She wanted to tell him she had known all along that he was not involved in Mr. Kenmure's murder, but of course, for a fleeting second, she had considered the possibility that he could have killed the man. How could she have not? She did not truly think he had done it, but what did she know of her husband, after all, beyond his violent past and his violent profession? She wanted him to protest his innocence as she had done the night before, but what he said was, "Yes, we are married."

She searched his face for his innocence, but could not find it in the hard, broken planes of his features. Her gaze traveled to his lips. She had the wild thought that he wanted to kiss her. She awaited the touch of his lips eagerly. There she would taste his innocence. She swayed toward him.

He took a step back from her. "Now that the dagger has surfaced as the murder weapon—and I am associated with it," he said in a cold, expressionless voice, "I am bound to be a target of suspicion among the general run of our acquaintance."

Her heart contracted. "No, that is absurd—" she began.

"Do you not find me an easy target, ma'am?" he interrupted, with just the raw edge of an emotion jutting out from behind the tonelessness. Her flush deepened, and he continued, "You must be prepared for what might await us in the coming days—now that we are married, as you point out."

Caroline realized her mistake. She should have defended him in private as well as in public, and now the moment had slipped by in which she could assure him she believed in his innocence without question. She took an indirect route. "You are not the target of everyone's suspicion," she said. "Most important, you are not a target for Chief Constable Locke, I think. He does not believe you are involved in Mr. Kenmure's murder."

Almost, the ghost of a smile hovered around Worth's mouth. "No, he does not."

"Then why did he have to... to *accuse* you?"

"He did not. Desford did."

"I did not think it was anything so *explicit* as an accusation," Caroline said. "And why did Chief Constable Locke follow through on it?"

"Locke was doing his duty," Worth replied. "I understood that and took no offense. He had to come and find out what he could find out. He apparently found out quite a lot."

Caroline sought an opening, any opening, the smallest crack, in the wall that seemed to stand now between her and Worth. "Do you think he believed my story that we were together at the probable time of Mr. Kenmure's murder?"

"Perhaps, but not necessarily."

"If he suspects me of lying, does that not make you—or me, or both of us—more of a suspect, rather than less? Still, I believe that he knows you did not do it."

Worth considered this. "Honor among army men, perhaps."

"Desford was an army man," Caroline pointed out.

"Yes," said Worth briefly. Then, "This morning, you encouraged me to attend Mrs. Shuttleworth's card party. I admit that I was not eager. Perhaps you are now feeling a similar reluctance to go out tonight." With a barren coldness that matched the November day outside, he continued decisively, "However, in light of this afternoon's developments, it is imperative that we attend the evening's engagement and that we appear together. We shall dine at six o'clock and be ready to leave at seven.'' He excused himself with a formal bow to go about his business.

Caroline felt the chill of the command down to her toes. She wondered, idly, if the appropriate response might have been to salute him or, possibly, to slap him. One part of her wanted to take him in her arms. In reflecting on this unfortunate exchange, she dismissed, as a flight of wishful thinking, the idea that he had been about to kiss her.

However, it was true. A desire to kiss his wife was with him constantly now. She did not guess that he had refrained from kissing her because of her statement, ''We are married now.'' He interpreted her mention of their legal bond as the sole reason for her loyal defense of him to Chief Constable Locke. He appreciated the quality of loyalty but wanted something different from her. He would not beg for it, and above all, he would not—he would *never*—protest his innocence.

Dinner was not easy. Both Caroline and Worth made an effort to keep the conversation afloat, but dark undercurrents kept dragging it down. Caroline had had several hours to imagine the full dimensions of the social horror that possibly lay ahead, and an undeniable coldness had come over Worth since Chief Constable Locke's visit.

Caroline was no heavy drinker, but this evening she had decided to fortify herself with a second glass of wine.

At one point, Worth remarked, looking at her levelly, ''Before engaging in battle, soldiers are known to relieve their fears in a variety of ways. Some men pray and take Communion. Some resort to self-inflicted wounds to avoid facing the enemy. Most drink themselves into a near stupor.''

Caroline put down the glass that she had just raised to her lips. She attempted a teasing note. ''Do you perhaps compare the evening ahead to a battlefield engagement?''

He did not match her light tone. ''No blood will flow.'' He focused his hard gaze on her. ''However, you and your fine sense of the social limits will be badly bruised.''

Caroline considered this. "About those limits," she said, "I always simply accepted them. Until I met you, I had never even pushed them. Tonight they may be fully tested. It will be...a challenge, I suppose. Perhaps even exciting."

Thus always spoke the brave, untried soldier. He made no response.

"You, sir," she said, "what did you do to calm your fears before a battle? Or are you going to tell me you were fearless going into the face of enemy guns?"

He replied, "I had little to fear in what lay ahead of me because, you see, the more deadly pistol of my past was loaded, cocked and pointed at the back of my head."

Chapter Seventeen

Worth had foreseen how Mrs. Shuttleworth's card party would unfold. He knew that once his association with the murder weapon, however circumstantial, was established, it would provide a forum for an open discussion of what had been whispered about all week: his sudden return, his hasty marriage and the dead bodies that littered his past. He knew that the mixture of the old scandal and the new was simply too potent and piquant not to start, and keep, tongues wagging the evening long.

Since Caroline did not have Worth's experience with scandal, no amount of conjecture could have prepared her for the reality of the evening. It was to pass as a strange and incomprehensible dream, one that teetered on the edge of a nightmare.

Arthur Devis had arrived early at Mrs. Shuttleworth's and enjoyed an unaccustomed popularity. Several factors converged to magnetize his presence: he had been duly visited by Chief Constable Locke that afternoon; he had met Worth leaving Desford House on the morning of Kenmure's murder; he could not recall having seen the dagger in question on Desford's library table after Worth's departure; he was rarely otherwise taken seriously and wished to maximize his celebrity; Mr. Shuttleworth was serving an excellent claret.

By the time Colonel and Mrs. Worth were announced and had stepped into the fashionable crowd, two camps of opinion had already formed. There were those who believed, along with Arthur Devis, that Worth had been involved in Kenmure's murder. Their explanations tended toward the fantastic, and when not fantastic, they were simplistic. Then there were those who dismissed any implication that Worth was involved in the murder. Their explanations relied on common sense and logic. The second camp was in the minority.

The arguments ran like this:

"But to be sure Worth is involved. Couldn't be otherwise. Stands to reason!"

"Reason is precisely what is lacking in your argument, sir. Worth's been gone these thirteen years on the Continent, while Gilbert Kenmure was in Leicestershire. Worth didn't even know the man. Why would he want to kill him?"

"Been in the army!" was the answer to that. "Used to killing!"

"But Worth has pursued an honorable profession these past years. Rode with Marlborough, distinguished himself at Bouchain. It was all the talk this morning at my club. It's all the talk, too, that he's returned to reinstate himself. He has a petition before the king to regain his title."

"Of course, the news about the petition is all over town! But it doesn't matter a jot that he rode with Marlborough. Lucky chap, though, I envy him that. But he'll never get his title back if it turns out he killed the duke's cousin!"

"Very true, which makes it highly improbable that he *would* come back to reinstate himself and then turn around and kill a man he does not know for a reason that does not exist!"

"Well, well, we're talking probabilities, are we? It wasn't probable that he'd return to marry as quickly as he did, either. But that's what happened. Against all expectations!"

"Now, look here, sir, marrying is one thing and killing is another. Everyone says that Worth fell in love with Miss Hutton at first sight. Why, just look at the pair. They're in love, man!"

"Disgustingly so!" (On this point there was agreement.) "But it won't last. His is an unstable character. Think of all the women he had before."

"Exactly! And they were quite a different lot from Miss Hutton. He's changed, I tell you."

"Interesting choice, the little Hutton! But now that I've had a better look at her, I see his point! Nevertheless, it's early days yet, and he's still enjoying all the usual satisfactions! But just wait until the bloom is off the rose. Worth's attentions will wander!"

"That remains to be seen."

"Can't change bad blood. Remember his father," was the response. Then ominously, "Remember the second marchioness."

As if there was something irrefutable in the mention of the old horror, arguments in support of Worth's innocence and character began to crumble. "Gad, man, who could have imagined such a thing? Such brutality all around!"

"Unthinkable! And now the man returns, as bold as you please! And if Worth didn't kill Kenmure, pray tell me who did?"

Since there was no answer to that, Worth's culpability was examined and reexamined among ever-changing constellations of people. The talk wove in and out of the old scandal and the new, swooped circles around Worth's life, loves and motives, looped Caroline Hutton into the narrative, inventing her life, her passions. She was no longer judged to be shy and uninteresting; she was now accounted secretive and unusual. Several gentlemen wagered to determine who among them would be the first, if Worth were convicted of murder, to comfort the rich and lonely wife.

Caroline had felt the tensions the moment she entered the room. As she and Worth circulated in the first few minutes, she realized that their presence was causing a mild sensation. This was the strange, dreamlike part: they were neither cut nor cultivated, but rather treated as special by all who acknowledged them, and not a soul breathed to them a word about the dagger. Mrs. Shuttleworth was plainly delighted that the most talked-about couple in London had been brave enough to come. Her party was assured of scandalous success.

Caroline was at first horrified by the kind of attention they were receiving, then, after some adjustment, interested by the effects of notoriety. The sensation of being the center of attention was not precisely contrary to her nature, and so she could not compare it to having her fur rubbed the wrong way or her feathers ruffled. It was rather that the sensation was entirely alien. She had never before felt glittery in public—or in private, for that matter. She felt glittery now, even gaudy, and the feeling of glittery gaudiness was not entirely unpleasant.

For Caroline, the evening was prevented from turning truly nightmarish only because a part of her was less preoccupied with herself and more interested in Worth. She was concerned for him. He was concerned for her. Since Chief Constable Locke's visit, a wall had been erected between them, not a solid wall, more like a lattice, but still effectively keeping them apart.

From behind either side of that lattice, each tried to hide the concern for the other, although in so doing, each betrayed more feeling for the other than they had when staging their "sweet illusion." Through a glance, a touch, an expression, they showed how they felt about each other. The signs were extremely subtle, discernible only to those who were interested, and in this case, everyone present was interested.

During a brief moment alone, Worth turned to Caroline. He had determined that they would attract less attention if they separated for the evening. "Should you object to it, ma'am, if I were to engage in cards?"

Caroline had come to the same conclusion. She readily assured him, "Not at all, sir! I am sure that many gentlemen present are *dying* to speak to you about your military career."

"To be sure," Worth said, adding politely, "I am only reluctant to leave you, since the mingling has been so pleasant."

She was aware of the many eyes upon them, both overt and covert. "Indeed, sir. Most pleasant." She knew that he could take care of himself, yet she hated the thought of what he might have to encounter, alone. It was only cards among gentlemen, but she imagined that facing the French at Bouchain had been easier for him. "Your reluctance is understandable."

Worth inclined his head and sketched a stiff half bow. "My reluctance is to leave *your* side, ma'am," he said meaningfully.

She looked up at him quickly, and blue eyes held hazel. In that moment, their separate concerns and their separate fears reached out, like tendrils, through the lattice between them, to touch their unfulfilled desire for each other. In the moment that these strands of emotion touched, they twined, and a braid of a tender love began to form between them.

Hardly conscious of it, but feeling breathless, Caroline said softly, "You need not concern yourself for *me,* sir. I'll be quite all right by myself. It's not been bad." To the quirk of his eyebrows, she amended, "Well, not *so* bad."

"You do not reassure me, ma'am," he replied.

Caroline suddenly realized that she would be more comfortable—though not happier—without his disturbing presence. She summoned a smile and said in a normal voice, trying to keep it light, "Go to your cards, sir! I cannot live in your pocket all evening, you know, without it being said that we are newlyweds in the worst of bad taste!"

He bowed over her hand and left her with a backward glance that caused the hearts of several ladies who had been closely watching the exchange to flutter.

Caroline sought first Martha Sheridan but was unsuccessful. She found refuge instead with several other of her more agreeable acquaintances. However, even that brief moment of ease was crazily upset. By sheerest coincidence, both Julia Stanhope and Angelica Gordon happened onto her group. With undisguised curiosity, they asked indiscreet questions about Caroline's marriage—attended by no less a personage than the Duke of Desford—to Colonel Worth, with whom, they were happy to inform the assembled ladies, both had danced on the evening of the London Assembly.

Curiously enough, it was the Duke of Desford who rescued Caroline. She had not noticed his arrival, and she was not quite sure how it happened, but presently she found herself seated on a settee with his grace, in private conversation. He mentioned nothing of the dagger taken from his library and nothing of Worth's possible connection to it. *And why should he?* Caroline thought. *His grace surely knows Worth is innocent!*

While responding to his polite, opening nothings, she reflected how perfect it was that, in the midst of the whirls and whorls of the evening's emotions, she should be seated with her secret love. With his gentle commentary on the fine intimacy of her small wedding, she thought that she would be sheltered from inquisitive eyes and from her confused emotions for Worth. She wanted to find the eye of her storm. She wanted to be harbored in her calm lagoon.

"And your very lovely home, are you putting it in order?" Desford asked, handing her the softest of soft questions.

"Oh, yes," she sang, in relief. "I have begun with the parlor, which your grace has visited. I spent the afternoon there, if you must know, very content among my porcelains."

Thus the conversation went. Caroline was surprised that she did not derive more satisfaction from it. Always before, her secret love for the duke had given her something. It felt so safe and perfect, this unrequited love. It was like having a secret garden, ever in bloom, unaffected by changing season, and growing no weeds. It was like having a hidden treasure. It was like a smooth and beautiful gemstone that she harbored in her breast, whose luster would never dim, sheltered from the wear and tear of the real world.

When there came a natural pause, she said, "But I have bored you, your grace, when there are more compelling topics!"

"Perhaps more compelling," Desford replied with a smile, "but hardly more pleasant. My conversations this past week have not all been so...pleasant."

Caroline was put in mind of the conversation the duke had had that morning with Chief Constable Locke. "Yes, and speaking of which, I must suppose you have heard the absurd talk tonight."

Desford smiled a polite inquiry. "I have heard no absurd talk tonight," he said.

Caroline felt a sudden twinge of discomfort in the duke's presence. "I mean the talk concerning my husband."

Desford's expression had not changed.

Caroline laughed somewhat apologetically, and said, "Oh, dear! This is hardly a topic as pleasant as household furnishings, your grace. However, in case you do hear the rumor going around, I wish to remind you that... that Richard and I were together at the London Assembly, if you see what I mean—" She floundered a little, but kept to her point. "That is, we were together and alone during the second interval in the dancing—why, just before you yourself arrived at the assembly, your grace. I remind you only so that you may mention that fact to anyone who might say something... untoward about my husband!"

"Remind me?" Desford queried. "Why, I know nothing about such an encounter, Mrs. Worth. How could I?"

Caroline could hardly say that she had overheard Worth tell him that very story on the evening of her wedding, and by the same token, his grace could hardly admit to having heard a story that cast her reputation into doubt. However, since she was now married to Worth and the account of his movements the night of the murder were of great importance, she hoped his grace would discreetly pass along the story, removing Worth from suspicion.

Before she could formulate an appropriate way of suggesting such a thing, he continued smoothly, "Now, before I leave you, I wish you will present me to your dear aunt. She is over there in a group with our hostess. If I did not know better, I would think she had been avoiding me."

It was a joke. Caroline smiled obligingly. They rose together and crossed the room to Lady Besant.

Since Caroline had no real desire to remain in her aunt's presence, she soon enough made her excuses. Before she left, Desford lifted one of Caroline's hands and brought it to his lips. The look in his eye was particularly warm.

Caroline retreated to another group not far away. When she looked back over her shoulder she noted that Desford and her aunt had become separated from their group and were, surprisingly, in private conversation.

"I thought you would have been pleased by the convergence of events and explanations, Esther," Desford was saying low.

The expression on Lady Besant's face showed the pleasure of a woman not usually honored by the Duke of Desford, but her tone was very far from pleased. "I had not thought you so stupid."

Desford's regard was hard. "And you are such a smart woman that I hardly need advise you not to outsmart yourself."

Witnessing this brief exchange, Caroline noted that Desford had said something that caused her aunt to turn away and leave him. Caroline felt swelling, troubled waves threaten the peace at the outer edges of her calm lagoon. She sought again the company of Martha Sheridan, but her search was to be in vain.

Martha Sheridan was spending the evening at home. She felt too pettish to circulate socially. It seemed too much of an effort to dress, to chat and laugh, and to keep an artful mask in place. Her thoughts were elsewhere, and she wanted to be alone.

Not completely alone, of course; but then she had been disappointed the night before when Chief Constable Locke had not come to see her after Lady Purcell's musicale. She had begun to think that he would not come this evening, either. The hour was late enough and her doubt strong enough that she permitted herself to be undressed. In the mood that swamped her, she asked for the most beautiful of her dressing gowns. It was ivory satin and immodest and greatly wasted on her alone. She had her hair unbound. She was far too fretful to make the pretense of trying to sleep. She slipped on a lace jacket to cover her shoulders and dismissed her maid for the night. Then she curled up with a pink satin coverlet on the pretty little sofa before the fire i⟩ her sitting room. She drew up her legs, hugged them and pu⟩ her chin on her knees.

Martha regarded the fire for a very long time, hardl⟩ aware when the inverted teardrop of a wall clock marked of⟩ ten dainty chimes, then eleven. She rose from the sofa an⟨ stepped to the hearth. She contemplated the fire, with it⟩ miniature caverns of delight and its hot temporary jewe⟩ gardens. A carefully limited combustion, she thought, wit⟩ its fire grate and bars, with its formal boundaries marked of⟩ by brass finials.

She thought of Gilbert Kenmure. She had chosen him a⟩ the perfect man to provide her with the carefully limite⟨ combustion she had been seeking. He was young. He wa⟩ eager. He melted in her presence. He was obscure. He wa⟩ discreet. He had plans, big plans, he had told her. He un⟩ derstood she had no desire to marry him. None. No matte⟩ how big his plans. He understood that she had been alon⟩ for some months. She had expected a decorous little seduc⟨ tion. However, no combustion, careful or otherwise ha⟨ occurred. At the time, she had wanted to tear her hair i⟩ frustration.

Her eye fell on the hearth salamander. She sniffed. Th⟨ salamander, a mythic beast with the power to withstand fire⟩ This one was brass. It mocked her. Over the top of it cam⟨ sparks shooting here and there. At the end of the arc woul⟨ come the small explosion of fine white powder that woul⟨ hold its bulbous shape only a moment before its randon⟩ specks were strewn across the hearthstones. She thought o⟨ phoenixes and firedrakes and Chief Constable Locke.

A small noise at the door to the room caused her to turn⟩ Stepping into her sitting room was a vision of the very ma⟩ she had imagined in the depths of the fire. She blinked⟩ Perhaps she had stared too long into the fire.

"Chief Constable Locke," she said aloud, moving awa⟩ from the hearth, unable to take her eyes off the vision.

The vision moved farther into the room. It had broa⟨ shoulders and well-muscled thighs. It spoke. It had a Scot⟨ burr. "Mrs. Sheridan, I find you at home."

She quickly gathered her wits. She said with what hauteur she could muster, "I gave instructions to my servants that you not be allowed into my house."

"I can always find a charge to drop," he said, "against the footman or the kitchen maid of any house I want to enter."

"But to come into my sitting room—"

Locke had stopped at the side of the sofa. "We were agreed on the terms."

"We were *not* agreed on—"

"We can play this your way, if you want," he said, cutting her off, "but I can think of better."

She gasped at his ability to make her gasp. A double gasp. She hated that he could so easily get the better of her. She was aroused by it, too, so much so that she had an aberrant fantasy that he could take her, now, on the satin coverlet and that she would enjoy it enormously. But not exquisitely. She, too, could think of better ways to play it.

"What do you suggest?" she asked. She drew herself up and stood before him in her beautifully immodest dressing gown. She was in the shadows. The fire, with its miniature caverns of delights and its hot jewel-gardens, was behind her. Even so, she thought, from the quality of his gaze, that he could see through the lace jacket and through the satin at her breasts.

He saw all that and more, and what he could not see, he could easily imagine. He came round to stand in front of the sofa. "We might start with Gilbert Kenmure."

"How did you find out I was there that day?" she asked.

"I didn't. I matched a description of the woman seen there to you. I took a guess, which you confirmed last night."

She was about to deny having confirmed his guess, until she realized that her power over him was not through words. "A description?" she prompted.

"It matched you, more or less," he answered. He was stingy with compliments. "I investigated."

"And what did you discover?"

"That you were a faithful wife for twelve years."

"Surprised?"

He did not answer that. "And that, since the death of your husband, your reputation is without a blot. Spotless."

"Surprised?" she asked again.

He assessed her womanliness, in a leisurely fashion. He knew she was not a woman who lived only above her neck, or down her spine, or between her legs, the way some women lived. He knew, from the way she moved, that she was a woman who lived in her entire body: in the slope of her shoulder, at the bend of her elbow, at the tips of her fingers, along the stretch of her thigh, within the arch of her foot.

The first time he had laid eyes on her, he had instantly known the value of her property. He knew the places she lived, and he appreciated all of them. Yet, he feared her, too, this womanly woman. It made him fear that he would not penetrate her so much as be swallowed by her. The fear sharpened his desire.

"Amazed, more like," he answered, "that you have gotten away with the spotlessness for so long."

She was attracted to his assessment of her, for no man had seen it so frankly; and she resented his frank assessment. She feared it, too, for if she gave herself to him, she could no longer have herself for herself. She might have to be his. It was a risk. "Do you think I killed Gilbert Kenmure?"

"Did he owe you money?"

She felt a surge of anger. "You, sir, are insulting."

"Oh? That depends on what your motives for being with him were, I suppose," he said. "Tell me."

He was baiting her with reverse suspense. Did he think she had killed the eager, young man, or did he not? "Tell you what?"

"For instance, the hour you arrived," he prompted.

"It was three, or three-thirty in the afternoon."

"Not quite the moment of a meal."

"No."

"No pretense of eating, then? Straight to business?"

She flushed.

"Why did you go there? Why did he not come here?"

"Because I don't like men in my rooms."

He bowed ironically. "Was it your first visit?"

"Yes."

"You arrived. No meal. Then what?"

She looked away a moment, then back at him. Her reaction to him, at this second look, was violent, shameful. She decided her course of action. "I took off my coat."

The first glimmer of a smile curved his beautifully molded lips.

Her shame evaporated in the heat of her lust. The violence remained. She licked her lips. She slipped the lace jacket from her shoulders. She was aware of the changes in her body as a result of his eyes upon it. She was proud of them.

"You took off your coat. And then, Mrs. Sheridan?"

She walked toward him and stopped a pace away. "Then undressed." She pulled the ribbon tie at her breasts. The satin relaxed over the curve of her breasts. She shrugged a strap off her shoulder.

Her breasts lay open to him, but he did not reach out. "And then?"

Her heart was pounding. "I undressed him." She raised her hands to his coat and slipped it off. It fell to the ground. Her fingers went to his collar and the buttons on his shirt. She undid them, one by one, then pulled the shirt ends from his waistband. She put both palms against his chest. He smelled sharp and clean, like late apples. Still he did not touch her. Her fingers fell to the fastening on his breeches. She looked up at him and stopped. The look in his eyes made her wet. He looked as if he had already had her many, many times.

"And then?"

She unbuttoned the first button on his breeches, then pushed him lightly. The back of his knees made contact with the sofa, and he sat down on it.

"I took off his boots," she said. She pulled off his boots, first right, then left. The effort caused the other strap to sag off her shoulder, exposing the rich surfaces of her earth. He was intoxicated.

"And then?"

She hiked up the skirt of her dressing gown and sat down on his lap, spreading her knees on either side of him. She arranged herself so that her hands could grasp the remaining buttons on his breeches. The position was awkward, but no less stimulating for both of them in the places her fingers touched.

"And then?"

She leaned toward him so that her breasts grazed his chest. "And then he touched me."

He found her hands with his, spread his fingers against hers, and slid his hands up the inside of her arms to her shoulder, causing her to shiver everywhere. Down her back, across her buttocks, to her knees, up the inside of her thighs, the curve of her belly, he explored the gentle landscape of her hillocks and rises, the swells and the rocky parts hiding sloping declivities and hidden clefts. It was the landscape of his home, the landscape of his birth. The beauty of it made him weak.

His hands came to rest on her breasts. "And then?"

"I kissed him." She had been hungering after the feel of his lips against hers. He tasted sweet and dark. He had been thirsting after the feel of her lips against his. She tasted of heather honey.

"And then?"

She paused. Her lips were still against his, but she was not kissing him. Their bodies could not have been more intimate without actually being joined. Heat shimmered between them. This was the dangerous moment. "And then, no more." She withdrew her lips and slid away from him, shinnying up his thighs. Her bottom rested on his knees. "We were interrupted."

His hands moved to grasp her shoulders. As he assimilated this new move, the look in his half-closed eyes changed considerably. He shifted the position of his hips and legs slightly so that she was no longer so clearly the aggressor, a position she had held only by his voluntary submission, but her heat still enveloped him. His impulse was to take her swiftly and thoroughly. However, his instinct for self-reservation had survived just enough to make him ask, "And the nature of the interruption, Mrs. Sheridan?"

The fire had not yet blazed out of control. His grasp on er shoulders became firmer, with a slightly resistant pressure. He was holding her away from him. Her eyes widened. Could it be that he would withhold himself from *her?* The humiliation of that possibility produced a complex reaction in her, ultimately increasing her desire. She had never felt so much at the mercy of a man. She loved it and hated it and loved it all the more.

He understood that he had her just where he wanted her. He would have her just how he wanted her. "The interruption?" he demanded.

"A messenger came with a letter."

His eyes roamed the loveliness of her face and body in her exquisite stimulation. He was aware of her spread legs round him. "A letter from whom?"

"It was from his cousin, I think," she said, breathing heavily, whimpering with building frustration.

He was still holding on to his control. He needed just a few moments longer. "The Duke of Desford?"

"Yes," she admitted, panting. She had dissolved. "It was important, Gilbert said. Important enough for him to leave me. At that moment. Immediately. Just like that."

His control was slipping away. He had all his answers. "So Mrs. Sheridan's record remains spotless?"

"Yes. Yes. Yes, yes, yes," she wept.

He leaned forward. He felt mightily inspired. "Almost," he said into her ear, "it takes the challenge away."

Then he gathered her in his arms and carried her into the next room, for he had determined to have her in her bedroom on her bed or not at all.

Chapter Eighteen

During the carriage ride back from Mrs. Shuttleworth's, Caroline and Worth exchanged little conversation. However, it was not a brutal silence that enveloped them, such as the one that had accompanied their return from Lady Purcell's; rather it was a lively, electric silence. For her part, Caroline was brimming with things to say, with things she wanted and needed to say, but there were too many, they were too chaotic, and she did not know where to start.

At last, the carriage drew up at St. James's Square. Caroline shot out and was halfway up the steps to the house when Worth caught up with her. The front door was opened for them, and Caroline tumbled into the dark entry hall, which was lit by a single candle. Like the proverbial man in the desert finding an oasis, she gasped, with exultation and relief, "Home! I thought we'd never make it!"

Worth took his wife's cloak and handed it, along with his, to the waiting footman. He instructed the man to douse the lanthorn at the front door, then dismissed him. Worth said to Caroline, "I gather you are glad to return."

She did not know whether to laugh or to cry. "Never *so* glad!" She blurted, "Oh, my word! What an experience! I am not sure that I can describe to you how I feel!"

"Should you like to try in the parlor?" he suggested.

"What an *excellent* idea! I cannot even *begin* to think about sleep! Oh, my poor head! It is bursting!"

Worth took the candle from the side table. He linked her arm in his and asked, "Headache?"

"No," she answered with amazement, "not at all. Isn't *that* remarkable! It's just that—just that—well, I have said that I do not think I can describe how I feel!"

"At a guess, I would say you feel invigorated."

She had to laugh. "Oh, dear God! I feel lucky to be alive!" She laughed again. "*That* is ambiguous—which is, in fact, a fair statement of how I feel. Suffice it to say that I have never experienced anything the like!" She looked up at him. "But I have already said that! You must promise to stop me every time I repeat myself or fall into prattle."

"I promise," he replied, "although, all in all, you seem to have taken the evening in stride rather well."

"Have I? If you say so—! It seems that I am not at all who I used to be but am whatever people say I am. I owe my existence now to reports and rumors!" They had arrived at the threshold to the parlor door, where they stopped. She looked up at him. "Is that what happens once you become the object of gossip—you become a projection of the talk?"

"Yes. To a certain degree."

"Well, after this evening, I shall never be the same. I feel so different—so *transformed!*"

Worth entered the chamber to light the sconces. When the glow had illuminated the room, they looked at each other and burst out laughing.

"I did not want to sit down anyway," she told him. "Why did I think the settee and chairs had already arrived? I must be deranged!" She walked to the harpsichord and stood in the curve of the closed wing, as Worth had done that afternoon.

"Something to drink?" he offered.

She threw her head back over her shoulder and said, "I would dearly like that second glass of wine now!"

"The second glass?"

"The one I did *not* have at dinner!"

"You drank nothing this evening? Brave woman!"

"Brave, nothing! I did not *dare,* with everyone staring at me and whispering about us," she told him. "I feared losing my control!"

He left the room in search of the necessary, and she went to the fireplace to bring the dying embers to life. She teased the flames, threw on a log and returned to her place at the harpsichord. She stood and surveyed her surroundings. Even empty, save for the jumble of boxes and cushions and pillows, the chamber felt very, very good to her. There was, of course, her china cabinet, already in order and in place. Her eyes fell on her favorite plate. They traced, with pleasure, the outline of the dragon, blue and winding. She sighed deeply.

Presently Worth returned with a bottle and two glasses. He took up a place next to her in the curve of the wing. There was room for two, and they were facing each other, more or less, as they leaned against the instrument. He filled the glasses and put the bottle on the floor next to him. Caroline took her glass, brought it to her lips, nodded to Worth over the rim and took a good sip.

"The best I have ever tasted," she pronounced. "You know, you were right about this evening being a battle. One thing I can say in favor of warfare is that, having survived, I have a distinct sense of being alive!" She took another sip, then gestured with her glass and said, "Is this what soldiers do, then, to entertain themselves afterward? Go to the nearest tavern and drown themselves in drink?"

He had just taken a sip and was looking at her in a way that made her realize how soldiers best entertained themselves after battle. Their eyes held a moment, before he lowered his and looked into his glass. "Yes, they drown themselves in drink," he said pleasantly.

The moment was a delicate one. In her heightened state, all her senses were sharpened, and she was aware of the very air. She felt it heavy with humidity, with just a shimmer of tension, as if, unseasonally, a summer storm was gathering. When he did not pursue the subject of how soldiers preferred to relieve their postbattle emotions, Caroline felt a spurt of curiosity and interest. It came to her as a watering in her mouth, as if she had just smelled her favorite meal of mutton pie and buttered beans and sugared plums. She glanced at him, while he was still looking down. His lashes were short and dark. In the flickering light of the fire, the leanness of his cheeks was pronounced.

She glanced away, suddenly aware of a bubbling inside. It was the familiar effervescence she felt in his presence. "And what an excessively strange battle it was!" she continued a little breathlessly, glossing over the moment. "I did not feel under constant fire or constant attack, but I did feel under constant surveillance! My every move! My every word!" Then, in a pugnacious aside, "But, you know, it was not as if *I* could not see *them,* too, and I must say that Catherine DeQuincy's dress was most unbecoming, and Lady Bonifant's tiara was horrid—as horrid as her second daughter's coiffure!"

Worth chuckled. "Tell me more," he invited.

Caroline recovered from her little outburst and said primly, "I am not usually so cattish."

Worth smiled and placed an elbow on the rosewood surface and leaned against his arm with his whole body. "Don't excuse yourself on my account. I enjoy the commentary and the light of battle in your eye."

"Well, it *did* feel good," Caroline acknowledged, "and with everybody talking about *us,* I do not see why we should not talk about *them!*" She turned so that her back was flush against the harpsichord, so that she stood at right angles to him. She looked out into the room, holding her glass with two hands in front of her, waist high. "But the talk tonight! It was beyond all belief! I mean, for anyone to have imagined for a moment—" she cocked her head and rolled her eyes over to him "—that is, for anyone to have imagined for *more* than a moment that you had anything to do with Mr. Kenmure's murder is crazy! And irresponsible, besides!"

He was leaning comfortably against his arm. "There is a strong streak of the soldier in you," he remarked. "I think you enjoyed yourself this evening."

Caroline laughed again, shaking her head, in part denying his statement, in part puzzling over her freak of temper. "I would feel differently if there were the least shred of possibility that you had anything to do with Gilbert Kenmure's murder. But you did not know him, he did not know you, and everybody knows it! You simply have no motive.''

She put both elbows behind her on the harpsichord and leaned against the instrument. She put her head back and took a deep breath. It was a liberating gesture, uncramping the stresses of the evening that had settled into her back. It was a provocative gesture, too, with her breasts thrust forward. When she wobbled her head on her neck, she felt good—not beautiful, but glittery and sparkly. She rolled her head over and asked, "What do you think?"

His voice was lazy, and the look in his eye unmistakable. "About what?"

Caroline felt strange. First was the water in her mouth, now came water in her knees, making them weak. Her glittery bubbliness seemed to be resolving itself into water and filling her body. At the moment she began to feel a liquid warmth seep into her breasts, she became aware of her pose. Slowly she pulled her elbows back toward her body and drew herself into a less exposed stance. "About the talk this evening," she said, as calmly as she was able, "linking you to Kenmure's murder."

"I agree that I did not know Kenmure, I agree that he did not know me, and I agree that I had no motive."

"You are agreeable," she said.

"I hope to be," he said, smiling agreeably.

"And impossible!" Before she was carried away by these very new emotions, she said sternly, "Now, listen! We need to think this problem through!"

Worth chose to appear suitably chastened.

Caroline nodded with approval. "It is obvious that *anyone* might have taken the dagger from the duke's library. Why, even Mr. Kenmure might have done so—for some unknown and unknowable reason!—and had it on his person when he was set upon by street thieves. He could have used it to protect himself and had it wrested away. Thus, the dagger could have become, ironically, the unhappy means of his death. The killer would have left it at the scene because it belonged to Mr. Kenmure anyway."

Worth considered the scenario. "Yes," he said, "that is plausible. However, no one mentioned that possibility this evening."

"Perhaps no one knows that Mr. Kenmure visited his grace that day." She began to shake her head. "I do not believe that anyone really and truly believes you are guilty. Your association with the dagger is more an excuse to talk about you."

"True enough. However, unless the real murderer is discovered, the stain of murder may remain on me for lack of a better suspect. People like their mysteries solved. I present a solution."

They considered the reality of that possibility a moment before they said, simultaneously:

"It's unpleasant, but we must consider possible murderers."

"I've wondered from the first who killed the man."

They turned to look at each other, brows raised at the convergence of their thoughts.

"If we are going to consider possible killers," Worth said, "I am going to get comfortable." Matching word to deed, he took off his jacket. He loosened his cravat, leaving a fall of lace askew at his throat, and shook out the lace at his wrists. He tossed the jacket across the rug and managed to hit the pile of cushions tumbling over one edge of the carpet.

Caroline fiddled with her glass. "I proposed Arthur Devis as a possible suspect this afternoon. He had access to the dagger and a motive—Mr. Kenmure's bad debt to him."

"Arthur Devis," Worth repeated, considering.

After a few moments reflection, they looked at each other again and shook their heads.

"No," Caroline said. "The motive is too flimsy. He's as rich as Croesus."

"The man's a drunken sot," Worth added by way of concurring with her judgment. "No strength. He could not have produced the slash in Kenmure's neck."

After a moment, Worth added, "Locke does not think it's Devis, either. I am sure of it."

"Let's eliminate Mr. Devis, then. So whom does Chief Constable Locke suspect?" Caroline asked, reasonably enough.

Worth made an equivocating gesture with his hand. "He's got a prospect or two, I would say. Nothing definite."

"But there is so much about Gilbert Kenmure's life that we simply do not know," Caroline said, not seeing an obvious way to go about solving the puzzle.

"Let us consider what we *do* know about his life," Worth proposed.

"Well, Mr. Devis mentioned that he saw a woman at Mr. Kenmure's window the afternoon of his murder. She may possibly be involved."

"Possibly."

"But—the slash in his neck." Caroline shuddered. "You said Mr. Devis could not have done it. Could a woman?"

"Depends on the woman. Depends on the intensity of the motive. Yes." Then, "But unlikely."

After a moment, Caroline said, "Mr. Kenmure was very excited that evening."

"About what?"

Caroline held up her hands in an empty gesture. "He did not have an opportunity to tell me." She smiled a little ruefully, remembering her flight of fancy that night. "Well, there were his charitable projects...."

"Which you told Locke about yesterday," Worth said. "However, it was an odd start of his, these charitable contributions, when he had debts all over town."

"Just Mr. Devis's horse," Caroline said, frowning. "And Mr. Kenmure was murdered before he had a chance to pay. I am sure he intended to make good."

"Devis was not the only man he owed," Worth said, "so say the rumors. I heard a few things over cards this evening. Nothing explicit. A word here and there. Some rather large figures were mentioned. Kenmure started borrowing within the first few days of his arrival in town last month, it seems."

"Why was he borrowing so much?"

"A country lad underestimating town expenses?" he suggested. "Desford is paying everything off, of course. It's not talked about much. Bad form."

"And it's better form, I suppose, to accuse *you?*" Caroline retorted. "If there is money involved—large amounts—then there is reason enough for murder. But—but *who?*"

They stood in silence, side by side, considering the question, with the fire crackling. At length, Caroline finished her wine and put down her glass with finality. "Only one name comes to mind," she said, "and it is most absurd!"

Worth raised his eyes to her. "Only one name comes to my mind, as well, and it is beyond absurd." With a little gleam in his eye, he asked, "What if they are the same name?"

Caroline took a breath. "Mine is Lady Esther Besant."

"Mine is Jonathan Wyndham, Duke of Desford."

Caroline rounded on him. "Desford. *Desford!* That *is* beyond absurd!" She was disgusted. "I mean—*Desford?*" When Worth did not react to her outburst, she cooled a little and asked, "Why on earth do you think it is Desford?"

Worth shrugged. "I don't know. Nothing specific. I've been annoyed with him several times in the past few days. Always a different reason." He glanced up at Caroline. The gleam in his eye became a glint. "Always something to do with you, come to think of it." He paused. "There now. I feel better for having gotten that off my chest. Why did you think of your aunt?"

Caroline frowned. "Well, I don't have any more specific reasons than you do, it's just...a funny feeling. I mean, I thought she had the most inexplicable reaction to Mr. Kenmure and then she had such strange suggestions to make about the...." She was about to say "the duke," but her voice trailed off. She could not finish her sentence. She shook her head. "No." Again, "No." She looked at Worth. "However, unlike you, I do *not* feel better for having voiced such an idea. In fact, I feel rather ashamed of...of accusing my aunt of murder."

"Do not apologize to me," Worth said. "She is capable of almost anything. But what did you mean—manipulating you and Kenmure?"

She waved it away. "Nothing. Nothing important, and certainly not pertinent to his murder. It's all crazy, and actually *I* started it. Then I believed her when I should not have, but it's all right now, I think— Oh, dear. What did you mean about being angry at the duke with respect to me?"

Worth straightened. He smiled, looked down at his feet, then back up, his eyes sweeping her. "Caroline," he said.

The disaster of the overheard conversation and the consequences for their wedding night loomed large in Caroline's mind. Suddenly, they were no longer discussing murder suspects but personal matters. Perhaps the discussion had been personal all along. The watery feeling was overtaking her. Agitated, she walked away from the harpsichord to stand in front of the fire. She was half-turned away from him.

He had studied his field position and judged it to be excellent. He had assessed her defenses and found them attractively vulnerable. "About that conversation you overheard..." he began, and let the half sentence hang there unfinished. He kept his eye on her. The moment lengthened.

At last, and after a severe struggle with herself, she turned to him and asked, "Why did you ask me to marry you?"

"Why did you reject me on our wedding night?"

"I asked you first!" she fired back. "Why did you choose *me?*"

He smiled. He was coming to know his Caroline. He imagined the courage it took to ask such a question. He walked over to her. He stood next to her without touching her. His best strategic instincts called for a sneak attack. He said gravely, "I think that sometimes, when a man and woman meet, some ill-defined feeling draws them to each other. They may not be fully aware of that feeling, as I was not the first time I met you, but the force of it exists and cannot be resisted."

Caroline stared into the flames. Then, keeping the corners of her mouth turned down, she replied with equal gravity, "That was a remarkably good line. Have you been working on it since our wedding night?"

"No, it came to me only now," he replied without hesitation, and disarmed her further by asking, "Did it work?"

Caroline gave herself over to laughter. She shook her head. "I'm not sure," she said shakily. The watery weakness in her knees had spread upward toward the pit of her stomach.

To distract herself, she reached out for the poker to stir the flames, but Worth took it out of her hand. "It makes me nervous to see such a weapon in your hand," he explained. "You understand."

"I was not going to hit you with it," Caroline said, miffed.

"I am glad to hear it, and I am sure I can defend myself admirably, but—"

"But—?"

"I would rather not have to." He put his hands on her shoulders and slid them down to her hands. He grasped her fingers.

Caroline was having difficulty thinking, and she had lost the ability to breathe normally. With Worth so close and touching her and with the light of desire in his eyes, she should have been frightened and resisting him. Where was the little fox? Why was it not clawing at her stomach, reminding her that she was ugly, undesirable? Had it gone to sleep? Was it drowned in the liquid trickling through her body?

She summoned her foolish courage one last time. "Why me?"

His eyes were intent on her generous mouth, and he had little on his mind beyond the memory of their kiss and the feel of Caroline when she was stretched out beneath him on their wedding night. He drew her closer, so that their arms were folded up between them, their hands and fingers entwined. "I don't remember," he said, bending his head and touching the curve of her neck with his lips. The sweet smell in the wrinkle of her skin enchanted him. "It was your neck. Yes. When we danced. The curve. Lovely. That's it. Must have been."

She tried to shrug him off. "No, I mean...I mean, that is, I am not beautiful."

That statement momentarily captured Worth's attention. He lifted his head to look at her. "You are not? I am feeling extremely agreeable tonight and refuse to argue with you. Let us agree, then, that you are not beautiful. No. But infinitely kissable and infinitely desirable."

Not beautiful. It seemed to Caroline, at that moment, like the most extravagant compliment. Worth bent his head again and kissed her, this time on her generous mouth. The opened palms of his hands slid down her breasts to her waist and then around her back. Her hands crept up toward his neck and the muscles at his shoulder blades. This time, it was not a storm cloud that arose between them, amorphous with unrealized moisture, but a force of nature where the dampness had taken definite shape, as in a flowing stream or a bubbling pool or a fountain seeping up from the ground.

The longer they kissed, the greater became their thirst, the more the waters rose. Their tongues met, and the waters took on patterned successions, to become wavelike, as if springing from great rocks above to descend to a beautiful meadow in the valley below. The waves moved slowly, lazily, lapping the wild hillside in their descent.

Worth was dazed by the force of the kiss. His hands went to her breasts, separating the lace of her bodice, fumbling, not finding an opening, and sliding his hands to the back fastenings. He wanted her bodice off. He wanted her skirts off. He wanted her white clothes off. He wanted her.

Caroline felt that some underground fountain had been tapped and was flowing between them. She brought her hands to his chest and found his skin. It felt like magic. Her hands tingled, and the tingle spread all the way through her. She was pressed to him, breast to breast, stomach to stomach, thighs to thighs. The little fox in her stomach—the vicious creature that kept her from pleasure—seemed to come alive. It surfaced.

She was frightened and drew away, but Worth grasped her more tightly and pressed her to him and his desire. The fox rose above the waters, swished his tail and dived back down, swimming deep, burrowing inside her. But it was no longer a fox. It had transformed itself into a different animal, a furry water animal, like a beaver playing by a dam or an otter slick with fresh water frolic. It was wriggling and wet and thirsty and playful and insistent.

She was excited, she was desirable, she was desiring. A remarkable, reckless idea flooded her brain and her being. He felt good. He tasted good. He was strong and needy. She could have him. He could be hers. It was legal. They were married. At the same time, it was deliciously illicit, given the love she harbored, in secret, for another man. This love of the lips and tongues and hands and bodies was tainted, not pure. This love was of musk, not flowers. This love was rough, not smooth. This love was flawed, not perfect. This love, unlike a secret garden, needed work, had weeds, withered in the sun, died in the cold. This love, unlike a beautiful gemstone, fractured along irregular lines. This love was no calm lagoon; its water heaved and churned. This love was here and now.

Caroline broke their kiss, clutched Worth's shirt and whispered into his neck, in what, for her, was a statement of desire and submission, "Shall we go upstairs now?"

He had unlaced her dress so that the bodice gaped open. One hand was on her breast, the other hand under the folds of her skirt. He opened his eyes, rather dreamily, and smiled into hers. "No," he said, shaking his head slowly. He looked beyond her to the pile of cushions and pillows. He nodded to them.

Slowly, slowly they undressed and fashioned for themselves an exotic bed of pillows on the floor before the fire. Soon they were afloat on the pillows, adrift on the Oriental rug, alone save for the company of the porcelain bestiary, delicately restrained in their grooves on the shelves. Caroline stretched luxuriously to receive Worth's embrace. He sought and found her fountain, and suddenly the animal inside her was nothing so familiar as the furry creature of the field and streams. Her desire snaked out. She was free. She had become strange and wonderful and blue and winding. She was Lung, the Mandarin water serpent. Her monstrous body was salty and marine.

The waters swelled and a submerged rippling began, rhythmic and harmonious. A blurred melody could be heard below the waters. It was her singing self, coming to life. She merged with the serpents to become a musical being. She was a nymph on the waters. She was a siren, singing beautifully.

When the ripplings began to wave and the waves began to sparkle and break upon the shore with successive shivering delights, she felt capable of hitting the high notes.

Chapter Nineteen

The fire had burned out in the grate, the candles had guttered in the sockets, and the frosty chill of the November midnight had stolen into the parlor. When a thrill of goose bumps harped over their skin as they lay entwined, and their musky waters could no longer keep them warm, they reluctantly decided to rise. They gathered their clothing, but otherwise left the signs of their lovemaking on the floor in the scattering of pillows. They mounted the stairs and found Caroline's bed. They rapidly warmed the clean, cold sheets, content at first to lie, quiet, in each other's arms, then no longer content to lie quiet.

Worth felt uncharacteristically ennobled by the woman in his arms. He had touched and kissed and possessed many women. However, touching and kissing and possessing this woman seemed to change him. He was no longer a mere cavalryman. He had become a chevalier, a knight upon a white horse. He was no longer in battle, a man among thousands. He was alone, on a quest. He was young and untried. He was mature and experienced. He was weak with innocence. He was strong with sin. He was afraid. He was fearless.

As in the romances of old, his surroundings were both familiar and strange. He had been at this crossroads many, many times; he had never been there before. He and his horse were lost in a glen, humid and fragrant. Man and beast slipped and scrambled down some rounded rocks, luxurious with ferns and foliage. Down they went, down,

down until they came to a still and secret pool, with its low mossy stones, with its peaks and freshenings, with its running waters. He was enchanted. He was awed. He was thirsty. He was ready to dismount. He wished to kneel, in purity, at the stream, to refresh himself in the waters.

As he swung his leg, his horse reared up, and suddenly the dark waters rushed in and closed around him. He thought he had been sent to save the maiden and slay the dragon, but at that moment, he revolted against all the teachings and shrugged with mighty force to abandon that false quest. The taste of salt and blood was in his mouth, and his male fountain rose confidently out of the secret pool. With a drive as deep and ungovernable as hunger, he knew his mission was to slay the maiden and save the dragon.

"Caroline," he breathed when he had met and mated with her water serpent. A rhythmic pulse of sensations—not words—coursed through him and they were: Warm. Safe. Satisfied. Home.

He slept, without dreams. No images of blood and gristle came to haunt him. No quicksilver peace beckoned to him to grasp at and lose. He awoke later with his hand splayed over the rise of a feminine hip. He was with the most splendid of his mistresses. He was suffused with an extraordinary feeling of contentedness. He had no need to rise today to plan a campaign, to fight a battle, to count the dead, to divide the spoils.

A cold, gray dawn was straining through the cracks of the curtains. He usually met the new day by mounting a rigorous defense against its depressing onset. This morning was different. He felt light, without armor. Buoyed and boyish. The wonderful sensation receded when he realized that he was in his wife's bed. His throat felt suddenly constricted, as if his cravat was too tight. The uncomfortable feeling remained until he remembered her waters. He wanted to be drawn again by her undertow. He wanted the strife of resisting its pull, of rising out above it. He rolled over and nuzzled her awake.

"Good heavens, Richard," Caroline murmured. "No."

"Yes."

"Don't. No. I'm bloated."

He moaned into the back of her neck. "You tempt me."

She laughed weakly. Her eyelids fluttered but refused to open. She felt heavy with drowse. She felt fleshy. She felt messy. She felt unclean and lovely and deep-down desirous, but absolutely unable to carry on. "I'm a limp fish, then. Don't. I can't. Have pity."

"A limp fish?" He kissed her nape. "Don't tempt me," he repeated, "unless you mean it."

Caroline snorted sleepily. "Men."

"Women," he replied, sliding his hand over her hip to her thigh.

Caroline's eyes cracked open. She could hardly believe it: he was serious. She rolled toward him, positioning herself to him so that she could get this over with, he could have done with her, and she could go gloriously back to sleep. "I'm all yours. What would you like?"

He was not going to let her get away with such uninteresting submission. He knew various paths to pleasure. He explored one. "Talk to me." Idly, he fondled a curve.

"What about?" she asked, still flushed with sleep and on the verge of multiple awakenings.

He eased onto his back and drew her into the crook of one arm. With his other hand, he raked his hair, then rubbed his unshaved chin. "Anything."

She burrowed into his side. "Well, you know, I was thinking," she said drowsily, "that last night wasn't so bad, after all."

"Thank you."

The tone in his voice brought her fully awake. She looked up at him provocatively. "Last night, at Mrs. Shuttleworth's," she informed him, without skipping a beat. "It was last night I discovered that, on the whole, it is better to be talked about than ignored."

"When were you ever ignored?"

"The last time I was in London," she said with no hint of self-pity. "But you could have guessed that."

"How?"

"By opening your eyes, I suppose," she said, as if he were a little slow. She did not care to press the point of her un-attractiveness when she was feeling so full and satisfied and well loved. She continued, "But now I am not being ig-nored, and I admit that I like it!" She sighed, "It's all been most extraordinary!"

"So now I have a wife who craves to be on the tip of ev-eryone's tongue and the target of everyone's eye?"

"It feels good for the moment," she acknowledged, "and I realize that it won't last. You and I will sink into comfort-able oblivion once the murderer is found."

"And if he isn't?"

"Then we can remove to Sussex, Hutton Manor."

"But that is very far from the center of attention," he pointed out.

Her head was against his chest. She smiled. "I like the quiet of the country, too."

Worth considered this statement. "From one extreme to the other," he remarked. Then, "Yes, I remember you say-ing when we danced together that night at the London As-sembly—"

"That infamous night!"

"—that you, as a Londoner born and bred, were sur-prised to find the country to your taste."

"I *was* surprised at how well I adapted to country life," she said. She added idly, smiling again against his chest, "But now that I am back in the city, I like this life, too. I do not know whether my nature is basically retiring or outgo-ing! A contradiction, perhaps, but true."

Contradiction. A woman of contradictions. He was star-ing into the middle of the canopy, where gathered in a tight center were the folds of chintz that spread out to the four posts. Caroline. The woman he held in his arms. A woman of contradictions. Not the most beautiful woman he had ever seen, and yet the most enticing. Both calm and stormy. Solemn and humorous. Vulnerable and strong. Shy and forthright.

Forthright. After last evening in the parlor, he appreci-ated her quality of forthrightness above all others. "Which reminds me to ask you a question," he said. With his free hand, he ran his fingers down her neck, to her breast, to her stomach. "Why did you reject me two nights ago?"

She did not immediately answer.

"You are right," he said to her silence. "It is more interesting for me to guess. Let me see. You have had bad experiences with men."

She shifted. "One man."

He took her chin in his hand and lifted it so that she would look at him. "Not your father, I hope," he said.

"Of course not, and you are shameful," she retorted.

"Not on that score," he replied meaningfully, "and I'm surprised it's only been one. So. I shall tell you how it went. Let me see. It was a man you knew well, a man you trusted. He was quite taken with your charms and thought to sample them." He still held her chin and was regarding her with a half lazy, half intent eye. "Am I right so far?" She nodded. He continued, "It was a man who always got what he wanted, and he wanted you. It was," he pronounced, as an image of Caroline's hand being kissed the evening before floated into his mind, "my good friend Jonathan Wyndham, the Duke of Desford."

Caroline blushed. Then she blushed at her embarrassment. Worth did not fail to notice her reaction. He had been teasing her. He was far from pleased. "I *knew* I had reason to be annoyed with the man," he murmured.

Caroline recovered. She shook her head. "You are absurd. It was a farmer in Sussex." She sensed his withdrawal from her. She wanted him back. She was amazed at herself, at how easily she had slipped into the ways of physical pleasure. Did it take nothing more than an attractive man, opportunity and a little desire? She began to caress his chest. She told him the story of the farmer's courtship, her rejection of his suit and the way he had chosen to express his hurt feelings. She came to the part with the milking stool.

"Ah, yes," Worth said, "the stool." He was lulled by her kisses and caresses, and the ring of truth of her story. Under the circumstances, he was willing to let his annoyance with Desford fade. It was difficult to think of anything other than the feel of her lying against him. However, at the mention of the stool, he remembered their wedding night. He remembered how she had been stretched out beneath him on this very bed, and he had looked into her eyes. He had not seen fear, but something very different.

"You imagined pain, I think, the other night," he said, "but you did not fear that I was going to harm you."

"I thought you were going to humiliate me," she replied.

"Humiliate," he repeated, absorbing this. He smoothed his hand down her stomach and slid his fingers in the seam formed by her crossed thighs. They lay still, trapped and happy. He thought back to her responses on the pillows on the floor in the parlor. "I don't understand."

She shook her head against him. "It's nothing now. Or, I might say, it's everything. You see, the incident occurred, oh, two months ago, I guess. The farmer spread his version of the story about the neighborhood, and I was humiliated."

At that he raised his head slightly and looked down at her. "This from the woman who has just asserted her enjoyment of notoriety?"

Caroline laughed. "You're right! I am thoroughly confused! It's *your* influence! After the experiences of last night—*both* at Mrs. Shuttleworth's *and* in the parlor—I am not quite the same! I said that I was transformed, did I not?"

She slid up his chest and, lying half across him, kissed him fully on the mouth. When he attempted to rise, in order to change positions, she pushed him back down. She shook her head. He submitted. His hands slid across her and came to rest in the small of her back.

"I find it very difficult to believe," he said between kisses, "that you were humiliated."

"But I was! It seems strange now that I should have cared what he—or anyone else—thought. However, had I *not* cared, I would not have accepted my aunt's invitation to visit her in town."

"Your aunt invited you? Is that how it was?"

"Yes, and the invitation came right out of the blue." She looked down at Worth. "Aunt Esther and I were never close, you see, and I would say we even rather disliked each other. In any case, *I* certainly disliked her!" Caroline made a face. "That is something of an understatement, since I was ready to accuse her of murder last night."

"So you accepted her invitation in order to escape the farmer's stories. What was her reason for inviting you?"

"Well, at first, I imagined that she wanted something from my father's estate, once it was settled. However, now that I come to think of it, when I told my aunt there was nothing, she did not seem concerned. So... why did she invite me? I don't know, and it is strange that I have not since thought to ask myself the question." She settled across his chest and propped her chin on the double fist she made with both hands. "Perhaps I have been too busy! Or perhaps," she said slyly, "I have been rather more vexed by the question of what my aunt has to do with you. Is she, somehow, the reason that you chose *me?* I do not believe your proposal had anything to do with my neck, as you told me last night—although the idea is very flattering!"

With her thighs next to his, her breasts pressed into his chest and her neck very close to his lips, he imagined, briefly, that he had proposed to her because he had known that she would be the most luxuriously gratifying of all women. He closed his eyes and breathed in her scent. His plan was that Caroline would give him access to Esther Besant. Yes, proximity. He wanted to be near her, to unnerve her, to titillate her, perhaps even to indulge in a dark, little affair, by force, if necessary. He wanted to compromise her publicly, to expose her and to demand that she retract the rumors she had spread all those years ago. His plan was not without its lingering appeal, but it had lost its teeth. It held no interest for him at the moment.

"I refuse to answer that question," he said, "on the grounds that I would risk lowering your opinion of me."

"You think, for some reason, that it is high?" she asked sweetly.

Without opening his eyes, he shifted her body so that it lay directly on top of his. They were suddenly entwined in a very stimulating position. "How charming of you," he said, drawing her lips to his, "to ask for the very thing I want to give you."

She experienced a quick flash of desire. "That was not at all—"

He cut off her protest. "I will tell you all, but not just now. You were recounting a far more interesting story—about your return to London. It had to do with humiliation, and your aunt."

"It is as simple as I have said—she invited me, and I accepted her invitation in order to avoid the pain of being talked about indiscreetly!" There was something oddly confessional in telling this story in this position. "I had no notion then that I would not be returning to Hutton Manor. I did not know that my father had gambled away the rest of the fortune."

He kissed her. "You did not?"

"No. It sounds idiotic, but I did not."

"And the farmer? What was he like?"

"Nice shoulders."

"Tell me. Did you ever kiss him?"

"Yes. Twice."

"Cruel woman. Poor man," he commented. "My murderous impulses toward him have just been transformed into sympathy. Speaking of impulses…" he said and shifted with intention.

They spoke no more.

Much later, they awoke to daylight. Caroline rose, wrapped a dressing gown around her and left the room for a few minutes. When she returned, it was to find Worth lying on his side with his head propped in the palm of his hand. It was disconcerting to see a man lying in what seemed a very feminine position. And in her bed, too. He was not what the world would call beautiful, but in that moment she found him so. She laughed at the beauty and the wonder of the moment.

"What amuses you?" he asked.

"You look very unlike yourself. Exotic. Like an odalisque."

He smiled and did not move. She slid back into bed, but did not shed her wrapper. Neither did she lie down. She settled back against the headboard and stretched her legs out. She took Worth's head in her lap. He relaxed against her. She began to stroke his hair, gently and intermittently. He leaned his head back to look up at her. He did not smile exactly, but a light of shared understanding came into his eyes and his facial muscles eased. He reached up a hand and touched her shoulder, companionably. He dropped his hand and lay still.

It was an extraordinary moment. Lying in her bed, with her husband's head in her lap, Caroline experienced a distilled moment of life, a concentrated drop of her history as a woman. It was a sedentary history, for the most part, with her pleasurable moments coming to her when seated. There was the cerebral stimulation of holding a good book in her lap and reading. There was the pleasant contentment of settling in her favorite chair, nestled with her knitting basket, full of bright skeins and skewered by nickel needles. There was the sensual surprise and warmth of a kid goat as it thrust its head inquisitively between her knees as she milked the mother.

That had been her history until last night, when she had completed these gentle pleasures with an experience of deeper bodily satisfaction. What she felt now, holding her husband's head, was all the stimulation, contentment and sensuality of her previous life as a woman with the added joys of being a wife. What she felt now was all of life. She held her husband's head where she would always happily join with him, where she would carry their children, where she would dandle their children's children. It was a moment of peace and fullness. It was a moment of grace.

It could not last, nor should it.

They rose, eventually, reluctantly but happily. They kissed and parted. They dressed in their respective chambers and tended to their respective affairs. Caroline had more than enough to occupy her in the parlor. There were deliveries to oversee, furniture to accept or reject, boxes to unpack, objects to dust and the room to arrange and rearrange. In her pinafore and kerchief, with her dustcloth in her hand, she hummed throughout most of the activity. At times, she would even break into a little song, embellishing it with a flourish or two.

At one moment, a mirror she had ordered was delivered. It had a carved and gilded frame, incorporating a barometer and thermometer and a bracket for a clock. She regarded it critically and decided to reject it. In the process of inspecting the mirrored object, she necessarily inspected her face, with her hair bundled away, a smudge on her chin, and her cheeks pink with activity.

She had never had a friendly relationship with mirrors. She guessed that a beautiful woman, seeing herself in the mirror, knows, "This is I." An ugly woman knows, with equal certainty, "This is not I." Throughout her existence, Caroline had tended to deny her reflection, to know, "This is not I." Today, by contrast, she was happy to acknowledge, "This is I." She did not fall into any extravagant conceit whereby she actually thought herself beautiful. No, she saw clearly the bump in her nose, her too-wide mouth and her coloring that would never be dramatic or fashionable. Yet she was willing to accept herself and to declare, "This is I."

It was a privilege, she thought, to please a man and be pleased in return. It was a blessing that the man should be her husband. She felt good about herself, as if her inner skin finally fit her outer skin. That was it: she fit. She had achieved a good fit. The perfect fit. It was as if, all these years, she had been living with a dress sleeve bunched up inside her coat; it had made her uncomfortable but, try as she might, she had never been able to reach the cuff to pull it down. Or, perhaps her inner self had been like the inverted lining of one finger of a glove that could not be worn comfortably. Now, the lining and the glove and fingers fit. With the fit, her years-long discomfort and self-consciousness smoothed away. The catch she was singing called for a little trill.

The afternoon advanced, and the settee for the parlor was delivered. The tradesman who accompanied this exquisite piece of craftsmanship explained, apologetically, that the matching chairs were not yet ready. Caroline, used to the ways of laggard tradesmen, and full of newfound authority, allowed the man to infer that the performance of his furniture makers was unacceptable.

The tradesman groveled. "Yes, Mrs. Worth. It is a grievous delay, Mrs. Worth. I would hasten to add that my wood turners and japanners combine the greatest speed with the greatest skill. I hasten to report, Mrs. Worth, that the delay does not come from the shop of Channon Brothers, oh, no, no! It is rather that the green silk was not immediately available when you placed your order Friday, Mrs. Worth. Friday of last week it was!"

Friday, last week? Caroline thought. Why, that was not even a full week ago. It was a startling realization. She would have said that she had placed that order a month ago, or even a year ago. Her imperious, queen-of-the-castle manner toward the tradesman struck her as absurd, then, on second reflection, majestic. She maintained her absurd majesty. With a confident smile, she informed the tradesman that today was Thursday—already!—and that she needed the chairs by Monday.

The abject tradesman left Caroline wondering how so much could have happened in so short a time. Her life felt crammed, like her sewing kit or poetic language. It was stuffed with meaning and emotion, not all of it happy, but so full and round. Had it only been ten days—not too many more—that she had known Worth? Only ten days? Or should she not say it "ten whole days"?—for ten whole days had been enough time to have lost a fortune and gained one, to have married, to have fallen out of love and in love.

The last snatch of a thought caught her: fallen in love? Or, for that matter, fallen out of love? She did a mental search for the secret garden but could not find it. There was no room inside her for it. She sought the calm lagoon. It, too, was gone, absorbed into other waters. And what of the gemstone of her love for the Duke of Desford that she treasured just below her breastbone? It was no longer there, but neither did the space feel empty.

So she had fallen in love—? No love, just lust, she chided herself playfully. That *was* all it took, then: an attractive man, opportunity and a little desire. All right, *a lot* of desire, and he was *very* attractive, her husband. And he fit so very well, she thought, not without a blush. More to the point: he had made her fit herself. Enough of the afterglow remained for her to imagine, in a burst of extravagant self-satisfaction, that she deserved such happiness!

When she pondered the lovely problem of why she loved Worth—that is, when she considered the spirit that dwelt behind the broken architecture of his face and that animated his touch, his kiss and his passion—she decided that it must be the immediacy of his pain and the raw courage that he hardly knew he possessed that drew her to him.

The doorbell had clanged the day long with deliveries and messages and lackeys seeking work. Unless a tradesman was come to see Mrs. Worth, Caroline was not disturbed by this activity, and thus she was not paying attention to any arrival in particular. At one point, late in the day, someone came, but Caroline was busily engaged in the parlor. She did not so much as demand of a passing footman the identity of the caller.

Minutes later, Caroline sensed a presence at the threshold to the parlor door. She looked up from her work. A happy smile lit her face to see her husband standing there. Her smile faded when she perceived the look on his face. It reminded her forcibly of the first time she had laid eyes on him. His face was devoid of expression and looked as dangerous as the edge of a cliff. His eyes, when they came to rest on her, were chips of blue ice.

His voice was cold when he said, "Why did you not tell me the truth about you and Kenmure that night at the London Assembly?"

Chapter Twenty

"The truth?" she echoed, surprised.

"About you and Kenmure at the London Assembly," he repeated.

"I have already told you all there is to know," she said, placidly enough.

He did not venture further into the room. "Have you, ma'am?" he demanded, from his distance. Neither his face nor his voice had altered.

Caroline laid down the picture frame she was dusting. She took several steps toward him. "Why, yes," she began cautiously but willing to humor him, for it suddenly occurred to her that a man of his violent past might be given to fits of irrational temper. "We shared the first dance together at the London Assembly. I have mentioned it to you, I am sure."

"You have mentioned it, yes," he replied. "It is a detail that might be confirmed by the entire Assembly, I note." His voice froze her to her marrow. "What you neglected to mention was that you were entertaining an offer of marriage from him."

Caroline felt the room spin momentarily. She steadied herself and tried to clear her head. Hardly knowing what to do or say next, she looked distractedly about the room. Her gaze fell on the maid. It made her feel effective to dismiss the girl, whose eyes had bulged to saucers. When she was alone with her husband, she asked, "Has my aunt just come? Was she the one who rang the bell about ten minutes ago?"

"Esther Besant?" he repeated, almost sneering. He moved from the door and took one step into the room. "No it was Chief Constable Locke who came calling."

She was dazed. "But how could Chief Constable Locke have known about Mr. Kenmure and the marriage proposal?"

The expressionless set of his features took on a cast of grim satisfaction. "Then it is true," he stated.

"No, it is *not* true," she replied. "Mr. Kenmure did not offer me marriage. Neither do I believe that he intended it!"

"I suppose you are going to deny, as well, that you had an assignation with him that night at the London Assembly?"

Her eyes were wide. "How could anyone have known *that?*" she said, as much from surprise as from honesty.

"No one does know that," he answered. "I pieced that little bit together myself."

"If I never mentioned it before, that was because it seemed . . . to—to complicate matters. It was irrelevant."

"Irrelevant," he repeated in a voice heavy with sarcasm. "You were on your way to an assignation with a man who wanted to marry you. He was murdered. And you call your movements and your relationship to him irrelevant?"

"I *had* no relationship with him," she insisted, "and he did *not* want to marry me. Yes, yes, I was on my way to a . . . a *meeting* with him, and he was going to tell me something—I do not know what!—but he never came. Of course that was because he was lying dead in the alleyway, as I soon discovered—to my horror, and to everyone else's! He was excited that night—remember how I told you that? That is all I know!" Caroline was afraid, but not of Worth. She took another step toward him. "Mr. Kenmure had no intention of offering for me. That is a story produced by my aunt, whose purposes I cannot imagine! It was just a . . . a coincidence that he was killed at the moment I was supposed to meet him! But I did not kill him, nor do I know who did! You *must* believe me!"

His smile was not pleasant. "I do, and you are under no suspicion," he said. His next words fell like boulders. " am."

"*You?*"

"Your relationship with Kenmure—despite your protests—seems to provide the motive that was otherwise lacking me."

Caroline's wits were not moving. "I am afraid that I do not understand."

"Kenmure wanted you. I wanted you. Kenmure was in my way. I killed him," he recited. When she opened her mouth to protest, he continued, "Of course, you are perfectly right to point out that I did not know the man. My lack of acquaintance, you see, only made it all the easier for me to kill him. That way, I got what I wanted at little cost or remorse." He paused. "So the story goes."

Caroline was making a great effort to put her thoughts into order. "But how were you supposed to *know* that Mr. Kenmure was in your way—which he was *not!*"

"Common knowledge," Worth answered promptly. "If I was interested enough in you, it was necessary only to make a few discreet inquiries at the assembly, and I could have determined which way the wind blew."

"Which would have informed you of something that I did not know myself?" Caroline demanded.

"So the story goes."

"*What* story?" she countered. "And what of *our* story? We are claiming to have been together at the crucial moment. Does Chief Constable Locke accuse us of lying?"

Worth's face lightened with a kind of ironic amusement. He shook his head. "No, he does not. Poor fellow! As a former army man, he has an abiding faith in me and a lingering respect for my authority. However, he has received this information about you and Kenmure from—shall we say?—a higher authority."

Caroline was becoming angry at Worth, at the world, at herself and at Chief Constable Locke. She put her hands on her hips. "I will repeat, with emphasis, that the one person who could have told the chief constable such a tale would have been Esther Besant! Could she, by some misguided notion, figure in Chief Constable Locke's mind as a 'higher authority'?"

Worth was shaking his head. "No, it is my good friend, Captain Jonathan Wyndham," he said, "the Duke of Desford."

Caroline frowned. "*His grace* told Chief Constable Locke this tale?" She blinked. "But why now? It seems a rather belated revelation."

"Precisely because Jonathan is my good friend," Worth explained, "he withheld this damning piece of information. He claimed to Locke that the possibility I had killed his cousin occurred to him almost immediately after my association with the dagger was established. However, naturally, he had no intention of accusing me outright. His delay was to protect me."

"As of yesterday, his grace only wished to *insinuate* that you were involved," she recalled with some asperity. "Why is he accusing you outright now?"

"Because, you, my dear, told Locke that Kenmure had visited Desford on the day of his murder. Locke naturally investigated that claim and discovered today from Desford that Kenmure had, indeed, paid him a visit that day. Desford was forced to divulge to the chief constable the nature of Kenmure's visit."

Only half of what her husband was saying to her made sense. She drew a breath to calm herself. "I believe that Chief Constable Locke has misunderstood his grace," she said. "I will be most happy to clarify several points for the chief constable. Have him sent in, Richard, if you please."

Worth shook his head. "Locke is gone. He is not ready to arrest me—yet. He came merely to inform me of the new development, so that I might discuss it with you. Very sporting of him, don't you think?"

"But Chief Constable Locke has confused what his grace must have said regarding Mr. Kenmure's wish to marry me. You see, his grace did not learn the nature of Mr. Kenmure's wishes that day."

Worth was shaking his head slowly. "No, my dear, it is very clear. Desford told Locke, quite unambiguously, that Gilbert Kenmure had come to announce his intention of marrying you."

Caroline frowned again. The image of the duke turned topsy-turvy in her mind's eye, but the effect was so unsteadying that she dismissed it in order to focus on the immediate problem. She steeled herself to point out, "If that is the case, then his grace was behaving . . . dishonorably, if I may say so, to have suggested me to you as an eligible marriage partner."

"Kenmure's visit came *after* mine, and it was only then that Kenmure first informed Desford that he intended to marry you."

"Well, then, his grace should have informed you of his cousin's intentions when next he saw you."

"When next I saw Desford, his cousin was already dead."

"No," she said. "*No!* This is all wrong. The idea that Mr. Kenmure wanted to marry me comes from my aunt. From my aunt, and no one else!"

"And how did your aunt arrive at such an idea?" Worth wanted to know.

"She got it," Caroline said, with infinite regret, "from me."

Worth's silence was stony and frightening.

Caroline felt she was fighting for something, but was not sure what. Taking several more steps toward him, she said, "I said it in jest, to spite my aunt. I said it with no thought that it was true. Oh, I had danced with Mr. Kenmure twice at the Birminghams' ball and twice with him at the City Assembly before that. I liked him, he liked me well enough, we shared interests. I said it because I had had enough of my aunt's scorn and pity and contempt that I was three-and-twenty and not married." There was something bald, but unselfpitying, in that last statement. She was standing before him. "I said it because my pride could bear no more. She used the story—told it to the duke—to incriminate you, don't you see?"

Worth did not see.

Caroline continued in desperation, "It was my aunt's doing! I am sure of it! There is something strange going on! Excessively strange! And now that I am telling you all, I may as well mention that my aunt said that the duke was going to offer for me on the day... on the day that *you* did. You came first, and I accepted you because—because—" She drew a ragged breath. "But that is of no moment, and in any case, I thought that *she* was maneuvering *him*, but then—no! His grace did not come to offer for me. So you see, so you see..." she faltered. "Chief Constable Locke has misunderstood something. It is Chief Constable Locke who needs to hear a clarified version of the story!"

After a very long pause, he said, "This is a fantastical story, Caroline."

"Fantastical, but true!"

"How am I to believe you?"

She was looking into his eyes, which were as unwavering and expressionless as if he had been aiming through the sights of a rifle. She suddenly knew what she was fighting for: his trust. She said the words that made the most sense to her, and she said them directly. "I have no reason to lie to you. I love you."

At that, Worth felt something fierce travel through him, like a lightning bolt. It might have been anger, but it might not have been. Whatever it was engulfed him totally.

"Love?" he bit off. "*Love?* I did not ask for your love!"

He did not trust himself to speak further or even to remain in her presence. He spun on his heels and left the room. He stormed down the vestibule, across the entry hall and out the front door, hardly noting the heavy cloak that was pressed on him by the waiting footman.

Caroline was left stunned. She looked around her helplessly. She saw no answers to her painful questions in the silent walls or in the ceiling or in the beautiful rug beneath her feet on which she had first made love with Worth. She opened her mouth to speak, to call him back, to unsay the string of foolish truths that had fallen so easily from her lips. No articulate sounds could be made. She felt as if she had been punched in the stomach. She doubled over with pain. She felt like a wounded animal who had stepped trustingly, idiotically into a trap and felt it clamp to lame her.

The maid reappeared, timidly, at the door. With an effort, Caroline straightened. She gathered the shreds of her dignity and said, "Yes, Abigail, you may come back in now. Colonel Worth and I have finished our discussion."

Her voice sounded normal, though somewhat faint, and she was enormously pleased. Emboldened, she proceeded to issue calm instructions. There were more boxes to unpack, brasses to polish, this to do, that to do, then the next thing.

She had no other choice than to continue what she had been doing. She was paler now, her hands shook, but there were no other outward signs of change. However, on the inside, her happy self-satisfied confidence of the early afternoon had shriveled. It was replaced with the stone weight of misery. The misery was doubled by the knowledge that she would have to face him again. And again. And again. Every day. Every day from now on. This was not a country dance to last half an hour. This was marriage.

She had offered him her love, plainly and without embellishment, and he had rejected it.

She was plain and unembellished. *What else could she have expected but rejection?* The little fox in her stomach woke up and demanded his vengeance.

No humiliation had ever been more biting. No humiliation had ever so thoroughly been brought upon herself by herself. Every brain wave trembled with the humiliation. Every cell of her body felt that it had been, individually, sliced in two. Now and again, like a scribble of static, thrust the thought: *One piece does not fit.* Then, the companion thought: *The duke is lying.*

But which piece did not fit? Which part was the lie? That the duke did know, or did not know, the purpose of Mr. Kenmure's visit to him on the afternoon of his murder? That he did believe, or did not believe, that she and Worth had been together at the moment that Mr. Kenmure must have been murdered? That he did believe, or did not believe, that Worth had murdered his cousin?

The afternoon drained into dusk, and dusk into dinnertime. When she was asked whether she cared for the evening meal, she accepted out of habit, and strained with every nerve against asking whether her husband had returned. She knew he had not. She sat down in a solitary state in the dining room, and stared at the dishes set before her. Midway through the second untouched course, she laid down her fork. She called for her cloak and the carriage and left the house.

Love? Worth repeated to himself, unbelieving, as he thrust himself out the front door and into the afternoon gloom.

He was angry. He was astonished. He was terrified. He had felt these feelings before. He knew all about rage and confusion and love. He knew all about deception and betrayal and love. He knew all about scandal and death and love. He strode blindly across St. James's Square and absentmindedly cast his cloak around his shoulders but did not secure the ties.

With the gray sky pressing down on him, the full horror, long suppressed, of the scene in his father's drawing room was squeezed out of the darkened corners of his mind to drench him. He remembered it all now: how he had opened the door to the drawing room; how he had escaped, by a fraction of an inch, the bullet his father had aimed at him; how he had seen the bodies crumple and fall, first his stepmother, then his father. His mind's eye ran red. His inner ear rang with the echoes of the shots. He remembered other sounds, too, sounds long-forgotten. Voices. A woman's and a man's. Familiar voices. It was the altercation he had heard, between his father and his stepmother, just before he had opened the door. His father's voice was shouting fire and unreason. His stepmother was sobbing, pleading, entreating. "But Vincent," she had cried pitifully, pitiably and to no avail, "I love you."

Then he had opened the door. He had escaped the bullet, but not the experience of its horror. How had he survived? He could not at first answer that question, for his mind moved tentatively, haltingly, wincingly, as bare feet over broken glass. When the answer came to him, it was accompanied by a kind of childish relief, as if he had found some treasured object of security: he had survived by forgetting. He had perfected the ability to forget. It was not easy. It took strength. He shook these memories off, as a dog shakes off water. He thought himself safe for a split second, until other memories, fresher memories jumped out from behind, memories of the second most horrifying experience of his life.

He was helpless to stem the tide of these memories. They seemed so immediate, as if he had just closed the door on them and walked away from them. He remembered a young woman's body sprawled half-naked across a bed, the white sheets seeping with a bright red. She was a beautiful woman, with fragile ivory skin and dark hair. She was delicate and near death. She was his mistress of several years. What was her name? He could not think of it. She was Flemish. She was flirtatious and well-born and pleased him greatly, that much he remembered. Also that she was married. Also that he had not been her first lover. To ensure that she knew how to play the game. So that there would be no misunderstandings. What was her name?

With renewed terror, he remembered her name was Caroline. No, no, not Caroline. Almost giddy with relief, he remembered her name was Yola. Yes, Yola. Beautiful, flirtatious, sensuous, possessive Yola. She had been his mistress for three years. They had pleasured each other well and with no misunderstandings. It had been taut and teasing between them until the day after he had announced his definitive return to England.

That day, he had found her with her wrists slit. He had found her in time for her to whisper, "Richard. Don't leave me. I love you."

He had found her in time to save her. He had fetched a doctor and relinquished her to the care of one of his underofficers. He had stormed out of the apartment he had bought for them in Antwerp and had flung himself out of the neighborhood. He had never wanted to see her again. He had left almost immediately for Utrecht. The last he had heard, she was going to live.

He shuddered and became aware of his surroundings. They were remarkably similar to those that had met him in the street that day in Antwerp. His memory jarred. No. That must have been springtime, for he had bought his release in late April, more than six months before. That was right. It had been springtime, with the trees a budding green. But it was not the tender fresh green of new life that he had seen in the aftermath of Yola's suicide attempt. It was the green of flowing bile, the green of wretched vomit, the green of rotting flesh, the green of sickness and unnatural death.

There was the similarity. He saw it now, looking around him, with the smoky veil of early evening descending on London. All was gaunt in this city square. It was winter, not springtime. It was inevitable. It was the sick and dying body six months later. The body had lost flesh and was black with decay. The graceless trees were obscene in their black nakedness. The black iron railings circling them looked like standing ribs of pork, the bones picked stark, slick of flesh. The gutters were choked with rank, wet black alley ashes, ground beneath his feet.

He shuddered again and realized that he had no idea where he was. He got his bearings and discovered that he was in the vicinity of High Holborn, not far from the craft shop of Roger Plenius, Harpsichord Maker. He craved music now as he had once craved alcohol. He knew he could go to Plenius to soothe the savage beast in his breast, but after that—?

He could not return home. He had to return home. Caroline was there. Caroline and her love. Was she telling the truth? Or had her declaration been to hide some further, sordid involvement in Kenmure's death? He was aware that he had made another strategic miscalculation: he had not thought ahead, to the moment after he had stormed the citadel and won access to the inner sanctum. He should have treated her as the defeated enemy. However, she had not been defeated. She had become his ally. She was his wife, not his mistress, that was the problem. And love? He should have spared herself—and himself—that. He liked her too well and admired her too much to love her. *But was she telling the truth?*

He had said that he had no fear going into battle because the pistol of his past was pointed at the back of his head. Somehow, it had turned—or he had. He saw now, vividly, that it was no longer behind him. Instead, it was pointed straight at him, and he was looking down into the long barrel of death. For him, believing in Caroline's love and acknowledging an answering love would have been the equivalent of opening his mouth and pulling the trigger. The image held him enthralled.

Then he shuddered, violently, a third time, for all the bodies that lay strewn across his past, for all the deaths that he had caused, for all the deaths that he had not caused. That third shudder eased the deep numbness. He could feel again. It hurt, but he could feel. It made him weak, but he could feel. The feelings were bunched, like muscles held too long in one position. He could not distinguish them. He could not tell profound happiness from great sorrow. But he could feel.

He considered the possibility that everything Caroline had told him was true. Suddenly implications cascaded, and disparate pieces of a puzzle came together, as if pulled by an unnamed centripetal force.

Pursue one great decisive aim with force and determination.

He had returned to reclaim his life. *No mistakes and no delay!* The music could wait. His life could not. High Holborn was not far from Lincoln's Inn Fields. Lincoln's Inn Fields and not far from Portugal Row, and in Portugal Row was the home of Lady Esther Besant.

Locke had warned him, once, that if he were to pursue the case of the London Assembly murder, he might not like what he would find. Locke was not precisely wrong. Nevertheless, when Worth turned his steps toward Portugal Row, he had a foretaste of the rigors of hand-to-hand combat, and he tasted it with relish.

Chapter Twenty-one

It had begun to drizzle. Worth flipped up the wide collar of his cloak against the rain, then smoothed it down again. He did not need the protection. The spit felt good, not like a cleansing exactly, more like an anointing. He ran his hand through his hair, bringing wet spangles to life as he passed under the light of a lanthorn. His body felt hot, like a well-stoked furnace. The surrounding cold felt good.

He arrived at Portugal Row and found the fashionable brick house with the black iron railing and green door. It was unlit, with no sign of life within, all the curtains drawn. He bounded up the few steps and pounded at the door. He waited a moment. He pounded again. The door cracked open, hesitantly. The sliver of a face appeared, one eye, half fearful, half suspicious, illuminated by a single candle held high.

"Lady Besant, if you please," Worth said.

"Her ladyship is not at home," was the old butler's reply.

"Not at home?" Worth repeated politely.

"Her ladyship has left town for a spell. Gone to the country, sir. Indefinitely."

Worth pushed the door, which ceded to him easily, and crossed the threshold. "Your efforts, though understandable, Marston—it is Marston, isn't it?" Worth returned unperturbed, "—are entirely wasted." He looked down at the old man and actually smiled, rather pleased with himself. "When I saw you last week, my good man, I could not remember your name. It just came to me now." He took the candle from Marston's unresisting hand and began to walk down the vestibule, throwing cavalierly over his shoulder, "You need not announce me."

A few steps farther, Worth added, "Oh, and Marston, do not follow me. There's a good fellow."

Worth traveled down the vestibule, rattled the door of the dining room, saw nothing, continued to the anteroom, where again he found only the dark lifelessness of an unoccupied chamber. He had the strangest awareness of walking upright, as if he had been a toddler but moments ago, hesitating, after crawling on all fours and now taking his triumphant first steps. The simple activity of walking felt good. He felt the stride of his legs. He felt the swing of his arms. This was re-membering: finding the members and putting them back in place. He worked his spine and flexed his shoulder muscles.

He strode farther down the vestibule, remembering with great clarity the same steps he had taken, on that day thirteen years before. He had been here, in Esther's house. He searched for the ghost of his former self in the shadows, hoping to find him, for he was wanting to punch the arrogant wastrel in the nose. It was fitting that he should be here in the place where he had been on the day that a part of him had died. It was the same place where he now intended to claim a new life. The symmetry pleased him.

He took the stairs two by two. He turned a corner, dredged a memory for the direction of Esther's bedchamber but came up with nothing. He figured that it must lie at the back of the house, where no light from the windows could be seen from the street.

He found it on his first try. He had not deliberately quieted his steps, for dissimulation was unnecessary. However, when he opened the door to Esther Besant's sitting-room, and she turned in the armchair where she was huddled before the fire, he read complete surprise on her face.

The room was relatively dark, lit only by the fire and a single branch of candle. Nevertheless, he had seen clearly the expression on her face. In addition to the surprise, there had been undisguised fear. When she perceived the identity of the intruder, the fear was replaced by a scurry of emotions, with curiosity chasing calculation.

He closed the door behind him with a little snap, bringing Esther Besant to her feet. The woolen shawl around her shoulders slipped to the ground. She did not bend to retrieve it.

"You were expecting someone else?" he asked cordially.

"I was expecting no one," she returned with admirable calm, but he saw her put her hand out to the arm of her chair, as if to steady herself. It had trembled, slightly.

"You must have been expecting someone," he persisted, "to have wanted him denied at the front door."

"I was expecting no one," she repeated.

"I think I know who it was, so there is little point quibbling." He smiled. "I am only surprised that you were not expecting me."

He dropped his cloak and looked about him. The surroundings were completely unfamiliar. A thought occurred to him. He said it aloud. "I've never been here before." Was that why she hated him so much?

"No, you have not," Esther Besant agreed.

From her tone and the expression of her face, he had his answer. He walked straight over to her and stopped a pace away. He looked down at her, leisurely. He admired her black and white beauty, the glossy black hair, the hard ivory of her skin, stretched smooth over angled cheekbones, with just the faintest lines of age. "You are still beautiful, Esther," he remarked. "Not much changed, really." His eye traveled the curve of her neck, followed her collarbone, exposed and fragile above the cut of her bodice. Then, conversationally, "Are you still as hungry and expensive, after all these years?"

When she did not reply but lowered her eyes, he answered his own question. "Of course, you must be. Otherwise, you would not have engineered such an elaborate scheme."

Her long black lashes swept up, and she made the mistake of letting him see deep into her onyx eyes. "Why have you come?" she asked.

"It seems we have some unfinished business between us," he said. He smiled again, but the smile did not reach his eyes. He reached out with one hand to touch her white shoulder. She did not move. His fingers smoothed themselves over her shoulder to settle into a light grip.

"You will permit me to object," she said, lowering her lashes again, "to your manner, sir, which is too familiar."

With his free hand, he took her chin and lifted it so that she would look at him. "You object, Esther?"

"To your motives, sir. I think I know why you have come."

"Do you?"

This was something of a check. She felt fear, yes, but curiosity, too, and frank interest. It would not do to expose her interest—just yet. The unfinished business could be either revenge or seduction. Or could it be both? Intriguing thought. "Shouldn't you be getting back to your wife?" she asked.

He shrugged and would not be drawn by the contempt in her voice. "She is, in part, why I am come."

Although her chin was raised against her will, she lowered her lashes again to cover her eyes. "You are come on an errand of revenge," she tried.

He considered it. "Revenge. There was a time—was it only this morning?—when I would have come for revenge. Just as there was a time when I liked being treated badly." One hand remained on her shoulder. His other hand left her chin to drop to her arm. He caressed it experimentally. He felt her breast, then her hip. "Still firm. No children. Very nice." The thought drifted idly into his brain that he could have her now on the floor, before he sent her on her way. The thought drifted on by and left, without an afterthought. He was in too much control. He smiled yet again, and this time the smile was genuine. It felt good to be alive.

"Yes, there was a time when I liked being treated badly," he repeated, "and you treated me very badly. Although once

I appreciated your methods, I fear you have repeated your self."

She looked up sharply. "What do you mean by that?"

"I am not likely to fall victim to your schemes and rumors twice, my dear Esther." His voice was pleasant. "Either you have underestimated me, or you are desperate. Whatever your reasons, you must understand that I am not likely to accept, in rage or despair or helplessness, the charge of murder."

"Murder?"

"Gilbert Kenmure's murder."

Her onyx eyes became calculating. "Ah, yes, I have heard the rumors."

"My dear, you have started the rumors."

She did not respond to that. "But the charge is not for you to accept or reject. The charge is against you, Richard."

"It remains to be proved."

"All the evidence points to you."

"Evidence?" he said dismissively. "There is no evidence pointing to me."

When she opened her mouth to protest his reading, he put a finger to her lips to silence her. "Before you say anything incriminating, perhaps I should mention that I know who did kill Gilbert Kenmure." He replaced his hand on her shoulder and looked down into her hard, beautiful face. "And so do you."

She did not struggle against him. If his purpose was not precisely revenge, she could facilitate the seduction. She gazed up at him with an unmistakable look in her eye.

He had once been susceptible to that look. He had once been drawn to it. She was still beautiful and magnetic, but the iron in him that had once been attracted to her had dissolved. He was not fully conscious of the remarkable alchemy that had begun to turn the iron in his heart to gold. He knew only that he was free of her pull.

He shook his head. "No, it is not going to work, Esther." When she squirmed, a little, at that bald statement, he continued, "On the other hand, you have nothing to fear from me. You have done nothing illegal—that I know of! You tried, but you failed, I think, did you not?"

She had been rebuffed and did not like it. At least she had committed herself to nothing. "What, dear Richard, are you talking about?" she asked. "You have barged into my house, you have intruded into my room, and you have rambled about knowing the identity of Gilbert Kenmure's murderer! You have even accused *me* of something, although I am not quite sure what! Whatever it is, you assure me that it is not illegal. Well! What am I to make of all of this?"

"You are to understand that your schemes are at an end."

"My schemes?" she echoed, her exquisite eyebrows arched.

He gripped her a little tighter, and all his pleasant bantering vanished. "Last month," he said, "you invited your niece to visit you. A purely social invitation, one might have supposed. However, your invitation was not entirely social. You had the notion to marry her off to Desford. Is that the gist of it?"

When she did not answer, his grasp became tighter still, though not yet hurtful. "How do you know?" she asked, and his grasp relaxed.

"Because I am not stupid," he replied, "and it is something in your style. You had a little game going with Desford, did you not? Nothing regular, nothing sure. Just enough to keep you both interested for a while. Then he began to tire of you."

"Me and Desford?" she said with creditable skepticism.

"You have always liked younger men who are just above your touch."

She struggled in earnest now, and he ceased her movements easily with two strong hands. His grip became hurtful to her. "Yes, just above your touch. You should have remarried years ago. To a man who would have been happy to have you! Your marriage was less than brilliant, as I recall, but you were always after the brilliant lover. So I can imagine that after Besant died, you wanted the match that had eluded you first time around. Well, now it is too late for you, and so you decided to make the match for your niece."

"You criticize me for wishing to making a brilliant match for my niece?" she tossed off haughtily. "And what was to get out of it?"

"Money. Lots and lots of money, and you could have kept your little game going with Desford—for the time being, anyway! The only way he would have come up to scratch on your marriage scheme would have been if you had had something to hold over his head. The word that comes to mind is *blackmail*."

"Meaning that Desford would not have wanted my dear niece on her own merits?" she said snidely.

"Meaning that Desford is not sufficiently discerning to recognize what they are. Meaning that Desford knows you know too much. Meaning that you thought, for one dreadful second tonight, that I was Desford and that I had come to put a period to the threat that your existence poses to him."

Esther Besant was torn between fear that she had been found out and relief that she had been found out. However, she was not yet ready to give up. "It's a remarkable tale you tell."

"Fantastical, I agree."

"And how do you expect me to respond?"

"I don't. However, I do suggest that you leave town for an extended period. Indefinitely, I think, was the idea you gave Marston."

That was it? Leave town? She was more disappointed than she was surprised. "What of your revenge? What of your plan to clear your good name and regain your title? Do you not intend to punish me in some unspeakable way? Do you not intend to have me recant my accusations of thirteen years ago?"

He chuckled softly. "How well we once knew each other," he mused. "Yes, indeed, what of that plan? I don't know. For the immediate future, I think you had better leave town—I recommend tonight, in fact—and perhaps when you return, you can say whatever you want to whomever you want about my past. I am not sure that I care any more."

He released her then, and her hands came up mechanically to cover her maltreated shoulders. He picked up her shawl from the floor and laid it around her shoulders. He took the branch of candles and crossed her sitting room to her bedroom. He found her wardrobe, opened the door and grabbed a tapestry bag from its depths.

"Here, pack this," he said, throwing the object on the ground and motioning to her from where she stood, astonished, by the bedroom door. She entered.

He returned to her sitting room and fetched his cloak. He was eager to leave her. Almost on an afterthought and with his hand on the doorknob, he called out to her, "What was the motive?"

After a moment, she appeared at the door between her bedroom and sitting room. "The motive? For what?" Her tone was the perfect blend of the provocative and the dismissive. It was hard, unchastened, self-confident and scheming.

"You are good, Esther," he said.

But apparently not good enough for you, Richard! was her silent response. From across the room, she allowed her regard to rest on the unusual beauty of his unfinished face. Watching him standing at the door, his broad shoulders set, his hips relaxed, she had a vision of the vitality leaping out from him. During the past several days, she had pictured a variety of scenarios for this inevitable meeting between them. She had imagined him in a variety of moods. He might be angry and passionate when he came to her. He might be cold and masterful. He might be teasing and titillating. She had feared some scenarios, desired others, but mostly waited in anticipation, plain anticipation. It seemed as if she had been waiting a long, long time.

She had imagined many, many ways this scene would play, but she had not imagined this nothing. No revenge. No seduction. No emotion. No demands. Just the suggestion that she should leave town for a while. Just indifference. She had deserved something more. Anything. Anger, at the very least. An ugly recrimination or two. Instead, she had nothing from him. She felt cheated, demeaned. She was not good enough for him now, just as she had not been good enough for him thirteen years before. The dissatisfaction was intense.

So, she was good, but not good enough? She would show him how good she was. With the same blend of the provocative and the unchastened, she said, "Why don't you ask him yourself?"

"I think I will," he replied, finding favor with her suggestion. Then he went downstairs, informed Marston to have Lady Besant's coach sent around and strode out into the night to his next destination.

Looking down into her tapestry bag, Esther Besant tasted her disappointment, as if it were a substance in her throat. She swallowed, but the bitter taste did not go away. Her hand shook as she threw a random dress, a pair of shoes into the bag. Worth was right, of course. She had to leave town. It was the only wise course to pursue, if she wanted to stay alive. She swallowed again and cleared her throat, but the strange taste remained.

"You are good, Esther," she muttered aloud, continuing to pack, and added savagely, "but not good enough!" *Not good enough for whom?* She wanted to spit, but the bitter disappointment could not be expelled so easily. She was good enough for anyone! *She* had been the most beautiful debutante of her time. *She* had been the wittiest. *She* had been the most charming. *She* had been the most interesting. *She* had had the most to offer! How was she to have known—no one did, in fact!—that the dashing Lord Besant supported his opulent style on next to nothing? How long did she have to pay for that one night as a giddy debutante when she had let Besant lift her skirts? All the young, unmarried women she knew had done the same. Only *she* had gotten caught! Only *she* had had to marry the rogue when she could have snapped her fingers at better offers! Only *she* had had the bad luck to make illicit love to a man with birth but no breeding or fortune!

And why had she not had better offers once her excuse-for-a-husband had suddenly and sensibly died? It remained a mystery to her. For years, she had looked around her and seen far less beautiful and amusing widows make exceptional matches.

She had been cheated, twenty years ago, thirteen years ago, tonight. Last week, as well, if she came to think of it. Particularly last week, in fact, since Worth had returned to spoil her most excellent plan. He could not have wanted to marry Caroline. He had just wanted to get at *her*.

Or had he?

She finished her preparations to leave and left her bedroom. No, Worth could not have wanted Caroline. *That* much she knew! It had been all too laughably easy for her, when Caroline was first out, to win away any eligible young man who might have been interested in her niece. And at her age, too! Not that she had even tried, for Caroline was a quiet, mousy thing. What man wouldn't want to flirt with a beautiful woman with wit and charm and good conversation? No, Worth did not want Caroline. She did not believe that we're-in-love story for a moment.

Esther frowned as she tied her cloak. Caroline had surprised her. What had possessed her to accept Worth's offer before she had received Desford's? Was she not infatuated with the handsome duke, like every other silly unmarried woman of her acquaintance? She had thought Caroline susceptible to Desford, but it was possible she had misinterpreted those doe-eyed glances Caroline occasionally sent him. Esther sneered.

So Worth had offered and Caroline had accepted. Her beautiful plan might still have worked if Desford had not double-crossed her. All he had to do was to protest Caroline's engagement, to acknowledge the purpose of his visit and to ask her to marry him over Worth. Instead, he had seen a way out and had fabricated a story about Gilbert's last visit to Desford House! That story was likely to hang him now.

Or was it?

Desford. One mistake after the next. Stupid, stupid, *stupid* man.

Stupid man. Desperate man. Dangerous man. And she had sent Worth to him. Now Esther smiled. The bitter taste in her throat did not go away, but she felt that it was somehow contained.

Chapter Twenty-two

Just as Worth left Lady Besant's house, Caroline was approaching it. Hardly more than twenty feet away from the door, she stopped and stood stock-still, when she recognized the man disappearing into the black drizzling mists.

Caroline had come by carriage to her aunt's in the hopes of straightening out the horrible mess concerning herself and Mr. Kenmure. She had taken the precaution of having the carriage stop at the opposite end of the street, so that there would be no inferences made, in the event that someone would be interested to identify the Worth carriage in front of Lady Besant's house. However, when she saw her husband leave that very house without looking right or left, as if not caring who saw him, her precaution struck her as unnecessary, almost vain. He had already told her he did not want her love. If he wanted to flaunt his relationship, why should she take steps to hide it?

Caroline knew this story by heart. It was the same old story about beautiful, slutty Aunt Esther and every man who had come Caroline's way. Her feet refused to move forward.

Caroline composed herself. This was different. Always before, her dignity had prevented her from competing with her aunt. This time her dignity would not allow her not to compete. She reminded herself: this was not a competition. He was her husband, and he needed her. He needed her to protect him against her aunt.

She moved forward and up the steps. She raised her hand to the brass ring and was surprised when the door opened before she had knocked.

Lady Besant was poised on the threshold. She was cloaked and carried a tapestry bag, as if ready for imminent departure.

The two women exchanged a wordless regard. Caroline stepped into the vestibule and broke the silence. "You are leaving, Aunt?"

Esther retreated back into the house, wondering just how much Caroline knew. "Yes. Did you not know that I would be leaving town, my dear?"

"Why, no, how would I?" Caroline replied.

"How, indeed?" Lady Besant returned, now with a slight smile. Caroline would have known if she and Worth had discussed it. "But if you have come to see your husband," she said silkily, "you are too late."

"I did not come to see him."

"You came to see me, then, my dear?"

"Perhaps my visit is superfluous," Caroline said. "Perhaps he came for the same reason I have come."

"I doubt it."

Caroline imagined that she was supposed to be disconcerted, but she fit too well inside herself to get rumpled by one of her aunt's insinuations. Whatever the purpose of Worth's visit, her aunt did not look like a woman who had gotten what she wanted. "When are you leaving?" she asked.

"Immediately."

"And when are you returning?"

"I will be gone indefinitely," she answered with a sly smile. Then, "Disappointed, my dear?"

"Yes," Caroline replied honestly. "I came to ask you a favor. I would appreciate it if you let everyone know that there was no talk of marriage between Mr. Kenmure and myself. It would be best to do it before you leave."

Esther Besant nearly laughed out loud. "My dear, why on earth should I do that?"

"Because it is not true and you know it. Because I fabricated that story about Mr. Kenmure wanting to marry me and you know it. You must be fair."

"I must be fair?" Esther Besant echoed, with a soft crack of laughter as if something had broken inside. "Fair, my dear? Why must I be fair?"

"Yes, fair. Because my husband cannot be charged with a murder he did not commit," Caroline said, "and you know it."

The bitter disappointment Esther had felt in Worth's presence was catalyzed, by her niece's presence, into something new. Like an infected abscess, all her festering anger, all her corroding dissatisfaction, all slights real and imagined that she had absorbed over the years, all her unrealized ambitions fused together and burst a fragile membrane of provocative charm and self-control. The powerful, hateful feelings rose in her gorge. She tasted her own fury and powerlessness. She knew it was poison. She did not care where the poison flowed, as long as it was out of her body.

"Because he cannot be charged with a murder he did not commit?" Esther repeated contemptuously. The poison oozed. "Which one are you talking about? His stepmother? His father? Or your pretty Mr. Kenmure?"

"All of them," Caroline said, surprised at her own response. "He is innocent."

Esther Besant focused a terrifying eye on her niece. Caroline was bedraggled from the rain. Her hair was limp, her nose was red, and her mouth was too wide for beauty. By what strange workings of fate had this unlovely creature married the one man who had always eluded Esther? What perverse twist in Caroline's timid little soul prompted her to plead Worth's case? She was too sweet, too good, too noble, too selfless, too loving for words!

"Innocent?" Esther jeered. "You, my dear, are the poor innocent! Look at you! Do you think that the man—or any man!—would want you? What for, I wonder? Did you never ask yourself why Richard Worth wanted to marry you? I can tell you! He married you to get at me. *Me*, my dear! I refused him years ago, and I refused him again to-

ight. You stare! Just *why* do you think he came to me tonight? If I am leaving town, it is to spare you the humiliation
of being played false in the first week of your marriage! You
should be thanking me, instead of asking me to do you a
favor that I am hardly disposed to grant. You should—you
should—"

*You should not be looking at me like that! You should not
be looking, for all your lack of beauty, so fresh-faced and
satisfied! You should not have had all the luck!* But the
words did not come out, for the poison choking her throat.
Abruptly, she picked up the bag at her feet, pushed Caroline aside and muttered, "I am finished with it! I have done
what I can, and can do no more! I wash my hands of the
entire affair!"

Caroline grasped her arm and pulled her up short. "Did
you murder Gilbert Kenmure?"

Esther Besant looked at her niece a moment, incredu-
ous. "Did *I* murder Gilbert Kenmure? Why would I do
that?"

"I don't know!" Caroline replied. "So that you could
force the duke into offering for me!"

Esther's black eyes narrowed. "*I* am not so stupid! I had
a much better plan in mind. One that would not have done
you any harm, either." Then, she rushed out the door,
nearly tripping down the steps in her haste to hurl herself
into the carriage that had drawn up in front of her house.

Caroline felt winded. She had to bend over to regain her
breath. She felt as if, for the second time today, she had been
punched in the stomach. Her aunt had known her vulnerable spot and had hit it with all her force. That spot, already
tender, felt battered. She left the house, leaving the closing
of the door to Marston, who had been cowering in the
shadows during this most extraordinary half hour in his
mistress's employ.

There had been just enough of a possibility of truth in
what her aunt had said for Caroline not to be able to dismiss it entirely. Wincing as she walked, she regained her
carriage, which was waiting for her at the end of the street.
There was only one place she knew to go.

Some time later, she was in Martha's sitting room, seated on the pretty sofa before the fire. Her hand was resting comfortingly in Martha's, and she was pouring out a tangled tale. Martha was listening with great attention and, remarkably enough, needed to interrupt Caroline's incoherent discourse not more than two or three times with questions of clarification.

When Caroline had finished this amazing recital on an exact repetition of her most immediate conversation with her aunt, Martha patted her dear friend's hand and said slowly, "I think Gilbert did mean to ask you to marry him, Caroline."

Caroline stared at her. "He did? How can you know that?"

"Well . . ." Martha said, trying to find a way to hedge exposing her own little part in this story, "you see, I might have known Gilbert better than some. That is to say—I, oh, it is not what you think—!" She laughed, and the sound was melodious. "Oh, all right, it *is* what you think! When I returned to society last month, I wanted comfort—I admit it! I saw in Gilbert Kenmure the qualities that had attracted me to Humphrey! No, Caroline," she said, shaking her head and blushing, "nothing happened, so you need not give me such a knowing look! But I had wanted something to happen, and Gilbert—eager young man that he was—was willing to oblige me." She stopped and slanted a glance at her friend. "Do I shock you?"

Caroline looked at Martha frankly and saw many things come into focus. "I almost wish I could say now that you *have* shocked me, but you have not. But why should you think that Mr. Kenmure wanted to marry me? Was he not more interested in marrying you?"

Martha shook her head. "It was never a question of marriage between us. He did not want it any more than I did. Oh, I don't suppose it was the fact that I am some years older than he was. Or even necessarily that I was a widow with more experience. I think it was rather that we did not suit. We did not share any long-term interests." Martha paused. "He admired you. He said so more than once."

"Admired me?" Caroline said. "I don't believe it!"

"Is that so wonderful?"

Caroline blinked. "I am not beautiful, like you. Or witty. Or sophisticated." She looked up at her friend shyly. "I cannot believe that he would have preferred me to you, or that he would have truly wanted to marry me."

"I have *never* liked Esther Besant," Martha said to this, "for she has certainly contributed to your low opinion of yourself. And do not ask me to apologize for insulting your relative! Furthermore, I refuse to give credence to her perception of your many qualities by contradicting her last ugly speech to you! It would please me far more to know what *you*—and not your aunt—think of yourself!"

Caroline looked into Martha's kind eyes and saw some of her own beauty reflected. She smiled. "I am not so bad," she said in a shy voice.

"Not bad at all!" Martha approved. "So tell me—did you have any reason to think that Gilbert wanted to marry you? Did he give you any indications? It is entirely within the realm of the possible, you know!"

Caroline thought back to all of the kind attentions that Mr. Kenmure had bestowed on her. She recalled their many conversations. She remembered how much she had liked him. She had never been in love with him, but perhaps her infatuation for his cousin had blinded her to the possibility. Now that her unreal, perfect love for the duke had been dissipated by the force of her real, imperfect love for Worth, she reconsidered what her feelings had been for Mr. Kenmure. She arrived at the conclusion that she had had genuine liking for him, but nothing more.

Had he given her any indications that he had wanted to marry her? Quite a few, if truth be told, and they must have been the reason, at least unconsciously, why she had told such a story to her aunt. However, it still struck her as highly unlikely that a man would be in love with her and that she would not return his regard, out of gratitude, if nothing else. The idea that a man truly wished to marry her dazzled her.

Caroline laughed and briefly covered her face with her hands. "Yes, it is possible, although I do not quite believe it, you know!'' She briefly related the strange, exciting words she had exchanged with Mr. Kenmure during their last dance and admitted, ''When he said, 'I shall *tell* you one thing, Miss Hutton, and *ask* you another,' I thought, at the time, that he was going to tell me of his love for me and ask me to marry him.''

Martha said matter-of-factly, ''Well, Caroline, what more do you need? I knew! I just *knew* it!'' She looked puzzled, ''But what caused you to think otherwise?''

She told of her conversation with the duke. Martha was noncommittal but advanced the idea that Gilbert had most likely not made his intentions generally known.

Caroline's heart had fallen to her stomach. ''Yes, but if you guessed it, would not others have known it, too? Oh, possibly not the duke, for why should he concern himself with me? But I mean anyone else! And if Mr. Kenmure *did* wish to marry me, could it mean . . . could it possibly mean that my husband is guilty?''

Martha regarded Caroline steadily. ''Again, I must ask you if *you* think he is guilty.''

Caroline shook her head. She pronounced a definite ''No.''

''Neither do I,'' Martha agreed, ''and I only inferred Gilbert's feelings for you because—well, the matter came up between Gilbert and me, so that there would be no ill feelings or misunderstanding!''

''But what has teased me this week past,'' Caroline said, ''was Mr. Kenmure's very enigmatic statement to the effect that he had discovered something remarkable that was going to change our lives.'' Caroline's brow wrinkled. She looked into the depths of the fire. ''I had thought at the time that it could be a declaration of love, but now I think it must have been something else.''

''There was something, yes, but he did not tell me, either,'' Martha said. ''I gather that it was important. We shall never know.''

Still looking into the depths of the fire, Caroline said the thought uppermost on her mind, and she did not bother to conceal her anguish, "Is it possible that Richard and Aunt Esther—?"

At that moment there came a sort tap on the door and in walked Chief Constable Locke. Martha did not register what Caroline said, for her head had turned and her entire expression changed swiftly. She relaxed back into the corner of the sofa.

At the interruption, Caroline transferred her gaze from the fire in front of her to the door behind her and in so doing, caught sight of Martha's expression. Then she looked at the chief constable. With her own new awareness, Caroline had no difficulty reading the look that passed between the two lovers. They looked capable of devouring each other. Although she hardly had time to absorb this extraordinary development, she was curiously pleased by it. It occurred to her, on a wry turn of humor, that she must have missed a hundred such glances in the past.

When Locke saw Caroline seated on the couch, he checked his step. It was, of course, too late to exit and make a less familiar entrance, but he could arrange his face into a more official mask. "Mrs. Sheridan, your servant," he said. He walked around the sofa to face them. He bowed, "And Mrs. Worth, a pleasure."

"But what a charming surprise, Chief Constable Locke. Do you care to sit down?" Martha asked him with a sultry smile and trilled her fingers in the direction of one of the delicate armchairs next to the sofa. "We were just speaking of something that may be of interest to you."

Before Locke had a chance to seat himself, Caroline had jumped up from her seat and crossed to him. She would have leisure later to mull over this fascinating situation between her friend and the chief constable. For now, she perceived the chief constable's appearance to be a godsend.

"I am so glad you have come!" Caroline said impulsively and launched into speech about the conversation he had had earlier with her husband and the various misunderstandings that were circulating.

It was not the smoothest explanation that Locke had ever heard, but he was given to understand, as Caroline wove a

rather inelegant explanation of how things had stood be
tween herself and Mr. Kenmure at the time of his death, tha
marriage was not officially in question. Therefore, he wa
to understand that her husband had no motive and—and—

When she floundered, the constable said calmly, "You
husband is under no suspicion from me, Mrs. Worth."

"But when he left the house this afternoon, he was con
vinced that he was the prime suspect and that the evidence
was mounting against him!"

Locke explained that he had had to relate to Colone
Worth the latest conversation with the Duke of Desford
"The devil of it was, ma'am—if you'll be begging my par
don—that your husband is a wee bit too experienced for his
own good. When I told him the new charge against him, he
accepted it without the least change of expression! It made
it difficult for me to flush him out—again, my pardon!—
and to catch whoever was at the source of the lie."

Caroline nearly gasped in relief. The chief constable's next
question, however, caused her anxiety to resurface.

"You'd make my task much easier, ma'am, if you'd tel
me where I could find your husband now."

"I don't know," Caroline replied truthfully, then with a
flash of insight, she said, "I think that he may have paid a
visit to the Duke of Desford."

Locke had considerable experience himself. He said very
smoothly and with a comforting smile, "Ah! That is a co
incidence, for this evening I was going to pay a visit mysel
to his grace." So naturally did he say it, that Caroline di
not give further thought to why Chief Constable Locke had
come first to Martha Sheridan's. "I'll be on my way, then,
and thank you, Mrs. Worth, for having made my task eas
ier."

Martha was not lacking in presence of mind, and she wa
mightily interested in Locke's reasons for coming to her. She
rose from the sofa and said, "Why, yes, thank you fo
coming, Chief Constable Locke. I shall see you out."

"That would be a pleasure, Mrs. Sheridan."

When Martha and Locke had left the sitting room together, she turned to him and said, "Were you truly on your way to Desford's this evening, Chief Constable Locke?"

"Not necessarily, Mrs. Sheridan," he said, "but I had to say something."

Her regard was frank, her voice serious. "Trouble?"

"No," he lied.

"Then are you returning here this evening, by chance, Chief Constable Locke?"

Locke looked down at her. "Well, now, Mrs. Sheridan," he replied, "that depends."

"On what?"

"Your answer to the question that I came here to ask you."

"Oh?"

"Do you wish for me to return, Mrs. Sheridan?"

"Yes, Chief Constable Locke."

"Then I'll return," he said, looking at her with his keen gray eyes, "on a condition."

She liked the sound of that. She liked the look in his eye. She took a step toward him, so that she was standing against him. It was quick, the fire that sprang between them. "Name it," she said boldly.

His beautifully molded lips curved into a smile. He was far from feeling the confidence that he radiated. If he weakened now and succumbed to her desire for him tonight, he could never have what he wanted from her. He stood in her heat and resisted it. When he knew himself in control, he looked into the blue mists of her eyes and said the most difficult thing that he had ever had to say to a woman, to this woman, the womanly woman of his dreams, "That you marry me."

Chapter Twenty-three

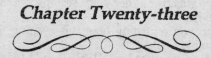

Worth was used to thinking himself invulnerable. He had led daring campaigns and survived years of bloody battles with little more than flesh wounds. He had seemed to know, with a sixth sense, beyond which hill and behind which bush lay the enemy. There had been times that he had gone into battle welcoming death, and yet he had survived, again and again. He accepted this with the usual irony that the ones destined to die were those who had the most to live for.

Thus, he proceeded to Desford House at Hanover Square with no thought to his personal safety. It did not occur to him to arm himself with a knife or a pistol. He was not wearing his dress sword, and he did not miss the feel of steel against his thigh. He felt whole without it, for he had his hands, his wit and his memory. His pace was surprisingly leisurely and unconcerned, given the perils of traversing London on foot at night. His manner was protection enough. Even when he crossed through districts where the streets turned mysterious and medieval, no lurking street thief or cutpurse judged him an easy mark. No drunk mistook him as a soft touch for a coin.

At length, Worth arrived at Desford House in Hanover Square. He was denied at the door by Jacobs, who informed him that his grace was not at home this evening.

Worth had already played this scene at Lady Besant's. "Desford will see me," he informed the butler pleasantly and swept past the loyal servant and into the entry. With a

ruly charming smile, he added, "You need not announce
ne. I won't be long."

Worth's instincts had served him well this evening, and he
ontinued to trust them. He turned a corner and traveled the
allway to the pale yellow oblong of light cast across the hall
rom an open door at the end. It was the library. He stopped
t the well-lit room. He allowed his eyes to circle apprecia-
ively the elegance of the chamber, with its tall bookcases
nd leather-bound volumes with lettered gold leaf, with its
vine-red carpet and burgundy leather wing chairs, with its
ire soughing on the hearth. Then he directed his gaze to the
ther end of the room, to the library table where sat his good
riend and old army chum, Jonathan Wyndham, the Duke
f Desford.

Desford's hand was resting on an unstoppered decanter
vhose crystal facets were winking in the mellow lights. The
ibrary table shone like a deep mahogany pool. The de-
anter and the crystal tumbler next to it appeared to hover
pon the rich surface. Desford was seated back in his chair,
eeming lost in abstraction, his hand stretched out and ar-
ested at the moment he was about to pour himself another
lrink. The movement at the door apparently roused him.
Ie looked up. His handsome face registered many emo-
ions, none of them welcoming.

"Good eventide, Jonathan," Worth said, stepping into
he room. "You are surprised to see me." Walking sound-
essly across the thickest of carpets, he remarked, "I seem
o be surprising everyone this evening."

Desford made an effort to pull himself together. He ut-
ered something inarticulate and half rose from his chair.
Worth waved him back in a friendly gesture as he sat down
n a chair next to the long table.

"So here we are again, Jonathan," Worth said, looking
bout him. "The last time I sat in this chair it was morn-
ng, late morning, just before the arrival of the morning
nail. I was asking you for names of eligible young women."

"If I am surprised," Desford returned at last, having re-
;ained his poise, "it is only that I was not receiving tonight."

"So I was told at the door." Worth nodded to the de canter. "You prefer your solitude."

"I have been grieved."

"That I can well imagine!" Worth said affably.

Desford's brow lowered. "What do you mean, m friend?" He sat forward. "Or, perhaps, I should ask wh have you come?"

"I thought you might wish for us to talk." With a shak of his head Worth declined the offer of drink Desford ex tended him. "However, now that I come to think of it," h continued, as if struck by a thought, "if you had wished t talk to me, you would have sent for me." He smiled. "Le us say, then, that I wished to talk to you."

"Evidently."

Worth smiled again and nodded.

Desford's face was unsmiling in response. If any emo tion could be traced on his impassive countenance, it wa wariness.

Into the silence, Worth said easily, "And this is what wished to talk about! You said that it would not be easy fo me to return to society. I fear, however, that you overesti mated my taste for a challenge."

Desford sat back in his chair. "You speak in riddles Richard."

Worth shook his head, minimally. "It was a mistake t accuse me of the murder of your cousin, you know," he sai conversationally.

"I have accused you of nothing, my friend."

"Did you think," Worth asked, looking at his old frien with a puzzled expression, "that I would not come, at leas to discuss with you your interpretation of the odd turning of events in the past several days?"

"Are you speaking of the dagger?" Desford queried.

"That," Worth concurred, "and the circumstances of m marriage to Caroline Hutton."

Desford held up his hands. "I have only recounted to th chief constable what lies within my field of knowledge."

"But your explanations fall very short with me, Jonathan," Worth chided his friend, "since I am the one person who can be sure that I did not kill Gilbert Kenmure."

Desford's face was shrewd. "How can I be equally sure?"

Worth did not drop his eyes. Neither did he directly answer the question. Instead, he said, "There are a number of unresolved issues in my mind. The first, of course, is the dagger. I have a perfect recollection of having seen it right here on your table the morning of Kenmure's murder. Why, I wonder, did you have it on your person that evening on the way to the London Assembly? I confess that it makes no sense to me!"

Desford's voice was politely incredulous when he said, "My friend, do I understand…am I really to think that you have come to see me tonight to accuse *me* of my cousin's murder?"

"Jonathan," Worth chided gently, "remember that I was there with you, when we both looked at Kenmure's body. I saw your cuff flecked with blood after you had touched his wound."

Desford affected puzzlement. "But we arrived in the alleyway very soon after he had died. The wound was still fresh. His blood had not dried."

"Flecks, Jonathan," Worth repeated. "Your cuff was stained with flecks of blood. You were there when the blood spurted out of his neck."

"You can't prove that," was Desford's immediate response.

Worth was shaking his head, in agreement with that statement. "You don't have the shirt anymore, I would imagine," he said. "No. That is true." He mused. "It is very strange. I think I could have overlooked your cuff if you had not thought to frame me with the murder. But there it is!"

"You persist in your accusation, Richard?"

"Have I not yet mentioned that, just before I came here tonight, I spoke to Esther Besant?"

"No, you have not." Desford's voice was no longer entirely pleasant.

"Ah, well, then, it is good that you know that she and I have had—what do the diplomats call it?—a frank discussion with a mutually profitable exchange of information." Worth considered his fingers a moment before looking up and across at his friend. "However, she failed to clarify all of my questions—which is why, as I have said, I have come."

"And have you brought Esther with you?"

"No, but where she is at the moment need not concern you. We will come to the problem of your future whereabouts later."

"Indeed? After I have answered your questions, perhaps?"

Worth nodded. "Yes, that would be good."

"Now, remind me of your questions, Richard."

Worth was helpful. "The dagger, for one. I hesitate to call it a clumsiness on your part, Jonathan, but I fear that using the dagger as the murder weapon was a—pardon me—fatal mistake on your part."

A portion of Desford's mask began to slip. An ugly look crossed his features. "Esther was inclined to criticize me on that point, as well."

"I do not envy you the tongue-lashing you no doubt received," Worth sympathized, "but what was your purpose? You chose to advertise your involvement in the murder with a highly recognizable instrument from your library table."

Desford pursed his lips, took a sip of brandy and set his glass down. He settled in his chair. "It was not so recognizable," he said after a moment. "No one had ever seen it in my possession, except you. I can't think why I had it out on my desk that morning, and I had actually forgotten that I had been toying with it in your presence. It was a dagger I brought back from the Continent, of course. In using it to kill Gilbert, I had meant it to look like the work of a cutpurse who had gotten the dagger from some returning soldier. It was common enough, for a stiletto."

"True," Worth agreed, "but how odd to have killed him before you arrived at the assembly, with so many people round, and with your arrival so closely timed with his murder in the alleyway, not twenty feet from the front door.''

"So far, my dear Richard," Desford said, "you are the only one to make such an association. I arrived at the assembly. I discovered that my dear cousin had been killed. I was in shock. Everyone was in shock.''

"Yes, but why did you kill him *before* you arrived? Why did you not wait until later, when there was no one about?''

Desford shrugged. "The contingencies of life, I suppose," he said. "I did not mean to kill him then. I had meant to do so later, as you suggest—that is, if he could not be brought to reason." Desford took another sip and became loquacious. "That night Gilbert had made an assignation, it seems. He was below in the hallway waiting for his ladylove, and he happened to go out in the alley just as I was arriving. To take a breath of air. To look around. Nothing more. He saw me. He confronted me. He...threatened me. He was in a volatile state that night. In love, or some other foolish thing! He told me that he was about to divulge to his ladylove the secrets of his heart, and then some other things!''

"And so you killed him.''

"It seemed as good a time as any. Before anyone could find out what he had to say. I left the dagger to make it look like street thieves. I had forgotten that—imagining the stiletto was retrieved—someone, namely you, could identify it as mine." Desford frowned. "It might have been the perfect crime otherwise.''

Worth was containing his curiosity. He did not yet feel the least inkling of fear. "Was it before or after I identified the dagger that you guessed that the woman whom Kenmure had had the assignation with was Caroline Hutton?''

"Gilbert had made his assignation with Caroline Hutton?" Desford uttered, in complete amazement.

It was Worth's turn for amazement. "You did not know?''

"Well, no! Of course, she was the first from the assembly in the alleyway, but I thought—well, that is to say—I thought Esther contrived that—such a coincidence, after all!'' Desford brightened. ''So you *did* have a motive.''

''Although I did not know it at the time,'' Worth commented. ''Which brings me to my second question, namely *your* motive.'' Worth composed his thoughts. ''You recommended Caroline to me in a deliberate attempt not to have to marry her yourself—for which I shall stand forever in your debt,'' he said. He moved on quickly, since he was disinclined to dwell on that particular subject. ''Esther was blackmailing you to marry Caroline so that she could have what she wanted from you. I gather that Esther was blackmailing you with the same information that Kenmure threatened you with. However, as thoroughly as I have pieced together this little episode, I still do not know what information both Esther and Kenmure had.''

Desford's face was so hard it was unrecognizable. ''It was a matter of the succession,'' he said flatly.

''I am not astonished to hear that,'' Worth said, although he was somewhat astonished nevertheless. ''I supposed it had to be something on that order, after all, to justify a murder. A hitch in the strict settlement, was it? You were not the rightful heir, but rather Kenmure?''

Desford leaned forward. Worth could not see his hands, for they were hidden by the table. When Desford laughed softly, the sound was scary, but Worth failed to become afraid. ''Esther should, by all rights, be strangled,'' Desford said. ''She was the one who stirred this whole thing up. I did not know of any of this until three weeks ago, maybe more, maybe less. How to describe Esther Besant to you?'' Desford looked at Worth and said, ''I hardly need to, since you know as well as I what kind of woman she is! Let us say merely that I had mentioned once that my grandfather was a twin. That was all I said. It was a chance statement. Another of the contingencies of life. But it was enough to send Esther to Leicestershire to dig through old church records. She discovered that my grandfather was born second, while Gilbert's was the first born. I was not the rightful heir.''

''No one had bothered to check that?'' Worth asked.

"When the succession was not at issue, no one bothered. The birth order on my side of the family was of no consequence."

"But what about four years ago, when your side of the family inherited?" Worth wanted to know.

Desford laughed again and the sound was crazed. "That is just it! We had grown up with the idea that my grandfather was the older twin, and Gilbert's the younger! Family jokes and lore were based on it, and our *grandfathers themselves* had grown up with the idea! Who knows where the confusion arose, but by the time the succession turned to me, all the relatives in my grandfather's generation were long dead! So no one questioned it. No one in my family. No one in Gilbert's. No lawyer. It took a mind like Esther Besant's to even consider the possibility!"

"And Kenmure found out, apparently."

"Esther's little trip to Leicestershire stirred his suspicion. That is where she made *her* mistake! What was an elegant town lady doing burrowing through old church records, after all? Gilbert wondered. He made it his business to find out, then he came to town and planned how he was going to depose me."

"But, Jonathan, why? Why did you kill him?"

Desford turned a glassy stare on Worth. "You ask me such a question? Why? Because the title is mine! *I* am Desford! Not Kenmure! He only showed his hand to me on that last day. Said he knew about the succession! Said he was going to take over! And, no, he would not hear of me paying him off! I would have paid him handsomely. *Handsomely!* But, no, he wanted it all! He had incurred heavy debts on the expectation that he would eventually have it all!" Desford stopped. His face was suffused a dull red. "He did not get any of it."

He turned on Worth and said in a voice that was losing control, "I was defending what was mine. How is defending *my* title and *my* estate against Gilbert Kenmure's claims any more criminal than what we did to the French or the Austrians or the Swiss Guards or God knows what mercenaries there were in the enemy camps? We spilled the blood of thousands of men for far less. Maimed them. Slaughtered them. I saw it. I did it. And so did you.''

"What you did was still murder," Worth stated.

Desford felt the red in his brain again, that same redness that he had felt when Kenmure had seen him and called out to him just as he was arriving at the London Assembly. The intense, murderous redness gave him a throbbing headache. He felt his thoughts clotting. The gloves were off now in this cordial conversation. "And just what are you going to do about it, Richard? Send me off somewhere as you did Esther Besant?''

"We might arrange to fake your death. You could leave town and begin life anew elsewhere.''

Desford showed his hands now. In one there was a silver-mounted pistol. During the recital of his deed, he had slowly opened a drawer at the side of the table and withdrawn the weapon. "Or we might arrange for your death, Richard," he said, "not a fake one, to be sure.''

Facing this gun, Worth felt the first real fear he had known in thirteen years. He thought of his life. It had been only this evening that he had known what it was to be alive. It was only an hour ago, perhaps, that he had conceived of his future and invested it with hope. He thought of Caroline. He thought that, at last, he had something to live for. It was only fitting, then, that he should die.

"Two deaths to account for, Jonathan?" Worth said. "You might have been able to skate past Gilbert's, but mine—?"

"I thought you were an intruder," Desford explained. "I have been jumpy of late, what with Gilbert's tragic death." Desford cocked his head and considered a new angle. "Or perhaps, once I discovered it was you who had broken into my home, I was afraid that you were going to do to me what you did to Gilbert, proving me right all along."

Worth was not going to give in without a fight. He did not judge Desford drunk, but dangerously unbalanced. He did not imagine being able to distract Desford at this point or trick him in any way. He knew the best defense was a good offense. His best hope was to lunge directly at him.

Calmly, Worth rose from his chair. Desford did not move, but kept the pistol aimed at Worth's head. At the moment Desford asked, "And your last words, dear friend?" there was a noise at the door and a shout of, "Stop! Don't shoot!"

At that, Worth threw himself across the table and grasped the wrist of Desford's hand that held the pistol. The struggle was short and brought both men to their feet. A moment later a shot was fired, and one body fell across the library table with another one beneath it.

With a *"No!"* ripped from his gut, Locke bounded across the room. He arrived at the two men and saw Worth lying on his back against the table, with Desford on top of him.

Locke knew a second of great sorrow, before he saw Worth shoving Desford's deadweight off him. Worth rose slowly and surveyed his dead friend's body slumped on the table, then looked down at the mess of Desford's entrails on his suit. When he looked up at Locke, his face was ashen.

Worth slowly peeled off his coat and began to mop ineffectually at his bloody shirt with a lace handkerchief. "There was a moment," he said heavily, "just the barest split of a second, when I thought, 'Why not? Let him shoot me. I'll never be able to explain my way out this one. Never. I'll be charged with murder.'" Worth fixed a gaze on Locke. "Did he win in the end? Am I to be charged with one murder, or even two?"

Locke shook his head. "What kept you going?" he asked instead.

Worth smiled sadly. "Jonathan was wrong." He looked down at Captain Wyndham's body. He closed his eyes and drew a deep breath. "There is a difference between killing a man on a battlefield and killing a man in a back alley. I do not know why. Someone far wiser than I may be able to explain it. But there is a difference."

Jacobs arrived at the door and behind him a host of Desford retainers. Locke took command. He ordered one retainer to find a sheet, another to find the local men of the watch, yet another to take charge of the other retainers before the shock wore off and emotional pandemonium broke out. Then he closed the door against all eyes and returned to Worth's side at the library table.

"And you, Locke? Is there anything in this for you?" Worth asked.

Locke pulled his ear as he, too, surveyed the dead body of Jonathan Wyndham. "A promotion, no doubt." he raised his eyes to Worth's. "Also ten pounds from one of the lads in my parish."

Worth shot him an inquiring look.

"I never thought it was you, man," Locke said. "Not even this afternoon. You play your cards close, I grant you that! Not a flicker of an eyelash to betray your thoughts when I came to you this afternoon. I laid ten pounds in a wager last week that it was his grace."

"Last week?" Worth asked. "Even before the stiletto appeared?"

"Aye, last week," Locke averred. "Who else could it have been? Although I do admit to having had one other strong suspect along the way." Locke smiled unapologetically. "It wasn't her. And you, Colonel?"

Worth's face was drawn, his voice weary. "I've one more body paving my road to hell." He laughed, without humor. "And in the meantime, it seems, I am doomed to a lifetime of sleepless nights."

"You'll feel better when you've told your story down at the station," Locke said, although he knew that nothing would immediately relieve the colonel's distress. "Come."

Chapter Twenty-four

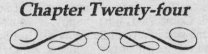

After a half laughing, half tearful, wholly extraordinary conversation with her dear, devious, delightful friend Martha Sheridan, Caroline returned to St. James's Square. She could have stayed on at Martha's, but she did not care to be there when Chief Constable Locke returned. Caroline was not sure how Martha was going to respond to the constable's condition of marriage, but Caroline saw that Martha was torn. Her lovely friend felt indignation at his bold move and imagined the glorious self-satisfaction of turning him down flat; she felt tremulous fear that she would not find a similar boldness inside herself sufficient to accept what she knew, deep down, was the best offer of her life. Caroline offered what advice she could: in her opinion, being the object of scandalous gossip was not reason enough for turning down the chief constable.

For her part, Martha was as helpful to Caroline as she was able: she could not assure her that Esther Besant had not been telling the truth, but she could surmise that Richard Worth had no cause to like the woman and, indeed, must hate her. Would his dislike of her prevent him from having a liaison with her? Unfortunately, Martha had not known the answer to that. Men, she had opined, were irrational creatures, and she had given up predicting, in light of Chief Constable Locke's odd start, what one of their species might do.

Thus it was that Caroline returned to St. James's Square in an ambivalent state of mind, somewhat comforted, though still dreadfully hurt after her double bruising.

She was happy for Martha, and yet she was jealous of her, too, in that her man was passionately in love with her. She was sad that she had no similar relationship to wrap herself in, although she felt a tinge of smugness that her love was her husband. Comforted, hurt, happy, jealous, sad, righteous. Caroline was in a muddle. Why did not being happy for her friend relieve her of her jealousy? And why, for that matter, did counting one's blessings *never* make one feel better?

She took these confused thoughts with her to her bed-chamber. She had nowhere else to go in the house at such an advanced hour, but she was not a bit sleepy.

While she was readied for bed, she wondered what it must be like to have a man truly, *truly* in love with you. Truly, truly in love with *you*. So in love that he wanted to marry you for you. Caroline thought of Mr. Kenmure. The knowledge that he had wanted to marry her gave her that secret feeling of glitter, but it was not enough. It was not quite right. It was not Worth's love and passion that she had inspired. It was not for *her* that he had married her.

Insatiable woman! Only last month she would have been grateful for any gentleman's regard and esteem. She would have been honored by any gentleman's offer of marriage to her, for her. Now Mr. Kenmure's probable offer did not seem satisfactory. Now she pined and whined after *one* man's regard and esteem, one man's offer, one man's love and passion. She was not sure how it had happened, but it had. Richard Worth had found a place in her heart, and all her experiences were measured with respect to their proximity to his relationship to her.

Why, there was even a time, in the not so distant past, that she would have felt very differently about all the warm regards and sweet hand-kissing that the Duke of Desford had bestowed on her of late. However, his attentions did not seem like very much now. Not real, anyway, or even very desirable, now that she was married. Why had he tried to rry her favor *after* she was married? Now that she was not iotically in love with him, she decided that she did not like e duke very much.

Humiliated! The word came to her, as she slipped into d. *That* was how she felt. She was about to blow out the ndles but realized that her humiliation would be more vid to her in the darkness. In the more tempering light of e candles and with her bedside pamphlet in her hands, she called that she had declared love for her husband in an surd and inappropriate way, and that he had flicked it off, if she had tossed him a repellent insect. The memory of s face and his gesture was sobering. She would certainly now better in the future how to conduct herself.

She was not precisely certain when that future would be. Vorth had not returned home, as far as she knew, and al- ough the hour was advancing toward midnight, she knew f no reason why he should return home. She had discov- ed that he was not susceptible to debauchery, even under ress, and so she was not worried that he was lying drunk some taproom. He had probably gone to Desford's, as e had suggested, and the two old friends had resolved their ifferences that had, of late, set them apart. Although that ongenial thought was accompanied by an ill-defined, ough rather strong anxiety, she was able to keep fear at ay in knowing that Chief Constable Locke had gone to [anover Square, hours ago, not long after her husband ust have arrived there.

The pamphlet of household hints failed to hold her inter- t. One moment she was staring abstractedly into the mid- e distance, and the next moment she turned at the sound f knocking at her door, to see Worth standing there, still loaked and damp and looking very grave.

Caroline's heart leapt in joy. Her heart sank in self- nposed restraint. To relieve the confusion of the contra- ictory impulse, she threw aside the covers and got out of ed. She reached for her dressing gown that was laid out ver the end of her bed and slipped it over her night rail. She ooked at Worth, standing there, her Richard, her man, her ove, her life.

At the sight of him, she felt the familiar effervescence in side her. This time, however, despite his gravity—or per haps because of it—she felt the feeling leaven, so that it wa not all sparkle on top, but had substance underneath it holding it up. The mere fact of his presence made the worl suddenly become a much more interesting place, a thicke place, with more plays of light, sweeter smells, finer tex tures and richer melodies. The world was a place in whic her life was worth living.

She made an effort that none of these rich, round, satu rated feelings should show on her face. As politely as sh was able, she asked, "Is there something you want, Rich ard?"

At her tone, Worth was unpleasantly jolted. Just the sigh of her had reassured him. He did not understand her cold ness. So much had happened to him in the past few hour that he had difficulty remembering whether she had caus to be angry with him. When the answer came to him, h frowned heavily. He groaned inwardly. Could it be that sh thought he had *rejected* her? Good God, whatever it was, h wanted her back, the Caroline who had offered him he love, plain and unembellished and unselfconsciously.

He understood that there was much to explain before h could expect anything from her. He would not—he woul never—force her to his will, but he needed her and her lov so desperately *now* that he did not know where to start o how to proceed or where it would end. Although he ache for the oblivion he would find drowning in her waters, h did not have the strength for seduction. What he wanted la beyond his skill as a lover anyway.

Not knowing what else to do, he crossed the room an stood in front of her. With all the artlessness of a small bo but with the directness of a man, he said simply, "I wan you to make it all better for me."

Her ears pricked at the note of anguish in his voice. Sh said nothing but lifted her brows, attentively, needin something more to go on before she responded.

"I want you to make it all go away," he said. At that, he let his cloak drop from his shoulders to expose his blood-stained clothing beneath.

When she overcame her initial shock and had plucked at the buttons of his shirt to reveal the smooth, unharmed skin beneath the rusty white linen, she grasped his lapels and dropped her forehead, momentarily, to his chest.

"How is it that you leave the house one way and come back like *this?*" she scolded. "Is every encounter in your life a battle? I confess that I had not thought all of them would be so literal!"

"But I have returned in one piece," he said. "It is not my blood you see."

She looked up at him quickly. The tone in his voice struck a chord she knew well. It resonated with her own hurt and doubt, strangely dispelling them. "Tell me," she said, nodding in understanding. "Tell me while I help you change."

He did so. While she undressed him and washed him and put him in his nightshirt, he told her of his encounter with Esther Besant. He told her of his plan for revenge against her. He told her of his freedom from all that she represented. He told her of his last conversation with Jonathan. He told her of her aunt's elaborate scheme, of the mix-up of the Wyndham grandfathers, of Desford's encounter with Kenmure in the alleyway moments before Caroline arrived.

He told of his remarkable experience, walking blindly through the streets of London, of his successive shudderings, of the evils he had witnessed and lived. He told her how Desford's pistol had been pressed into his neck, into his heart, into his gut before he had turned it, and it had exploded into his friend's body. He told her that at that moment, he had reached the center of some whirlpool into which he had been drawn, and he had found, to his profound horror, a void. Nothing. That center, the center of life, Desford's reason for living, Desford's reason for killing, that center was empty, null.

She held him in her arms and drew him to her bed. She cradled him, wordlessly, while her singing self silently wept a song of pain without self-pity. He might not love her, but

he needed her, and to be needed by him was all that she
could expect from him. She knew better than to ask anything of him. She thought many long thoughts, and among
them was the realization that her self-doubt had almost
caused her beloved husband's death. She could have pieced
the clues together herself, except that she had been too easily persuaded that Mr. Kenmure did not want to marry her,
and she had been selectively deaf—nearly disastrously so—
to the many false notes struck by Desford's character and
actions.

The candles had long since guttered in their sockets.
Richard lay quiet in Caroline's arms. Neither spoke. Neither moved. Neither was asleep. Into the still blackness, he
said, "When I left the army, I vowed never to see another
bloody body. A man can only take so much, after all. Since
my return, I have seen two such bodies. One was a friend of
mine. His death was caused by my hand."

Whatever had been blocking her hearing and causing her
deafness was now removed. She heard his words with no
obstacle from her head to her heart. She did not attempt to
deny his part in Desford's death or the pain he felt as a result. She said, simply, "You have met the enemy one last
time, and you have won."

"I won," Worth repeated dully. "To what purpose?"

She had been listening, and she had understood. Strok-
ing his hair, she said, "I think you lost your purpose with
Desford's death. He was trying to preserve what was not his.
You have been trying to restore what you thought was yours.
His purpose and your purpose seem parallel to you now, but
I am not sure that they are. However, I am not sure that they
are not. You would not kill to obtain all that you lost, but
that is not the point. I think it does not matter to you any-
more. You have been left with nothing more than your life.
Is that it?"

That was it. As Worth lay comfortably across the bed and
in his wife's arms, he had that sensation of re-membering
again. He felt his arms and his legs and his spine and his
scalp. He felt the blood pulsing in his veins. He felt like a

ree, with the sap flowing. He was glad of that much, but
merely having his life did not seem to be enough anymore.

"The king was going to make a ruling on my petition today," he said. "I was going to have Esther Besant proclaim
my innocence. Now I do not care. I do not care about my
title. I do not care about social position. I do not care."

To the despair in his voice Caroline said, "I weep for your
crippled heart."

Worth blinked in the blackness. His ears pricked up. He
felt his muscles on the alert, as if tensed for action. "Will
your tears heal it?" he asked, in a slightly altered voice.

She shook her head. "I am equally lame and bruised. I
fear my tears will not help you."

"Together we might make a whole," he suggested, turning half-around to look up at her, although nothing could
be seen in the darkness. Their presences could only be felt
and touched.

"Two halves of a whole?" she said idly.

"Two halves of a whole."

She paused. "What are you saying?"

"I don't know," he admitted. The strange and wonderful treelike feeling strengthened. He felt himself grow roots.
He felt branches sprout. He had little experience with this
new emotion, but he thought it might be love. Of a sudden,
the branches began to break. The roots immediately coiled
back and withdrew, as if they had touched something re-
pulsive. Love, it was deep and dark and destructive. Love,
it was passion, ungoverned and fatal.

"I don't know," he said again.

For a moment, her heart had leapt toward a new, joyous
note. At his response, her heart settled back, a little bruised.
She could not seem to shield herself from hurt. She shook
her head again, holding him and her pain. "It will be all
right," she said reassuringly. "Do you want to sleep on it?"

"I don't know," he said, a third time.

She did not respond. Time passed. It might have been
several minutes. It might have been several hours. She was
neither content, nor discontent to be holding her love. Her
pain receded and was replaced by a feeling as strong as pain

and that still hurt, but it was infinitely more complex, and
she recognized that its hurt came precisely from its strength
It gave her a perverse pleasure to like it so much, this strong
feeling. She could not say that she was happy. She could no
say that she was unhappy. Her personal happiness seemed
irrelevant. With his head lying against her breast and hi
shoulders enfolded in her arms, she felt his internal strug
gle. She wanted him to win it, whatever it was. Whatever it
outcome, she wanted him to win it.

So he lay there. The tree feeling came back to him. Th
roots grew down. The branches grew up. He did not resist
His trunk felt solid. Scarred, but with many strong rings
The branches sprouted leaves, thick and green. He though
of the one bullet he had not received, all those years ago, a
it spewed with anger and hatred and impotence from hi
father's gun. He thought of the many bullets that ha
whizzed by his ears and his arms and his legs during count
less battles on foreign battlefields. He thought of the sin
gular bullet that had not hit him this night.

He felt something wet on his nape. He was sure that it wa
not raining. The thought was absurd, for he was inside, no
in a leaking military tent. He was in his bed. In his wife'
arms. They were Caroline's tears, dripping silently, sweetly
on him. The realization electrified him.

"My God, Caroline," he said, sitting up, for he could li
still no longer. He turned to her and put his hands on he
shoulders. He could just discern the glisten of tears on he
cheeks. It was the most beautiful water in which he had eve
bathed. It was the most compelling water produced by he
body for him. "I had thought myself the most unlucky mar
alive. For years, you understand, I had thought I wa
damned." He was dazed by a wholly new understanding o
the events of the past years and weeks and days. "But I wa
wrong. Incredibly wrong. I don't think I'm stupid, but—i
just occurred to me. You see," he said, almost breathles
with the wonder of it, "my life is charmed. Completely an
utterly charmed."

Caroline gulped a silent sob. "I am glad," she managed. She let out her breath in measured moments, in order to hide what she could of her emotion.

He grasped her shoulders tighter. He wanted to shake her so that she could see. He thought himself superhuman, all his senses sharpened, for her face was becoming ever more distinct to him in the darkness. He could just see its outline and the two silver streaks down her cheeks. "Another man would have died somewhere along the way! Tonight, even. I should have received that bullet tonight. But I did not. There was Locke's timing—well, yes, I realize that *you* sent him to save me—but it was extraordinary! Out of normal life! I lived, and before he died, I even *thanked* him!"

The tightness in her chest was nearly unbearable. "Thanked him?" she managed again. To let out the emotion would be a vast relief. To let everything out. But she could not. He did not ask it of her. He did not want it.

"I thanked him, by God!" he said again, almost joyous. He laughed. "Before he died, I thanked him! He gave you to me. He *gave* you to me! Just like that! Handed you over! And I had enough presence of mind this evening to have thanked him! That was very decent of me! By God, I'm a decent fellow!"

Caroline had some difficulty following this. The tightness had eased somewhat, and she was able to say in a level, though somewhat watery, voice, "Well, no one exactly handed me over to you, you know. I had to accept your offer, after all."

Worth waved this away. "You had no choice. You were meant for me. Jonathan offered you to me. Thank God I had the wit to take you. I," he pronounced with deep satisfaction, "am a devilishly clever fellow, with an extraordinary amount of insight."

He blinked again and saw Caroline's face clearly. He glanced over at the window with the undrawn curtains and frowned. "Oh, it's daybreak," he said, with the disappointment of a little boy discovering that his magician's wand was a plain hickory stick. "I thought I was having miraculous night vision, seeing you so clearly." He laughed again. "Perhaps it *is* a miracle that I have lived to see this day."

Caroline drew back from him, in the ever-lightening room. She attempted to hide her face and wipe her tears.

Worth wanted to see her face in front of him and was impatient of even a moment of its absence. He wanted to see her face and trace every line with his eyes. It was the dearest face in the world to him. It was the most precious face. Her face. Plain and unembellished. Like her love. It was the most precious gift he had ever been given. It was the most precious gift imaginable. It was the most precious face imaginable. He put his hands on either side of her chin and turned her so that he could look at her. Without comment, he wiped away her tears with strong hands.

He said the first thing that came to mind. "Caroline, will you marry me?"

Caroline's heart swelled. Why did it hurt so much? No, that was not hurt. That was joy. "We *are* married, Richard," she felt compelled to point out.

He waved this away, too. "Legally, I suppose," he said dismissively. "Will you marry me and take my name and have my children?" His voice was urgent. "Caroline, please say 'yes.'"

"Yes."

"Good. That's settled."

"Does this mean," she said, before her heart burst, "that you love me?"

"I don't know what love is," he said. "Maybe." He said the word experimentally. "Love?" He shrugged. "Perhaps. Love, but no passion," he added definitely, shaking his head. "I do not want any more of that destruction. I do not want either of us destroyed by passion. All right, then, love. I love you. I love your forthright, sustaining love, Caroline. I love you. Forthrightly and with sustenance. Yes. Love. Yes."

"Richard, I am glad," Caroline said, urged again by a compulsion to state the obvious, "but I am afraid that I *do* feel passion for you."

He laughed again, joyously. "Well, now, I am feeling extremely agreeable! I'll agree to passion, if you'll agree to ,ing for me today."

Caroline nodded.

"All right, then. In this case. Yes. Passion." He pushed her back into the pillows.

The last thing Caroline saw through the windows with their undrawn curtains were bolts of sunlight piercing through the heavy mists and spreading like an Oriental fan across the spine of the low buildings opposite on St. James's Square. As she closed her eyes to kiss her husband, she imagined she saw the monstrous body of Lung, golden and benevolent, unfurl itself across the magnificent web of the sky.

* * * * *

Harlequin Historicals®

COMING NEXT MONTH

#131 TEXAS HEALER—Ruth Langan
Morning Light, sister of a great Comanche chief, had vowed
never to trust a white man. But Dr. Dan Conway's soothing
touch soon healed her bitter, lonely heart.

#132 FORTUNE HUNTER—Deborah Simmons
Socialite Melissa Hampton and impoverished Leighton Somerset
both profited from their marriage. Yet, was Lord Somerset the
one plotting Melissa's demise—or had he truly fallen in love
with her?

#133 DANGEROUS CHARADE—Madeline Harper
Beautiful Margaret Hanson had told Steven Peyton a pack
of lies. Why should he believe her now, when she claimed
he was a missing prince and begged him to save his tiny
European country?

#134 TEMPTATION'S PRICE—Dallas Schulze
Years ago Matt Prescott chose adventure over the girl
he'd been forced to wed. Now he was back—and one look at
sweet Liberty told him that *this* time, she wouldn't be so easy
to dismiss. . . .

AVAILABLE NOW:

**#127 THE LADY AND THE
LAIRD**
Maura Seger

#128 SWEET SUSPICIONS
Julie Tetel

#129 THE CLAIM
Lucy Elliot

#130 PIRATE BRIDE
Elizabeth August

COMING IN JULY
FROM HARLEQUIN HISTORICALS

TEMPTATION'S PRICE
by Dallas Schulze

Dallas Schulze's sensuous, sparkling love stories have made her a favorite of both Harlequin American Romance and Silhouette Intimate Moments readers. Now she has created some of her most memorable characters ever for Harlequin Historicals....

Liberty Ballard...who traveled across America's Great Plains to start a new life.

Matt Prescott ... a man of the Wild West, tamed only by his love for Liberty.

Would they have to pay the price of giving in to temptation?

AVAILABLE IN JULY WHEREVER HARLEQUIN BOOKS ARE SOLD

HARLEQUIN

Romance

Harlequin's Ruth Jean Dale brings you THE TAGGARTS OF TEXAS!

Those Taggart men—strong, sexy and hard to resist . . .

There's Jesse James Taggart in **FIREWORKS!**
Harlequin Romance #3205 (July 1992)

And Trey Smith—he's **THE RED-BLOODED YANKEE!**
Harlequin Temptation #413 (October 1992)

Then there's Daniel Boone Taggart in **SHOWDOWN!**
Harlequin Romance #3242 (January 1993)

And finally the Taggarts who started it all—in **LEGEND!**
Harlequin Historical #168 (April 1993)

**Read all the Taggart romances!
Meet all the Taggart men!**

Available wherever Harlequin books are sold.   DALE-R